UNFORGIVABLE
LUST & RESTRAINT

Book 2 of the *UNFORGIVABLE SERIES*

UNFORGIVABLE
LUST & RESTRAINT

Book 2 of the *UNFORGIVABLE SERIES*

SHAY LEE SOLEIL

Soleil Publishing
Belle River, Ontario,
Canada, N0R 1A0
www.shayleesoleil.com

Copyright © 2016 by Shay Lee Soleil
First Edition-2016

All rights reserved.

No part of this publication may be reproduced in any form, or by any means, electronic or mechanical, including photocopying, recording, or any information browsing, storage, or retrieval system, without permission in writing from the publisher.

This is a work of fiction. Names, characters, places, and incidents either are the product of the author's imagination or are used fictitiously, and any resemblance to actual persons, living or dead, business establishments, events, or locales is entirely coincidental.

Cover design: Damonza.com

Library and Archives Canada Cataloguing in Publication

Soleil, Shay Lee, author
    Unforgivable lust & restraint / Shay Lee Soleil.

(Unforgivable ; book 2)
Issued in print and electronic formats.
ISBN 978-0-9952342-1-5 (paperback).--ISBN 978-0-9952342-2-2 (ebook)

    I. Title. II. Title: Unforgivable lust and restraint.
PS8637.O4223U447 2016   C813'.6
                             C2016-906499-9
                             C2016-906568-5

ISBN
978-0-9952342-1-5 (Paperback)
978-0-9952342-2-2 (eBook)

Fiction, Erotic Romance
Distributed to the trade by The Ingram Book Company

DEDICATION

To my mother in-law Pearl (January 10 2015) You taught me so many things in life, but the one thing that stands out the most is to be stubborn and don't give up. I've always loved your tenacity. I hope you're giving them hell up there. We all love and miss you. You are, forever in our minds and hearts. To my husband and children. I love you! Thank you for letting me follow a dream.

ACKNOWLEDGMENTS

To my editor Lynne Melcombe. You had me laughing quite a few times with your comments. You are a genius. This book has improved tremendously because of your talent and skill. I appreciate it more than words can say. Thank you!

To the best readers an author can have, thank you for supporting and encouraging me to continue.

To Chrissy at Damanza.com for designing a magnificent cover for me. Sorry for being difficult, but I had a vision and was hoping someone could create what I was looking for. You did that, working day and night to perfect it. Thank you for formatting my manuscript and the endless revisions. It looks professional now. You've made me one happy author. I will definitely use Damonza's services to design the cover of book 3. Thank you again. My appreciation is endless.

1

ON THE WAY home from Barrie, after I've told Leena everything that happened with Bryce and I have a moment to myself, I hide my phone behind my purse and scroll through the text Bryce sent me. It's torture not knowing what it says.

In it, he says he had to get Lindsay out of there, away from his family, that she's thrown too many fits around them and they've had enough. He says he searched for me at his parents' house and then his house, and it killed him when I wasn't there. "Bullshit!" I whisper. I look up from my phone to see Leena grinning at me. "What?"

"Nothing," she says.

"It's all bullshit anyway." Furious, I shove my phone back in my purse and try not to think of Bryce and the look he gave Lindsay.

The drive home to Huntsville is mostly silent. We start out listening to music, but every song reminds me of what I thought I had with Bryce. When I turn the music down Leena gives me the look, but doesn't say a word.

She knows not to mess with me when I have so much on my mind.

My parents died when I was eighteen from a head on collision with a logging truck. I was in the car that fateful morning, but wasn't feeling good, so I got out and went to bed. My whole world fell apart in an instant when I got the call. I was devastated. I wanted to die with them.

My grandparents came to live with me for a couple of months until Gram got sick. She died shortly after. It was the worst year of my life. I've been living on my own ever since.

Leena and Katie, my best friends since kindergarten and Gramps, my only family member still living, have been my rocks to lean on, helping me through the grief.

At that time, I had to quit my part-time job to get a full-time job as a receptionist to pay for the mortgage on my parents' home. I was stuck in that job because it paid well. The moment I got the settlement from the logging company, I quit that job, because my boss gave me the creeps. He'd ask me out for dinner twice a week and he'd rub against me, making sly perverted comments and I felt very uncomfortable. I can remember praying for someone or something to help me out of that situation.

It was a miracle when I got that settlement. I paid off the mortgage, renovated the house, and bought my Journey.

On the outskirts of town as you travel along Highway 11, you'll see more jagged rock face and a familiar landmark of tall pine trees in perfect rows. The sun is starting to slip behind the trees and it's almost dusk.

Preparing to swerve or stop in a moment's notice is normal where we live, when deer or moose venture out onto the road.

Once you see the red and blue, welcome to Huntsville sign, you know it's only ten more minutes to home.

As we drive through town, Leena points out one of the two houses my stalker set fire to.

It is a brown brick home, with the front windows shattered and the roof is partially caved in. The debris is scattered on the front porch and below the windows.

Most of the damage has been confined to the front of the house. The yellow caution tape still surrounds the yard while the investigation continues. I hope no one was hurt during the incident. My stalker is interfering with people's lives and I'm worried someone is going to get hurt-or killed. I hate that he's using me as a pawn in his demented obsession. He seems to know when I'm with Bryce, and lashes out by leaving a note professing his undying love for me, while at the same time, setting a fire that destroys the property of people I associate with.

The police and Bryce have been trying to catch him, but he's too quick and cunning. He knows how to slide in and out of sight without detection. If he wasn't a skilled arsonist to begin with, he's quickly becoming one.

My mind flips to when I first met Bryce in the grocery store. I was singing a song out loud that I'd heard on the drive over. "She don't love you she's just lonely. She wasn't once upon a time." I remember saying, yeah, story of my life. At that point and time, I was lonely, and I was praying for someone to come into my life. I had always dreamt of a relationship like my parents had. They got along great. Never fought.

At that moment, in my peripheral vision, I saw someone staring at me while I was reaching to the top shelf. I stopped singing and automatically looked.

Mr. Tall Dark and Gorgeous, the nickname I gave Bryce before I knew his name, was staring back at me.

I was mesmerized by the way he was looking at me. There was such a hunger in his eyes it made me shiver. The only time I looked away was to see if he was actually staring at me. There was no one else in the aisle. We stood stock still staring at each other. Neither one of us could look away.

Austin, his brother ruined our moment by pulling him

away. I left the grocery store dazed and confused. No one has ever affected me like that before. When I went home that night, I couldn't stop thinking about him.

Our second encounter was at our favourite bar when Leena, Katie and I were coming out of the washroom. I almost fell over when I saw him. I stopped abruptly and they piled up behind me.

I was hoping he would have been there. And there he was, leaning against the bar in the sexiest pose. I couldn't believe how my body was reacting. His intense stare, bore through me all night as he watched us dance, but he never approached me. I left, feeling disappointed.

My third encounter with Bryce was the day after the bar. I was blindfolded and held captive in a cabin and was allowed to go to the bathroom. I was scared, thinking my stalker had drugged and kidnapped me. When I stormed out the door, ready to claw my way free, I was met by Mr. Tall Dark and Gorgeous.

I was so mad at the time, I fought to get free. Somehow he calmed me.

And then, he seduced me.

My walls that were built so high over the years because of Jake almost raping me, crumbled.

I later found out, Bryce saw the way my stalker was acting that first day in the grocery store. And he knew he had to act fast. I remember when I left the bar that night feeling dizzy and hot, like I was going to pass out. I did.

I fell into Bryce's arms.

I shake my head grumbling, scolding myself to stop thinking about Bryce.

Leena gives me that look again and then she smirks at me. She knows I'm thinking about him again.

Leena and I drive to my house to make sure everything's fine, but on our way down my street I find myself checking out every vehicle, looking for my stalker's blue pick-up truck.

I didn't have too many worries before, but the notes my stalker has left behind in several locations, have opened my eyes and increased my fears. We suspect Bryce ruined his plan to kidnap me that night at the bar. Bryce has protected me ever since, but now that I'm on my own again, I have to pay attention to every detail, especially now that he's getting more aggressive, setting more fires, and showing up to public places undetected.

The last note my stalker left was on the windshield of Bryce's truck when we came out of the Royale Inn after our first official date. Bryce was having a fit, thinking he damaged his truck, but to our surprise he left only a note.

> You don't know how much it killed me to see you dancing with him and sitting on his lap. The way you look at him is the way you WILL look at me. I'll be dancing with you, and you'll be sitting on my lap, looking deep in my eyes.
>
> YOU BROKE MY HEART!
>
> You're not listening to me when I told you to get rid of him. I know you don't want me to kill him, so he'd better disappear. I won't wait forever. I'll take care of the problem myself and then you'll be mine! We'll be so happy together. You'll love me, until death do us part.

I couldn't believe he had the nerve to come into the Inn that night to watch me and Bryce.

When we get out of the car, Leena runs up beside me, holding my arm, pulling me from my thoughts and we creep up the back deck. "I don't like this," she whispers, shivering and gripping my arm tighter.

"You worry too much. We'll be in and out," I whisper.

"If you're so confident why are we whispering?"

I unlock and open the door as quietly as possible and on our way through the kitchen, Leena grabs a big knife out of the wood chopping block. We search my living room and spare room first, the closet, and even the shower. My room is last. First thing I check is under my bed. Leena grips my waist tighter as she makes me go first into my walk in closet. I sweep my hand through all the clothes and shine the flashlight on the shelf above. Better safe than sorry. Relief washes over me and I finally relax. I quickly pack, shoving random clothes in the bag. All my stuff is at Bryce's house. I raced out of Bryce's parents' in a frantic state, not even thinking to stop at Bryce's to get my clothes.

Leena has convinced me to stay at her house tonight. I'll decide if I'm going to go see Gramps in the morning.

"I don't like being in your house without Austin and Bryce. It freaks me out," Leena says, rushing me along.

"Fine, let's get out of here." I grab my bag and keys, lock everything back up, make sure the security system is functioning properly, and head for the garage.

I pull onto the road, following Leena's car.

As we pass Mr. and Mrs. Fisher's, I notice the lights are on and start thinking about how Bryce noticed smoke coming from the back of their house that day. When he went to investigate, he saw their wheelchair ramp on fire. He rushed to get Mr. and Mrs. Fisher out of the house safely.

I was so proud of him.

All the signs pointed to arson when the gas can was found in the woods by police.

Later, at my house, Bryce didn't have to work very hard at seducing me right there on my kitchen table.

The memory makes me shiver. I scold myself to stop thinking about him.

Tonight, to keep myself busy and my mind off Bryce, I'll go to see how Mr. and Mrs. Fisher are doing, and then I'll go back to my place to check out the surveillance footage on my computer. I didn't want to take the time while I was there, with Leena being so paranoid.

When we get to Leena's house, her mom is waiting for us at the front door. She holds out her arms for me and I walk into her embrace.

"Hi, Ma."

"How are you? I've missed you." She holds me at arm's length and looks at me.

"I've been better."

"I heard. But you know what? We're going to have a girl's night. We'll have some munchies and a few drinks, and I made a dessert."

"You're the best, Ma."

Just like Ma, always trying to cheer people up.

"Come inside."

Leena's mom has been my second mother since my mom died. When we were kids, I used to stay over at Leena's house at least twice a week. I even had my own room, adjoining hers. I can see why, when Leena's parents divorced, she chose to stay with her mom even though her dad wanted her to live with him in paradise, at the resort he built in Aruba.

We sit around Ma's old wooden kitchen table, drinking, talking, and munching on warm chili cheese dip. Ma doesn't ask what happened with Bryce, so I don't offer anything. She knows I don't like to air out my dirty laundry for everyone to see.

After a couple Pina Colada's, the doorbell rings and Ma goes to answer it.

A deep voice says, "Hello Mrs. Ericson. It's so nice to finally meet you. I'm Austin and this is my brother, Bryce."

I almost choke, taking a sip of my drink.

"Oh, my," Ma replies in a giddy school girl voice.

My eyes widen as Leena bolts for the door.

What is he doing here? He drove an hour from Barrie to Huntsville, and for what-to talk to me?

I'm slipping into my coat and shoving my shoes on when I hear, "Keera, Bryce is here."

Without answering, I leave out the back door into the complete darkness.

I don't want to talk to him but if he catches up to me, I might have to, and I don't want everyone else to overhear our conversation.

My pace is fast as I walk down the sidewalk to the street. I pull out my phone and use it as a flashlight because there are no street lights here. It's not only pitch black, but very cold. Winter is well on its way. I'd be surprised if it doesn't snow tonight.

A truck crawls by me slowly. I don't realize I'm holding my breath until I look up, see that it isn't Bryce, and feel my body relax, as I exhale.

I need more time to think, but I have to face the inevitable. He's here to talk to me. What if he catches up to me? If he touches me?

I walk faster, trying to keep warm.

Another truck crawls beside me.

Jesus, this is a busy street.

Then I hear, "Hi Angel."

"*Fuck!*"

For a moment, only the sound of his engine disrupts the silence. I keep walking.

"Angel, are you going to talk to me or are you going to keep running?"

When I don't answer, he guns it and pulls the truck in front of me, scrambling out quickly. His powerful sexy strut as he approaches me, almost pulls me toward him. The electricity charging between us sends a familiar tingle throughout my whole body.

When he reaches out his arms to hold me, I back up, and he holds his hands up in the air. "Okay, but can I talk to you? Please? I was so worried when I got back to my parents' house and you were gone. Then I went to my house and you weren't there. It ripped my heart out. It devastated me, Angel."

Silence descends upon us. He's waiting for me to respond, but I don't.

"You wouldn't answer my calls or text. I'm sorry, Angel. I should never have left you. But I had no choice, I had to do whatever I could to calm her down. I've seen that look in her eyes before. Christ!" He runs his hands through his hair. "I've never told anyone this, but it was the same look before she slit her wrists. She did it right in front of me, for Christ's sake. I'll never forget that look in her eyes-the anguish and helplessness. It was my fault, I had just broken up with her."

He waits for a response. And I'm about to say it's not your fault. Don't you see how she's playing you? She's using her mental illness to keep you, and you just don't see it. But I change my mind and don't say a word.

"It's still no excuse, but if I'd gone back in the house to tell you I had to take her home, she would have lost it. I know her. I know what she's capable of."

A shiver runs through me. I'm so cold now that I've stopped walking.

Bryce steps toward me to wrap his arms around me, but I

back up again. He lifts his hands in the air again, as if in surrender. "Okay, I won't touch you, but can you get in my truck, please. You're freezing, Angel."

A truck crawls beside us with the window rolled down. "The little lady doesn't want you touching her! So get you're fucking hands off her and keep them off!"

It's my stalker! Bryce lunges for the door handle, but he guns it, spinning the tires, and we watch as he disappears down the street.

Bryce pulls out his phone and calls Austin. "That motherfucker was watching me and Keera. He took off down the street. Come get my truck, I'm down about ten houses to your left."

I hear Austin say, "We'll take Leena's car."

"Leave out of Leena's driveway to the right. Blue pick-up." Ending the call, Bryce turns back to me.

"Angel, please. Will you get in the truck with me? It's not safe for you out here."

Realizing he may be right, I walk silently toward the truck.

Once inside, Bryce turns to me. "Did I do something else to piss you off?" He hesitates. "Please, talk to me."

I pause for a long time deciding whether to say anything at all. "I saw the way you looked at her. You still love her."

"No I don't. I never loved her. Don't you see, you saved me. You're what I asked for, the angel in my dreams. I didn't know what love was until you came into my life."

I close my eyes trying to blink back the tears.

Don't cry, Keera. Don't do it. Be strong.

"That look you gave her will be imprinted in my mind forever. I can't be with a man who loves someone else."

Bryce gently rubs my knee. "Don't do this. I love you."

My chest constricts. I feel myself actually aching for him, but is he only saying this to win me back? I feel bad for putting him through this, but he has to know what this has done to me.

"I gave her that look so she'd come with me. You've got to

understand, she's had too many episodes around my family, which they don't appreciate and the best thing for everyone's sake was to get her out of there. It's hard to explain."

"I'm all ears."

"When she tried to commit suicide, I had just broken up with her. I felt like a heartless bastard, so I stayed with her."

"Is she taking meds?"

"Sometimes. She stops taking them when she feels better."

"Do you ever think she uses her illness to keep you where she wants you?"

"Yes, I did think of that. With the help of my family and the fact that I finally grew a set, I know it's over and I'm never going back. Now all I do is damage control."

"Yeah, well, because of that look you gave her, she thinks you still love her, and so do I."

"What will make you think differently?"

"Well, Bryce, you said it. Do you ever think cutting all ties with her would be less damaging in the long run?"

He pauses, but says nothing.

"Who am I to tell you what to do? I've got to go. Bye, Bryce."

Slamming the truck door, I start walking back to Leena's. I hear the other door slam behind me and in seconds, Bryce is in front of me holding my arms.

I back up and stare at him.

"Why are you being such a hard ass? I've never seen this side of you."

"Let's just say I'm protecting myself from being hurt."

"Are you starting your period soon?"

I scowl at him in disbelief. *Did he really just say that?*

Bryce back-pedals. "I'm sorry for that comment, but you seem different."

"Well of course I'm different. I gave up my virginity to a man I thought really cared about me, and now it turns out he still loves his ex-girlfriend."

"I swear to God, I don't love her, I never have. I love you and only you. I'm going to tell you over and over how sorry I am. I never meant to hurt you and I hope I never do it again. Angel, how can I fix this?"

"We need time apart." I can't think straight when you're standing right in front of me, but I don't tell him that. "You need to figure out who you want to be with, and I have my own things to work out."

"Oh, hell no! We are not breaking up! I know who I want to be with. You!"

I close my eyes, trying to hold back the tears.

"I have to work tomorrow, but I'm coming back Friday night. Please, Angel, don't do this."

I can't hold back any longer. My tears start to fall. I tried to be strong. Bryce picks me up in his arms, carries me back to the truck, and places me on the seat. Once he's climbed in his side, he leans over me and wipes away my tears with his thumb. "I said I wouldn't hurt you, but I did. I'm sorry Angel. Please don't cry."

He moves to the middle seat and pulls me on his lap, cradling me in his arms. "Don't you see how much I love you?"

I finally get a grip and stop crying. "That disappeared when I saw the way you looked at her."

"I guess I'll have to convince you that I don't. I love you Angel. I'll keep telling you over and over until one day you believe me. I'm not giving up on us. We'll grow old together and that's a promise."

"Tell me something."

"Anything."

"Why do you still have her picture by your bed?"

"Because I'm a fucking idiot. I was so busy with you for the past few weeks that I wasn't paying attention and when I saw it there I shoved it in the drawer."

"You've been broken up for two months and you never thought to get rid of it?"

"I did. I threw it in my closet. When Lindsay broke into my house to steal my phone, she must have put it back on the table and I didn't notice. I haven't been spending a lot of time at my house lately."

"Oh," I say softly, feeling a little foolish.

"Do you believe me? I always tell you the truth and I hope you will always tell me the truth."

"Yes, always."

"It's getting late. Let me take you back to Leena's."

Moments later, we pull into the driveway. Turning to me, he says, "I'm coming back as soon as I'm done work. Can we stay at your place?"

"Yes."

"I don't want you going anywhere without someone with you."

"Okay."

"Did you and Leena go to your house?"

"Yes, I needed a few things."

"He followed you."

"I looked for his truck down my street, but I didn't see anything."

"He could have been hiding anywhere."

Leena's car pulls in beside us and we all get out. Standing next to Bryce's truck, Austin looks at his brother and says, "Nothing. That fucker's slippery."

As we walk to the front porch, Austin wraps his arm around my shoulder. "Hi, Blondie."

"Hi, Austin."

"Did you forgive the big dumbass?"

"Yes, she did," Bryce says.

"We're still working on it," I say.

On the front porch, Austin turns to Bryce. "What the hell happened?"

"That motherfucker pulled up beside me and Keera, rolled

down his window, and told me to get my fucking hands off her. I grabbed the door handle, but it was locked. I'm telling you, if I ever get hold of him, he's dead!"

As Leena opens the door and we step inside, Ma approaches. "Would anyone like something to drink?"

"No thank you, Mrs. Ericson," Bryce says. "We have to get going. We have to work in the morning."

"Okay, have a safe trip back." She disappears.

Bryce pulls me behind the wall. "Are we okay?"

I look down at my hands. "We'll have to see."

He lifts my chin, forcing me to look at him. "Can I kiss you?"

"Yes."

His kiss is desperate and passionate. It makes my muscles clench and my toes curl.

Unfair. He knows exactly how to bring me to my knees.

"I don't want to leave you, Angel."

"Go to work. I'll see you tomorrow."

"I love you."

I give him a half smile. "I'll see you tomorrow."

When we walk to the front door, I look up and see that Austin has Leena pinned against the wall in a hot and wild kiss.

Ignoring them, Bryce continues, "I'll text you when I'm on my way, okay?"

"Perfect timing bro," Austin says sarcastically.

"Yeah, we've got to go." Bryce gives me one more scorching kiss. "I'm coming back as soon as I'm done work." He stares deep in my eyes, squeezing my hand, then he heads out the door.

"Bye, Blondie."

"Bye, Austin."

Suddenly I feel sad. *What is wrong with me?*

Leena must sense I'm a little off. "Let's get a drink."

"I need a drink after that."

Ma joins us at the kitchen table. She can't get over how handsome and polite Bryce and Austin are.

Leena is dying to know what happened, but she doesn't pry and I don't share. Breaking the awkward silence, she says, "So tell me, what happened with your stalker?"

"I wouldn't let Bryce touch me because I knew I'd be toast if he did. He was trying to be calm, cool and patient with me and then my stalker pulled up and said, 'the little lady doesn't want you touching her so get you're fucking hands off her and keep them off.'"

"Holy shit! Bryce must have lost it! I wish I would have been there."

"I'm telling you, if he'd caught him he would have ripped him apart with his bare hands. He was so mad!"

"Shit. I missed all the excitement. Damn it!"

Ma plops a crystal bowl down in front of us. A graham cracker truffle with chocolate cake, whip cream, cherries, and hot fudge drizzled over it, and bits of Snickers chocolate bar scattered on top.

Leena and I look at each other with wide eyes, "Thanks, Ma," we say enthusiastically.

"This is going right to my hips," I say digging in like the chocoholic I am.

"Thish ish aweshome, Ma," Leena says around a mouth full of cake and whipped cream.

"Mmm, yeah just what I need, a chocolate-filled coma." My mind shifts quickly. "Hey, what are you doing Wednesday?"

"That's the only day I don't have to work. Why? What's up?"

"Did Austin talk to you about their hockey game, Cops vs. Firefighters?"

"He must have forgotten with all the excitement."

"Want to go?"

"Hell, yeah, but let's keep it a secret. I want to surprise him."

I stay overnight with Leena and Ma. We don't venture out in case my stalker is watching.

I call Constable Grant to let him know I'm back from Barrie and tell him about the encounter Bryce had with my stalker. I also tell him I forgot the last time we spoke, to mention this guy has been following me around since April.

"Tell Bryce not to take things into his own hands," he says. "Let the police deal with it."

"Do you have any more leads?"

"Yes, but that's all I can say."

In the morning, I wake to a text from Bryce. *I love you.* Later in the day, as he leaves work and heads to Huntsville, he texts me again. *I love you. Stay at Leena's until I come get you.*

I can feel myself getting excited knowing he's on his way. *Control yourself.*

He needs to know that no matter how good his explanations are, I will not be his second choice and if he ever leaves me again for Lindsay, we will be done.

I have no idea how I'm going to prove my point with Leena and Austin staying at my house with us, but then it strikes me. *He can sleep on the couch. No sex. I can't be alone with him and I can't give in to him.*

As I'm packing my things, I think about Mr. and Mrs. Fisher. I want to go and see how they're doing, but opt out of it. The best thing for them would be for me to stay away, since they were already a target. If anything ever happened to them because of my stalker's sick obsession for me, I'd lose my mind. It's better for me to keep my distance for now. Hopefully, their kids are helping them out.

God, I'm rearranging my life because of this lunatic. At first I thought Bryce was a little paranoid, but now-I have to admit, I'm scared.

When Leena gets a text from Austin saying they're five minutes away, we lock up, and I place my bag in the back of my Dodge Journey.

While we wait for them to show up, I find myself looking around suspiciously, acting as paranoid as Bryce.

They pull into the driveway and Bryce shuts the truck off. He's over to me in an instant.

"Hi, Angel."

"Hi."

That familiar tingle radiates through my body and the electricity crackles all around us. Nothing else matters. It's just me and Bryce, lost in the moment. Everything else disappears.

He hesitates, searching my eyes, maybe trying to assess if I'll let him touch me.

I don't know what he sees, but his lips find mine in a hard, desperate kiss.

I faintly hear Austin say, "You come with me. Bryce can go with Blondie."

I pull away and see that Bryce is shaking a bit. *I hate dragging him through this and causing him pain, but does he have any idea what he put me through?*

"We'll meet you over there," Leena calls out with a smile.

I just finished telling her not to leave me alone with Bryce. Damn her, she never listens to me.

Walking around, I get into the driver's seat and Bryce sits in the passenger seat. "We need to talk."

2

"I'LL DO THE talking. I couldn't sleep. I was awake most of the night, thinking. I wanted to call you just to hear your voice. I can't ever lose you, Angel, I'd go out of my mind."

I swallow the huge lump in my throat. I have to drive, listen, and stay in control while Bryce talks.

"Today was the longest day of my life, not knowing how you felt about me. It was like my heart had been ripped out of my chest and I couldn't get here fast enough for you to replace it. I know I screwed up and I'm going to make it up to you, every day that we're together, which will be for the rest of our lives. I'll show you I love you and only you. You're the best thing that's ever happened to me. I need you like the air I breathe."

By the time I pull into my driveway, I'm blinded by my tears. As I shut off the ignition, Bryce leans over and runs his thumb over my cheeks to wipe my tears away. "I'm sorry Angel, it'll never happen again. I promise."

He hands my keys out the window to Austin, who pulled in beside us, so they can get into my house. "We'll be in, in a minute," Bryce says.

Turning back to me, he wraps his arm around me and kisses my forehead. "I love you, Angel. You're going to get so tired of me saying it, but I swear I'll show you, forever."

He rubs another tear off my cheek. "I wasn't supposed to make you cry. Please don't cry. Come here." He gently tugs me over the console onto his lap and holds me tight, kissing every inch on my face while I try to breathe, and stop crying.

"Are you okay?"

I nod.

"Are you ready to go inside?"

"Yes."

"I'll put your Journey in the garage after."

Leena and I make soup and sandwiches while Bryce gets us a drink and Austin sets up our movie. After eating, we move into the living room and Bryce tucks me into his side as we cuddle up to watch the movie.

I melt as I feel his hard body next to mine. It feels so right to be wrapped in his arms, like it's meant to be.

I try not to let my mind drift to "that look" again. I have him in my arms and he promises he'll never let it happen again, so I need to let it go.

After the movie, Austin goes into the kitchen to check the surveillance footage from last week. "I thought about this while we were watching the movie. I'm dying to know if your stalker had the balls to come here while we were gone."

Leena and I clean up while Austin searches.

"Angel, where are your keys, I'll put your Journey in the garage."

I hand them to him. "Thank you."

"You're welcome. Be right back."

When Austin finds something, he calls us over. "Look at this jackass," He says as Leena and I gather around to view the screen.

Leena shivers. "He gives me the creeps."

When Bryce comes back in, Austin rewinds the footage. "Bryce look at this, he most likely parks down the street. It shows him walking up the driveway every time."

Bryce watches as my stalker walks toward the back door, looks inside for quite a while, and then retreats, focusing his attention on the garage before leaving.

Every second day at dusk he shows up again and goes through the same routine, looking through the windows.

"He must know we're back," I say, looking up from the monitor. "What if he comes here tonight?"

"Oh, he knows we're back. He'll see my truck in the driveway and the lights on. I don't think he'll try anything, Angel, but maybe I shouldn't say that. He is unpredictable."

"If anyone hears anything tonight, wake everyone else up," Austin says as he walks to the back door to make sure it's locked and the security system is set.

Bryce checks the front and then tugs me behind him to my bedroom. As he closes the door behind us, I can feel butterflies in my stomach. This is the first time I'll have to deny him sex, but I have to prove my point.

As he pulls me toward the bed, he must feel the resistance in my body. "Angel, I just want to talk. Can you lie in the middle of the bed?"

He climbs in beside me, propping his head up. His other hand caresses my knuckles, which lie across my stomach.

"I know you're still hurt and I'm sorry. I screwed up huge, but I promise I'll never do it again. I can fix this."

"I just need a little time Bryce."

"You've put up a wall and I can't break through it."

"I need to know you don't love her."

"I'm going to prove that to you. That's a promise."

I hesitate. "Bryce, I have to ask you something."

"Anything."

"Can we sleep separately tonight? I'll go sleep on the couch." He sighs heavily. "No. I'll sleep on the couch."

"I'm sorry."

"I understand." He gracefully rolls out of the bed and so do I.

I grab an extra pillow and blanket from my closet and hand it to him.

"Goodnight, see you in the morning."

"Goodnight," he says, kissing me on the cheek before he heads for the couch in the living room.

Why am I doing this to him? I can see he feels terrible, and he's dealing with so much. A crazy ex-girlfriend, my stalker, and me. I feel overwhelmed by guilt, terrible for what I'm putting him through.

Other than this one mistake, he been the perfect boyfriend.

A part of me wants him to come back in and sleep with me. I toss and turn, but I can't get him out of my head. I want to go to him and tell him I've changed my mind.

Suddenly the door bursts open and Bryce stands in the doorway. He hesitates for a moment, his eyes boring right through me. He closes the door and locks it.

He prowls toward the bed and climbs on top of me, holding himself up with his strong arms. "I can't sleep without you, knowing you're in here. I need to be with you."

Searching my eyes, he says, "I love you."

Before I can respond, he lowers his lips to mine. His kiss is slow, sensual. Pleasure ripples down through my body and echoes in my groin.

Aww, shit!

My resistance melts away and I surrender like I did when we first met. I kiss him back, our tongues tangling and dancing in circles, every kiss hot and wild, breathless for the next one.

When he finally pulls his mouth away from mine, he takes my hand and places it on his heart. "Feel that? It beats hard for you and only you."

My chest constricts, tears well up in my eyes, and a lump forms in my throat. "Babe."

Bryce grinds his thick, hard-as-stone cock against my pussy. "See what you do to me? You drive me crazy. I can't stand to be separated from you for more than five minutes. I can't breathe without you."

He kisses me again, long and hard, like he desperately needs to. When he pulls away, he looks in my eyes. "Angel, let me make love to you."

"Yes." My body trembles. I need him. Desperately.

I'll be pissed off at myself tomorrow for giving in to him, but for now I'm going to enjoy every inch of his gorgeous body.

He gets out of bed and holds his hand out to help me up. We're so hot for each other that we shimmy out of our pajamas in seconds.

My gaze rakes over him and his over me.

His eyes glimmer with desire as he closes the gap between us. He lifts his hand and glides it gently down my cheek. "I thought I lost you, I thought you gave up on me. I love you, Angel."

I close my eyes, feeling guilty for the pain and distress I've dragged him through, but also because I haven't told him I love him yet. I'm not about to until I know he loves me and only me.

When I open my eyes, he's gazing deep in mine.

"Please let me make love to you."

"Yes," I whisper.

His fingers weave through my hair and he holds the back of my neck while his lips gently seal with mine. He kisses me slowly, tenderly, making me feel precious to him. His other hand makes its way gently down my back, awakening every nerve ending. He reaches my butt and pulls me close to his hard cock, which presses between my stomach and his. My nipples are hard, poking against his warm skin. He holds me tighter, so our bodies feel skin on skin. Then he guides me, step by step backwards until the back of my knees hit the bed. He gently lowers me with his strong arms, his lips still fused to mine.

I realize in this moment that he could hurt me again and I'd eventually go back to him, but I'm not about to tell him that.

I'm weak when it comes to Bryce. He's my addiction. A habit I never want to give up.

He holds his own body weight while lifting me to the middle of the bed. His large thigh spreads my legs and he nestles between them, his hard cock laying between my spread pussy lips and his hips flexing to give me the perfect amount of pressure to drive me wild.

Rocking back and forth while he kisses and nips my neck, I feel unimaginably hot and ache to have him deep inside me.

"Bryce, I need you."

I feel him smile against my neck, but he's silent.

His kisses begin to move down my body, but stop at my nipples, where he alternates between biting, nipping, and flicking his tongue over the tight peaks.

I buck my hips to let him know I can't take much more.

I feel his smile on my chest before he begins sliding his lips down my abdomen.

I let out a heavy sigh.

"I'm getting there. I want to make sure you're ready for me."

"I'm ready. Trust me."

He smiles again before continuing his slow painful journey down my abdomen.

I shiver as he spreads my silky moist folds with his gentle fingers. As his tongue traces circles around my clit, my body convulses and my pelvis jerks.

A low moan escapes my lips.

His finger probes and teases at the entrance of my pussy.

I buck again and he inserts it slowly, moving it in and out of me lazily.

Flattening his tongue, he licks from my entrance to my clit. "Mmm, so wet, and so damn sweet."

He lingers there for a while, fluttering his tongue, tasting, teasing me, then suddenly he slides up my body and positions his hard cock at my entrance.

"When I thought I lost you, the only thing that got me through it was smelling your juices on your pretty pink thong. It was my lifeline. I kept them in my pocket day and night."

His confession has my heart tightening again. Aching. I close my eyes to keep the tears from seeping out of the corner of my eyes.

Suddenly, he plunges deep inside me. My eyes fly open and I gasp and moan.

"You're ready for me."

My nails dig into his back, scratching all the way down to his tight ass cheeks, and I squeeze, pulling him deeper into me.

There's no way I can control the tidal wave of desire crashing over me. I pull him down and kiss him with shaking desperation and he kisses me back with the same ferocity until we're both breathless and need to pull away.

We find the perfect rhythm, with my hips rising and falling hard as he drives his cock into me.

My muscles clamp down on him and he stops moving.

"Angel, we've got to stop. I'm going to come. It's too soon."

In one swift motion, he rolls me on top, making sure we stay connected. "This is better. I get to see these beautiful tits and your gorgeous body." He cups both my breasts in his hands. "Nothing better than this, Angel."

He pinches each nipple with his finger and thumb as I begin lifting and lowering. "That's it, ride me."

I start with a slow rhythm and then progress faster as I feel his fingers grip tight on my hips and I see the expression on his face change. I know he can't hold out much longer.

I slide up and down his thick shaft, feeling the wide head of his cock scrape the slick walls of my vagina. I hold onto his large pectoral muscles for support while I change the angle, then I ride him hard.

He lets out a regretful groan and then tackles me to the bed. He flips around in a split second and his hard cock glistens with a bead of pre-cum right in front of my lips.

"Sixty-nine, Angel, both of us pleasing each other at the same time. Another one of my favourite positions."

I wrap my fingers around his hard shaft, lick my lips, and take him into my mouth as far as I can.

He moans. "Your mouth is heaven on my cock."

His head lowers and his tongue dances over my clit. His finger circles my entrance, teasing me, until he gently eases inside me.

I have no idea how much time is passing as we pleasure each other.

With all the craziness and excess baggage in our lives, this is when we forget it all. It's just me and him, lost in ourselves, lost in the moment. It's as if time matters as little to Bryce when he's making love to me, as it does to me. There may be an urgency in the way he touches me at first, but then he takes his time as if he wants it to last forever, his hands have to touch every part of my body, as if he can't get enough.

I can't get enough either. My body aches to touch every inch of his sculptured, hard muscles.

Bryce changes position, making his way to my feet, slowly kissing my toes, working his way up my legs, feathering his lips across my hips, up my belly, across both my breasts, up my neck, and onto my cheek.

My God, he's so good at this.

The feel of his warm breath on my ear and the smell of his cologne is driving me nearly insane.

"I want you to feel every inch of my love. I want to possess your whole body, from head to toe. I want you to want me, as bad as I need and want you. So you'll never leave me again. You're mine, Angel."

I'm stunned by his admission.

His heavy warm body lifts as he straddles my body. "Flip! On your stomach."

I do as he says, feeling like I'm his to command.

His body hovers over mine and I feel his hard cock gliding over my sensitive skin as he pulls my hair to the side, kisses my neck, and tugs at my ear lobe with his teeth.

I feel his tongue run along my neck just before his warm breath gusts against my ear. "I'll be right back."

Bryce moves quickly and then I feel tickling as he kisses my feet. He doesn't spend too much time there as he knows I'm ticklish and I'll giggle and squirm. Instead, he leisurely kisses his way up the back of my legs, stopping as he approaches my butt. He kisses between words. "How. I. Love. This. Sweet. Sweet. Ass." His large hands cup my rear, and caress it gently.

His tongue runs up my spine, leaving goose bumps in its wake, and I shiver. "You like this, don't you?"

"Mmm, yes. You can do this to me any time you want."

"I take it that's an open invitation to worship your body."

"Anytime you'd like."

He smiles against my shoulder pulling my hair to the side, gently skittering his lips along my jaw. I feel his tongue dart out, gliding around my neck. "I love tasting you. I want to taste every inch of your body."

Not a romantic, eh?

His cock lays heavy in the crease of my butt and he lifts, flexing his hips so I feel that delicious tease of his plump head gently rubbing and caressing up and down my sensitive skin, setting it on fire.

He straddles my thighs and his large, strong hands massage my back, covering every inch. He works his fingers into my lower back, loosening the tight muscles, then moves to my butt and massages it for a while. He leans in, once more teasing me with the sensation of his cock skimming gently in the crack of my butt, as he works out the tight muscles in my shoulders. His large hands caress down both my arms from shoulders to hands.

I want him inside me. All this sensual touching sets my skin on fire.

I'm trembling all over and my pussy quivers for just a touch from him.

"Bryce?" I can't help the begging sound in my voice, because that's exactly what I'm doing. I'm begging. "I need you to touch me."

"I am touching you." But I hear it with a smile. He enjoys tormenting me like this.

I feel him get off the bed and my attention is automatically diverted to him and that body. I try to see what he's doing. He's standing in front of my lounge chair sifting through his overnight bag, but his large body is obstructing my view so I can't see what he's searching for.

He turns and sees me watching. "Eyes forward, or I'll put a blindfold on you."

Not that it would be a punishment. I like it when he blindfolds me. It brings my senses to life.

Since he's been teasing the hell out of me, I think I'll test the waters, so I keep staring intently.

He turns his attention back to what's in the bag and, just as he's about to turn around, he sees me. "What did I tell you?" he says sternly.

I smile mischievously, squinting my eyes and showing my dimple. He drops whatever he had in his hand back into the bag.

"Oh you're asking for it," he says, smiling. He unzips the side of the bag and pulls out a blindfold.

I'm on my belly, kicking my legs back and forth, quite proud of myself for derailing his plan. Now I might get a punishment, which I can't wait for.

Bryce climbs back on the bed, positioning his knee, oh so close to my crotch, and I feel the heat from his thigh.

He leans over, putting his full weight on me, and whispers in my ear. "You've been a bad girl."

"I know."

He slips the wide blindfold on and ties it tight. "Can you see?"

"No."

"Good."

I feel movement on the bed and then nothing. He must have left the bed. I hear him rustling around in the bag again and then he's back kneeling between my legs.

"On your knees and open wide. Bum up."

I get into position.

His finger strokes down between my pussy lips and he parts them, then he slips something inside and I moan. It's fairly big and stretching me a bit. All of a sudden, it starts vibrating inside me.

I drop my head onto my hands, moan, and circle my hips. "Babe, it feels so good."

"I knew you'd like it."

"I don't know how much longer I can hold out."

He shuts it off. "I'm not done with you yet."

How did he shut it off without touching me?

I clench in anticipation and wonder what else he has planned for me.

Whatever's inside me already, starts vibrating again and then I feel another vibrator between my pussy lips.

I feel it stroking over the sensitive tissues on the outside. He holds it at an angle so it vibrates my clit. I am overstimulated. So many sensations. Too many sensations. My body starts to tremble and shake.

I can't hold out any longer. A whimper escapes and I cry out. "Bryce."

"Let it go, Angel. Give it to me."

A scream escapes, but I bury my face in the pillow, quivering.

He waits until my aftershocks subside, then he shuts off both vibrators.

I collapse onto the mattress and he leans down and whispers in my ear.

"I love hearing you. I love every little sound you make and when you scream fuck, Angel, I get so hard."

"I can't believe how long that lasted. That was amazing, Babe."

He kisses my cheek. "Leave the blindfold on and kneel up."

My legs are still shaking as I get up on my knees.

"I need you to push it out." Bryce's hand reaches between my thighs waiting for it to come out, and then I feel a tugging motion. "There it is. I've got it."

"What is it?" I ask curiously.

"It's a surprise for the next time."

"Oh."

I feel the bed shift. I think he's hiding it and I smile because he likes to surprise me.

"On your back," Bryce commands.

I flip onto my back and he yanks me by my legs to the middle of the bed, like I weigh absolutely nothing.

He pulls the blindfold off. "Welcome back, Beautiful."

He positions himself and impales me.

A gasp escapes my mouth from his cock filling me so fast.

"Fuck, Angel, you feel so good." He moves his hips slowly, thrusting deep.

Then he stops moving, looks deep in my eyes and hesitates, as if he's going to say something, like he's struggling for the perfect words. "Don't you see, Angel? I won't ever give you up. You will always be mine."

A tear slides down my cheek and he sees how he's affecting me, but in this moment I don't care that he's insanely possessive. I wouldn't want him any other way.

He holds my ankles wide open to the sky. What a sight to

behold! His muscles strain everywhere as he pounds his cock into me, hard, balls slapping my ass.

"Babe! It's so good."

"Grab that vibrator next to your head and place it on your clit."

I frantically fumble for it, revving it up.

He's giving it to me hard. The sound of flesh against flesh fills the room. His skin is misted with a sheen of sweat, his breathing laboured like he's been running a marathon.

I see the features on his face tighten. "Angel?"

"I'm with you, Babe. Don't stop!" My muscles contract and squeeze around him and my body convulses.

He slams into me as long as he can, remembering my request.

I feel his cock jerk as he releases his warm cum inside me. When he finishes, he collapses on top of me and we both laugh.

"Wow Babe, you can go forever."

He lifts his head and smiles at me wickedly. "I'm not finished with you yet. I just need to catch my breath."

"Is that a promise?"

"Christ, if anyone can go forever it's you, Angel."

His cock slips out as he rolls to his side and then onto his back with his fingers twined together behind his head, giving me full access to his beautiful body.

I hurry to straddle his hips. His semi-hard cock lays between my pussy lips and I take full advantage of grinding on him.

"Nothing more beautiful than you on top of me."

I smile and grab a handful of his meaty pec muscles and squeeze. "I've never seen such a beautiful body." I shake my head. "Mmm, mmm."

"I'm glad you like. I don't mean to change the subject, but I need to know-are we okay now?"

Men! They think sex can fix everything-although I do feel more relaxed.

"Bryce, if you ever wanted another woman, you'd be honest and break up with me first. Right? That's all I ask, please."

"Angel, listen to me closely, I'm telling you right now you're the one. The only one. The only woman I will ever love. I'll never cheat on you and that's a promise I will never break."

I open my mouth to say something and he quickly shuts me up with his finger over my lips.

"Angel, you've got to understand when I sleep, I dream of you. When I'm awake, I'm constantly thinking about you. When I'm not with you, all I think about is getting back to you the fastest way possible."

Tears start to well up in my eyes.

"I've got to admit, I've lost my balls to you. I don't even look at other women now because my search is over. I love you."

A tear drops onto his chest.

"Oh, no you don't." He tickles and tackles me to the mattress and I can't help but giggle.

The phone rings and I reach over to pick it up, "Hello," I say, still giggling.

There's silence on the other end.

Bryce continues tickling me, and I grab hold of his hand, mouthing for him to stop.

"Hello?" I say, but there is still silence at the other end of the phone.

Bryce sees the smile fading from my face and says, "Angel? Who is it?"

I hold the receiver away from my ear, my heart starting to beat a little faster. When I answer Bryce's question, I hear my own voice cracking. "I only hear breathing."

"Give me that," Bryce says, gently taking the phone from my hand. He sits up against my headboard. "Hello?" Bryce's voice is deep and husky.

I lean in and listen closely.

"I told you not to touch her. She doesn't want you. She wants me. Didn't you get the hint when she wouldn't let you touch her? It's her way of telling you to fuck off! She wants to be with me."

My eyes widen and my heart is racing.

"Why don't you come here right now and we'll talk, man to man," Bryce says.

"You're not a man!" he yells. "You think you can come into her life and take over? We have a relationship, and a lot of history between us. She's trying to get rid of you and you're not listening to her wishes. Why don't you bow out gracefully and then I might think you're a man."

"Should've known better. You'll never meet me face to face. You're scared of me." The calm in Bryce's voice as he tries to coax my stalker to come here is really surprising me.

"We'll be seeing each other very soon," he says.

"Great! I'll be waiting." Bryce listens for a moment, waiting for my stalker to speak again. Bryce hangs up, wheeling the phone across the room. "Fuck! I wanted to keep him on the phone longer."

"I can't believe he had the balls to call here," I say.

"I don't put anything past that fucker."

I clamber out of bed and saunter over to pick the phone up off the floor.

Bryce takes the phone from me and gently places it on the nightstand. "Sorry Angel, I've got to learn to control my temper." He slides his black pajama pants on, while I slip into mine. "I need something to drink."

Leena and Austin are sitting at the kitchen table.

"Guess who called," Bryce says.

"Jesus, no. He's calling your house now, Keera?" Leena says, her eyes wide. "You don't think he'll show up tonight, do you Bryce?"

"We can't put anything past him, anything's a possibility."

"What did he say?" Austin asks.

"He said, 'I told you not to touch her. It's her way of telling you to fuck off. She wants to be with me.' He said, 'you think you can come into her life and take over?' He thinks Keera and him have a relationship. He says they have history together. He's frickin' delusional."

"I've never talked to him. He's always watched me from a distance."

Bryce holds my hip. "In his mind, he believes it. Like I said, delusional."

"I'll set the security system to sound an alert when the motion lights pick up any movement outside," Austin says. "Tomorrow I'll go to the cop shop and let them know what he's been up to."

"Thank you Austin, I feel so much safer when you guys are here. So does Leena."

"This whole thing has scared the crap out of me. I didn't want to come in the house without you guys. It gave me the creeps when Keera and I were here earlier. I couldn't wait to leave."

Standing next to the kitchen counter, Bryce turns so he's gazing in my eyes and he takes hold of my hand. "He's scaring you, I know. He's getting under your skin and frightening you. It's okay to admit it. He's getting under my skin, too."

"Yes, I'm scared, and I hate that I have to rearrange my life because of him."

"I know, Angel." He wraps me in a tight embrace and kisses my forehead. "Don't worry. We'll get him."

3

THIS MORNING, WE woke up to a foot of snow blanketing the ground, surprising us, and catching township employees off guard because the first snow usually falls in November, not October. Last night we played cards for a few hours waiting for my stalker to show up, but for some unknown reason, he never ventured out to pay us a visit. I guess the snow storm deterred him.

There were no visible signs of footprints in the snow around my house, leading us to believe my stalker was lying low for the moment.

The unplowed snow made it a little difficult for Austin to get to the police department first thing in the morning as planned. He had to wait until well after noon before my road was cleared.

Leena and Austin head to the police station on slick roads, while Bryce and I take my snow blower out of the garage to clear my driveway.

From the moment we walked outside, we could smell the clean mountain air and the pine trees, an aroma more prominent by the snowfall. "Mmm, I love that smell," I say, breathing it in deeply.

"I know. There's only one other smell I love more." Bryce wraps his arms around me tugging me close. I look up and he's grinning at me.

"And that is?"

"You," he says in that deep, sexy voice.

I snake my fingers around his neck and pull him down for a kiss. His luscious lips are soft and the kiss revs up my hormones. He nuzzles in my neck, inhaling my scent.

The snow that had fallen all night was thick fluffy snowflakes that accumulated quickly and are great for throwing snowballs. When Bryce isn't looking, I gather some into the perfect snowball and throw it at him. With my bad aim, it hits his shoulder, exploding, and some gets him in the face. He turns and gives me the cutest and most mischievous smile I've ever seen. His dimple forms on his right cheek and he raises one eyebrow at me. "You want to play that game, eh?" A moment later, I'm tackled in the snow and we're lying there kissing and hugging.

"I'm sorry." I wipe the snow off his eye lashes and give him little kisses all over. "It wasn't supposed to get you in the face."

"That's okay." Bryce gives me a quick kiss and then stands, holding his hand out to help me up. "Come on, I don't want you catching a cold lying in that snow." He pulls me up and flattens me against his body, holding me tight.

Reaching up, I hold his face in my hands and stare into his beautiful hazel eyes. "You're always thinking of me."

"Always." Bryce lowers his lips to mine.

Just then, a snowmobile cuts through my yard, circles my house, and parks twenty feet away from us.

Bryce gets close to my ear. "Who is that?"

"I have no idea."

We watch, waiting for him to take his helmet off. When he does, my muscles tense and shock overwhelms me.

Jake!

Bryce gives me a look of concern as my mind floods with bad memories of that summer night when I was fifteen in Algonquin Park when Jake almost raped me.

Jake closes the gap between us, and wraps me in a hug. I tense and stiffen more. "Keera, I'm so happy to see you. I've missed you."

"Jake?" I back out of his embrace. "What are you doing here?" My voice sounds angry, but Jake doesn't notice.

"I bought a house a few blocks away."

"Jake, this is my boyfriend, Bryce."

Bryce holds out his hand. "Pleased to meet you."

"Good to meet you," he says, giving Bryce a firm handshake.

Jake turns and wraps me in a hug again. "I was hoping you still lived here."

I pull away again, but Jake still holds my arms. I'm uncomfortable, and I wonder if a diversion will disguise how I really feel about him. "Would you like to come inside for a beer, coffee, or hot chocolate?"

"Sure, I'd love to."

Bryce pushes the snow blower to the garage and I follow, asking Jake questions, distracting him because I need and want Bryce with me. I don't want to be alone with Jake.

"So how are your mom and dad?"

"Mom died a few years ago and Dad still lives in Temagami."

"I'm sorry to hear that. She was a good woman. How'd she die?"

"Cancer."

"I hope she didn't suffer."

"She died within three months of finding out."

"I'm sorry, Jake, I didn't know."

Bryce closes the garage door and we walk toward the back deck.

Jake gets ahead of me, stops, and holds his arms out. "I'm

sorry about your parents, I wanted to make it to the funeral to see you." He hugs me again as Bryce watches, not saying a word.

"I was so caught up in getting my business off the ground and I was travelling a lot and couldn't make it here, but that's no excuse. I'm sorry."

Bryce walks around us to the door and opens it.

I back away from Jake and walk up the steps. "Thank you. I'm fine now. It was tough, but time helps to heal."

Inside, as we take our winter clothing off, Jake stares at me. I peek up at Bryce and see that he notices, too.

Jake finally focuses on the house. He walks from the kitchen to the doorway of living room. "Damn, this looks totally different from when your parents owned it. You did a really good job of renovating."

"Thanks. What would you like?"

"It's past two. I'll take a beer if you have it, please."

"Babe, what would you like?"

"I'll get it, you sit." Bryce pulls out a chair for me.

There's a method to his madness. He wants me to sit so Jake can't see me behind the table and he'll quit undressing me with his eyes.

Jake comes around the table, pulls out a chair next to me, and sits down.

Bryce plops Jake's beer on the table and gently places mine. Then he stands against the counter, leaning in that confident sexy pose that shows off his impressive package.

I turn my chair to face both of them, and move closer to the wall, away from Jake. "So you started a business?"

"Yeah, it's been up and running and doing well for a few years. I have my buddy run it now and I go in and check on them every once and a while."

"What kind of business is it?" Bryce asks.

"Robinson Sports. I have a dealership for ATVs, snowmobiles, and motor cycles. We buy, sell, maintain. If you need a part, I can get it. I'm located in North Bay."

"That's where my grandfather lives."

"I know. I've driven by his house a few times. He's got a new Dodge pick-up."

I look at him with a confused glare.

"Remember both our families went to visit your Gramps when we were kids? So I thought I'd drive by and see if he still lives there. I saw him out in the yard. I check up on him to make sure he's okay."

"Thanks," I say, blandly.

He places his hand on my knee. "Anything for you."

I peek up at Bryce and his glare floats to where Jakes hand is on my knee.

Jake sees Bryce's icy stare and quickly takes his hand away. "And what do you do for a living?"

"Barrie firefighter."

"Oh, yeah? That must be exciting."

"Yeah, it is."

"So how do you get time off to see Keera?"

"We make it happen. Sometimes she comes to stay with me at my house."

Jake sips his beer.

Just then, Leena and Austin come in the back door, saving us from the awkward silence. "Whose snowmobile is that? Jake!" She stops dead and leans against the counter gripping it. "What the hell are you doing here?" Her voice is angry.

Jake saunters over to Leena and wraps her in a hug. "Well, it's nice to see you too. I came to visit Keera. I bought a house a few blocks away."

Jake holds out his hand to Austin. "I'm Jake. And you are?"

"I'm Austin, Leena's boyfriend."

"Nice to meet you. Have you tamed this one yet?"

"I see you're still a jackass."

"Oh, Leena, you love me and you know it."

"Yeah, Jake, like a heart attack."

Jake laughs. "Well, I've got to be on my way. I have to keep an eye on my renovators."

Jake walks back to me, moving in for a kiss, but I turn quickly and he hits my cheek. He stares directly into my eyes. "I'll be seeing you around. I'll come visit, and when my house is done I'll have you over to see it." He walks over to his snow pants and boots, tugging them on. "It was nice seeing you again. You're just as beautiful as you were when we were teenagers."

My skin crawls from the sound of his voice and the way he's looking at me, and I wish I had it in me to be direct and honest like Leena, but I literally don't know how to be rude to people. My politeness gets me into trouble all the time.

"See you, Leena."

"Yeah. Thanks for the warning, Jake."

Jake chuckles as he grabs his coat off the hook and makes his way out the door.

Bryce looks at me. "So, I take it he's a family friend?"

"Our families went on vacation together."

We hear Jakes snowmobile start and Bryce looks out my kitchen window at him. "I'm sensing your uneasiness toward him."

We hear Jake's snowmobile fade into the distance.

"Well, yeah, he almost raped her," Leena blurts out.

"I knew I didn't like that fucker, and not only because he's got it bad for you. What did he do, Angel?"

Bryce stands in front of me at the kitchen sink, rubbing my waist, waiting for me to answer.

I hesitate, not knowing whether I want to share the way the ordeal with Jake affected me. How for the longest time, I wouldn't let a man into my life and that I'm still damaged because of it. Leena, Katie, and my parents were the only people I've ever told and that was difficult. At the time, I was a sheltered, naïve teenager, who trusted everyone. But after what happened with Jake, who I'd trusted as a good friend, I put up a wall. I couldn't trust any man, other than my dad and grandfather. It screwed me up for a long time. I sometimes still have nightmares. My way of dealing with it was to dismiss it from my mind. Forget that it had happened. But now that Jake is back, my mind will relive those terrible memories.

Maybe if I start to talk about it, instead of keeping it bottled up inside, I'll find a way to finally heal.

I take a deep breath. "Both our families were camping in Algonquin Park and I woke to Jake in my tent on top of me holding my mouth so I couldn't scream. He already had my pajama top unbuttoned and he yanked my bottoms down before I knew what the hell was going on. I tried to fight him off, but he was as big as he is now at fifteen years old. His clothes were off, he spread my legs, and he was just about to… I could see the look in his eyes from the lantern. They were so dark and evil. He was a different person at that moment. I started to cry and that's when he snapped out of it. He stopped and apologized over and over again. He said he read me wrong. He thought that was what I wanted. When I told my mom, we never went on vacation with them again and shortly after that they moved to Temagami."

While I'm speaking, the angry frown on Bryce's face, relaxes and his voice softens. He holds me in a tight embrace. "That's what you meant when you said you were facing your fears. Christ, Angel, the way I came on to you that first day we were together… I could have ruined us before we even got started. I'm sorry." Lowering his voice, he asks, "Why didn't you tell me?" He rubs my arms.

"I don't like to talk about it. I'm okay. I got over it." I put on a brave face for Bryce. "But don't leave me alone with him. I don't feel comfortable."

"I could tell by the way you were acting. I want you to text me right away if he comes over here again. Do you want me to kick his ass?"

"No, Bryce."

"Okay, but I'm telling you if he ever touches you again, even the knee touching, I'm going to lose it."

"Bryce, he's a family friend. You can't."

"I don't give a shit if he's a family friend. He almost raped you. I wanted to kill that fucker right here in your kitchen and at the time I didn't even know what he did to you. Wait until I see him next time."

I rub his arms. "Babe, you've got to calm that temper down."

"I know." He kisses and hugs me tight.

Austin clears his throat. "So the cops are coming Monday to set up the wiretap on your phone. Constable Grant said he'll call your cell so you can let them in."

"Thank you, Austin."

"No problem, Blondie."

"Did Grant say if he had anymore leads on her stalker?" Bryce grumbles.

"He's tight-lipped. He said they have a couple new leads, but he didn't give any details."

Bryce wants to go to the grocery store to draw out my stalker so we venture out, even though it's still snowing and the roads are slick. He playfully spins the truck, doing doughnuts and fishtailing down my road, and I watch as he maneuvers the truck with expertise in the parking lot. I love seeing the playful, carefree side of him.

We don't see him at the store, but when we return to my house we see fresh foot-prints in the snow leading up to my deck. A note is taped to the door and we all huddle around to see what it says.

She'll be mine soon.

Laughing and giggling with me.

How are you going to feel knowing she's in my bed, making love to me? That's the only reason I've let you live, so you can

die a slow, painful death with your heart ripped out!

Austin takes the note off the door, using his sleeve to avoid getting his fingerprints on it.

"That mother fucker is still watching every move we make." Furious, Bryce shoves the door open and we carry the groceries in. Austin places the note on the counter.

As we take our winter clothing off and unpack the groceries, Bryce comes up behind me, pulls my hair to the side and whispers in my ear. "I want you to come home with me."

I turn to gaze in his eyes. "I have to be here to open the door for the cops."

"I don't want to leave you here alone."

"Keera can stay at my house all week," Leena offers.

"Someone will be with her, always?" Bryce asks.

"If I'm at work, my mom will be there."

"I still don't like it."

"Babe, I'll be fine at Leena's. I'll only come out to open the door for the cops."

"I want Leena with you when you do. I'm telling you, I'm getting a bad feeling about this fucker. If you see or hear from him you call or text me right away. That goes for your other boyfriend too."

"Babe!"

"Not only do I have to worry about a crazy-ass stalker-slash-arsonist, now I have to worry about a rapist still trying to get into your pants."

I smile at him because he's too cute when he's jealous.

"I'll be fine. You worry too much."

"I want you two to be alert."

"Yes, sir!" Leena puts two fingers to her forehead and salutes Bryce.

How she loves to antagonize him, but Bryce lets it go.

We watch the surveillance video and see my stalker walk directly to the back yard, up the deck, and tape the note to the door.

Austin points at the computer screen. "See, he's not looking around. He knows we weren't here."

Bryce gives me a peck on the cheek. "I'll be right back. I'm going to take a quick look down the street to see if that fucker is hanging out watching." He walks to the back door to put his coat and boots on.

"Wait, I'll come with you." Austin kisses Leena. "Just a quick look and we'll be right back."

"We'll start dinner," Leena says as they take off out the back door.

"Jesus, I wonder what Bryce would do if he caught him?" I say, a little worried.

"Austin would be by the book and bring him in to the cops, I would think," Leena says proudly.

"I think you're right, but I bet Bryce would give him a beating before Austin took him in."

"Yeah, I don't doubt that. He's got quite the temper, don't ya think?"

"Whenever we get a note from my stalker, he gets angry, possessive, and jealous, yes." I think about when we started this relationship. Bryce warned me about his possessive tendencies and his jealous streak.

In my mind, I replay every incident with my stalker and how Bryce has reacted. I think it's a coping mechanism for him so he doesn't go out of his mind. "But he never gets mad at me. He's always calm and considerate with me."

"Yeah, I have noticed that. He loves you."

Leena and I prepare our garlic mashed potatoes and chicken dinner, and then are waiting for it to cook when the guys come through the door.

"Didn't see him," Bryce complains as he hangs his coat up at the back door.

"After dinner, we'll get a coffee at Timmy's and look for him then," Austin adds.

Just as we're cleaning up after dinner, we hear sirens, so we rush out to the front porch to see what the commotion is.

Bryce immediately dashes back inside to get his coat on and then runs over to my neighbour's house on the north side of mine. The Stevenson's garage is fully engulfed in flames. Austin runs after Bryce, while Leena and I hurry to get our winter gear on and rush outside to see the fire department running hose and trying to put the fire out.

I stand next to Bryce and his arm snakes around my waist, tugging me closer. "You think he did this?" I ask.

"I have no doubt. It's him."

We watch for a while as the firefighters dowse the flames, extinguishing the fire and then they sift through the hot spots. I catch Bryce scanning the crowd for my stalker.

Leena grabs my arm. "Let's go back in the house. It's cold out here and I'm freezing."

Bryce looks at me and rubs my arm. "Go back in the house and get warmed up. I'll talk to the chief and police."

When Leena and I get back in the house, I instantly notice a few things out of place. I search around, confused, and when I walk into my bedroom I see my underwear drawer open and some lingerie hanging out. I take inventory and notice that my light blue thong and bra are missing.

Leena walks in and I see the look on her face before I see the note she's holding with the tips of her fingers.

4

"*H*E WAS IN here as soon as we went outside. Oh my God, Leena! I can't believe this!"

"What if he's still here?" Leena whispers. "I don't know about you, but I'm freaked out."

"Yeah, I'm scared."

Leena grabs my arm and pulls me to the front door.

"Come on, let's get the hell out of here!"

Leena pulls me next door, until were about twenty feet away from Bryce and Constable Grant, who are busy talking.

"Keera, you've got to read this," Leena says, holding the note with the tips of her fingers.

> Like my diversion to get everyone out of the house? I knew it would work. These are my favourite, thanks baby. I wish you had worn them. I want to smell you. I love smelling you. I'll be back for more.

I'll add these to my collection.

Love, Your Romeo.

"Oh my God, Leena. He started the fire to get us out of the house. This proves he's been here before and he's taken a few things."

"You've never noticed things missing before?"

"Yeah, but you always think they'll show up, that maybe you misplaced them."

"This is too fucking freaky. Let's go show them the note." Leena says, pulling me closer.

The moment we walk up, Bryce turns to me, and Leena holds up the note.

"Bryce, he started this fire to get us out of the house, and the moment we came out, he went in," Leena explains.

"He stole two articles of my lingerie," I say softly.

Constable Grant grabs a police officer close by. "10-70. Go do a complete sweep of Keera's house. He may still be in there."

He turns to speak to me. "I want you to wait until it's all clear and I'll need a detailed description of everything that's missing. You can send it to me by text or e-mail."

"This is the second note in one weekend and now he's calling and trespassing. I'm worried, and scared." My voice falters and cracks.

Bryce pulls me into his side, consoling me.

Constable Grant hands me a business card. "Were getting closer to this guy. You've got to have patience with us Keera. We'll get him."

I shake his hand. "Thank you."

As Bryce is searching the faces of people in the crowd that's gathered on the road, Constable Grant says, "I'll have a car circle the neighbourhood and I'll get the van here to set up surveillance for the night."

"Thank you," I say.

Bryce is trying to be patient, but I think he's lost faith in the police.

When we get back in the house, Leena and I show Bryce exactly the way my stalker left everything.

"Christ." He runs his fingers through his hair.

"Un-fucking-believable! If I ever get a hold of that fucker, I'm going to stuff his balls down his throat."

I rub his back to calm him down. "Let's go have a beer. He's trying to antagonize us, and we can't let him win."

Austin places three beers on the table and a wine cooler for Leena. "Let's see if the camera's picked up any sign of your stalker setting the fire next door."

Bryce and Leena look over Austin's shoulder at the computer monitor, while I walk toward my bedroom.

"I'm going to take inventory to see if anything else is missing from my room."

I search my drawer, my closet, and my bathroom. When I exit, and I'm standing in the doorway, I notice a rope hanging out of Bryce's bag. I pull everything out of it, place it on the bed, and look everything over. A vibrator is missing, so I walk to the kitchen and ask Bryce to come into the bedroom.

We stand over everything laid out. "Are we missing anything else?" I ask.

"Why? What are we missing?"

"I don't see the blue vibrator."

"That's the only thing missing and I remember cleaning it and putting it back in there."

"Well, I'm not telling the police he stole a vibrator. It's hard enough to tell them about my bra and thong."

He pulls me against his strong body and kisses my forehead. "We don't have to tell them."

"Good."

We reload Bryce's bag with our sex paraphernalia, hide it, and then head out to the kitchen with my laptop so I can e-mail Constable Grant.

"Nothing on the cameras of him setting the fire," Austin says, "but look at this. As soon as Leena and Blondie come out the front door, he sneaks in the back. Time shows four minutes and he wrote a note in that time, so he's definitely been inside your house before. He's fast and efficient. He knows his way around and knows exactly where to find what he needs."

"Did you find anything else missing?" Leena asks.

"No," Bryce and I say at the same time.

"I'm going to make a copy of this footage and take it to the cop shop," Austin says. "It might help in the investigation."

Austin wants to catch my stalker as soon as possible. He doesn't want us to lose faith in the ability of the police so he's doing whatever he can to help out in the investigation, even though it's not in his jurisdiction.

We call it a night because Leena and I can't stop yawning.

Bryce must be tired, too, because he gives me a kiss, holds me, and falls asleep instantly. I don't think he's getting much sleep lately.

During the night, I feel something hard against my butt and butterfly kisses on my cheek and when the daze wears off and I'm fully aware of my surroundings, I know just how hot Bryce is.

"I need you," he says.

"Then take me," I reply.

He turns the bedside light on. "I want to see your beautiful body." There's a desperate need in his voice and touch and it has me wondering why.

Is it because we almost broke up? Because he has to leave me? Because my stalker has been here, set another fire, and left a couple notes? Or is it Jake that's bothering him?

Whatever it is, they all lead back to me. I'm the reason he's not getting any sleep and he's worrying so much.

I try to reassure him as we make love. When we finish, he kisses me hard, holds me tight, and falls back asleep within minutes.

I lie there thinking about how hard this relationship is on him and wonder why he hasn't given up on me. It's at least an hour before I finally fall back to sleep.

Sunday morning, we wake to the smell of bacon and I'm still wrapped tightly in Bryce's arms, my head on his chest. I look up to see if he's awake and he's staring down at me.

"Good morning, Beautiful."

"Good morning, Mr. Tall, Dark, and Gorgeous."

He smiles and I see his sexy dimple. "Smells like Austin's making us breakfast."

"Mmm, it smells good. I'm starving. Our mid-night sexcapade has given me quite an appetite. But before we go in there, can I ask you something?"

"Shoot. Ask me anything," he says in that deep sexy voice.

"But will you tell me the truth?"

"I told you, we will always tell the truth. No lies, Angel."

"I've noticed you're not getting much sleep. Is something bothering you other than my stalker?"

"That fucker keeps slipping through our fingers. He's coming in your house for Christ's sake, as soon as we leave. And according to his note, he's been here before, taking a collection of your lingerie."

"Anything else bothering you?"

"Yeah, Jake-the-snake rapist. That fucker better not come over here either."

"Babe, he didn't rape me. He stopped."

"Don't defend him. He's scum. I can feel it." Bryce growls.

"Anything else bothering you?"

"I almost lost you because I was a fucking idiot."

"Don't beat yourself up. I'm still here."

"I want you with me. It kills me to leave you. I can't protect you when I'm an hour away." His voice is angry and he's short on patience, but I think it's his coping mechanism for all the things he can't control in his life.

Changing the subject, I try to get him in a good mood. "Would you like me to come see your hockey game Wednesday?"

"Yes, I want you there and then I want you to stay the rest of the week."

"Umm, I was thinking I'd drive back with Leena on Thursday, but we'd stay overnight."

The scowl on Bryce's face proves he's not impressed, but he quickly recovers. "At least I'll get to sleep with you one night. Then maybe I'll convince you to stay the rest of the week."

You can try to convince me, but I've made up my mind, I'm coming back to Huntsville with Leena. I don't want to argue with him, so I let it go-for now. "Don't tell Austin, we're coming, Leena wants it to be a surprise."

"My lips are sealed."

"Sealed for the kiss I want to give you?" I climb on top of him, straddling his hips and grabbing a handful of his meaty pecs.

"Never for that, Angel. Come here." He pulls me down and our lips fuse together, tongues tangling in a slow dance. When we separate, we're breathless.

"Come with me. We'll have some breakfast."

I roll off of him and we get out of bed.

"Now if only I could get Mr. Stiffy to go down. You'd better get dressed or it'll never go down."

I chuckle and smile. "You're so cute."

"Thank you, Angel."

The weather cooperates for their trip back to Barrie. "I hope it's just as good Wednesday for the game," I say to Bryce. "I don't want to be travelling in a snow storm."

I lock the house up and make sure the surveillance system is activated before we walk to Bryce's truck and Leena's car to say our goodbyes.

Bryce kisses me so hard I think my lips will bruise, only releasing me when we hear a snowmobile circling us.

"For fuck's sake." Bryce glances at his phone to check the time.

Jake swings his leg over the seat of his snowmobile and takes his helmet off, flipping his hair back. "How's everyone doing today? Looks like your heading out."

I know Bryce and Leena are itching to say something to him, so before they do I say, "Yeah, we're heading out for the week."

Bryce tightens his grip around my waist and I hold his hand to keep him calm.

"So when are you coming back?"

"We'll be back sometime next week."

"Okay, I'll come see you then. I want to talk to you about something."

Bryce's hand lifts off my waist but I tighten my grip and hold him there.

Jake slides his helmet back on and straddles his snowmobile, lifting his face shield. "Bye, Keera. See you next week." He speeds off, kicking up snow, and Bryce swears up a storm as we watch him leave.

"If that fucker thinks he's talking to you alone, he's got another thing coming. That's not happening!"

"Jesus, I thought you were going to deck him!" Austin says excitedly.

"I was, but Keera squeezed my hand."

"That's it, Blondie, keep him under control."

"I wasn't leaving here until that fucker was gone," Bryce spits out.

"Yeah, I know. That's why I kept my mouth shut," Austin says smirking.

Austin and Bryce always seem to know when they can tease and push each other's buttons, and when they need to back off.

"Well, we'd better be going." Bryce kisses me hard, and then whispers in my ear, "I love you. I'll see you Wednesday."

"I'll text before we leave."

He closes his eyes like he's in pain, but I know it's because I can't say "I love you" yet.

I hug him hard, so he knows I just need time.

He looks over at Leena and Austin, who are still lip-locked, so he kisses me again. When we pull away, we're breathing heavy.

"I'm going to miss you. I'll text."

"I'm going to miss you, Babe."

"Come on, let's go," Austin says. "We could stay here all day." Austin grabs Bryce by his coat and they load up in Bryce's truck.

We climb in Leena's car and wave as they pull out of the driveway.

I get a text from Austin as we're driving through town:

We waited down the road to see if your stalker would follow, but nothing. You're in the clear.

I text back.

Thanks. Have a safe trip back and thanks for watching out for us. Text me when you get to Barrie.

Will do, Blondie. Take care of Leena for me.

K, bye.

Leena and I head to the grocery store, then to the beer and liquor store, gabbing each other's ears off as we try to overcome our sadness from our boyfriends leaving.

We decide that to keep our minds off of them, were going to make Ma a nice dinner. We'll sit around drinking and maybe watch a movie.

It turns out, Bryce was right about my period. It starts right after he leaves. He noticed the signs of my PMS before I did. How does he know my body and mood swings better than I know myself?

He calls me while we're watching the movie. I take the call in my bedroom to avoid disturbing Leena and Ma.

I think he's feeling a little insecure because he tells me he loves me three times and then he repeats that I should text him if I see my stalker or Jake, twice.

I tell him not to worry, everything's going to be fine and I'll stay put at Leena's.

Constable Grant calls me early Monday morning to set up a wiretap, so Leena drives me over to my place. Afterwards, she has to work so she brings me back to her house and I hang out with Ma.

Bryce either calls or texts me morning and night every day. Before we know it, Wednesday has rolled around and we're excited about seeing the game.

Once we get to Barrie, the GPS in Leena's car helps us find the arena, and we make it there with ten minutes to spare, before the guys step onto the ice for warm up.

Settling in on the middle bleachers, Leena and I sit between the two teams and people watch as family members and friends file in and fill the seats to see the game. Shortly after, two women around our age sit behind us, two rows up.

The one behind Leena is a little loud when she says she can't wait to get his hot muscular body beneath her again.

Leena nudges my arm when we hear her say, "To see his silky black hair between my thighs again and his tongue on me, oh God, Angie, that mouth of his. It's heaven. Nobody's ever made love to me like that."

Leena and I scoot back on our seats, leaning, so we can eavesdrop more than what we are. We're dying to know who she's talking about.

"To see that hard body naked, you'll just die, Ange. They're like twins, so I'd say they both have the same equipment and Jesus, is he hung. They both probably treat their women the same and he's kinkier than hell, and that's what you want. You don't want someone who's boring in bed. You want him to take control of your mind, body, and soul. God, Ange, to have those hands all over me again. I fantasize every night. Look! I've got goose bumps just thinking about him."

Angie speaks up. "Sidney, why'd you break up?"

"We didn't go out, but I will get him again. And when I do, I'll have Austin talk to Bryce about you."

My eyes widen and I can see Leena's eyes doing the same at her comment. We both tense.

Leena makes a fist like she wants to hit Sidney, and her facial expression changes dramatically. I place my hand over Leena's to calm her down.

"There they are," Sidney says, as the two teams skate out onto the ice. "You look for Bryce and I'll see if I can find Austin."

I search for Bryce and identify him instantly by the way he carries himself and how graceful he is on the ice. His jersey is number #8 and I watch as he shoots on the net and gets it past the goalie, effortlessly into the top left corner of the net.

I search for Austin on the other team. He's not hard to find either, because Austin and Bryce have the same style of skating. He's number #24.

When they're done warming up and shooting on the goalie, Bryce searches the bleachers, and then, seeing us, skates in our direction.

We hear Sidney and Angie behind us. "Ange there they are. They're coming our way."

"Oh, God, Sid, they're so fucking hot!"

Bryce's eyes lock on mine as he skates toward the bench. He smiles with that gorgeous ear-to-ear smile, showing me his dimple, and then he nods, melting me to my core with his sexy-cool persona.

"Did you see that, Syd? Bryce looked at me and smiled. He is so gorgeous. I've wanted him since grade two."

I smile and wave at Bryce, ignoring Angie's comment. Every muscle from the waist down tightens and contracts. I want him right now.

Bryce stands against the boards facing us while he talks to the guys on the bench. He glances up into the bleachers periodically to look at me.

Austin follows Bryce's line of sight to see what he keeps looking at and that's when he sees Leena. Austin skates to the boards where we are and crooks his finger at Leena.

She jumps down four rows of benches and stands before him, talking through the glass. I hear him say, "What are you doing here?"

"I thought I'd surprise you. I want to see you play."

"I'm glad you're here." Austin takes his glove off and lays his hand on the glass, splaying his fingers.

Leena puts her hand against the glass over top of his. The affection they show toward each other is sweet and I'm glad I introduced them.

Austin skates over to Bryce and gently punches him in the ribs, then stands beside him. Austin nudges Bryce and I see they're hot in discussion. They both look up and I know what the conversation is about: Austin's probably giving Bryce shit for not telling him Leena was coming.

Leena climbs back up the bleachers. "I guess Sidney and Angie didn't want to sit behind us anymore."

"Of course not. She probably wants to kick your ass for stealing her boyfriend." I nudge Leena and give her a wink.

"Fuck buddie." Leena corrects. "Not boyfriend. At least, that's what it sounds like to me. It was a one-time thing."

"Sorry. I think you're right. It did sound like it was only one time." I try to reassure her because the claws are coming out.

"Unbelievable, eh?" Leena looks up and to the left at Sidney and Angie. "What the hell did he ever see in her? She's loud and obnoxious."

"I wouldn't worry about it. He's got you now and the way he looks at you, tells me his search is over. He's found the only one that matters. The rest were stepping stones to find his perfect soul mate."

"Why is it you always know what to say to calm me down?" Leena asks.

"Because that's what friends do. I've always got your back." I lean into her.

Leena looks up to her left again. "Fuck, is she ever shooting darts at me. If looks could kill…"

"Just ignore them. Look Bryce and Austin are facing off together." I grab Leena's arm.

I guess it's easy for me to say. I have to admit, when I didn't know who they were talking about, I was a little anxious and my jealous meter was shooting through the roof. But when I found out it was Austin and not Bryce, relief washed over me like a tidal wave.

After the players assemble into position, Bryce and Austin lean in with their sticks, ready to dual for the face-off.

Bryce wins and passes it to a player on his team. Austin checks Bryce, but Bryce regains his stance almost immediately and skates toward the net. Two players for the firefighter's team pass the puck with precision back and forth, shoot on net, and bounces the puck off the goalie's pads. Number #4 for the Firefighters gets the puck and passes it to Bryce. Bryce shoots it into the upper right corner of the net, just as Austin checks Bryce again, and he scores the Firefighters' first goal in the first two minutes of the game.

Bryce's team mates congratulate him with a slap on the back.

I search for Austin to see his reaction to Bryce's goal and he's smiling, shaking his head.

As the game goes on, Bryce and Austin get intensely physical, pushing and shoving at each other. I can see the competitive edge they both possess even though they're laughing when they check each other. I wish I could hear their trash talk. I'll bet it's hilarious.

Throughout the game, the Cops try hard to get a goal and in the third period they do. Austin is on the ice and he assists in the goal to number #15.

It's almost like they get their second wind because not even two minutes later Austin pops one in the upper left corner of the net. The score is Cops 2, Firefighters 1.

Austin turns to see Bryce's reaction. Bryce smiles at his big brother.

Bryce gives everyone on his team a pep talk and they seem to get their butts in gear. They're checking harder and skating faster. The intensity of the game shoots through the roof and Leena and I are on the edge of our seats screaming and yelling.

I watch Bryce battle for the puck again and when he's out of breath he skates back to the bench.

Number #4 nudges Bryce on the bench and when he takes his helmet off, he stands and waves at me. It's Dante! I return the wave and Bryce pulls him back down to sit.

Dante's a good hockey player.

After a couple of minutes, they switch lines and the face-off is Bryce and Austin again. Bryce backhands it to Dante and he takes off down the ice with Bryce hot on his heels. Austin skates close to Dante and Dante passes the puck to Bryce. They continue closer to the net and then Bryce makes out like he's going to shoot on the net, but at the last second he fakes them out and passes the puck to Dante. Dante shoots the puck in between the goalie's pads to score their second goal. It's 2-2 with only six minutes left in the game.

Bryce's mom said he was something to see and she's right-he's good. Watching his amazing abilities on the ice makes me so hot, all I can think about is his hands all over me. I squirm restlessly in my seat. I felt the same way when I watched Bryce carry the baby out of that house fire.

They all congratulate Dante and when he skates in front of

us, he takes a bow and blows me a kiss. I quickly glance at Bryce and he's looking up at me shaking his head, smiling. I smile back.

"Who's that?" Leena asks.

"That's Dante. He's quite the character. You'll learn that soon enough. He works with Bryce. They're all really good friends."

"I was wondering, because it looks to me like he has the hots for you."

"I think he likes to piss Bryce off."

They sit on the bench to catch their breath and Bryce wrestles with Dante, capturing him in a head lock. Bryce looks up at me smiling. Dante squirms, but Bryce's strength holds him in place until Bryce decides to let him go.

The other players battle on the ice for the puck, but no one scores. When Bryce and Dante's line comes back onto the ice, so does Austin's line.

Bryce faces off with number #20 from the Cops' team, winning the face-off, so Bryce quickly passes the puck to number #9. Dante and number #9 pass it back and forth until Bryce catches up with them. Austin's right behind Bryce, covering him.

Austin checks Bryce into the boards and they wrestle to the ice. The refs break it up and they get sent to the penalty box with two minutes for fighting. They argue the whole way there. Brotherly love. They're so cute.

My cheeks hurt from my face-splitting grin.

I'm not even paying attention to the game now. I'm watching Bryce and Austin arguing back and forth through the glass at each other in the penalty box. It's quite a show.

When they've served their two minutes, they're both out the doors and chasing down the puck to the Cops' end, where Dante passes to Bryce. Bryce passes to number #9 and he slaps it in the net, top shelf with thirty-two seconds left on the clock. The Firefighters dive onto number #9 sending him to the ice. The Firefighters on the bench stand and cheer, slapping the boards with their sticks.

I glance at Austin and he's shaking his head, disappointed.

When the Firefighters extricate themselves from the player, his helmet has fallen off and I see it's Jax. They help him up, put his helmet back on his head, and skate back to the bench.

It's Firefighters 3, Cops 2.

The Cops come out fighting to get another goal, but with only thirty-two seconds left on the clock, they don't get it.

Leena and I wait in the lobby for the guys to come out of the dressing rooms and we notice Sidney and Angie waiting in the crowd.

As we're standing against the wall, I feel someone grab my arm and turn to see it's Bryce and Austin's sister, Ciara.

"I thought that was you," she says as she looks at me and then Leena.

I give her a hug. "Ciara, good to see you. This is Leena."

Ciara hugs Leena. "I'm so happy to meet you."

Leena doesn't get a chance to comment back because Ciara's tugging us by our hands toward Bryce's mom and dad.

"Mom, Dad, this is Leena."

Deana wraps Leena in a hug. "So happy to meet you dear. You can call me Deana, and this is Garrett." Deana slaps Bryce's dad on the chest.

Garrett extends his hand into Leena's. "I'm so glad to meet you."

"Glad to meet both of you. Now I know where your boys get their good looks from." Leena looks back and forth at Garrett and Deana.

"Oh, I like this girl," Deana says.

Just then the guys burst through the doors, laughing, from the insults flying back and forth amongst them.

Would you look at that? Bryce is walking toward me with his hockey bag slung over his shoulder, sticks in hand, his hair wet and falling over one eye. His t-shirt is tight, showing every delectable muscle underneath, and his nipples are hard from the climate change. My eyes scroll down to the way his jeans fit to perfection, accentuating the bulging package between his legs.

My heart!

5

MY HEART IS pounding so hard right now. He's too sexy for his own good.

It is really unfair how he does this to me. I shiver, unable to take my eyes off of him.

When he gets close enough, the scent of his body wash and cologne nearly makes my knees buckle underneath me. The electricity crackles all around us.

"Good game." I say, smiling.

"Thanks, Angel." He envelopes me in a tight embrace and kisses me hard. "Do you feel that?"

"The electricity? Yes. And, oh, I feel that too."

Bryce grinds his cock into my pelvis and smiles wickedly down at me.

I see a hand tapping Bryce on his shoulder and it has him spinning us to see who it is.

Dante says, "Hey, what about me, don't I get a hug?"

"Back off," Bryce says as he playfully pushes Dante away.

Dante laughs, blurting out, "Hi, Keera."

"Hi, Dante."

I divert my attention to Leena and Austin kissing and hugging and then I look to my right and see Sidney and Angie. They're scowling at us, but Leena doesn't pay attention because Austin is now introducing her to everyone.

Jax runs his hand gently over my elbow. "Hi, Keera."

"Hi, Jax. Good goal."

"Thanks. Hey, it's good to see you're keeping this big guy in line."

Aw shit, Bryce must have told him about our fight. Does he tell them everything?

Dante butts into my thoughts. "I don't get a 'good goal'?"

"Good goal, Dante," I say with a smile.

Bryce holds one finger up to me. "I'll be right back, Angel." Then he wraps his arm around Dante's neck, tightening the headlock, pulling him over to the guys. Dante squirms and protests, until Bryce lets him go. I can hear them recapping the game, trash-talking and shoving each other around. Watching them makes me smile.

Deana makes her way over to Leena and me. "I told you they were something to see."

"Oh, yeah," I say. "They can play the game. They're good."

"I'm glad I came," Leena says. "I really enjoyed that."

"We'll have to make this a weekly ritual." I state.

"Yes, and then if you can stay another night, you girls can have dinner at our place." Deana nudges Garrett in the ribs.

"Yes, we'd like that," Garrett says, blowing out a breath.

Deana doesn't mention how I left abruptly the last time I saw her, which I'm still thoroughly embarrassed about. I let out a sigh of relief when the subject of Lindsay doesn't come up in the conversation.

After his recap with the guys, Bryce maneuvers between people, finding his way back to me. His hand slides to my waist, pulling me against his hard body. "Ready to go?"

"Sure."

Deana reaches up, to give her son a kiss, and then Bryce shakes his dad's hand and ruffles Ciara's hair.

"Don't! You're messing my hair," she protests.

In the parking lot, after Bryce throws his equipment in the truck, he slaps Austin on the back.

Once Austin and Leena head off to his house in her car, we're finally alone.

Tugging me close, Bryce wraps his arm around my waist and slides me across the seat of the truck. "I've missed you, Angel."

"I've missed you, too. I have to tell you, I really enjoyed watching you play hockey. I don't know what it is about watching you in action, but damn, you get me so hot."

"Hold that thought! We'll be home in a few minutes."

We grin at each other and Bryce winks at me.

"Austin says he's beating our asses next week."

"It was a close game. When you guys were down, I thought if you lose, Austin will never let you forget it."

"That's why we've got to win next week, to take him down a few pegs. Hey, you'll stay with me at my house next week, right?"

I hesitate for a second, thinking. "Won't you be working most of the time?"

"I'll get to sleep with you a couple of nights."

"Sure."

When we get to Bryce's house, he hangs his equipment up to dry downstairs. When he comes back up, I'm sitting on the stairs with a beer in my hand for him.

As I hand him his beer, he stands back and stares, eyeing me up and down, then he holds his hand out for me to take. I slide mine into his and he pulls me up the stairs, down the hall and to his bedroom.

I stand in the middle of the room, raking my eyes up and down his beautiful body as he does the same, inspecting me. He takes a swig of his beer, his eyes never leaving mine.

"You were right about my period. How did you know before I did?" I ask.

"Your personality changed. You were different. But I wasn't completely sure because of our fight."

"Umm, I'm just finishing. If you don't want to-"

"You think a little blood could keep me away from you?"

He absent-mindedly places his beer bottle on the nightstand without looking where he's placing it, as his eyes scan my body, worshipping it. He steps toward me. "Let's get you naked." He unbuttons my shirt, slips it down my arms and lets it fall to the floor. His fingers go to work, pulling my jeans down. Bra. Gone. Flung onto the chair. His thumbs slip behind the material of my thong, and he slides it down slowly, setting my skin on fire with his caress.

I stand before him totally naked and place my hands on his muscular chest. "I want to undress you."

"I'd like that." His voice is deep and husky, making me hotter than what I am already.

I run my hands slowly down his tight abs until I reach the hem of his shirt and lift slowly. Lifting his arms, he backs away to help me pull the shirt over his head. I swing it around my finger and fling it across the room.

My eyes move from his smile to the smattering of hair between his chiseled pecs and I run my fingers through it. My hands roam freely across his pecs, grazing over his nipples, which harden at my touch. I look up to see that he's gazing down at me with half-lidded, hungry eyes.

My inquisitive fingers make their way down his washboard abs and I have to touch every inch. My finger circles his belly button and then follows his happy trail until I'm stopped by his jeans.

I undo the button and zipper and hook my fingers in the waistband of his boxers pulling them both down. His rock-hard cock springs out, hitting my cheek as I bend. He kicks his pants out of the way.

I look up from my kneeling position and lick my lips. My fingers wrap around the shaft and I take him to the back of my throat.

His low, pleasurable moan tells me he likes it.

"Your mouth, Angel. It's so warm on my cock."

I pull him out and take him deeper, making him slick and wet with my saliva.

After a few minutes of licking and sucking, his balls tighten, telling me my performance is shattering his control.

He lets out a mournful groan and pulls me up, snatching my lollypop out of my mouth with a sound of lips smacking.

"Babe, I was just getting started."

He holds my lower back with one hand, his other hand holding steady at my mouth. He runs his thumb along my lower lip, which is wet with saliva. He studies my reaction.

His eyes move from my lips to my eyes. "I've been dying without you."

"So have I."

"Three days is too long without you, Angel."

"I know."

His eyes and thumb once again move to my lips and he gently slides it back and forth.

He's killing me with that sexy as hell, pantie-combusting stare, but I feel loved and cherished.

His lips devour mine and my body explodes with burning desire.

He picks me up and gently throws me on the bed. I bounce a little, and his playfulness has me giggling.

"Fuck, how I love that sound." He crawls stealthily up and over me, like a panther ready to pounce on its prey, and settles between my legs as I open wider to accommodate him. "Right where I want to be, between your legs. I've been thinking about this all damn day. All week."

His cock lays heavy on my pussy lips and I instantly grind

into him, wanting more-wanting some kind of relief from my achy, needy body.

"You need me, don't you, Angel?"

"Yes."

"You want my cock?"

"Yes. God, yes."

"Good. That's good." He smirks. "But not yet."

I sigh.

His lips meet mine and he separates them with his tongue. Our tongues dance in slow circles around each other. Just as I'm about to deepen the kiss and go wild on him, he pulls away and continues down my neck, alternating between licking and kissing.

His stubble scrapes gently along my skin and he automatically adjusts so he doesn't hurt me. His lips run across the mound of my breast to my puckered nipple, he flicks it with his tongue, and then he gently bites with his teeth, pulling, until it grows half an inch. He then switches, torturing the other nipple.

I grind harder, to let him know I need him. He peeks up at me, smirking against my breast, my nipple captured between his teeth.

Bugger. He's enjoying this.

His tongue jets out and circles around my nipple. He teases each breast as he hovers, and his hard cock skims ever so slightly across my thigh. His tongue then follows a line down my belly.

I buck my hips under him. "Babe!"

"I know, but you'll have to wait, I'm getting there."

I sigh and he resumes kissing across my hips, looking up at me just before he settles between my legs.

He likes to see my reaction when his tongue goes deep inside me and my response is always a satisfied moan of pleasure.

My head falls back and my fingers weave through his silky, jet-black hair. I grab on almost painfully but he doesn't seem to mind.

He looks up at me. "You need to come, don't you, Angel?"

"You don't know how badly."

He looks up at me with those gorgeous eyes as his finger penetrates me. "Oh, I think I do." He says slowly, probing around inside me. "So wet for me."

His tongue finds my clit, and swirls around and around it.

My fingers slide through the long strands of his hair and I hold on for dear life as I circle my hips and grind into his luscious mouth. His finger finds the perfect rhythm inside me.

My breathing quickens as I work up a sweat. I feel like I'm on fire. I'm getting closer and closer to orgasm, the sensation building, bringing me higher and higher. I squeeze my muscles around his finger. The delicious sensations are too much to suppress. I can't hold out any longer. My whole body starts to convulse. My legs shake uncontrollably and I grasp the sheets because I don't want to hurt him anymore than what I have, by tugging too hard on his hair. I buck my hips and my pelvis jerks. I'm amazed that somehow during all of this his mouth has stayed securely fused to my pussy as I quiver through the last few tremors of my orgasm.

My arms and legs are as limp as a ragdoll's. I'm vaguely aware of Bryce yanking me down to the middle of the bed.

He opens my legs, positions himself at my entrance, and plunges all the way in.

I gasp.

"So tight," he moans, "We fit perfectly."

"Babe! It's so big, and hard."

"I'm not too much for you, am I?" He teases.

"No! Just pull out a little and give me a second to adjust."

Bryce pulls out to the tip, then leans forward so his chest and my breasts are skin to skin. He nuzzles in my neck, breathing me in. He begins thrusting his hips ever so slightly, in and out, teasing me with the head of his cock. I breathe deeply, trying to relax and ready myself to take every inch of him inside me. I run my nails down his back until I reach his butt and then pull him into me.

He lifts his upper body, grabs onto my ankles and extends my legs up and out, spreading me wide. No matter how often he does this, I never cease to be amazed by the sight of his muscles straining everywhere. He gives it to me hard, pounding relentlessly. His skin is damp with sweat like mine. His breathing is harsh and laboured and the sound of slapping flesh and moans fill the room.

My orgasm is so close that as soon as I clamp down on him he lets out a regretful sigh and rolls me on top of him. "I don't want you coming yet. I want you on top so I can see this beautiful body, these beautiful tits."

He cups my breasts in his big hands, running his thumbs over my hard nipples. "Perky as ever and getting harder by the second."

"Well, yes, when you do that to them."

"They're so responsive to my touch."

"All you have to do is blow on them anymore and they pucker immediately."

"I love it," Bryce says in that husky voice I adore.

I place my hands on his tight abs, bracing my legs and feet on both sides of his hips, and then lift and lower myself onto his stiff shaft.

His large hands grip my butt cheeks, guiding me to the perfect rhythm.

Our orgasms build with every thrust and our panting sounds bounce off the walls, echoing throughout the room.

As soon as I clamp down on him he rolls me again.

"Hands and knees," he commands. "I want you from behind."

"Babe!" I know what he's doing: he's prolonging our orgasms so they're stronger, but he's driving me insane.

Bryce positions himself at my entrance and teases me by swiping his cock across my pussy lips, then he runs the head down the crack of my butt. "Someday, I will have your whole body." He smacks my butt with his cock.

I tense and feel my eyes widen, knowing he can't see my face from behind.

He leans over my back and holds my throat, whispering in my ear, "I want every inch of you. Of your body."

He lifts off of me and smacks my right butt cheek. "You're mine! Every inch."

Oh, Bryce, what is going through that mind of yours? It's almost scary, like he flips a switch and his dominating personality rears its head.

He positions his cock at my entrance again and sinks balls deep into my pussy. I moan at the intensity of it.

His hand caresses the globes of my ass and then lands hard, smacking my butt cheek. "Do you feel how hard my cock gets when you let me do that? Fuck!" He pulls out and rolls me so now I'm lying on my back again, and he's settling between my legs and sliding his cock deep inside me. "I want to see your beautiful face when you're coming apart."

He hands me my vibrator. "I want us to come together."

I fire up the vibrator and place it on my clit, moaning from both delicious sensations.

Continuously running my finger across his nipple, it hardens immediately. "You ready, Angel? I won't last with you doing that to me."

"Ready, Babe. Fuck me hard!"

His amazing abilities not only show through in everyday life, but also during our beautiful lovemaking. He's so talented at everything he does. He gives me exactly what I want, continually ramming deep, tilting my hips so he hits my sweet spot deep inside. He doesn't stop even when I clamp down on him as I milk his cock into ecstasy. I can see how he's struggling to hold on, to keep his control, but as soon as I scream out his name, he lets go and so do I.

My finger-nails scrape down his back. When I reach his butt cheeks, I grab two handfuls of that perfect ass, pulling him deeper into me.

His cock jerks inside me, releasing spurts of cum. "Angel, I love you." The words sound hoarse and broken up as they spill from his mouth. His powerful lunges ram into me a few more times, taking his intense orgasm as far as it will go.

Then he collapses his full weight on top of me, his lips gently sliding across my neck.

My body quivers and shakes underneath him from my mind-blowing orgasm as the last few tremors subside.

My lips find the crook of his neck and I kiss tenderly. "Wow. You. Are. Unbelievable," I say between kisses.

I can feel his mouth curling into a smile against my neck. "I don't know if my heart can take this."

He pulls out and off of me, rolling onto his back. I settle beside him lifting my head so I can cuddle against his chest.

"I'll give you plenty of exercise to keep that heart strong." I rub his bulging pec muscles.

"I bet you will. It's a full-time job keeping this sweet pussy satisfied, but I'm your man and I'll die trying." He grabs a handful of my pussy.

My hand gently rubs his abs and we lie in silence as time drifts by. We're both totally satisfied, lost in the afterglow, lost in our own thoughts.

After a while, Bryce clears his throat, breaking the silence. "Angel, I want you to stay with me."

"Umm, I was going to go back with Leena to stay at her place. You'll be working anyway."

He hesitates, like he's trying to be patient or to find the right words. "I don't want you alone. I've got a bad feeling about you going back alone. But if you're here, I can keep you safe."

"I won't be alone. Ma or Leena will always be with me." My body shifts so I can look into his beautiful eyes and I run my hand down his cheek to reassure him. "I'll be fine. We'll see each other in a couple of days. We could go to the cabin. Remember when you said you wanted to fulfill one of your fantasies? Well, I'm your girl."

"Yes, you are my girl. But I want you with me. I can't protect you when you're not with me."

"How about we compromise? Next week, I'll come stay with you."

"Tell me something? You're choosing not stay with me because of my fuck-up, right?"

"Babe, it's only two days and you'll be working around the clock anyways. We'll be together again after that."

Bryce closes his eyes like he's in pain. When he opens them, he's glaring at me with a furrowed brow and anger in his eyes. "You didn't answer me."

I hesitate. "Well, in some ways, yes. But mostly, I need some time to think."

"You're punishing me."

"No."

"Yes, you are."

"Babe." I climb on top of him, straddling his hips and desperately try to recover his good mood. I lean down and touch my nose to his, my hair forming a blanket around our faces. "Please, I just need a little time alone. Two days. That's all I'm asking."

"Fine!" Bryce radiates anger. He changes the subject. "You haven't seen your stalker?"

"No, but I haven't been out of Leena's house."

"Good. I want you to stay put until I come get you."

"Okay." *Mr. Overbearing.*

"What about Jake-the-snake rapist? Have you seen him?"

"No, Babe."

He physically relaxes.

Jeez, is this what he was talking about when he said he gets jealous and possessive?

I bend down, kissing him slowly. Still angry, he kisses me back, reluctantly.

I deepen the kiss and grind suggestively to distract him from our conversation. His cock hardens underneath me and his defensive wall crumbles. His tongue probes deeper in my mouth.

Once he's recovered his mood, our sexcapade resumes for another hour, though at a gentler, less frantic pace, until we're both exhausted and fall asleep wrapped with our arms and legs entangled.

The next morning, Leena and I are heading back to Huntsville, because Bryce and Austin have to work.

As we set out, we're gabbing, but eventually we both fall silent, lost in our own thoughts. I'm thinking about Bryce hesitating to let me leave, and how he continually reminded me of his love for me. And then my thoughts focused on our beautiful lovemaking, well into the night.

There's a grin on my face that I'm sure must look ridiculous, but I can't get rid of it.

When I look at Leena she has the same ridiculous grin plastered across her face. She must be thinking the same thing.

We break out laughing.

"I know what you're thinking about," I say.

"Yeah, you're thinking the same thing by the fuck-me expression on your face."

After a few moments of silence, I ask, "Did you resolve the Sidney problem with Austin?"

"Yeah, he just wasn't that into her. Kind of got on his nerves, you know? A one-time thing. But she still hounds him whenever she can. Next time I see her, I might tell her to back-off, he's taken!"

"I can see you doing that. Maybe I should try that with Lindsay. I wonder how well that would go over."

"Keera, I don't think it would be a good idea. Talking to Sidney is one thing-she's just a loudmouth. I can handle her. Lindsay on the other hand is a little unstable."

"She's not just a little unstable. I've seen her outbursts first hand. But I get your point. It's probably best for me to just stay away from her."

"So you and Bryce are good?"

"We're getting there."

"Maybe I shouldn't say this, but of course, I have no filter so I'm going to tell you any way. I feel bad for the poor guy. Keera, the way he looks at you-God, he doesn't see anyone but you. There's no way he loves anyone else."

"I know. I need to see it for myself, though. I'll find out the next time we see Lindsay."

When we get to town, we quickly stop by the grocery store to pick up a few things for the rest of the week.

Both Leena and I scan the parking lot for blue pick-up trucks and the store for familiar faces, but we see nothing. My stalker is nowhere in sight.

I text Bryce to tell him we made it home safe. He tells me to stay at Leena's again, as if I didn't hear him the first or fourth time, but I think it's the way he reassures himself. Either that or his dominant personality takes over and he likes to tell me what to do. At the end of our conversation, he tells me he loves me and he'll text tonight.

While Leena gets ready for work, I make dinner. She eats quickly and leaves, so I hang out with Ma for a while before heading to my room. After my shower, I climb in bed, firing up my laptop and transfer some music to my iPad.

Bryce texts me when I'm almost finished:

How was your day?

I text back:

Good. How is yours at the station?

Bryce texts back:

It would be better if I could see you.

The guilt trip.

I go to bed with a smile on my face knowing I'll see Bryce tomorrow afternoon. He also said he loves and misses me.

Just as I'm falling asleep I hear Leena come in from work and she quietly gets ready for bed.

A disgusting odour fills my mouth and nose, waking me out of a dead sleep. The stench of a chemical on a cloth is draped over my face and my natural instinct is to fight back. My head thrashes from side to side as I try to escape the hand and the pressure he's exerting.

Enough light floods from the kitchen into my room for me to see that it's my stalker hovering over me, holding some chemical-soaked cloth tightly to my nose and mouth.

My fingers dig into his hands and I try desperately to release them from my face.

I struggle to get free, but his strength overpowers me and my hands fall limply to my chest.

He whispers in my ear. "Shhh, Baby, everything's going to be fine once I get you out of here. I won't hurt you, I promise."

6

I WAKE FROM A painful prick in my arm and then a warming sensation surging through my veins. I can't move a muscle. My limbs feel numb. I'm dazed and confused and it demands all my strength to stay awake.

I'm vaguely aware of being hoisted over my stalker's shoulder. I want to scream, but my mouth doesn't work. I'm frozen and only a garbled mumble comes out.

As we pass by the kitchen chair my foot snags on the wood back rest and it crashes to the floor making a loud noise.

Please let Leena or Ma hear that. Please help me!

I wake again, disoriented and groggy. My eyes dart around the room, frantically searching.

Slowly, what's happened comes back to me-he drugged and kidnapped me out of my bed at Leena's house. I start to shake and my attention is drawn to the ropes securing my legs and arms to the bed. I'm cold and I shiver. When I look down, I see I'm wearing only my bra and thong, and my skin is covered with goose bumps.

I've lost track of time and have no idea how long I've been unconscious for-hours? Days? Do they even know I'm missing yet? How will they find me?

A whisper passes through my lips. "Bryce!" My heart wrenches. Oh, God! This will kill him.

My eyes dart toward the door because of the sound beyond it of a creaking floor.

Here he comes. Calm, keep calm, I repeat over in my head.

With the drugs surging through my veins, it is not difficult to stay calm. I close my eyes and breathe slowly, like I'm still asleep.

The door opens and I hear footsteps. The bed dips as my stalker sits down beside me. He's too close, my skin crawls, but I use every ounce of my will power making sure I don't move a muscle.

He runs his hand down my cheek and then over my hair. "So beautiful. Baby, you don't know how long I've dreamt about this." He kisses my lips gently. His hand runs down my neck, across my chest, and between my breasts. His finger slips inside my bra and he runs it across my nipple.

This is the most difficult thing I've ever had to endure. I fight the urge to flinch every time he touches me. He has to believe I'm still drugged and sleeping.

His hand runs down my belly and slips into the top of my thong. His hand instantly stills as he lifts the fabric. "I can't fucking believe this," he yells. "You were supposed to save that for me!"

I feel him get off the bed quickly. I risk a peek, opening my eyes a fraction. His face is beet red. He's so frustrated and angry that he's pacing, grabbing a handful of his hair and pulling. He punches the wall, opens the door, and disappears down the hall, swearing.

He left the door open. Holy shit!

My eyes search desperately around the room. To my left is a window, but it's covered with wood and no light shines through.

I have no idea if it is day or night. If I could somehow get myself untied from this headboard, maybe I could get out that way. I try grasping the rope that's tied to my wrist, but fail. I can't reach it with my fingers to loosen it.

On the nightstand to my right is a lamp, a glass of water, a syringe, and a glass vial with clear liquid in it. The room is not clean at all. There is dust everywhere. The mattress I'm lying on has no sheets and it is filthy.

And then my attention diverts to the shrine of blown-up pictures of me on the wall. Me coming out of the grocery store, me cutting wood in my back yard, and me walking down my driveway to get the mail. A collage of smaller pictures of me is strategically arranged in the shape of a large heart that covers a complete wall. I shiver. Oh, dear God, help me!

I shake my head. How stupid? I've been oblivious all this time to my stalker's obsession. But Bryce knew. Bryce saw the way he looked at me, saw it in his eyes and in the way my stalker was acting that first day we met at the grocery store.

I study the picture of myself cutting wood in my backyard. I'm wearing my favourite tank top which I threw out two years ago when I repainted my living room.

Holy fuck! He's been watching me for two years now?

I hear footsteps and the creak in the floor, so I quickly close my eyes again.

He closes the door and locks it, then sits beside me. He's touching me again and I'm trying not to cringe. "He did this to you. I know you would've waited for me. I envisioned a night of drinking champagne, dancing, me seducing you, and later we would both shave each other and make love. I wanted us to lose our virginity together. I had this all planned out and he ruined it for me!"

He kisses my cheek. "I forgive you, baby."

What the-? Holy crap, he's delusional!

"I had my suspicions when I found that bag on your chair

with the sex toys. I had a feeling that you lost your virginity to him. But this confirms it. He'll get his though. Karma's a bitch. I'd love to see the look on his face when he finds out I took you and he'll never see you again."

Bryce, I'm so sorry to drag you through this ordeal. Please, dear God, Mom, and Dad if you're listening, get me out of this. Let me live long enough to see Bryce and to tell him I love him. A huge lump forms in my throat and I can't swallow it. *Do not cry Keera, he'll see you. Be tough and you'll make it through this. Don't you dare cry!*

I feel him untying my ankles, so while I know he's preoccupied, I sneak a peek. What the hell?

He's naked.

What is he going to do to me?

He opens my legs wider and straddles my right leg. I feel his balls rubbing along my thigh. His body weight falls down on me and he kisses my neck, my cheek, and then my lips. "You're so beautiful and you're finally mine." He lifts back up and focuses on rubbing my pussy behind the fabric of my thong, so I peek again.

He's stroking his cock. *Please, dear God, don't let this happen! Please let someone save me.*

"This pussy is mine now." He grabs a handful and squeezes.

I feel movement on the bed, something bumps against my clit, and I hear a sharp intake of breath. I peek a fraction again.

He's smelling me. The bed shifts quickly again. "Baby, you smell as sweet as I imagined you would."

The bed shakes slightly, but I don't risk a peek. I stay still, not moving an inch, eyes closed, still breathing slowly, like I'm sleeping.

His breathing quickens to rapid pants as he pulls down the cups of my bra, exposing my breasts. "My baby has perfect tits. They're getting hard for me, that's it baby, make me come." He pinches my nipple.

I hear his laboured breath come to a halt as he gasps for air. I feel something warm spurting across my belly and tits.

A minute later, the bed shakes and I feel him wiping it off of me. He falls beside me, kisses my cheek, and nuzzles in my neck. "Baby, I can't get enough of touching and smelling you." He wraps his arm and leg across my body.

I lie there listening to his breathing as it changes from the rapid breath of orgasm to the deep inhalations of sleep. He's snoring.

My eyes dart around the room frantically, trying desperately to find a way out of this situation. My arms are restrained above my head, but my legs are untied.

Maybe I can convince him to untie me later so I can go to the bathroom? Maybe I can fight my way out of here like I did with Bryce.

And how'd you make out with that situation?

Maybe he's not as strong as Bryce?

He is strong, remember? You couldn't fight him off at Leena's.

That's because I was under the influence of the drug he injected me with. I think I'm much better now. I hope it's wearing off.

What if I make out like I'm still drugged and incapacitated? He might let his guard down. And he might not rape me.

Yeah, right. He's got one thing on his mind.

What do I do?

Watch and learn, Keera. Pay attention to his personality and how he treats you. If he loves you as much as he says he does, he might not hurt you.

My mind is a scrambled mess. One minute I'm trying to find a way out of this, the next I'm thinking about Bryce and what he's going through at this very moment. My heart aches in my chest.

Bryce, will I ever see you again? I never had the chance to tell you I love you because of my stupid, jealous pride. My poor baby, I knew I loved you, but I didn't know how much. Just to have you hold me one more time.

No, who am I kidding? Once wouldn't be enough. I know that.

I think about what we've been through in the past six weeks

together as if I'm replaying a movie in my mind. Tears well up in my eyes and streak down the side of my face.

Shit, Keera, you've got to stop this before he wakes up.

He moves slightly. "Baby, I need you," filters from his mouth.

I close my eyes and listen for him to speak again.

He falls back asleep for about five minutes and when he wakes he hugs me. "You're still here, you're not a dream. I love you, baby." He rubs my arm. "We're going to be so happy together."

He gets out of bed and opens the door, and then I hear water running. He disappears for a minute and then I hear his footsteps approaching the bed. He places a cold cloth on my forehead and water runs down my cheek. "Baby, I need you to wake up. I need to get you to the bathroom."

This is my chance to escape!

My eyes flutter like I'm still under the influence of the drug.

"There's my baby. Welcome to my home." He stands back, staring, hesitating for a moment, and then unties my wrists. "I'm going to help you get up." He pulls me to the edge and swings my legs off the bed. He lifts me up, but my body feels lifeless, so he cradles me in his arms.

My head falls against his chest and I groan.

"You feel so right in my arms. We were meant to be together."

Over my dead body. I'm out of here, the moment I can escape.

He carries me to the bathroom and places my feet on the floor in front of the toilet, holding me so I don't fall over.

I lean against him, even though he disgusts me. I've got to make him believe I'm still drugged and incoherent.

He pulls my thong down and sits me on the toilet. My head bobs to one side limply. He holds my shoulders. "Okay, baby, you can go pee now."

Oh, fuck, I never thought of that. He's not going to let me go in case I fall over.

I start to pee.

"Good girl." He reaches for some toilet paper.

Oh shit, now he wants to wipe me. *You never really thought this through, did you Keera?*

When I'm finished, he spreads my legs and wipes. "See, baby I'll probably be doing this when we're old. I'll take good care of you for the rest of our lives."

Like Fuck! That is not happening!

He picks me up in his arms, carries me back to the bedroom, and places me gently on the bed, then takes hold of my wrist and ties it. I groan in protest. He ties the other one.

"I'm sorry, baby. I have to tie you. I don't want you running away from me. You're mine! I'm never letting you go. But after we make love, I may trust you more. Then I might untie you from the bed." His eyes scan my body.

My eyes close and open like I'm struggling with consciousness. I lie as if I'm lifeless on the bed.

"I'm going to get you something to eat. I'll be right back." He disappears down the hall, leaving the door wide open.

My eyes scan the room once again searching for a way out of this and then I look up to see how my hands are tied above my head. I try to untie them, but I can't. I try to slip my hands through, but the rope bites into my wrists, tightening even more.

After about ten minutes, I hear the creak in the floor and quickly close my eyes again.

He loosens my ropes and props me up with pillows so he can spoon feed me. "That's it, baby. We've got to get something in that belly of yours. I wouldn't want you to wither away in front of me."

Some soup dribbles down my chin and he wipes it off.

"You have no idea how happy you make me, do you?"

I stare at him blankly.

He puts the soup down and hugs me tight. "I don't know if you heard me before, but I love you. I've loved you for a couple of years now. From the first time I laid eyes on you. I didn't know how to approach you. I've never been with anyone before, so it was hard for me."

It's like I'm seeing him for the first time. I inspect his facial features. He's kind of good looking. *Why hasn't he had girlfriends? Listen to you, Miss Unapproachable. Obviously guys are scared of you. Why? Maybe he's shy.*

He has brown hair, cut short, and styled to perfection. His eyes are deep chocolate brown. His teeth are white and perfectly straight. His body is tall and thin with the right amount of muscle. I don't get it. Why hasn't he had a girlfriend?

He picks up the bowl and feeds me again. "Eat up, baby. As soon as you finish this, I'm going to have to leave you for a bit, but I'll be back as soon as I can."

My stomach flutters with excitement, but I show no emotion.

When I'm finished, he places the bowl on the nightstand, takes some pillows away, and pulls me down so I'm positioned in the middle of bed. He ties my ankles and tightens the ropes for my wrists. I groan again so he knows I don't want to be tied.

"I know, baby. When I get back, I'll take these off and let you go to the bathroom again."

Another groan escapes my mouth because of sharp stabbing pain in my arm. Fuck, he's drugged me again. Warmth fills my veins.

The feeling of cold metal against my skin at my shoulders causes me to open my eyes slightly so I can see what he's doing. He cuts my thong in two spots at the hip and then I feel the cold metal between my breasts. He yanks my bra and thong away viciously.

Those small scraps of fabric were the only protection I had from him and now they're gone.

I thought he was leaving. What is he going to do?

My eyes flutter and I see him standing over me naked again.

"So beautiful. I could stare at you all day." He takes a picture and then drops the camera on the bed beside my ribs. He kneels, straddling my leg, and then he starts stroking his cock. I'm fighting to stay awake.

His hand cups my breast and the bed shakes continuously, and it's the longest minutes of my life not knowing what he's going to do next.

When he finishes he hugs me. "I love you, baby." He jumps off the bed and wipes up his cum.

"Baby, we're going to be so good together. Just wait and see. I've got to run out now to get some condoms because that fucking prick had his cock in you. Never know what kind of disease that loser is carrying. We didn't need them before because we were virgins, but now that I know you're not, I've got to protect myself until I get you tested. I love you, baby. I'll be right back." He kisses me on the lips and leaves out the door.

I fight to stay awake, to keep my eyes open, but they close slowly and all light and sound fade to nothing.

I wake to hear the door bust open and hit the wall. "She's in here."

"What's he doing in here? Get him out!" someone says in a deep commanding voice.

"No fucking way I'm leaving. Fuck-you! Get off of me."

Bryce? Babe is that you? I can't open my eyes, they're so heavy. I can't talk, but I can hear everything.

There's a scuffle and the bed gets shoved over, making my body jerk.

"Fuck, just leave him alone." Austin? It sounds like Austin is in the room. Oh God! I'm naked!

"Jesus Christ! Are we having a party in here? Just Bryce! Everyone else out!"

"Bryce!" escapes my lips, but it comes out in a whisper.

"Get me a fucking blanket to cover her," Bryce yells.

Babe, I love you!

I feel warmth from my breasts to my groin. I smell Bryce's

cologne and him. Am I dreaming? My eyes flutter open to see Bryce arranging his coat on top of me.

They found me! Thank you God, Mom, and Dad. I love you.

"Angel, I'm here. I love you so much!"

Bryce covers me with a blanket and unties my hands and legs. He picks me up in his strong arms, and holds me tight. My head falls to his chest. "What the fuck did he give her?"

"Don't touch anything. Leave it for the investigators."

Oh God, he's trembling. Bryce is trembling for me. So hard his whole body's shaking. He sticks his nose in the crook of my neck, takes a deep breath, and holds me tighter.

Please tell me Bryce isn't crying. I've never seen him cry. My heart aches. I feel as if I've been ripped wide open.

"Ambulance is here. Get her on the gurney," someone says in a deep, furious voice.

"She's fine right here in my arms," Bryce growls.

"Bryce, you have to let the paramedics check her out."

"I'm not letting her go."

"Austin, talk some sense into your brother."

"I don't think he's letting her go until he gets her to the ambulance."

"Clear out! Let the investigators do their job."

I wake slightly to a loud bang and then I hear Bryce's angry voice. "Fuck! Why won't she wake up?"

"Bryce, calm down! You know she wouldn't want you hurting yourself. It doesn't do you or her any good."

"Listen to Leena, Bryce."

The door opens. "What was that loud noise? Did you punch the wall? Look what you did! Now you're bleeding. I'll be right back to bandage you up."

"I'm fine," Bryce says in his husky voice, sounding irritated.

"Here, Bryce. Take this."

"Thanks, Leena."

"All right, then. No more punching walls there, mister. Oh, Dr. Liberty, I was just leaving. Did you need me to stay?"

"That won't be necessary. Thank you, nurse."

You're dismissed! Get ta skippin bitch.

Jesus! Listen to me. What's wrong with me? I don't have a filter on my mouth anymore. Shit, I wonder if I said that out loud?

Phew, I'm still fucked up. When's this shit going to wear off?

"Hello, I'm Dr. Liberty, I've been assigned to Keera as her physician until her family doctor is available."

"I'm Bryce, her fiancé, and this is my brother, Austin, and Keera's best friend, Leena."

Fiancé? What? Did I miss something? Like a proposal. Christ, how long have I been out?

"Well, I wasn't supposed to release any information if you weren't family, but since you're practically married it should be fine. We did a sexual assault evidence collection kit on her and there's no signs of vaginal or anal tearing, no bruising, no semen in either cavity, only on her extremities, her breasts, and her abdomen. Blood tests have been collected, but we're still waiting for the results of what's in her system. That shouldn't be too much longer and as soon as I receive it, I'll let you know. Any questions?"

"When will the drugs wear off?"

"It's hard to say. Everyone's different. Keep talking to her. That will help guide her out of it."

"Thank you."

"I'll let you know about the blood tests."

I hear the door open and close.

"Fiancé?" Leena asks.

"Yeah. I knew they wouldn't release any information and they'd most likely kick us out of here. Unless one of us were family."

"Quick thinking," Austin says.

There's another knock at the door.

"How is she?" Constable Grant asks in a concerned voice.

"Hard to tell. She won't wake up."

"Do you want to go out in the hall to hear what the investigators have found?"

"You can tell us in here. She can't hear you," Bryce says sadly.

"First, let me apologize. I'm not allowed to release too much information during the investigation, but now that this is over with, I can tell you more. That's morphine in her system. He injected her three times based on the number of syringes we found and he's been watching her for more than six months, going by all the evidence we've collected. That room lit up like a Christmas tree. We found semen from one end to the other. We had no idea how bad his obsession was for her. The reason he left the house was to buy condoms, they were in his hand when he came back from the store. He got a huge surprise when he saw us set up in the room waiting for him. We had to Taser him. He lost it when he saw Keera was gone. But we have him in custody now and he won't be getting out for a while. They've started the investigation at the Ericson's house, but no report yet. I'll keep you informed."

"Thanks for dropping by and telling us," Bryce says.

"No problem. Text me when she wakes up. I need to know if she's okay, and I'll need to take her statement."

"Will do." I hear the door open and close.

"I told you!" Bryce says loudly. "Finally. They see how long he's been obsessed for." Bryce hesitates. "If only I could have saved her this time." His voice is deep and filled with regret.

"You did," Leena says. "Quit beating yourself up. You saved her."

"Angel? Can you hear me? Wake up, Beautiful."

"Leena grab me a cold cloth. I'll run it across her face."

"So what did you make of the doctor's report?" Leena asks.

"You mean that he only jacked off on her because she was drugged?" Bryce asks.

"That's what it sounds like to me. Maybe he wanted her awake and coherent," Austin says. "I don't think she was raped."

"The only way we'll know for sure is when she wakes up and tells us," Leena says. "But give her time Bryce, let her tell you. That's if she remembers anything."

"Angel, please wake up." I feel cold running down my cheeks and across my forehead. My eyes flutter, but they don't want to stay open.

Bryce runs the cold cloth across them.

"There you are! Hi, Angel." He wraps me in a tight embrace and holds me for several minutes. His big body shakes and I feel wetness on my cheek.

Bryce wipes his eyes quickly and looks deep in my eyes.

"I love you!"

A tear slides down my cheek. In a voice barely above a whisper, I say, "I love you, Babe!"

He climbs onto the bed, half on me, draping his leg over mine, holding me tight. "Say that again."

"I. Love. You."

7

BRYCE CLOSES HIS eyes and swallows hard.
"She's awake. Hey, Blondie, you scared the living hell out of us."

I give Austin a crooked half smile.

"Keera, I'm so sorry, it's all my fault. I must have left the back door open when I got home from work." Leena leans over and holds my head close to hers. "I was so scared when I woke and you were gone. I knew he took you when I saw the chair on the floor." I can feel her whole body trembling.

"Don't cry, I'm okay."

Leena wipes her eyes. "I'm sorry this happened."

"It's not your fault. If he hadn't done it this way, he would have found another way. At least, now, he's in custody and the worst part is over."

"Angel, do you want me to call your Gramps?"

"No, I don't want him to know. It would kill him."

"I'm going to go get Ma in the waiting room. She's probably going out of her mind with worry. I'll be right back." Leena gives Austin a look and he lets her tug him out of the room.

Nice diversion. She's giving me and Bryce some privacy.

"Can I get a drink of water, please?"

Bryce discreetly wipes his eyes as he gets off the bed and pours some water.

Oh God, he's crying. Crying for me. My heart aches for him.

He places the cup at my lips and I take one sip and then another, until it's gone.

"Jeez, I guess you were thirsty. Would you like some more?" Bryce is trying to lighten the mood.

"Mmm, no, I think that's good. Maybe I'll have more in a little while."

"Are you hungry? I can send Leena and Austin to get you something."

"Maybe a sandwich."

Bryce pulls his cell phone out and calls Austin. "Can you run down to the cafeteria and grab Keera a sandwich? Great, thanks."

I shuffle around in the bed and then slide my legs to the side.

"Where do you think you're going?"

"Pee! I've got to go bad."

"Here, let me carry you." Bryce picks me up and holds me. "You feel so good in my arms. I love you, Angel."

"I love you. I thought I'd never see you again." Tears streak down from the corners of my eyes.

Bryce snuggles my face into the crook of his neck. "That would never happen. I'd search for you for the rest of my life."

He carries me to the bathroom and sits me down on the toilet.

When I'm done, I try to stand, but wobble on my feet.

"Oh no, you don't," he scoops me up in his arms and carries me to the bed, placing me gently down onto it.

Bryce sits on the bed with one knee up. He's facing me and holding my hand in his. "You've never said you loved me before."

"I know. I'm sorry. I knew that I loved you a while ago, but after the Lindsay thing, I had to know that you loved me for sure. That's why I held off."

"Can't you see how much I love you?" Bryce stares directly in my eyes. "I will love you and only you for the rest of my life."

"Yes, I see that now." I say softly.

"I'd give up my life for you, Angel." He hugs me again, holding me for a while and whispers in my ear, "I love hearing those words from you. Please, don't ever stop saying them."

"I won't."

He smiles, but then his face turns serious. "Angel, do you remember anything?"

"I remember almost everything."

I tell Bryce every detail from beginning to end and everything my kidnapper said. The whole time, he holds my hand.

I can tell he's struggling to keep calm. His facial expressions show his anger, but he stays in control because he wants to know.

I try to gather my thoughts to add more.

"Please continue," he says. "I need to know so I can help you through this. We might need some counselling."

What he means is, I might need a shrink.

"I'm okay. Drugging me was the only thing he did to hurt me. But tell me something: why is it the guys I come in contact with want to restrain me?"

"Because once we get you, we don't want to let you go. When you fell into my arms in the parking lot, I knew I wasn't letting you go until you fell in love with me. That's why I tied you up. I didn't want you to wake up and bolt out the door while I was preoccupied. Angel, you got me so fucking horny, I set a new personal record. Three times in one hour just from looking at you tied up. You stirred up some amazing fantasies that I didn't even know existed in my mind."

I chuckle because he's adorable when he's so honest.

"I think the experience with Jake, and you, helped me get through this." I smile and nudge him.

"Are you trying to be funny?"

"I'm trying to lighten the mood."

In my mind, I compare the time when Bryce kidnapped me-or as he prefers to describe it, kept me safe-and when my stalker kidnapped me. I was scared both times, but my stalker made my skin crawl. With Bryce, I had a delicious tingle running down my spine and when I saw it was him, my walls crumbled down and my insides melted. I surrendered totally to him.

"What are you thinking about?"

"You do remember that I was drugged when you kidnapped me."

"I didn't kidnap you. I was keeping you safe. But yes, I remember."

"Both times the drug felt the same."

"This confirms it. He was going to kidnap you that night and I ruined his plans." Bryce runs his fingers through his hair, frustrated. "I wish I could have saved you this time."

"You did, Babe. Thank you." I run my hand over his cheek.

Bryce is deep in thought. I know he's thinking if I hadn't been so damn stubborn when he wanted me to stay at his house in Barrie, none of this would've happened. He's biting his tongue, fighting the urge to tell me. I know it, but he stays silent.

"So did they catch him?" I ask.

"They had surveillance on him the moment he left the house. That's when we stormed it to see if he had you there. They cleared the area around the house of all police vehicles after we got you in the ambulance. Surveillance followed him back to the house, where the police were set up in the bedroom waiting to arrest him.

Grant said he had to Taser him because he lost it-went completely crazy when he opened the bedroom door and found you gone, and knew we'd rescued you."

"That's probably because in his mind, he loves me. He thought we'd spend the rest of our lives together. Did you see all the pictures on the wall?"

"Yes. He's been obsessed, watching you for a while now."

"Two years at least," I say.

"How do you know that?" Bryce asks.

"Because there's a picture on the wall of me cutting wood. I was wearing my favourite tank top, which I threw out two years ago when I spilled paint down the front of it."

"Two years. Two fucking years he's been obsessed with you." Bryce shakes his head.

"I had no idea it was this bad until you came into my life."

"I'm sorry Angel, but I have to ask. Did he rape you?"

"No. He didn't rape me. Do you think this is finally over?"

"I hope so. I hope they charge him with everything they can and he spends years in jail, away from us."

Leena, Austin, and Ma come walking through the door.

Ma comes around the bed and gives me a hug. "Keera, honey, we were so worried. I've been going out of my mind."

"I'm okay, Ma, just a little hungry and thirsty."

"Well, you let me know if you need anything and I'll bring it for you tomorrow."

"I was kind of hoping to be out of here by tomorrow."

Leena places my sandwich on my lap. "How's an assorted sub sound?"

"Perfect! I'm starving." I dig in immediately. "How long was I missing for?" I say with a mouthful.

"Damn, I guess she is starving. Look at her." I look up at Austin, who has a ridiculous grin on his face, and then focus my attention back on my sub.

"We figure he kidnapped you around four a.m. Friday," Austin says, getting serious now. "It's now Saturday night. You were admitted around three, and it's now seven, so he had you for approximately thirty-four hours."

"That's why I'm so hungry. He fed me soup, but that's all I've had since Thursday night, when I ate with Leena and Ma. Here, Babe, you eat the other half. I'm already getting full." I hand Bryce half my sub while I finish off the rest.

Little miss helpful nurse comes in with another young nurse to take my blood pressure and check my chart. "You're not supposed to be eating until the doctor marks it on your chart that you can eat solids."

"Too late!" I say, giving her back a snotty attitude. "I'm done." I pop the last bite in my mouth and grin.

But the real reason for their visit becomes clear when they blush and focus their attention on Bryce and Austin.

Leena nudges me and gives me the eyes. I give them back to her and shake my head.

"Just so you boys know," Little Miss Helpful says as she's turning toward the door, "visiting hours are over at eight."

"Just so you know," Bryce says, "I'm not leaving."

The door opens. "Well it's good to see you're awake. Nice to meet you, Keera. I'm Dr. Liberty. How are you feeling?"

"Nice to meet you, too. I'm good. When can I go home?"

Dr. Liberty chuckles. "When they ask that question, I know they're feeling fine. We have to wait for your blood pressure to normalize. Right now it's very low, which is why you might feel a little unsteady when you stand or walk. I would think we'd be able to let you go tomorrow. After you go home, you can do a follow up with your family doctor."

"Okay, great. Thank you."

Dr. Liberty disappears out the door.

"I'll be out of here first thing in the morning," I say.

Bryce shakes his head and then looks at Leena and Austin. "I'll call you with the details."

Leena, Ma, and Austin give me hugs and kisses before saying their goodbyes and heading out the door.

When we're finally alone, Bryce climbs on the bed beside me. He props his head up with his hand, extending his elbow above my head, and looks directly in my eyes.

Uh-oh, serious talk again.

"Leena wanted to take you to Aruba to get away from all of

this, but I told her we have to wait and see how you'll react once you're out of the hospital. I told her you might have nightmares, that you could be traumatized over this. I think she finally realized it was too soon and backed off."

"Once she gets an idea in her head it's hard to shake her of it. She's stubborn."

"I called into work and told them I'll need some time off. They told me to take as much time as I need."

"Babe, you didn't-" My words are cut short by Bryce's warm, lush kiss.

"Yes, I'm staying with you. We'll get through this. Together."

I give him a hug and kiss. "Thank you."

"You're welcome. Did you want to take a shower? I can help you."

"Yes, please, I feel dirty."

Bryce helps me to the bathroom and props me up against the shower enclosure. He takes off my hospital gown and runs the water against the wall, waiting for it to reach the perfect temperature. "Are you okay if I let you go for a second?"

"I'm fine. I can stand on my own now."

He strips his clothes off and climbs in with me. "I need a shower too. When I got the call, I got dressed and drove like a mad man to get here."

"All I could think about was you, Babe. How you had that bad feeling and hesitated to let me go. And the hell I was putting you through. I'm sorry."

Bryce puts one finger to my lips and shakes his head. "No, shhh." He wraps his strong arms around me and holds me in a tight embrace. "You shouldn't be sorry for anything. You didn't put me through hell, he did. All I could think about was finding you and getting to you fast enough."

Tears start to flow again. I can't stop crying. "I thought about our relationship and how you've had to deal with all this crap, with all this baggage and bullshit, and I wonder why you haven't given up on me."

"Never! We'll be together forever. We'll look back on this when we're old and grey, and we'll think it was another tough time we survived."

"I love you!"

"I love you, Angel. And as long as we have love, we can conquer anything."

"I couldn't ask for a better boyfriend."

"Fiancé," Bryce chuckles.

"Oh, you're cute." I sniffle.

"Angel, I'm serious. I want to marry you. On my way here from Barrie, which was the longest ride of my life, I swore that when I got to hold you again I wouldn't hesitate, I'd ask you."

"Umm, don't you think we should get to know each other better first?"

"Is that the only thing that's holding you back?"

"Yes, I think it's important. We should know every little mood swing we both have before we say I do."

"Good, then its settled. Since I already know what your moods are like and you've seen all of mine and haven't run for the hills yet, tomorrow on the way home from the hospital were going to pick out rings."

"This is too fast. You're making my head spin."

"Okay, I'll cut you some slack. I'll let it sink in for a while and then one day I'll surprise you. I just needed to know you're not totally against the idea."

"Well, no, someday I'd like to get married."

"Good." He hugs me again. "We'd better wash up before the nurses come back in here."

My head is spinning while Bryce washes my body. Holy crap! He wants to marry me?

After he washes my breasts and stomach I take the wash cloth.

"I... need... to scrub... hard... to get his..." I look up into his eyes and see pain and anger. "off of me." I couldn't say "cum." Bryce is having a hard time with this.

Bryce places his hand over mine and we scrub together.

"We'll get through this, Angel. Together."

His hard cock rubs against my skin occasionally and thickens as my body arches toward his.

I want him right here and now in this shower. I wrap my arms around his neck and grind suggestively on his thigh.

He clears his throat. "You don't know how bad I want you too, but I think we should wait to see if you're okay."

I reach down and grab his perfect ass cheeks, squeezing them, tugging him tighter to me so I can grind against his cock. "Really, I'm okay, but I'd be even better if you gave me this." I reach down and wrap both hands around his stiff shaft and stroke.

He groans. "Angel, this wasn't where this was headed. I need to wash you. When I get you home, we'll see how you're feeling and go from there."

Denied! Boy, if that isn't a brush off, I don't know what is!

"You don't want me anymore? Because of him?"

"Fuck! Don't even say that. I want you! You don't know how bad I want you right now. You're not making this easy for me. Just let me get you home and see how you're doing, okay?"

Jesus, I'm not a porcelain doll. I won't break. I'll be fine.

"Fine." I say, pouting.

When we finish our shower, Bryce dries me off and I wrap a new hospital gown around me. I comb out my hair while he quickly gets dressed. He guides me back to the bed and helps me onto it.

I scoot over and pat the space next to me. "I want you to sleep with me."

"I think that can be arranged." Bryce takes his phone off of his hip and places it on the nightstand. He climbs in bed and we talk for a bit, reconnecting and reassuring each other that everything's going to be fine, and then fall asleep in each other's arms.

I jump, twitching from a vision of my stalker hovering over me. My eyes search the room frantically, my chest heaving for my next breath. Sweat forms at my temple. I turn to see Bryce and physically relax when I realize it's a nightmare. I melt into his body beside me. I stare at the ceiling, trying to calm down and to think of something else. After a few minutes, I hear that Bryce has a text. And then another, and another. I reach over and grab his phone so it doesn't wake him.

He probably hasn't had much sleep.

I scroll through and see the texts are from Lindsay. She must have bought a new phone, because she's been texting since Thursday. The texts start out with "Hi, Bryce, how are you, I just got my new phone and I wanted to see how you're doing." So nice and sweet. When Bryce doesn't answer, she sends a few more nice ones that he still doesn't answer. Then she asks why he isn't answering her. She can see he's reading her texts and her anger shows through in her responses, with the use of shouty capitals and exclamations to get her point across. I can just see her throwing a hissy fit and whipping her phone across the room.

Bryce moves to a different position and wakes up. "Good morning, Beautiful. How are you feeling?"

"Good morning to you, too. I'm good. How'd you sleep?"

"Okay, considering how small this bed is." Bryce says.

"I know, eh. I tried to scoot closer to the edge to give you more room."

"I probably ended up half on top of you anyways."

"That's how you like to sleep. And I like it too." I say, lowering my voice seductively.

"How'd you sleep, Angel?" Bryce asks, ignoring my tone.

"Good, even though I've been sleeping steady for two days now."

"The drugs have to be out of your system by now."

"Yeah, I don't feel groggy anymore."

"Well, let's see if we can get the doctor to discharge you."

As he gracefully lifts himself out of bed, he sees I'm holding his phone.

"I didn't want it to wake you. Lindsay has been texting you."

"She's been sending them since she got her new phone. I haven't answered them."

"I see that. Maybe you should change your number." I hold up my hands in surrender. "Just saying."

Maybe I should zip my mouth. What happened to my filter?

I hand him his phone.

"Good idea. On the way to the cabin I'll run in quick and get it changed."

"Oh, we're going to the cabin?"

"Yes. Just you and me, Angel. Austin and Leena are heading back to Barrie. She's going to stay with him for a couple days and then head back because she has to work."

"Oh," I say, trying not to sound disappointed.

"I'll go see if I can find when the doctor will be in. I'll be right back, Angel."

"Okay."

Bryce is gone for a bit, so I head to the bathroom. *"Jesus, I look like hell,"* I say, looking into the mirror. I run a comb through my hair and then a thought hits me. I have no clothes. They brought me in here with a blanket on.

The door opens. "Don't tell me she's gone already?"

"I'm in here."

Leena wraps me in a hug. "We brought you a suit-case with some clothes and toiletries because you'll be going to the cabin. I don't want you going to my house while they still have the yellow tape up for the investigation."

"Thank you so much. You must have read my mind." I look to my left and Ma and Austin are standing in the doorway. "Hi Ma, hi Austin."

"You're not getting away that easy. Give us a hug." Austin wraps me in his big, strong arms and then Ma holds me as if she never wants to let me go.

"Jeez, I like all of the attention I'm getting. This is great."

Bryce comes back in. "The nurse will be here in a few minutes to take your vital signs, and then the doctor will be in shortly after that with the discharge papers. Then, we can leave whenever you're ready."

Bryce lifts the suitcase on the bed. "Thanks for getting this together for us."

"No problem," Leena says as she sits on Austin's lap.

Bryce is always prepared. He's always thinking ahead and thinking of me and my needs. My heart constricts with overwhelming love for him. He obviously asked Leena to pack a bag for me before it even dawned on me that I needed one. It surprises me every day of how much he thinks about me.

Bryce hands me my clothes. "You get dressed and I'll tell the nurse you're ready to go."

I run my fingers over his hand in a silent thank you.

When our eyes connect, I see that I-want-you-right-now stare and give it right back to him. Our eyes stay locked on each other for a couple of seconds before he shakes his head and looks away, as if he's trying to dismiss the thoughts from his mind.

I know if we weren't in the presence of company, he would have shown me how much he appreciated that look. But for now, he's back to being Mr. Take-Control of the Situation. I think he's anxious to get out of here too.

We say our goodbyes downstairs in the hospital lobby with hugs and kisses and promises to exchange text.

"Sorry I turned your life and house upside-down because of this investigation, Ma."

"Oh, I don't mind. It brought some excitement into my life. Besides," she says with a little wink, "I really don't mind seeing the good-looking police officers inside my house."

Bryce holds the door of the truck while I clamber in. He reaches over, handing me my seatbelt and closes the door. Then he climbs in and we head through town, to the grocery store.

In the parking lot, Bryce holds my hand hesitating, before getting out of the truck. "I can run in. You don't have to come in with me."

"No. I want to go in. I need to get my life back. This incident isn't going to rule my life. I want to feel the freedom of coming and going as I please. I don't have to look over my shoulder anymore. I need this."

"Okay, let's get some groceries. Can I help you out of the truck like I did before?"

"Sure, but Babe, you treat me like I'm going to break. I'm fine, no damage is done. I'm still the same as before."

The thought of my nightmare runs through my mind again and I try to banish it.

He squeezes my hand. "I'll try to remember that. I love you."

I squeeze him back. "I love you."

After our grocery excursion and another quick stop to change Bryce's cell number, we're on our way.

The drive to the cabin is about fifteen minutes away, travelling North East on Highway 60 from town. The roads are paved most of the way, until we come to the familiar turn off that we take to the right. From that point on, the roads are gravel and they twist and turn. The region is very hilly and scenic with an abundance of pine trees and rock face cut out along the side of the road. There are many lakes and a few bridges we need to cross. A moose sloshing through the water has me noticing the ice is starting to form along the banks from the cold temperatures.

Once Bryce's truck reaches the clearing in the trees, the cabin is in plain view, set back from the road. The forest green, peak, metal roof, and the medium stain on the logs catch your eye the moment you see it.

Bryce drives the truck down the asphalt driveway to the door of the garage, which is a replica of the log cabin up front. Bryce hits the button for the garage door and we pull right in.

We haul the luggage and bags into the cabin and I put the groceries away while Bryce gets the fire going.

"Holy crap, is it cold! Is it always like this before you get the fire going?"

"With the temperature below freezing, it might take a bit to warm up in here."

I rub my hands together to keep them warm.

Bryce loads the wood stove in the living room and I watch from the kitchen which is at the back of the cabin.

The bathroom and Bryce's bedroom are also at the back. The living room at the front has huge peak windows and to the left, down the hall, is the work-out room and Austin's bedroom. I can remember the first time I saw the interior of the cabin. The heated granite floor in the bathroom, the huge Jacuzzi tub, and granite counter tops had me thinking, whoever owns this place is certainly not hurting for money.

When Bryce and Austin built this cabin, they cut labour costs by constructing the interior themselves, so they could use their money elsewhere to have the best quality inside and out.

"Come with me, little girl." He tugs me over to the couch, where he's laid out a blanket. Slipping my coat off my shoulders, he tosses it on the other side of the sectional, and then lies down urging me to do the same, facing him. He covers us both with another blanket and I'm surrounded by his warmth.

"This is where I want to be, wrapped in your warm arms, against this gorgeous hard body." I rub his chest.

"I couldn't wait to get you home to do this." He gives me a squeeze.

"I know how we could warm up real fast." I grab his ass cheeks and pull him into me, circling my hips and grinding suggestively against him.

"What am I going to with you?"

"I gave you a suggestion. Do you need me to spell it out?"

"Angel, you have a one track-mind."

"Oh, and you don't?"

"You're not making this easy for me." He runs his thumb along my lower lip. "My plan was to have one night together, no sex, just the two of us enjoying each other's company, getting to know each other better. But that's all gone to hell. We can't be in the same room together without having sex."

"And what's wrong with that? It means we can't keep our hands off of each other. It's called love."

"So my plans have changed. This is what we're going to do. We're going to lie here enjoying each other's company and, get to know each other better, with no sex."

I sigh.

Bryce smiles. "Wait, I wasn't finished. We'll lie here to warm up, with no sex, and then we'll make some dinner. And then after dinner, if you're up for it, we'll make love."

"Okay, now were getting somewhere! Promise?"

He smiles and hugs me. "Yes, I promise."

"So now that were getting to know each other. Let's see. Hmmm. What do I want to know about you, other than you have a rock-hard body and you make me hotter than I ever thought I could be?"

"Angel," Bryce says sternly. "Play by the rules before dinner, or there will be no dessert after dinner."

"All right." I grumble. "So how long have you been with the fire department?"

"Eight years now. I was hired after my nineteenth birthday."

"Wow, that's young! Isn't it hard to get hired at such a young age?"

"Yes it is, but I had a little pull from my dad."

"What do you mean?"

"My dad worked at my station before he got promoted to investigations."

"I had no clue your dad was a firefighter."

"I guess you wouldn't unless you saw the shrine downstairs at my parents' house. I'll have to show it to you next time."

"I can't believe it didn't come up in conversation."

"I know. He fought fires for twenty-five years, never got hurt once. Then one day when we finished gutting a house that burnt on Arbour Street, the bathtub from the second floor came down on him. They say if he hadn't been in such great shape, it probably would have killed him. But he's a tough old bugger. He came back with a vengeance. It broke his leg and arm. That's why you see that bit of a limp. Other than that, he's good. Do you want to know how stubborn he is? The casts weren't off yet and he was already working out so he could come back to work. My mom talked him into taking the investigative side to keep him safe, but I can see how he misses it when he asks a lot of questions about what went on at the scene."

"Were you there when it happened?"

"Yeah, that was tough. I was venting the ceiling and wall about twenty feet away and when I heard the loud noise, I turned and saw my dad go down. We all rushed over to get the debris off of him and-do you believe this? The crazy bugger wanted to get back up and go to work until he realized he had a few broken bones. Stubborn old man. It was hard seeing my father hurt like that. I mean it's hard seeing any of my guys hurt, but my own dad."

"I'm sorry you had to see that. You're right though, he is tough. I would have never known that he was hurt if you hadn't told me. I can see his stubbornness in you."

"What do you mean?"

"Oh come on-you've never noticed that you're exactly like him?"

"Well, maybe a little. Hey, you getting warm now?"

"Oh yeah, toasty warm. Wouldn't want to be anywhere else."

"Angel?" He hesitates. "I'm sorry I wasn't there for you." Bryce kisses my forehead.

"Oh, no." I pull away to look deep in his eyes. "Please do not blame yourself. You were there for me. You rescued me. You're my hero. If I wasn't so damn stubborn, I would have been sleeping at your place for the rest of the week and this would've never happened."

"Just the thought of him with his hands on you. I get so pissed. I'm losing my fucking mind over this." Bryce closes his eyes, and when he re-opens them, they're filled with regret and anger. "He was bound and determined to kidnap you. I told you I'd protect you, keep you safe. I failed you."

8

I LOOK INTO BRYCE'S eyes. His forehead is furrowed, and the corners of his mouth are slightly turned down. I wish I could take his pain away. How can he possibly feel he failed me? Without him, I might still be in that lunatic's clutches.

"You didn't fail me, Babe. You saved me. I knew you'd find me."

"I would've never stopped looking for you."

"I know." I stop and think about it for a minute. "How did you find me?"

"Leena had already called Constable Grant, and while I was driving like a mad man to get here, Austin was on the phone with police getting information and finding out what their next move was. The cops told Austin they knew where your stalker lived, and when we got to the cop shop they said they had a surveillance team set up. Only thing was, they were taking their sweet-ass time setting up a team to go in. You should have seen me. I was going nuts because it was taking them so long. Austin had to pull me outside so I could get a grip. He said the cops were on the verge of throwing me in jail. So I calmed down. When they finally got their shit together, we followed them to the command centre where they'd set up a block away. And we waited… and waited."

"They kept telling me to calm down, that they had to make sure you were at this location because he might have you held somewhere else and if they stormed the house without that information, we might never find you. I calmed down for a bit, but then it seemed like we were at a standstill. I lost it again. I grabbed the head honcho negotiator by his shirt and shook him. I told him that mother fucker could be raping you right now. I was just about to punch him when Austin stepped in and stopped me. They told Austin to get me out of there, so he dragged me off to my truck where he tried to reason with me. He told me I wasn't doing you any good by flipping out. That's when I realized I had to calm down or I wouldn't be allowed back in. I apologized to the negotiator and was allowed to enter the command centre again. After that, I just sat there, glued to the monitors, waiting. Then around two-thirty, your stalker came out the front door and got in his truck."

"They had a team following him to see if he was going to a different location. They told me to stay at the command centre, but that wasn't happening. When the team piled into the truck to go over to his house, me and Austin hopped in my truck and followed them over. As soon as they stormed the house, I forced my way in with them. My heart was ripped out of my chest when I saw you lying on that bed. I'm sorry, Angel."

Tears flood my eyes. "You found me and you saved me. I was drugged, but I heard your voice and everything else that was going on in that room. I said your name, but with all the commotion going on you probably didn't hear me. I was so happy, I wanted to wake up and hold you, but I couldn't move. I wanted to tell you that I loved you, but the words wouldn't come out."

Bryce runs his fingers along my arm. "When I got to hold you, it was the best feeling ever. I had to contain my emotions and there was no way I was letting you go. I'm not ever letting you go again. I want you with me, always. If that means I'm being a possessive bastard, I don't give a shit, so be it. You're mine and I'm never losing you again."

"I want to be with you too, always."

Bryce wraps me in a strong bear hug. "You don't know how happy I am right now."

"Yes, I do. I feel the same way. But what we need to do now, from this day forward, is to quit beating ourselves up over this and move on. He's been under our skin for a while now and we need to forget and start fresh with our lives, me and you."

"I'd feel a lot better if I could've beaten him to a pulp. But maybe not, it's better this way. I'd probably be charged with murder right now because I wouldn't have been able to stop."

"You're right. I need you with me, not in jail." I run my fingers across the frown at his eyebrows, and I feel his facial muscles relaxing from my touch.

"Tyrone wouldn't mind sharing a cell with you, a gorgeous, hunky fireman like you-oh yeah, you'd be his bitch. I'm having a visual right now."

He tickles me. "Are you trying to be funny?"

"No, no. Please stop." I roll backwards, giggling, and almost fall off the couch, but Bryce catches me.

"Oh no, where do you think you're going?" He hugs me and whispers in my ear. "I love you so much."

"I love you. And you're right, we can make it through anything if we have a love as strong as ours."

"Yes. I don't mean to change the subject, but I'm curious why your parents decided on only one child?"

"My mom had difficulties when she was pregnant. She miscarried three times and then they got lucky with me. I was born five weeks early and they didn't think I'd survive. After that, the doctors advised her not to have any more children." I shrug my shoulders. "So this is why I'm an only child. They wanted four children, but..."

"Well, I'm the happiest man alive. You survived because the big guy upstairs has a plan for you and that plan is to be with me for the rest of our lives."

"I think you're right. The day my parents died I was in the car with them, but I wasn't feeling good so I got out and went to bed. When I got the call, my whole life was turned upside-down and ripped away instantly. I wished I'd never gotten out of that car. I wanted to die with them. But as time went by, I thought maybe I was spared for a reason." I hold his face in my hands and stare deep in his eyes. "And now, I think you're that reason."

"I think so, too. I think you were spared so we could be together. Angel, I wish I would've known you then. You must have been devastated, and I would have helped you get through it."

"I wish I would've known you then too. My parents would've loved you."

Bryce hugs me. "It's getting a little hot in here. Do you want to make dinner now?"

"Sure, I'm getting a little hungry."

"Yeah, my stomach's grumbling."

"I can hear it."

I roll off the couch, stand up, and extend my hand to help him up, but he tugs me back down onto the couch and kisses me. "See, that was very productive, we're getting to know each other."

"Yes, we are."

Making dinner with Bryce-while he was wearing his pajama bottoms hanging low and showing that sexy V muscle on his hips-was a true test of my self-control. Fantasies of him touching every inch of my skin, of him throwing me on the counter and fucking me senseless ran wildly through my mind until it was downright unbearable and I pounced on his bare back, wrapping my arms around him and grabbing his meaty pecs.

"Babe, I can't take it anymore, you're teasing the hell out of me."

Bryce laughs. "And you're not? I think you went to put those little shorts and skimpy tank top on just to send me over the edge. I'm really struggling to make it through dinner here without throwing you on this counter, spreading you out, and having dessert first."

"Huh. I was thinking pretty much the same thing."

Bryce turns in my arms and I feel something hard covered in silk.

I look down.

"I was starting to worry that I'd lost my sex appeal, that you weren't interested anymore, but-"

"But you see what you do to me." His hard-as-stone cock sticks straight out of his pajama bottoms, the fabric straining like a teepee pulled tight to the ground around a center pole. "And me losing interest in you? Angel, that would never happen. Look at this thing. I've been hard for you since I held you in my arms, but I'm trying to be a gentleman and ease you back into sexual touching. It would kill me if my touching you triggered a flashback and freaked you out."

I can't keep my hands off him. I pull at the waist band and slip both my hands inside, wrapping my hands around his hard shaft. I stroke up and down.

Bryce groans. "Angel, that feels so good." His body jerks from my touch.

I pull his waist band down to his muscular thighs and his cock springs free.

"It would be a shame to waste this, don't you think?" I drop to my knees and take him deep in my mouth before he has a chance to protest.

His hands grip the counter and he leans back for support.

"Christ, Angel! Your mouth... aw, fuck. That's so good, just like that."

I devour his cock, sucking and stroking it and listening to his moans of pleasure as I reach down and fondle his balls with my other hand. They tighten immediately.

Tasting pre-cum on my tongue, I look up to see the expression on his face, to see if he's close.

He lets out a regretful groan. "Fuck! You distracted me." Snatching his cock from my mouth, he pulls me up by my arms. "I can't think straight when you're around me. You mess with my head. We're supposed to ease into this. Take our time. See if you're okay."

I lift off my shirt and pull down my shorts, kicking them away. Then I rip off my bra and stand naked before him. His eyes widen.

"Don't I turn you on anymore? Do you not want my body?"

"You're all I think about! And, yes, I want you. Jesus, I want you so bad I'm shaking! Can't you see that I'm losing my mind over this?"

"Why? Because that lunatic had his hands all over me and now my body disgusts you?"

"Christ Angel, how could even think that? How could that idea ever enter your mind?"

"Because of the way you're looking at me. You've been hot for me from the moment we've met, but it's gone. That look is gone!"

His strong hands shake from the adrenaline rush. "Never!" Bryce lunges, holding the back of my neck in one hand and my lower back in the other, crushing me into him. He kisses me passionately as I press back against the counter, and then he grinds his cock on the perfect spot, pinning me down with the expert roll of his hips. I moan in his mouth.

Hot and breathless we pull apart, panting, gasping for breath.

Bryce's eyes quickly scan the counter. With one swoop of his arm, he pushes everything out of the way, clearing the counter, pots and cutlery clattering to the floor. He lifts me up under my arms, sitting me with my butt and feet on the edge of the counter. "Lean back on your hands." He quickly strips the remaining of his pajama bottoms off and stands back with a smoldering look in his eyes, admiring the position I'm in. "So fucking sexy, spread wide open for me on my counter. You don't know how many times I've pictured you like this."

That look is back! The look that says he adores and cherishes me.

His beautiful eyes examine me, drinking me in. He hesitates for a moment and then his mouth lowers to my pussy. Roughly. Impatiently.

Yes, this is what I want. Finally!

His magical tongue goes to work flicking and sucking. It grazes down my swollen clit and my pelvis jerks at his expert touch.

I lean back on my elbows. It's not very comfortable, so I adjust and flop down onto my back on the cold granite counter top. My toes curl around the ledge and I grasp a handful of his silky, jet-black hair and tug gently. My breathing quickens until I'm gasping for little breaths sporadically. I circle my hips, enjoying every sensation of his luscious mouth on me. His tongue darts out, spearing inside me. Then he licks up one side and then the other. When he sees I'm close, his finger rims the outer edge of my entrance. He pushes it in deep, and pounds the hell out of me keeping with the same rhythm. His mouth latching onto my clit, flicking it wildly. My orgasm builds and builds to the point where my butt lifts off the counter and every muscle in my body is tense. With all these sensations desire unfurls from deep within my pelvis, taking me by surprise as I explode and fall apart, shaking uncontrollably. I realize I'm grinding too hard against his beautiful mouth and I loosen my grip on his hair. He doesn't seem to mind. His tongue and finger don't stop until he sees I'm pushing away from the sensitivity of such an explosive and satisfying orgasm.

"I guess you needed that. What got you so excited?"

What the hell kind of question is that? I sit back up and frown. "You! I haven't had you since Wednesday and the way you tease me with that gorgeous body of yours is unbearable. I can't even think straight when you're around me. My body aches for you and your touch. All I think about is getting your hard cock inside me again to relieve it."

"Good answer. Now come with me." He lifts me off the counter and I slide down his body. He bends his knees and pokes my pussy with the head of his rock-hard cock. "Open," he commands.

I open my legs and his cock slides between my thighs grazing my pussy lips. We slide back and forth to the same rhythm, relishing the feeling. Our tongues dual in a sensual assault. We start out slow but as we get hotter our aggression intensifies until we pull away breathless.

"Come," he orders, pulling me by the hand from the kitchen to the living room. "This couch will do. On your back."

I lie down and he spreads my legs wide, nestling his large body between them.

He kisses me slowly, working me up into a frenzy again as he grinds against me.

"Babe!"

"I know, Angel. You want this don't you?"

"Yes, please." I spread wider to accommodate him.

The head of his cock tests my wetness and then he gives it to me, inch by inch, until he's balls-deep, filling me.

I inhale sharply from the exquisite stretching as my hips strain toward him and my nails claw down his back. My lips and tongue run along his neck, tasting him, and then move up to his waiting mouth. I can't get enough. We kiss hungrily, devouring each other.

When we separate, I gaze deep in his eyes, hesitating. There's something I want to say, but I don't know if I should. I don't know how he'll react, but finally blurt it out. "Babe, I need you to help me wash away the sickening thoughts of him touching and hovering over me."

"Oh, Angel." He hugs me tight. "Tell me how I can help you?"

"You're doing it already. I need your touch and your kiss. I need you to make love to me to erase him from my memory."

"My, Angel." He hugs me again.

I pull back to gaze deep into his eyes again. "I need to know that we're okay and nothing's changed between us."

"Angel, don't ever think that. Nothing's changed. I want you more with every breath I take. It almost suffocates me with how much I want you. I was worried about how you'd react to touch so quickly after that ordeal. I don't want you to freak out and I don't want to fuck this up. I need you."

"Babe, I'm okay, I promise. Please make love to me."

"Let me start here." He kisses my lips slowly, passionately, like I'm the most precious thing to him in the whole world. "And here." He kisses that tender spot behind my ear. "What about here?"

"Yes, I like that. I love you."

"I'll give you anything that you will ever need. I love you, Angel."

We're lost in our beautiful lovemaking for a couple hours, until we're exhausted, and we collapse on the bed smiling, breathless, and sweaty. We tangle our legs together and gaze up at the ceiling, each lost in our own thoughts.

My thoughts turn to how Bryce always tries to prove his love for me with such force and greed that it brings tears to my eyes. I know he would do absolutely anything for me. I see how much he loves me. I turn to look at his beautiful face and realize this horrific ordeal seems to fade with every passing hour that Bryce and I are together. Every kiss Bryce gives me, every caress, seems to dull the bitter memory of my stalker's touch.

I want to forget and move on. The horror of this ordeal is fading, yet, I know this will be another bad memory that will never completely go away.

Our stomachs growl simultaneously and we laugh, bringing us back to the here and now.

We'd put dinner on hold because we couldn't keep our hands

off of each other. There was a desperate need to show one another that nothing has changed in our relationship, and that our love is stronger now than what it's ever been.

As we sit at the breakfast bar eating our sweet and sour chicken stir fry in the buff, Bryce rubs my thigh and absent-mindedly rubs my foot with his. "So, since I'm off work for a week and you seem to be handling this ordeal well... what do you think about going to Aruba with Leena and Austin?"

"Really?" I can't contain my excitement. I'm almost hopping off the bar stool and my cheeks hurt from smiling so hard. "I'd love to."

"I wanted to surprise you, but I had to make sure you were okay with the idea."

"Babe, it's a great idea, thank you."

"Well then, it's settled. Do you want to text Leena or do you want me to? She said she'd make all the arrangements."

Before Bryce can finish his sentence, I jump off the bar stool and practically run to the bedroom to get my phone. "I'll text her."

As I'm walking back to Bryce, I check my phone. Leena's been texting to see how I'm doing, but I was too caught up in making love in every room of this cabin to hear it.

I climb back onto the bar stool and lean into Bryce, showing him the text from Leena as I stroke the inside of his thigh. "She's worried about me."

I text her back:

Sorry I didn't see your text, I was busy sexercising. I'm fine, better than fine. And we're going to Aruba, Baby! I'm so excited. Can't wait!

Leena texts back:

Really? Holy crap. I'm on it! I'll text back with the details. Get ta-packin', Sista. Most likely we'll be flying out tomorrow. I'm so pumped!!!

K. I'll let you do your magic. Bye. I'm so excited!

I turn to look at Bryce and he still has a smile on his face.

"I love seeing you this excited, Angel. You're so beautiful. When you smile, the whole room lights up."

I turn and run my hand down his cheek. "Thank you, Babe. You make me so happy. I'm so lucky to have you."

Our lips fuse together in a soft kiss. When we pull apart, I hug him.

"We should get dressed and get to your house so you can pack. Not that you're going to need many clothes. I want you naked most of the time. And no thongs under those dresses and skirts."

"Okay." I say softly, wanting to be naughty for him.

As we drive through town, that angry, suspicious look has finally faded from Bryce's face. He looks like a weight has been lifted off of him. He's not as stressed now that my stalker's out of the picture and locked up. He's happy and relaxed. I love seeing this side of him.

In a moment of reverie as we drive to my house, I examine the features on his face. His nose is, not too large, just perfect. His jet-black silky hair falls perfectly over his forehead. His eyebrows are full, but not too full. His jawline, cheekbones, and chin are all as sculptured as a statue of Adonis. And those lips-those luscious, kissable lips, so soft, smooth and full. I think about him kissing me and what it does to me. I think about his lips skimming over me, caressing my skin, going down on me. When his lips are on me-oh, God! I squirm in my seat.

This gorgeous Greek God can't be meant for me, can he? I'm the luckiest woman in the world.

Bryce glances over at me, smiling. "Keep looking at me like that and see what happens."

"Is that a promise?"

"I'd give anything to know what you're thinking right now. And yeah, that's a promise I'll love to keep."

"I was thinking how gorgeous you are and how lucky I am. And somehow I think my parents had something to do with steering you my way."

"Angel that goes both ways, because I think I'm the luckiest man alive. Whenever I wake up, you're the first thought that pops into my mind and you stay with me all day until I fall asleep at night. And then, I dream about you."

I move his coat to the other side of me and scoot closer across the seat, running my right hand down the thick veins on his forearm, loving how he tells me everything that's going on in his mind. My left hand glides across his thigh and my finger grazes the impressive bulge through the crotch of his jeans.

"I think you're right about your parents though. It was the strangest thing when we met in that grocery store. I told Austin I wanted something different to eat and for some strange reason we ended up going to the other grocery store, clear across town from the one we usually go to. Austin bitched me out, but then humoured me because he thought I was a little unstable at the time. So yeah, it was weird that we ended up at that store, almost like I was being pulled to you. Like magnets."

"Well, I guess you found something different to eat." I smirk at him.

Bryce does a double take. "I love it when you have dirty thoughts and say them out loud." He snakes his fingers down my jeans, caressing my pussy lips through the fabric. "I heard you singing a song that day. You looked so sweet and innocent and I couldn't take my eyes off of you."

"You heard me?"

"Yes, that's what caught my attention. The sweet sound of an angel. I knew then I was never going to be the same and yes I found you, and you are my favourite thing to eat. I could eat you for breakfast, lunch, dinner, and snacks in between. I could eat you all damn day, if you'd let me."

I'm just about to say, who's stopping you, when I get a text from Leena:

Be at Pearson Airport in Toronto at eleven a.m. tomorrow. We fly out at one p.m. We return Saturday night at eight p.m.

Okay, we'll be there. Going to my house to pack. If I have any questions, I'll text. Thanks, hun, for taking care of the arrangements for us. Let me know how much I owe you and I'll transfer it into your account.

No problem. You know I love taking care of this and no need for cash. Bryce already paid.

K, we'll text when we get close to the airport. Thanks again ttyl.

I gaze up at Bryce. "I know I'm probably wasting my breath, but let me pay you back. This is my treat."

"Nope. End of discussion."

"Stubborn!"

"You have no idea Angel. You're not paying for anything, so don't even try."

Back at my house, Bryce is supervising my packing. Every time I pick an article of clothing, he has a comment. "Not going to need that, or that. Hopefully you'll be naked most of the time."

"Well, in case I do have to wear clothes, I'll bring it."

"All right, if you must," he says with a sigh.

On the drive back to the cabin, I cuddle close to Bryce and rub his thigh, grazing my fingers along his denim-clad big bulge. I look up to see his reaction and he looks down to see mine. I give him a smile that I hope looks mischievous, dropping my head down to the side, and peering up at him.

"Angel, you keep lookin' at me like that and you're going to get it."

"Really?"

"You're asking for it. I wish I were hands-free right now. I'd tickle the piss and vinegar out of you."

"Oh, yeah?"

Bryce shakes his head again, smirking at me. "What have I created?"

"You've created one horny little bitch and I need this." I wrap my fingers around his growing cock and stroke up and down.

"Don't let me stop you."

Bryce pushes the seat back and I undo his pants. He lifts his butt and I help him shimmy them down to his knees.

I take hold of his growing cock, lick my lips, and drive it deep in my mouth to the back of my throat.

"Ah, fuck, Angel. I'll never get enough of you. You're so good to me."

His praise spurs me on. I want to give him one of the best blow jobs of his life. "Your mouth wrapped around my cock is the sexiest thing I ever felt."

As his excitement grows, I feel the truck leap forward and accelerate. Then he lets off and we coast, then we accelerate and leap forward again. "Christ, Angel, I've got to pull over."

I don't stop. My head bobs up and down and my hand strokes his rock-hard shaft.

He pulls the truck off to the side of the road and puts it in park before his grip tightens at the back of my head. I know he's close. I wonder if he'll deny me his release, but to my astonishment he doesn't tell me to stop.

"Angel, you're going to make me come."

His fingers splay through my hair and his grip tightens, as I lift and lower my mouth onto his steely cock. I cup his balls and they tighten with my touch.

"Aww, fuck, fuck, fuck. Angel!"

I feel warm cum spurting to the back of my throat and I swallow quickly, keeping up the same rhythm to give him a strong orgasm. I swallow again, taking it all, only stopping when he rubs my back gently.

"Angel? You are my Angel. Sent from heaven. You know that? Damn woman, can you suck cock good."

I lift my head, wipe my mouth with the back of my hand and smile proudly. "So you like?"

"Oh hell, yeah. Now wait to see what I have in mind when we get back to the cabin."

The anticipation is killing me.

9

WHEN WE GET back to the cabin, we set up our luggage at the back door so it's ready for tomorrow morning and then Bryce takes my hand and leads me to the bedroom.

He pulls a white Victoria's Secret bra and thong out of the drawer of the "kinky cabinet." Sparkling jewels are strategically placed on the fabric and there's a matching garter with silk stockings. "Can you put these on in the bathroom for me and I'll set up the room for our fantasy."

"Okay," I say excitedly.

"I'll come get you."

While I dress, I hear furniture moving in Bryce's bedroom next door. "What's he up to now?" A smile forms on my face as I do up the garters. When I stand straight and look in the mirror, I'm amazed at how beautiful it looks. "*Wow, Bryce you sure do know how to pick out lingerie."* I quickly spray on some perfume and brush my teeth.

Bryce comes in wearing a black thong and I zoom in on his magnificent bulge. My eyes rake up and down his gorgeous body.

Finding it hard to look away, from any part of him, but it feels like my eyes keep darting back to his bulge.

"Angel, you're beautiful. I knew it would fit perfectly. I can't stop looking at you." His eyes bore through me, travelling the length of my body. He drops to his knees and wraps his arm around my hips, holding me in place as he gently caresses my exposed butt cheeks. He kisses each cheek as I look in the mirror with my head turned, watching him. His teeth latch onto the ruffled silk strap of the garter, and he pulls it out, letting it slap against my skin. His tongue darts out and he licks his way to the other garter. He spins me so I can see in the mirror as he takes the other strap in his teeth. He pulls it out farther, and lets go. Him on his knees, admiring and worshipping me is an erotic sight that will be in my mind forever.

"How I love this ass." He kisses tenderly a few more times and then straightens.

"Come." He pulls me to the bedroom, where I'm surprised to see he's moved the bed tight against the wall. A swing hangs from a set of ceiling carabiners.

"Oh, wow! That looks like fun." I run my hand over his washboard abs and they tighten further with my touch. "How did you move that bed by yourself? It weighs a ton."

He lifts his arms and assumes a pose. "Muscles, Angel, muscles."

I stand in front of him and gently squeeze his flexed hard biceps. "Oh, and how I love these muscles."

His strong arms wrap around me. "Oh, and how I love you."

From the moment we entered the bedroom and I saw the swing hanging there, I noticed his breathing had changed, his eyes were glimmering with excitement, his cock looked so hard it must be painful, aching for release. He was so excited for me to see the room. *This is the fantasy that tops them all and I want to be the woman who gives it to him. I want this to be his ultimate fantasy,* exceeding all his expectations, because he's given me so much. Anything I could ever need, he's given it to me.

His lips lower to mine. He weaves his fingers through my hair, holding me in place at the back of my head, and we kiss slowly, tenderly.

"I wasn't sure if you'd like it." He runs his fingers across my cheek, caressing. "I thought maybe it was too soon. This isn't the best timing. If you don't want this, we'll wait."

"I'm okay. I want this. I'll be fine."

"You're amazing." He runs his thumb along my lower lip as he gazes deep in my eyes. "I want you to bring this fine little ass over to the swing and I'll lower it." He gently rubs my ass as if he's shining it.

"You're sure it'll hold me?"

"Yes, I tested it myself. I almost couldn't get out of the frickin' thing. If it can hold my weight, you've got nothing to worry about. You're like a feather inside it."

"You're adorable. I wish I could have seen you, but that's okay, I'm having a great visual right now." I run my hand gently down his cheek. "Always thinking of my safety."

"Yes, always." His stance changes before my eyes as he spreads his feet hip-width apart and stands erect, shoulders back, transforming from my sweet Bryce into a deliciously, dominating sex god. His eyes rake up and down my body, greedily.

"Let's take these off first so I can have access to my sweet, sweet pussy." He crooks his finger and gently runs the underside between the fabric and my pussy.

He bends his knees, lowering himself with perfect control as he slides my thong slowly down my legs, gently skimming his fingers down every inch of my skin through the stockings. He holds my hand to help me out of them so I don't fall, a real possibility in these four-inch, fuck-me heels, and he tosses the thong onto the dresser.

Then he walks over to the swing and lowers it. "Come here."

He clasps the ropes onto another position at the back of the swing so he's hands free, helping me climb in. "That's it, lower that sexy little ass right in here."

I hold onto the ropes and clumsily maneuver my butt into place, sinking down into a comfortable position while he holds the swing so it won't take off. The swing cradles me in a slightly angled sitting position. It also has a cut out where my butt sits for easy access, I presume.

Bryce extends the metal stirrups and positions my high heels in them.

I lean back and relax. "They thought of everything when they made this swing."

"Yes, and so did I when I bought it." Bryce walks to the back and raises it, then clasps the ropes into another position, elevating me.

"Woo-hoo, I'm pretty high now."

"Just lean back and relax, Angel."

Bryce grabs his phone off of the dresser. "Can I take a few pictures?"

"Sure."

"Angel, you're amazing, do you know that? Damn! You turn me on. I've always dreamed about this, but I never thought it would come true. You're everything I could ever want in a woman."

"You say the nicest things to me."

Bryce gently swings me.

I giggle. "This is fun, I like this."

Bryce switches from videotaping to taking pictures at different angles. "So sexy. Do you have any idea what you do to me?" He places his phone back on the dresser, stops the swing from moving, and stands between my legs. "Look at this. Perfect height for me to devour this pretty pink, luscious pussy. I'm going to get you so worked up that when you lose control you're going to squirt in my mouth, like the last time I drove you insane."

"I did what?" I'm horrified at the thought. "I'm sorry. I didn't... I don't have control over what my body does when-"

Bryce reaches up and covers my mouth with one finger. "Shh, I loved it and I want more. I can't stop thinking about it. You don't know how much it turns me on."

"Bryce?"

He shakes his head at me, silently ordering me not to talk. "Angel, do you know how many guys would love it if their girlfriends or wives squirt? You're every man's fantasy."

"Is that normal?"

"You're the ultimate woman, Angel. I couldn't ask for more."

"Why didn't you tell me?"

"I did."

"I mean, when it happened?"

"Well, at the time, I was a little busy. I wanted to tell you, but I didn't want you feeling self-conscious. I want you to let go, like you usually do. And then eventually we'll work up to having you squirt more, every time you cum."

"So I should feel self-conscious about this?"

"No, Angel. Let's forget I said anything and just concentrate on this."

Bryce lowers his mouth to my pussy and I forget everything else. "Oh, my. Ooooh," I moan.

All my worries are obliterated when Bryce's luscious mouth is on me.

He holds me in place with one hand at my lower back while his tongue and finger do their magic, working me into a fever pitch. When he notices I'm close, he stops.

I whimper and he grins at me. "Not yet."

He reaches down under the swing, where I had seen an assortment of toys earlier in the pocket below. "I think you've seen enough." He saunters around the swing to my head and slips the blindfold over my eyes.

All my senses heighten immediately and I feel an excited giddiness flow through me, almost like an adrenaline high. I wait impatiently for a touch. And wait. And wait.

Nothing.

What is he doing? I know he's still in the room, because I hear subtle sounds of him doing... what?

I hear music faintly and then I feel Bryce's warm breath against my ear. "Don't be scared, I want you to listen to some music for me."

I nod yes and he places the head phones on my ears. The music is something I've never heard before, but it's amazing. I'm teleported to a different world.

I feel something cold at my entrance. He holds it there for a moment, driving me wild with anticipation, and then pushes it inside-not slow, not fast, just deftly, steadily pushing, stretching me as it goes in. It starts to vibrate and the feeling is exquisite. I moan appreciatively and it stops. I sigh, knowing he's teasing me. He starts it back up again. It's pulsing low, and then a little higher, and then so high, I don't know if I can take much more.

I start to squirm, but Bryce holds the swing steady by gripping my butt.

His mouth seals onto my clit and he flicks it relentlessly with his tongue, hardening it, then he sucks gently. He doesn't stop. He coaxes my body to the brink of orgasm over and over again and then eases me back by slowing when he notices I'm on the verge, and speeding up when he wants to work me into a frenzy again.

I swear he's working with the rhythm of the music that's being piped into my ears. My body is overheating, my skin is misted with sweat, and my breathing has changed from fast pants to shallow intakes, where it's almost ceased. I reach down, snaking my fingers through the silky strands of his hair, and tug him into me, holding him in place. The music is at a climax-and so am I. I scream, "Bryce, oh God, Babe! It's so good." I dig my nails into the side of the swing as my legs start to shake and quiver uncontrollably. My body bows from the onslaught of delicious sensations. I feel him tighten his grip on my butt so I don't swing away from him, and he laps up every drop.

When Bryce notices that my body has gone limp, he stops the vibrating, pulls the toys free from my body and lowers the swing.

He lifts the headphones off my ears and slips the blindfold off my eyes. "You're unbelievable, do you know that?"

"Babe, holy crap, wow! It keeps getting stronger. Did I?"

He pulls me out of the swing and holds me in a tight embrace. "Yes, and I loved every minute of it. Angel, you have no idea what this means to me, do you? Let's just say that if I were to tell Dante or Jax… they'd be all over you, more than they are now. Forget the brotherhood bullshit. They'd back-stab me in a second to have you."

My curiosity is getting the better of me as I think of Bryce telling Dante and Jax everything. "You don't tell them anything that goes on in our sex life, do you?"

"No, I learned from my last mistake. They try to get me to talk. It doesn't work. This is between you and me. Like I said, I don't want to fuck this up."

His lips fuse with mine in a slow, sensual kiss as he backs me up to the bed, while he unclasps my bra, pulling the straps down, and tossing it to the end of the bed. Lowering us to the mattress, Bryce gently holds my weight and his as he stares deep in my eyes, stirring me up again. I can't imagine any other man doing what he does to me. His seduction skills melt me to my core.

I know I have nothing to compare him to, but I see how gentle and considerate he is of my needs, which he always fulfills. And then just below the surface, when his arousal grows, the dominant sex god appears and I know he's everything a woman could ask for. He's my perfect lover.

His lips lower to mine and he kisses me slowly and tenderly as he hovers above, gliding his hard cock along my leg.

Just that simple touch and it sets my blood on fire. I want his cock inside me, stretching me, filling me, fucking me hard.

I can't take much more. I reach down and wrap my fingers around his cock and touch my pussy lips with the head.

Bryce mischievously smiles at me, his head tilted slightly, showing his dimpled smirk. "Are you dying for my cock, Angel?" His voice is deep and seductive.

"Yes."

"Do you want me to shove it hard in that tight little pussy of yours?"

"Yes."

"Do you want me to give you every inch of my cock so I fill you, until you can't take anymore?"

"Oh God, yes."

He settles between my legs which are open wide and positions himself at my entrance, hesitating, teasing me.

"Do you want to feel my cock stretching you? The head of my cock scraping the walls of your juicy pussy?"

I'm shaking with desperate need. "Babe, please."

Bryce gives me what I want, positioning his cock at my entrance, teasing me with the head, and then plunging in until I'm completely full.

"Babe, my spine is tingling. You feel so good inside me."

Sweat starts to form on Bryce's skin and beads on his forehead. He's breathing heavily, but keeping up with the same hard pace. I can see he's close, as we stare lovingly into each other's eyes.

He holds himself up, supporting all his weight with only his arms and feet. A powerful pose, impressive and magnificent to watch as he tunnels deeper with every thrust, hitting that aching spot inside me.

"Angel, I don't know how much longer I can hold out."

"I'm with you Babe, let go."

My muscles contract, squeezing him like a vise. I reach between us and circle my clit with my finger, feeling my arousal build again until I explode. Somehow, he holds out, watching my orgasm unfold.

I'm a quivering mess as my body unravels and falls apart.

He slams into me, pushing me harder into the mattress. Our lower bodies are sticking together from sweat.

Every muscle of his is strained, contracted. His eyes close and then open again. He gasps for air and then thrusts again- once, twice. His cock twitches and jerks as he empties himself deep inside me. "Angel." Escapes from his lips as he comes, long and hard.

I run my nails down his back, soothing him, and then grab his ass cheeks, pulling him into me. "How was that Babe?"

Bryce falls down onto me, smiling into the crook of my neck, and then kisses me gently. "Wow, Angel!" He runs his tongue along my neck.

"I know it was amazing for me. I'm still shaking."

"Sorry I couldn't hold out longer, but seeing you in that swing… I almost blew my load just looking at you."

"Babe, you can come whenever you like, you shouldn't feel obligated to satisfy me first."

Bryce lifts his upper body to stare directly in my eyes, making sure his cock stays securely connected inside me. "Aww hell no, the man always satisfies his woman first. And I will be the best for you. I don't ever want you wondering if some other guy could please you better. Angel, you make me want to be a better man. And I will succeed! I will be your everything for the rest of your life. Anything you need, I will do whatever it takes to get it for you."

"Babe. You're such a romantic. What you say goes straight to my heart. You are my everything. I'll never ask for more. You're perfect."

Bryce rolls to his side and pulls out. "Let's keep that romantic crap between us. We wouldn't want to ruin my reputation as a bad ass, would we?" He raises out of bed, grabs a handful of Kleenex from the dresser and cleans me up.

I chuckle, placing one finger over my lips. "My lips are sealed."

"Good. Let's take a quick shower and then get to bed. We have a long day tomorrow."

As we approach the airport, Bryce notices my nervousness. "Angel, are you okay?" He squeezes my hand.

"Yeah, I've got butterflies in my stomach. I've never been on a plane before."

"You'll be fine. This is my second time. First time was to a hockey tournament when I was fifteen, states-side in Michigan. I think I had butterflies then, but you relax once you get in the air."

"I think I'm going to need a drink."

"Seriously? You hardly drink."

"They serve alcohol here right?"

"Don't worry. We'll find you something."

I text Leena as we park the truck and head inside to find her and Austin. We make our way through inspection without a problem.

After clearing security, we find a restaurant that serves alcohol at eleven-thirty in the morning.

I suck back two Bud Light Limes immediately, hardly tasting them, but I'm feeling fine, less nervous. We grab a bite to eat and talk about all of the excursions Leena has planned for us. Before we know it, it's time to board the plane.

Bryce ushers me down the aisle in front of him. When we find our seats, I notice we have a window seat. "Babe, do you want the window?"

"Angel, you take the window seat. I want you to see this."

"I'm not sure I want to see this."

He squeezes my hand. "You'll be fine."

I settle into the window seat and Bryce sits beside me. Leena and Austin are right in front of us.

"Shit, Babe, I think I need another drink."

"You're funny. I've never seen you this worked up before."

"Yeah, I'm surprising the hell out of me too. I'm not usually such a wimp. Get a grip, Keera. It's no big deal. Right?"

"Right," Bryce says, looking sideways at me with that gorgeous smirk.

When everyone's seated, the engines start and the announcements come across the speaker.

"Shit, I wish I could see Keera's face," Leena hollers from the seat in front of us. "Bryce, video tape her, so we can laugh later."

My eyes widen and I reach for Bryce's hand. "Holy crap, Babe."

Bryce grins at me from one ear to the other and starts to video tape me.

"What are you doing? Oh, you're enjoying this aren't you?"

"Yes I am."

We start to move.

My grip tightens on Bryce's hand. "Oh shit!"

"Haven't you ever been on a roller coaster?"

"Yeah, we went to Canada's Wonderland for a grade-eight field trip and I went on every roller coaster with no problem."

"Well, this will feel almost the same."

We taxi down the run-way and pick up speed.

I'm white knuckled, gripping Bryce's hand tighter. "Holy frick."

Bryce stops videotaping and shuts his phone off. "You're hilarious, Angel."

"Oh shit, shit, shit. We left the ground."

"Damn, woman, you've got a good grip." He repositions our hands so I'm not squeezing so tight. "See no problem. Everything's fine." He pats my hand.

We level out and I start to relax, loosening my grip. "I'm okay now."

When the stewardess comes around, I ask for another beer and Bryce laughs at me.

I glance sideways at him. "What?"

"Nothing. I'm just thinking how cute you are when you're nervous."

"And what would you like today?" The flight attendant smiles at Bryce and touches his arm.

"I'll have a Labatt's blue, if you have it?"

Oh, here we go. Can't dress him up and take him anywhere without women throwing themselves at him. Maybe I'm over-reacting?

The flight attendant retrieves a beer from the fridge below, and hands it to Bryce touching his shoulder. "You let me know as soon as you need another and I'll get it for you."

She reaches over the first person and practically sticks her tits in Bryce's face, watching his reaction, not even looking at me when she hands me my beer.

Nope, not over-reacting.

Bryce turns his head to look at me and takes the beer from my hand. "Here, Angel, let me open this for you."

The stewardess sees that Bryce has no interest and moves on to the seats in front of us. "Oh my, there's two of you. Are you twins?"

"No, but I'm the older, better-looking brother," Austin replies.

The flight attendant laughs and touches Austin's arm. "And what can I help you with?"

"I'll have the same as my twin back there and a wine cooler for my girlfriend, please."

I watch over the seats and see her touch Austin's cheek. "Oh, you're so funny, darling. I'd love to take you home with me."

Between the seats, I see Austin unclenching Leena's hand, and then he pats it and gives it a squeeze. I bet she's biting her tongue like I was.

The flight attendant leaves, walking to the front of the plane, so I stick my hand through the seats and touch Leena's shoulder.

She looks back at me between the opening in the seats. "I'm

telling ya, one of these days I'm going to blurt out what's really on my mind and it's not going to be pretty."

"I knew you were biting your tongue," I say chuckling.

The flight attendant returns with Leena's wine cooler and does the same leaning scenario with Austin as she hands Leena her drink. She touches Austin's shoulder again. "Oh my, you obviously workout. Well, hun, you let me know if you need anything else," she says in a seductive southern drawl, before moving on to the next seat. When the flight attendant has moved down the aisle, Leena undoes her belt and turns to stand up, looking at me and Bryce. She shows us, measuring with her finger and thumb. "I was this close to losing it on her."

"Get her Leena, get her for me, too," I say smiling.

My nerves settle down after another drink and landing doesn't seem to bother me as much as taking off did.

The moment we step off the plane and walk through the tunnel to the airport, we can feel the heat and humidity.

We make our way over to pick up our luggage at the baggage claim and then find a washroom. We're still dressed for Canadian winter, and I need to change into something more suitable for Aruba weather. Leena and I drop our suitcases to retrieve a change of clothes.

When I emerge from the washroom, I'm wearing my little jean shorts and a white tank top.

Bryce looks me up and down and swallows hard. He wraps his arm around my waist and pulls me close into his hard-on. "You wore that the first time we met in the grocery store."

10

"I'M LOVING THIS vacation already." Bryce grinds into me as he kisses my temple.

"We'll be right back," Austin says as he and Bryce disappear into the men's washroom to change.

When Bryce and Austin emerge, they're wearing shorts and tank tops and look absolutely amazing.

I look Bryce up and down appreciatively, raise my one eyebrow, showing my dimple, and grin seductively. "Yum, I can't wait to get you alone."

Bryce tugs me close and whispers in my ear. "And what are you going to do to me?"

"You'll see."

"I sure hope so."

We share the bus to the resort with some colourful characters, including an older man with a monkey on a leash performing tricks, entertaining us.

Our bus driver seems to think he's a NASCAR driver, gunning it all the time, taking curves without slowing down, and shoving us forward with abrupt stops. We laugh as we bounce out of our seats and Bryce scrambles to hold me down.

The grounds at the front of the resort are beautifully landscaped with large rocks, colourful flowers, trees, and plants in large terra cotta pots. Two straight rows of fifty-foot palm trees line the concrete driveway to the resort entrance. In the main lobby we stop to admire a waterfall cascading over rocks, which catches my eye because of the bright lights changing colour beneath the water. We check-in at the concierge desk, and Leena's dad appears to greet us.

Leena hugs him. "Hi, Dad! How are you?"

"Good. You look amazing as usual-just like your mother. How is she? How was the flight?"

"Good," Leena says quickly, but he's already diverted his attention to me.

Leena's dad's mind and body are always in overdrive; he never stops. Now I know where Leena gets it. Whereas Ma is so laid back. I never noticed it when we were kids growing up, but I see it now. Pops is wearing a suit and styles his brown hair to perfection, and with the strong jawline, tiny eyes and goatee, I see that he is still a very good looking man for his age. He looks a lot like Kris Kristofferson.

"Keera, honey, it's so nice to see you again."

"Hi, Pops, how are you? Your resort is amazing. I can't wait to see it all." I give him a hug. "Pops, this is my boyfriend, Bryce."

Pops grabs Bryce's hand and they shake hard and fast. "Glad you could come. You need anything and I'll get it for you."

"Thanks for having us."

"Dad," Leena says, "This is Austin, my boyfriend."

"Glad to meet you, son. You keeping my baby happy?"

"I'm sure trying to, sir. It's nice to finally meet you. Leena talks about you all the time."

"That's great, but none of this 'sir' nonsense. I'm Pops to Leena's friends."

"Yes, sir. I mean, Pops."

Pops shakes Austin's hand firmly and then slaps him on the back. "We'll have dinner tonight at six-thirty in the paradise lounge. We'll get to talk more then. I want to hear about what you do for a living." Glancing at Bryce and me, he adds, "I gave you the best bungalows in the resort-great views. I've got something to take care of right now, so get checked in and I'll see you tonight."

He wraps Leena in another hug, kisses her, and disappears as quickly as he'd appeared.

"Busy man, eh?" Austin observes.

"Definitely," Leena says, "He's so wound up, I don't know how he sleeps at night."

The concierge gives us the key card for bungalows twenty-nine and thirty, and says if we need anything we only have to call and someone will bring it over right away. We follow Leena through part of the hotel and then the other, and make our way outside. She's so animated and excited, pointing out everything along the way.

It's almost too much to take in; there's a botanical garden, several ponds, waterfalls, wooden walkways, and bridges, Japanese garden statue's, big-bellied Buddha's, dragons, and pools with colourful pergolas for shade. I've never seen anything so beautiful, other than Leena's face. She's beaming with pride over the paradise her dad has created.

As we approach our bungalows, the last two after the largest pool, I thank Leena for inviting us. "This is absolutely amazing," I say, giving her a hug.

"Let's change into our bathing suits and swim up to the bar for a drink. It'll take a couple of days to see everything, so we'll start there."

"Okay, we'll meet you back here."

The front porch of our bungalow faces the pool, with two lounge chairs slightly hidden behind the railing of the composite wood deck. Bryce drops our luggage and takes out the key to open the door, he then surprises me by scooping me up in his arms and carries me inside.

I giggle. "Babe, can I ask why you always carry me through the door? I know you said tradition, but what did you mean by that?"

"Growing up, I watched my dad carry my mom through doors when we went on vacation and sometimes at home and I'd see how happy she was when he did it, so I thought I'd start my own tradition."

"So you never did this with any other girlfriend?"

"No. Do you like it or do you want me to stop?"

"I love it! Please don't stop."

Bryce gives me a quick peck on the lips. "Good. I love holding you in my arms."

He places me back on the floor gently and brings our luggage in.

"Wow, eh?" I throw my luggage on the rack and search every room. "This is nice."

The bungalow has a huge bedroom, large bathroom, and a living room with two sets of French doors. One set opens up against the backdrop of the tropical forest.

When we venture out further, we see it's beautifully landscaped, with a hot tub. The patio, surrounded by a six-foot fence, has plenty of privacy.

"We're going to have fun in here," Bryce says, lifting the lid. "Perfect temperature."

The other set of French doors, off the north side of the living room, opens to a magnificent view of the turquoise water.

"This is unbelievable."

Bryce saunters over to me and wraps me in a hug. "You look so happy. I love seeing you like this." His lips lower to mine in a slow, sensual kiss. When we pull away we're hot and breathless. He slaps me on the butt. "Go get dressed. Let's go swimming."

When I emerge from the bathroom, he's changed into swim shorts. His eyes zoom in on the small scraps of fabric that make up my blue corona bikini. "You call that a bathing suit? Look at this, you're popping out everywhere." His fingers run along the plump globes of my breasts.

"I thought you wanted me naked?"

"I changed my mind. Only when we're alone. Inside. And alone."

I tug him by the hand out of the bedroom. "Come on. Let's go swimming."

He stops dead in his tracks. "Wait!" He tugs me to his chest. "Aren't you going to change?"

"Oh, Babe, you're funny. Leena's going to be wearing her teeny bikini. I don't think Austin will have a problem with that."

Now that I've added Austin, whom he idolizes, into the mix, it might make him think how ridiculous he's being. Cheap shot, I know, but if it works, why not?

"Fine, but you stay right beside me."

"You're so cute when you're overprotective and jealous." *Wait until he sees my light pink bikini, he'll have a coronary.* I stand in front of him and rub his muscular chest. "You're half naked."

"That's different. Come with me." He leads me outside to the pool.

Leena sees us and waves us over.

When we walk around the pool, the way people are staring makes me feel naked. Maybe they're staring at my gorgeous boyfriend, or at the two of us because we make such a cute couple. I feel so uncomfortable from the intense scrutiny that I dive right into the water. Bryce follows and we swim up to Leena and Austin at the bar.

"Try this." Leena hands me her drink and I take a sip.

"Mmm, that's good. I'll take one of these, please," I say to the bartender.

We hang out by the pool drinking, swimming, and tanning for a few hours, and then we walk along the beach. The weather is a balmy eighty-seven with light cloud cover. When the breeze whips up, it's exhilarating. After being in the sun too long, we duck into the shade whenever we can as we make our way back to the bungalow to shower and dress for dinner with Pops.

Bryce stands in the doorway of the bathroom watching me apply the finishing touches of my make-up. I glance sideways at him. "Is something wrong?"

"No, but I was thinking that I don't know why you put make-up on when you're perfect without it."

"You're so sweet. I just need a bit since we're meeting Pops' new girlfriend. You know, I've got to make a good first impression."

"Will you do something for me?"

"Anything."

Bryce opens a box containing two sets of pink and purple plastic ben-wa balls. He takes the pink set out and places them in my hand. "Will you wear these?"

An instant thrill shoots up my spine. "Sure, but how'd you get them through customs?"

"Suitcase. The pink set are the lighter ones." Bryce places the purple set in my other hand. "Feel the difference in weight? We'll work up to the heavier ones later."

I hold one between my finger and thumb and shake it, noticing the metal ball inside the plastic ball. "Good quality." I picture in my head Bryce roaming around the naughty shop looking for the perfect toy and it makes me smile.

"Only the best for my Angel." Bryce takes my hand and leads me over to the bed. "Bend over and spread those sexy legs for me." Lifting my dress up and placing it on my lower back, he bends down and runs his hands up each leg, grazing my pussy lips, firing up every cell in my body. Then he stands and leans his hard body over mine, whispering in my ear, "So sexy." Holding me in place on my lower belly, his other hand rubs the globes of my ass, and I feel his expert probing fingers insert a ball.

The feeling is exquisite. I grasp the comforter, moaning and circling my ass.

"Aw fuck, Angel. I'm so hard for you right now."

He inserts ball number two and pushes them both deep inside me. Deeper and deeper his skilled finger probes and massages, trying to go up further.

"Babe, it feels so good."

"I don't know if I'm going to make it through dinner. You've been teasing the hell out of me all day."

"Good, maybe we can finish what we started earlier."

"It's a date." He smacks my ass.

"Ouch!"

My mind wanders back to the look he gave me when he first saw me in my bikini, and then in the pool when we snuck off to the grotto, underneath the cascading waterfall. I think about how hard he was when I wrapped my arms around his neck and ground my pussy into his hard cock while kissing him ferociously, how hot and breathless we were when he almost succeeded in pushing his cock inside me.

We were interrupted by a group of people, so we tried to find another secluded spot, without luck, but we were so hot and worked up I almost didn't care if anyone saw us. I had to force myself to think of Leena and how embarrassed she'd be if we were escorted off the property for fucking in the pool.

It's a good thing Bryce had on a loose-fitting swim suit because it helped to conceal the wood he'd been sporting all day. I kept standing in front of him to defuse the situation, but I couldn't resist rubbing my ass against him, which made it worse.

With the ben-wa balls tucked inside me, he pulls my dress back down.

"Put a thong on, in case they fall out."

I quickly close the gap between us. Reaching up, I run my hand through the hair at the back of his neck while my other hand caresses the tee-pee that's formed in his dress pants. "You've been hard all day."

"Yeah, I think I have blue balls."

I'm chuckling when our attention turns toward a knock.

"I've got to get this fucker to go down." Bryce adjusts his cock in his pants and goes to answer the door.

As I'm looking for a thong, I hear Leena and Austin's voices, so I quickly slip it on and meet them in the living room. "Hey, guys. Look at you! You're both looking pretty hot."

"So do you guys. You ready?" Leena asks.

"Yup."

"Good. Let's go eat," Austin says. "I'm starving."

As we file out the door, Leena says, "Austin you're always starving."

"Starving for this hot body." Austin envelopes Leena in a hug. "Can't we get room service?"

"Didn't get a quickie in, eh?" Bryce teases. "That's okay. We'll have blue balls together." Bryce slaps Austin on the back as we stroll past the pool.

As we follow Leena through the gardens and into the hotel, Bryce alternates wrapping his hand around my waist with resting it on the small of my back. Every time he shifts, I feel chills up my spine. I look up at him and he gazes down at me with a knowing, mischievous smile. His eyes glimmer and shine and his right dimple forms on his cheek. *This man is too sexy for his own good.*

As we stand in line waiting to be seated at the restaurant, Bryce bends to whisper in my ear. "How do my balls feel?"

"I'm dying with the way you're looking at me and how they're moving inside me when I walk. I want you so bad right now."

"Good." Bryce brings me around to stand in front of his hard cock, which is jutting out and making a tee-pee again. He whispers in my ear. "I want you as worked up as I am. Feel that?" He pulls me in a tight embrace and I feel his hard cock rubbing against my butt and lower back.

My head turns and I smile. "Oh yeah, I feel it. I want it."

"There you are. George, let them in." George unhooks the velvet roping and we follow Pops to our seats.

Leena hugs her dad. "Thanks for having us."

"Anything for you, baby." He ushers Leena and Austin to sit next to him and his girlfriend. "Sit. I've already ordered drinks. This is Brooke." He waves his hand, pointing us out. "My beautiful daughter, Leena, and her boyfriend, Austin. And this is Leena's good friend, Keera, and her boyfriend, Bryce."

We all shake her hand. "So nice to meet you."

Brooke, who is maybe in her late twenties is beautiful. I'm stunned by how much she looks like Ma. But a younger version of Leena's mom. The resemblance is uncanny. Obviously, this is the first time Leena has met her too, because of the look on her face as she shakes her hand. Leena must be freaking out right now. I keep glancing at her as she's checking Brooke out. My gaze floats over to Brooke and then back to Leena. What is she thinking right now?

Bryce and I sit at the end of the table and listen to the conversation unfold.

"So Austin, how'd you meet my baby?"

"Keera introduced us."

"And how'd you meet Keera?"

Oh shit. Here we go. You never know what's going to come out of Austin's mouth. I start to blush. Our drinks come and I take a big gulp before hiding behind my menu.

"Bryce and I met Keera at the grocery store in town. We have a cabin on the outskirts of Huntsville, but we live in Barrie."

"So what do you do for a living, Austin?"

"Ontario provincial police officer in Barrie."

"Impressive. I bet you've got some good stories to tell."

"Oh yeah, it gets a little crazy sometimes."

The waitress comes to take our order and Pops gets us another round of drinks.

"Bryce, what do you do for a living?"

"Barrie firefighter."

"Bet you see some sticky situations."

"Never a dull moment."

"Well that's good. I'm glad you both have good jobs. I have to make sure my girls are taken care of."

"Oh, Dad."

"That's sweet, Pops, always watching out for us."

"You're my girls and I always want to know what you're up to and if you're taken care of. While I was busy building my paradise, I worried for years, but your mother had it all under control and did a great job of raising you. Now that you're older, you can come visit me any time you want and you can stay as long as you want. Maybe permanently. I built this for you and your m…" He stops talking.

"Dad, you know I could never leave Mom."

"I know dear. Bring her with you, next time you come to visit."

I glance at Brooke and her face drops from happy to pissed off. Jeez, I hope they haven't been going out that long. I'd have to kill Bryce if he ever did that to me.

"Excuse me." Brooke stands and shoves her chair back. "I've have to hit the powder room."

I glance at Leena and then Pops, who's clueless and doesn't skip a beat as he takes Leena's hand in his. "How is she? I know she'd love it here. Bring her next time you come. Tell her not to worry about the money–I'll pay for everything."

"I told her the last time you asked me to. She said she'd think about it."

"Really?" The excitement in his voice rises. "Well that's a start. Tell her I miss her."

"Okay, I will. So how long have you and Brooke been going out?"

"Not long, but don't worry. I'll send her away if your mother comes."

Brooke is gone for about ten minutes. When she returns her eyes are red and puffy.

I feel badly for her.

Our dinner comes and as we eat and drink, the conversation roams all over the place.

All seems to be forgotten with Brooke until I see Austin stiffen. I look down the table and from my view I can see she has her hand on Austin's cock.

Oh shit! I glance at Leena, who is across the table from us and looking at Austin strangely.

Austin takes Brooke's hand off his crotch and then gets up to go to the washroom.

Leena, Pops, and Brooke are engaged in conversation, so I whisper in Bryce's ear. "Did you see Austin stiffen up?"

"Yeah."

"Brooke had her hand on his cock."

Bryce's eyes widen. "You're shitting me?"

Austin comes back to the table after a few minutes, shifts his chair closer to me, and then sits.

Another round of drinks comes and already I think I'd better slow down, because this evening could get really interesting and a little crazy once Leena finds out.

Pops stands with his drink. "Come, let's go out on the terrace for the festivities."

We follow and I watch Austin and Leena whispering into each other's ears. Then Leena's face turns red and she looks like a volcano ready to erupt.

We place our drinks on the table set up for us and are about to sit when Leena grabs my arm. "Come on, let's dance."

I pull Bryce with me and we follow Leena and Austin to the other side of the dance floor, out of Pops' and Brooke's sight.

"Do you fucking believe that bitch? Just because my dad can't let go of my mother, she decides to grab my boyfriend's cock. I'm so pissed right now. I want to go rip every strand of her hair out. Did you notice how much she looks like my mom?"

I shake my head and rub her back to let her know I feel for her, but I don't say a word because I know with how pissed off she is right now, anything I say is not going to matter.

"Damn, woman! When you get all worked up, it stirs something inside me." Austin wraps her in a tight embrace and kisses her ferociously. When they separate, she physically relaxes.

"Don't worry. I'll sit beside you and you can grab my cock." Austin grins down at her.

Leena reaches down and runs her hand along the outline of Austin's cock. "I want this right now."

"I know, but we'll have to wait for your father to leave. Or we can say we've had a long day in the sun and we're tired."

"Good idea."

We dance our way slowly through the people. I pull Bryce down and talk against his ear. "I'm so excited that we get to leave. These balls are moving around and they feel so good, but I want this instead." I reach back and run my fingers along the length of his hard cock. "I've been dying for this all day."

"As soon as Austin gives us the cue, we're out of here." Bryce's voice is deep and husky.

The song ends and we exit the dance floor to sit down at the table. I sit next to Brooke this time, Bryce on the other side of me, Leena across the table from Brooke, next to her dad, and Austin beside Leena.

The sound of drums beating, diverts our attention to the dance floor, which everyone has vacated.

Large drums surround the outer edge of the floor and the pounding reverberates with a beat I can feel in my stomach. Acrobats and fire dancers in scantily clad costumes fill the dance floor and stage, jumping over each other, performing somersaults. The women are wearing a bra and a thong with a grass skirt, which doesn't hide much. The men are wearing suede Tarzan sarongs and are showing off their wash board abs. Every man and woman in this performance has a head piece on and grass covering from their knees to their ankles. I check out every performer and wonder where they found so many dancers who are so good looking and who are in such great shape. Then my attention flips to Pops, who's beaming with pride. He most likely hand-selected his performers. It strikes me then that every employee I've seen so far at this resort is extremely good looking.

Bryce squeezes my knee and talks above the music. "I guess we're not leaving yet."

I give him a small pout and turn my chair so I can see better. Once I'm situated close to Bryce, I take his hand in mine, splaying our fingers together.

There's so much to see that our eyes dart from one spot to another, trying to take in all the performers. The show is amazing.

Later in the show, a female dancer with long black hair leaves the stage, dances her way over to our table, and stands before Bryce and Austin, giving them their own personal performance. Shortly after that, a very good-looking male fire dancer stands next to me, staring deep in my eyes, giving me my own personal performance. It's strange, and the competition between the two has me wondering if they're boyfriend and girlfriend trying to get each other jealous or if Pops asked them to interact with us? It seems odd that no other performer has left the stage and dance floor.

Once the show is done, Pops asks us what we thought of it. We all express our excitement and gratitude as he gushes with pride. He then tells us he has another surprise and wants us to meet him for dinner tomorrow night. Leena tells him if we're back from our excursions, we will.

The look on his face, suggests that not too many people say no to him. Leena tries to smooth it over with a hug and a kiss and he noticeably relaxes.

We say our goodnights and then walk through the lobby. As we turn the corner, the female performer who gave Bryce and Austin a personal dance is standing alone against the wall, looking freshly showered and wearing a low-cut dress, showing off ample cleavage. Her eyes light up when she sees Bryce and Austin. I peek at the guys, but they don't notice her. Leena and I do, though. We glance at each other and Leena scowls.

Walking through the gardens, Bryce has his arm wrapped around my waist and with that simple touch he has me on fire. Standing in front our bungalows, Leena says, "See you at eight, don't be late, we've got a full day ahead of us." Seeing her dad in full commanding form, I know where she gets it from. Surely not Ma. Why didn't I notice this when we were younger?

Bryce closes the door to our bungalow and stands in front of me, just inches away, not touching me, eyeing me up and down. "You look so sexy in this dress and these nipples have been teasing the hell out of me. They've been hard all night." His eyes zero in to my fully erect nipples.

"You noticed?"

"I think every man that came in contact with you noticed, but especially me. I've been hard for you all damn day, and night."

I crave his touch, but I think he's trying to set the mood and build anticipation, so I try to wait… but I can't.

"That's what you do to me. Seeing you half naked all day and feeling you in the pool-Babe, the way you touch me. I'm ready to explode."

"Well, I wouldn't want that to happen, so let's take this off." His fingers skim my sensitive skin as he slips the spaghetti straps off my shoulders. I shimmy out of my tight dress and it falls to the floor, pooling at my feet. I stand before him with my thong and high heels on. "Christ, Angel, that body! What it does to me. I ache for you. I'll never get enough."

A smile crosses my lips and butterflies flutter in my belly.

Bryce surprises me when he lunges toward me and picks me up in his arms. Strutting to the bedroom, he tosses me onto the comforter, staring down at me with dark lust-filled eyes. "We're going to take care of each other right now and then we're going to make love in every room of this bungalow. Hot tub last. Because I'll be toast by then."

11

WE DON'T MAKE love in every room and we don't make it to the hot tub, but Bryce promises me before this week is done that we will do just that. Exhaustion takes over after we make love twice. Too much sun and getting up early to make our flight, is the cause, I think.

As we climb onto our Harley, for a day of sightseeing, Bryce whispers apologies in my ear.

"Are you kidding me? Babe, if you had more energy I wouldn't be walking today. Didn't you see how satisfied I was?" I wrap my arms around him, grab his meaty pecs, and yell over the rumble of the engine. "Was. But now I want more."

Bryce turns his head and smiles at me. He faces forward again and shakes his head. His hand covers mine. "Hold on tight."

We surge forward out of the parking lot behind Leena and Austin and then pull up beside them.

A squeal of delight escapes my lips. "Woo-hoo! This is frickin' awesome!" Leena and I touch fingers every once in a while as we drive.

My head spins from one side to the other trying to take in all the scenery. It is breathtakingly beautiful. After a couple of hours, we stop at a restaurant on the oceanside to stretch our legs and grab a bite to eat. Bryce and Austin park with all the other Harleys in a row.

As we ease off the seat and straighten, I rub my butt to get the circulation moving again.

"Let me do that," Bryce says in a sexy drawl as he massages my buns.

"Oh, that feels so much better. Turn, let me rub yours."

"Will you two cut that shit out?" Austin complains. "Somebody might be looking out the window. We're supposed to be tough bikers, so suck it up."

Bryce fiddles with the strap of my helmet, pulls it off, and places it on the seat. It leaves me wondering why we're the only dumb Canucks wearing helmets when practically everyone else we've seen on the road was letting the wind whip through their hair.

The restaurant's interior décor is a nautical theme with fishing memorabilia and seascapes along the walls. As we settle into an open booth, the waitress informs us that the soup of the day is popular, so we all decide on that and a sandwich.

Back out on the road, we visit the lighthouse, Alto Vista Chapel, Casibari rock formation, Frenchman's Pass, Savaneta and Baby Beach. Leena and I take out our cameras and capture some fantastic pictures.

After returning the Harleys, we venture onto a luxury catamaran for several hours, stop to snorkel at Catalina Bay, and sail by the largest shipwreck, the Antilla.

When we make it back to land, we call Pops so he can make reservations for us and then head back to the resort with just enough time to shower and look presentable. Pops must have told George to keep an eye out for us because as soon as we step into line, George has us walk around the velvet ropes and ushers us in.

Before Pops can tell us where to sit, I pull out the chair beside Brooke and sit down. Leena gives me those eyes and a thank you grin.

During our dinner and after the main course, Bryce's ring tone blares sirens, so he looks at his phone to see who is calling. He squeezes my knee and gets up to find a quieter spot and I watch him disappear behind a wall that leads to the washrooms. He's gone for a few minutes and when he returns, he bends to talk to Austin. They both turn to stare at me.

"You have to tell her," Austin says. "Shit, Leena's mom."

"What's wrong?" I say.

I hear Pops voice clearly across the table. "What about Leena's mom?"

"That was Constable Grant telling me Keera's kidnapper escaped from the emergency psychiatric room at the hospital. I told him we're in Aruba until Saturday and he sounded relieved. He set up surveillance at Leena's and said he'd keep a close eye on your mom."

"What the hell is going on? Start at the beginning." Pops' voice deepens.

Bryce sits down beside me again and runs his hand down my leg. "Are you okay?"

"I'm okay, but I thought he was in jail."

"He was taken to the emergency room at the hospital."

Austin tells Pops everything from beginning to end. His face turns red and he looks angry. "I've got to call Shawna." He rises from his seat and Leena grabs his arm. "Dad, she'll be fine. Constable Grant will watch over her."

"Oh, yeah? If he got to Keera, he can get to your mother."

Pops turns and books it toward his office, and Leena follows.

Brooke stands, shoving her chair back so hard it almost tips over. "Tell Dean I've gone back to the suite and I won't be back!" She turns and storms off.

"Oh shit, she's pissed," I say, raising my eyebrows.

"Wait until she sees that she's a carbon copy of Leena's mom." Austin pipes up.

"Yeah, that's not going to go over well."

"Angel, you sure you're okay?" Bryce asks.

"Yeah, I'm fine. I thought he was in jail? How did he escape?"

"He attempted suicide and was taken to emergency. I guess the infirmary at the jail doesn't have the facilities to deal with a suicide attempt. Once he was stable and they were getting ready to transport him back to jail, he asked to go to the washroom. Somehow, he managed to overpower both a male nurse and a security guard. And then he was out the door, he just disappeared."

"He was a little unstable, but I doubt he was suicidal," I say. "I'll put money on it that he faked the suicide attempt as part of a plan to escape."

"All I can say is they better catch him before we go home or you'll be staying with me in Barrie until they do," Bryce says. "Grant said he'd keep me updated."

Leena and Pops return to the table and Pops' eyes glance at Brooke's empty chair.

"Brooke went to the suite, said she won't be back. How's Ma?" I ask, trying to distract him.

"She's good. They've already set up surveillance outside the house. She sounds really good," Pops repeats with a smile. "Said she'll seriously think about coming to visit me. And I'll want all of you to come back for a visit, too."

He sits and starts up a conversation immediately and I note that it doesn't seem to bother him that Brooke left. He's happy that he got to talk to Ma.

I had no idea how much he still loves her.

Our dinner arrives-filet mignon and lobster with a garlic dipping sauce which I use for each of them because it is both delicious and addicting. They practically melt in your mouth. The conversation flows easily as we talk about our excursions. Then after dinner, Pops ushers us to a small auditorium, where we sit in the front row for the magic show.

We all laugh when the illusionist brings Leena up on stage for one of his tricks. Pops seems carefree and happy when he isn't with Brooke.

As midnight descends upon us, we head back to the bungalows, exhausted from another full day in the sun.

Bryce and I climb into bed and he holds me tight. Just as I'm falling asleep I hear him whisper, "I promise I'll protect you."

When morning comes, we're full of life again and we venture out to one of the many restaurants on the resort for a big breakfast, which we then work off in the spacious workout room. Bryce stays close at breakfast and at the gym because he doesn't approve of my skimpy workout attire. He hops on the bow flex while Austin starts on the weights and I run on the treadmill next to Leena. I glance over at Bryce and see the same female performer from the other night standing next to him, giving him instructions, then she switches to Austin.

She wears a name tag on her tight workout shirt that says "Fitness Instructor" with the name Fiona below.

I have to admit that her helping Bryce makes the hair on my nape rise and my claws instantly come out. It's something about the way she moves. She has an exotic sex appeal-a screaming body with long, black, silky hair and perfect facial features, not to mention her flawless dark skin and major cleavage. She also seems to be trying to get both Bryce and Austin's attention.

I nudge Leena with my elbow.

"What?" she says in an irritated voice as she reluctantly diverts her attention away from Austin to look at me.

I raise one eyebrow. "Looks like she's working on a threesome with twins."

"Over my dead body. Watch this!" Leena saunters over to Austin and straddles his hips.

Fiona backs up.

Leena places her hands on Austin's chest. "Hun, can you show me how to use the bow flex when you're done?"

Austin places the weight back on the bar. "I'm done." He runs his hands along Leena's thighs and she gyrates on his cock.

Fiona's attention reverts to Bryce as he moves from the bow flex to the weights.

Oh, no you don't. He's mine!

I watch Leena and Austin move to the bow flex as I take a swig of my bottled water. Then I saunter over to a piece of equipment that I have no clue how to use. But a very nice man with tattoos and long, brown hair, neatly pulled back, has no problem showing me. I thank him with a smile and climb aboard.

As he instructs me, I notice his voice lowers, changing to a sexy tone and his eyes are intense, staring deep into mine. His gentle touch lingers on my skin longer than it should and that's when I notice how big his muscles are beneath the tribal tattoo. He hits a few buttons on the screen, programming it for me and backs away so I can try it. His eyes bore through me, making me feel uncomfortable, so I look away.

Before I know it, Bryce is standing by my side asking me if I'd like to try some other piece of equipment.

Left Fiona in the dust, eh? I would have been pissed if that hadn't worked.

I thank Mr. Tattoo and move over to another piece of equipment, which Bryce enjoys showing me how to use.

Bryce glances over at Mr. Tattoo and whenever he finds him looking at us, Bryce pours on the charm, showing me major affection-staking his claim, I presume. He never leaves my side after that.

Leena gives us a break from the excursions for a day so we can relax by the pool and I wear my slinky pink bikini to make Bryce think of me and not Fiona. For some reason, I'm jealous of her and her perfect little body, but I think it's the way she flirts with them to get their attention that bothers me the most.

As we're swimming, in the pool we notice some band equipment, backdrops, tables, and cameras being set up at the other end of the pool area. "What's going on?" I ask.

"I don't know. Looks like a party with a band." Bryce confirms.

"We'll have to ask Pops. He'll know."

We swim to the bar to get a drink with Leena and Austin and watch as a bunch of guys with long hair and tattoos push each other into the pool.

"I take it that's the band," Bryce says with no emotion on his face.

A couple of them swim up to the bar, pretending to drown each other.

Bryce stands next to me, shielding me from the splash of water.

Mr. Tattoo, grabs both of his buddies and puts them in a head lock. "Cut that crap out, you guys. You're splashing these two lovely ladies. Sorry ladies. You can dress these guys up, but you can't take them anywhere. We just finished the last leg of our world tour and they're a little anxious to start partying."

We smile. "No problem."

"Colt, let us go!"

"Are you going to behave?"

"Are you frickin' kidding me? You know what numbnuts is like when he's around beautiful women."

Leena and I smile at each other.

"Yes, I agree, but promise me you'll go over there and play."

"Fine, we promise."

"Don't lie to me." Colt tightens his grip on his buddies. "I'll bang your heads together."

"We're not lying," they say in unison.

Mr. Tattoo lets them out of the head lock and extends his hand to Bryce. "Colton Von Jobin."

"Bryce Hamilton."

"Nice to meet you. Where are you from, Bryce?"

"Barrie, Ontario, Canada. And you?"

"Canada? We were there about two months ago. Beautiful country. We're originally from Vegas, but we haven't been there in a while. We're either on a bus or a plane, touring."

"What's the name of your band?" I ask, thinking maybe I've heard of them before.

"Von Jobin. And what is your name, beautiful?"

"Keera."

Colton takes my hand in his and shakes it. Then he holds it steady with his other hand. "Nice to meet you officially. I met you this morning in the gym, but we didn't introduce ourselves."

"Yes, you helped me with the equipment."

"You remember me."

"Yes. Thank you for the help."

His fingers gently glide through the palm of my hand as he lets go, slowly. "Anytime."

He looks at Leena. "And who is this lovely lady?"

"I'm Leena and this is my boyfriend, Austin."

"Pleased to meet you." Colton extends his hand for them to shake.

"What kind of music do you play?" Leena asks.

"Rock. We'll be playing by the pool for the next three days while we're shooting our video. Tell me you'll come to watch."

Leena pipes up. "We'd love to."

"Good. I look forward to seeing the Canadians at the video shoot."

Colton turns and swims away toward the other guys, playfully drowning them.

"He's very nice," Leena says expressing her thoughts.

Bryce and Austin say nothing.

"Yes, that was very nice of him to invite us don't you think?" I say, trying not to sound too excited.

Bryce lets out a slight groan.

After we down our second drinks, we swim away from the bar with a glow on. Bryce and I wanted to finish what we started in the pool grotto underneath the waterfall, but we'll have to wait because the pool is a little busy right now.

With my arms around Bryce's neck, and my legs wrapped around his waist, Bryce holds me, bobbing in the water to our end of the pool. His hard cock rubs deliciously on that perfect spot.

We decide to sun bathe on the lounge chairs for a bit and Bryce fusses over me getting too much sun, so he plasters me with sunscreen. I can feel the strength in his hands as he rubs me down, and I can't help but let out a moan of pleasure.

"You're enjoying that way too much." Leena holds a bottle of sunscreen to Austin. "I want some," she says, almost whining.

"I don't want that crap on my hands."

Leena bats her eyes at Austin. "Please?"

"Fine."

After Austin's done rubbing Leena down, he asks, "Would you like another drink?"

"Mmm, yes please," I say as I roll onto my stomach and undo my string.

"Sure, that would be great," Leena says as she assumes the same position.

"That's okay. We don't mind being your slaves for the day," Austin complains.

Leena grabs Austin's calf. "Thanks, Hun."

"Thanks, Babe." I gently caress Bryce's foot.

"No problem." Bryce and Austin walk around the outer edge of the pool to the bar.

This is one of those days that you know if you're in the sun for more than twenty minutes you will pay dearly for it later. The breeze whips up every once in a while and it's cool and exhilarating for a moment.

"Damn! This is the life," I say.

"Yes it is, but if I lived here, Pops would make me work."

"I don't doubt that," I say, chuckling.

Just then, a large shadow covers our sun from behind. "Wow!" a deep voice breaks the silence.

My head turns to see two figures staring down on us.

I quickly tie my top and flip over.

"Double wow!"

Colton nudges his buddy in the ribs. "My brother wanted to meet you ladies. This is Reese, my younger brother and lead guitarist." Colton waves his hand toward us. "This is Keera and this is Leena."

Reese sits down on my chair and I quickly lift my legs to scoot over. He wraps one arm over my legs and holds them close to his side. "Colton said you were beautiful, so I had to come see for myself. Wow! That's all I can say. Wow!"

"Nice to meet you, Reese." I extend my hand to shake his and he grabs it, giving it a kiss.

I smile. "Aren't you smooth?"

Colton laughs as his intense eyes devour my body, making me feel uncomfortable. "You have no idea. We call him Mr. Casanova."

"I can see why."

"Tell me you'll be in our video," Reese says quickly.

"Umm."

"Please?" Reese puts his hands together like he's praying and gives me the cutest begging smile I've ever seen.

"I forgot to tell you, he's very persuasive too," Colton adds.

I look at Leena and smile.

"We'd love to be in your video," Leena says.

Reese waves his finger up and down my body. "Can you wear this bikini?"

I grin and look up to see Bryce and Austin walking over with our drinks. My eyes scan the length of Bryce's muscular body, stopping at his wash board abs for a second, appreciating how good he looks with just his swim shorts on. "Thanks, Babe." I smile and take the glass from Bryce's hand.

Bryce gives Reese, who still has his arm draped over my legs, an icy stare.

Reese jumps to his feet and extends his hand to Bryce. "I'm Reese, Colton's brother. Lead guitarist."

"Bryce, and this is my brother, Austin," He says with irritation in his voice, but I don't think Reese notices.

Reese then shakes Austin's hand. "We came over to ask the ladies if they'd like to be in our video."

"Oh, yeah?" Bryce says plainly.

"Leena said you'd love to be in the video, so we'll see you in a bit, right? We'll start in about an hour." Reese can't hide the excitement in his voice.

"We would have started earlier, but these guys don't get out of bed until noon." Colton nudges Reese.

"Yeah, right, like you'd let us sleep until noon."

"We'll take a quick shower and be over." Leena confirms.

"See you then." Colton inspects my body before he turns, and then they both dive into the pool and swim toward their end.

Bryce sits in the same spot that Reese vacated and looks at me. "You don't really want to go over there do you?"

"It could be fun."

Bryce whispers in my ear. "I thought you might want to swim in the grotto, since they'll be busy with the video."

Leena stands before Bryce can change my mind. "Let's go take a shower and head over there."

"Okay." I stand, taking Bryce's hand and as we walk toward the bungalow. I notice his mood has changed. "Aren't you curious how they make a video?"

"I guess." Bryce opens the door and we slip inside.

I close the gap between us, holding his arms, searching his face for a clue to his mood, waiting for him to speak.

Seconds later he says, "If we go, I want you to stay right beside me."

"O-kay." I try to read the look he's giving me.

"I don't like the way that guy looks at you."

"What guy?"

"Colton. He looks at you like you're his next meal."

"Oh Babe, you know I only want you, but I'll stay right beside you."

"Good."

It's mid-afternoon and very warm. We're thankful for the cloud cover and the occasional breeze. The festivities are in full swing as we walk along the pool, noticing everything that's changed in the last hour. They've set up a wraparound bar with stools. Free standing posters of every band member and the instrument they play are strategically placed along the outer edge of the pool, with their names at the bottom of each poster in large letters. The huge backdrop banner is the length of the stage and has a picture of the band on tour with a sea of fans. The name Von Jobin is written across the top.

When we walk up toward the band, I see Colton is the lead singer. He smiles and winks at us as we stand behind the crowd that's gathered to see them. We listen for a bit and then Bryce talks close to my ear so I'll hear him over the music.

He asks me if I want a drink and tells me to stay right where I am and he'll be back in a couple of minutes. Austin goes with him.

The song ends and I see Colton talking to a man with a head set on. Shortly after the band starts another song, the guy with the head set comes to me and Leena and tells us Colton wants us up front. I look over at the bar to see if Bryce is on his way back, but he's waiting at the bar with Austin. And Fiona.

I elbow Leena to look.

Fiona has nudged her way between the both of them and seems to be advising them on building muscle, or that's how it looks with her touching their biceps.

Instantly, my claws come back out and I'm pissed. I don't know what it is about that bitch that gets me so riled up.

Leena tugs me by my arm and we follow the guy with the head set to the front of the crowd. He places us right in front and I notice the scowls of the two girls whose places we're taking, but Colton looks happy.

I'm torn between having a good time and going to rip her hair out, but since I'm not a violent person, the good time wins. We start to dance and all is forgotten. There are cameras everywhere recording different angles. One camera man gets a little too close and I feel like covering up, but he's quickly gone, capturing a shot of someone else.

The women in the crowd are chanting the band member's names. I try to place each one with a name from their posters. In the process, I notice how good looking each one is.

When the song ends, Colton hands his ear piece to the guy with the head set and saunters down the stage and over to us. "So what do you girls think?"

"Wow, you guys are good!" I say.

"Amazing!" Leena adds.

Colton lets go of a throaty, sexy laugh. "I thought you'd like it. Now how about we get a shot for the camera?"

He maneuvers his way between me and Leena and wraps his arms around our waists.

He's smooth, like his brother.

His hand moves a little lower and he gently massages the skin underneath my bikini bottom with his finger. I wonder if he's doing the same thing to Leena.

We smile for the camera while they take a few shots and when they're done, I turn to see Bryce glaring at Colton's hand on my hip. *Oh, crap!*

Bryce hands me my drink and I move out of Colton's reach. Bryce's arm protectively wraps around my shoulder, squeezing me close so he can whisper in my ear. "You left me."

I glance up to see Colton watching our every move, now that he's backed up and moved away from Bryce's icy stare.

My hand reaches up and slides through Bryce's hair, pulling him toward me to whisper in his ear. "Sorry. They wanted us up front for their video."

"You mean Colton wanted you up front so he could drool." His facial expression changes. He's angry now.

I look into his eyes. "Babe."

"What? That motherfucker can't take his eyes off of you." He gently tugs my arm. "Come with me."

As we pass by Leena and Austin I say, "We'll be back in a couple minutes."

"K," Leena says as Austin grinds up against her to the music being piped into the pool area when the band isn't playing.

Bryce takes my hand and when we walk past a table he plops our drinks down on it. He leads me through the gardens and out to the deserted beach. After we pass a few tiki huts, I get frustrated at all the tugging, and ask, "Babe, where are we going?"

"To find a place where we can be alone." He pulls me inside the tree line of the tropical forest and abruptly turns me so my back rests against a leaning palm tree. He holds the tree with one arm, moving in closer to me. His eyes are dark and angry. "Do you want him?"

12

I FROWN. "NO. I only want you."

"That's not what I see."

"Babe, I don't want anyone else, only you. I love you."

"You took off to be with him as soon as I went to get you a drink."

"I saw that Fiona was keeping you company," I spit out, furious from his accusation.

"Who?"

"Miss perfect fitness instructor. The one who was touching your biceps."

His eyes search mine and then he lunges for me and snakes his fingers through my hair holding me steady at the back of my neck. He kisses me ferociously, as if he's been starved for weeks. I kiss him back with the same ferocity. When we pull away, we're breathless, our chests heaving for air. Bryce bends over, holding his knees like he's run a marathon.

"Babe, are you okay?" My hand reaches for his shoulder.

He looks up at me from his crouched position. "Fuck, Angel,

you drive me crazy! I get insanely jealous and I can't control it. You're fucking with my head."

"I know what you're going through. When she's around you, I want to rip every strand of that long black hair out."

"Come with me. I know what we need." He pulls me further into the trees, away from everything. When we find a huge boulder, he flattens me against it.

Our lips seal together in a frantic kiss. His hands shake with desperation as he searches for the crotch of my bikini bottoms. He pulls them to the side and feels to see if I'm wet. Then he yanks down his bathing suit bottoms and his glorious, hard-as-stone cock springs out.

Looking deep in my eyes, he takes hold of his cock and pokes my pussy with it. "I don't ever want to lose you."

Our foreheads touch. "I don't ever want to lose you, Babe."

"You're mine, Angel."

"Yes, yours. And you are mine." I quickly slide down my bikini bottoms.

Bryce pulls them down further and hoists my leg over his arm, leaving my bottoms hanging on my right foot. He shoves me hard against the big rock.

He sinks slowly into me, inch by inch, his cock penetrating deeper and deeper. "I'll never let you go."

I suck in a long breath, closing my eyes and tilting my head back. My body bows at the exquisite feeling. When I gaze into his eyes again, he's looking at me intently. He pulls out and shoves his cock back in deeper. "Oh, God, Babe. Mmm, that feels good."

He fucks me hard, pushing me farther up the rock as he holds my legs straight out and apart. What a sight this must be. From my angle, this looks pretty frickin' hot.

Bryce is working up a sweat as he relentlessly thrusts deeper with every stroke. His muscles strain and bulge, and I observe attentively where we're connected, his cock disappearing inside me. I watch as he struggles with his self-control.

When I can't take anymore and I'm ready to explode, my fingers circle my clit. I clamp down on him and he lets out a regretful groan. He pulls out quickly and I sigh.

"Not yet."

He slips my bikini bottoms down off my foot and hands them to me. "Scoot up the rock."

I quickly shove them behind the string of my top and lean back on my hands to watch his magical mouth go down on me. He's at the perfect height to devour my pussy and he does just that, his tongue expertly flicking my clit and his finger sliding deliciously in and out at a fast pace, driving me closer to orgasm.

All of a sudden, my eyes catch movement about thirty feet away to my left.

I'm mortified by the intrusion into our privacy, but try not to react in case I'm mistaken. When I look again, I see a large, muscular arm with a tattoo partially hidden from behind a tree. It's Colton's tribal tattoo.

I don't let on that I know he's there because Bryce would lose his mind. The thought of the two of them in an altercation, scares me.

Colton is as big as Bryce, with huge muscles, and he seems to be a badass. I wouldn't want to see the angry side of him. The thought of them exchanging blows causes me to fear for the safety of both of them, especially with Bryce's temper. They wouldn't stop until one of them was beaten beyond recognition.

I can't let Bryce see me looking at Colton, so I pretend Colton isn't there and devote my attention to Bryce and the unbelievable sensations flowing through my body.

My hips move to the rhythm of his relentless pounding finger and my hands weave through his hair, tugging gently. Sweat forms at my temple and my skin feels clammy. My breathing almost ceases as my orgasm builds and builds, but it stays at a plateau, suspending me high above as my mind wanders to Colton.

I can't stop thinking about him watching. I chance a quick look to see if he's still there, and he sees me.

Colton steps out from behind the tree, shoving his shorts down around his ankles, and starts stroking his massive, thick cock. He purposely moves sideways out in the open so I can see him pumping his cock as he looks on hungrily.

That is hot!

I can't risk Bryce seeing me watching him, so I look periodically.

Colton's stroking faster now. He's coming, shooting in the air.

My orgasm builds like a volcano, ready to erupt. I clamp down on Bryce's finger and my legs start to shake. I scream out in ecstasy. "Babe. Don't. Stop!" My words come out slow and shaky.

He doesn't stop until my legs fall limp on his back.

Bryce doesn't give me time to collect my thoughts before he roughly helps me down and bends me over so I'm facing the big boulder. "Hold onto the rock, this is going to be one hard fuck."

He slams into me balls deep and pushes me forward. "Hold on tight, Angel." He warns me. I spread my legs wider, holding the rock and my stance steady.

The sound of sweaty, slapping flesh on flesh and heavy breathing reverberates throughout the trees, while I get the best fuck of my life.

Bryce holds out as long as he can. When he wants me to come again, he reaches around and circles my clit. "Come with me." I turn my head to look at him pounding the hell out of me and then peek over my shoulder to see if Colton is still there. He is still stroking his cock.

I guess his voyeurism has got him as worked up as it has me. Risking another glance at him, I see a look of pure hunger as he shoots long and hard again.

I push back with the same rhythm as Bryce and it sets me off, spinning me out of control. I scream out, "Babe."

"Fuck!" Bryce's voice is deep and husky as he slams into me

two more times. He rears up, lifting me onto my toes as he holds me in place at my hips. "You. Are. Mine!" He growls.

When he's almost finished emptying himself inside me, he falls down on my back and gently bites my shoulder. "Fuck, you drive me crazy." He hugs me and then pulls out. He pulls me up and spins me around so I'm facing him. He's pressing his hard body up against mine, pinning me to the rock. He holds my face with both hands and searches my eyes. "I think I love you too much. The thought of you with someone else…" He trails off closing his eyes like he's in pain thinking about it. His eyes open. "It would kill me."

"I think that's why we get insanely jealous. We love each other too much."

"We stay together from now on," Bryce says in his deep, commanding voice. "If I get us a drink, you come with me. If you or I need to go to the washroom, we go together. Okay?"

"Okay."

"I love you, Angel."

"I love you, Babe. You always seem to know what I need." I hug him and plant a wet kiss on his luscious lips.

"Let's go back to the party," he says, clearly in a better mood.

He notices I left my sandals back at the pool so he picks me up in his strong arms and carries me back. As we pass by the tree Colton's behind, I look to see if he's out of sight. He's disappeared and I'm relieved there won't be an altercation between them.

Bryce carries me all the way back through the trees. Once we make it to the beach, he sets me down on the soft white sand and takes my hand. We walk down the boardwalk and through the gardens. My mind wanders back periodically to Colton with his shorts down around his ankles and his cock in his hand, stroking himself. That hungry look in his eyes and the way he shot up in the air. What a sight!

Stop thinking about it, Keera!

Guilt overwhelms me.

I've got to get that vision out of my head. Maybe I should tell Leena what I saw. Maybe she can give me some insight and help me get over this because right now I'm struggling. It feels like I've done something wrong. No, I can't say a word. She'll tell Austin and then Bryce will find out and... aw, hell.

Once we get to the pool, Bryce turns to look at me. "Angel, is something wrong?"

"No, I'm fine. We should find Leena and Austin. They're probably wondering where we ran off to."

We dance our way through the crowd. When the song ends, Von Jobin comes back out to play again. The crowd goes nuts when Colton comes out from behind the large backdrop. The drums bang and the guitars start to play. Colton stands in front of his microphone, playing his guitar and singing. We find Leena and Austin dancing close to the band so we slide right in beside them.

"Where the hell did you go? Back for a quickie?" Leena asks.

I smile and turn red.

"Un-frickin'-believable!"

I glance up at Colton, who stares directly into my eyes. I turn away. *What's wrong with me? I can't even look him in the eyes now?* I try again and he holds his stare way too long, so I look away again.

Bryce and I dance and I try to erase what just happened out of my mind.

When the song ends, Leena grabs my arm. "Come with me back to my bungalow to go pee."

"I'll come with you," Bryce says, and I know the meaning by the look in his eyes.

Bryce sticks to me like glue, most likely because of the tipsy state I'm in and because he doesn't want Colton anywhere near me.

Later, the band announces that they'd like to video everyone out on the beach for the sunset and a bonfire.

We dance around in the sand with our drinks held high as Colton sings an acoustic version of one song.

Damn, he's good.

By the number of women standing in the vicinity of him, I'd say he's giving a monumental performance, tugging at the heart strings of every woman at this party with his sexy baritone voice.

It's almost like he knows when I am going to look at him because, he's already staring at me.

"You know, I'm getting really tired of that fucker staring at you," Bryce growls.

"Babe, it's okay. Ignore him. Like I'm trying to ignore that Fiona's dying to get you alone. But I'm not leaving your side. We're together and nothing's separating us, because we're in love."

Bryce hugs me. "You're absolutely right." He looks deep in my eyes and then our mouths meet in a sensual kiss.

When we separate he says, "Well, if they didn't know we were in love before, they know it now with that kiss."

"Yes, I would say so."

The night descends upon us and it's late-well past two in the morning. The guests at the party have been dwindling, so we say our goodnights and head back to the bungalow. It's a good thing we don't have to drive anywhere. I'm giggling and staggering a bit, but Bryce guides and protects me from falling over and then helps me to bed.

My body jerks, waking me from a bad dream. I sit up quickly and scowl down at Bryce, who is in a dead sleep. My mind does a replay and then I realize it's morning and the bad dream isn't real.

In my dream, I was searching everywhere for Bryce, but couldn't find him. When I finally did, Fiona was leading him by the hand, out of an elevator. He totally ignored me when he passed by. I called out his name and he turned. Fiona laughed and then tugged him by his arm. They left me standing there. Alone.

He left me for her!

The look of pure evil satisfaction on her face brought my blood to a boil.

I throw the comforter off, stomp to the bathroom, and stare at myself in the mirror. *It's a bad dream. Bryce would never do that to you. But how do you know? She does have a fit body. She might have a better personality. And her seduction skills are definitely better than mine.* I shake my head to get the bad thought out. *Quit! You'll drive yourself crazy.*

I have a strong desire to get my body in great shape, to look better than she does, so I decide to go for a jog on the beach. The sun is rising so I set up the coffee pot for Bryce and leave him a note to come join me if he wakes up.

I sit on the front porch drinking my tea and wait for the sun to rise so I can go for my jog. It's already warm and humid so I go back in and change into my white bikini. I check to see if Bryce is awake, but he's not. He's still sound asleep.

I start jogging from the garden trail to the beach. When I get to the waterline where the sand is harder, I jog along there. The sunrise is magnificent and I make a mental note to do this every morning because the smell and feel of the breeze is amazing first thing in the morning. But also, I want to avoid running into Fiona in the workout room.

There's no one in sight, so I jog past four hotels. When I've worked up a sweat, I head back.

As I get closer to our hotel, in the distance, I see someone sitting in a lounge chair. My heart skips a beat when I think it's Bryce waiting for me, but when I can finally make out the figure, I see it's Colton holding a video camera. Fuck!

He is not videotaping me jogging, is he? I stop jogging and start to walk.

Colton places the camera on the lounge chair and walks toward me. "Good morning, beautiful. Gorgeous day, isn't it?"

"Good morning. Yes, this is perfect. What are you doing up

this early?" I say breathless. "Thought you said you don't get out of bed until mid-morning?"

"No, not me. I was talking about the rest of my band. I'm an early riser. I don't sleep well. I've got too many things on my mind."

He looks into my eyes so deeply, I have to look away. "Hey, I hope you don't mind me videotaping you for different shots in the video. I got some great shots of the sunrise and you running on the beach."

"No," but really I do. Shit! How do I tell him that?

"I'll send you a copy of the finished version if I can get your e-mail address."

"Oh, okay."

"Yeah? One sec, I'll write it in my book." He strolls over to the chair, picks up his book and pen, and struts back with that sexy walk.

Christ, I can see why women throw themselves at him.

The. Man. Is. Fine! Those eyes and that smile and all he's wearing is low-hanging shorts. His chest is perfect, he has eight-pack abs, and below is the sexy V, and-aw, crap! He notices me staring. I look up at his gorgeous face. He has a knowing half smile with a dimple showing.

Oh my lord, look at that dimple. I shake my head to dismiss my thoughts.

He hands me the book and chuckles.

Brat! He knows he's irresistible.

I search, but there isn't a spot to write in it.

I turn to look at him. "You write your own songs?"

He flips it to the front of the book, where there's a blank page. "Yeah, me and my brother, but every one of us has a creative part in the whole musical process."

Colton stands next to me with his side plastered against mine. He wraps his arm around my waist and holds my hip. *Aw, crap, too close.*

I stiffen. "Umm, I'm a little sweaty from running. You might not want to get too close to me." There. I warned him!

"The closer I get to you, the happier I am. You think sweat bothers me?"

I quickly write my e-mail address and hand his book back to him, then move away out of his grasp.

Facing me, he places one hand back on my hip. He looks anxious as he hesitates, collecting his thoughts. "Can I talk to you about what we experienced yesterday? I can't stop thinking about it. We shared something beautiful and I want more."

Damn it! How do I get myself into these situations? I think about what I want to say, so I don't lead him on. "I couldn't tell Bryce you were there. He would have lost it."

"I know. I'm stepping on his territory and he doesn't like it, but you and I connected. I know we did. You feel what I feel. You can't deny that. I saw it with my own eyes."

"Colton, I love Bryce."

"I know, but would you give me a chance? A couple days could change your mind."

My eyes glance down the beach and I see Bryce running toward us. "Bryce." My head motions toward Bryce and I move away.

Colton's hand drops off my hip.

Turning to see Bryce, Colton let's a quiet, "Fuck," slip from his lips.

Bryce stops in front of me, his eyes turning icy as they meet Colton's. "Colton." He nods his head and then turns back to me, wrapping me in a bear hug, picking me up off my feet, swinging me around in a circle. "I missed waking up to you this morning. You ready for our jog?"

I'm saved. "Sure, let's go." I wave to Colton. "Bye."

"You two have fun." Colton says as he looks me over with that hungry stare.

Bryce put on a show for Colton, but I know he's pissed that he found us talking. He probably wants to rip Colton's head off.

We jog down the beach, past a few hotels. When we're out of Colton's sight, Bryce stops.

I stop with him and pace.

"Why wouldn't you wake me up?" Bryce yells. "He's the last person I want to see you talking with."

The whole time we've been jogging, he's been seething, his anger surfacing, and now it's erupting.

I keep my voice calm. "I know, I'm sorry, but I was a little pissed off this morning and I needed to jog. He wasn't there when I ran by the first time."

"But he was there when you came back."

"Yeah."

"And he just started talking to you?"

"Yes."

"What did he say?"

"He was telling me he got some good shots of the sunrise… and…" Shit! Should I tell him or hide it from him? "… and shots of me running on the beach. He asked if I mind and I automatically said no, but then I thought about it and didn't know how to tell him I did mind."

"That fucking asshole! What else did he say?"

"Umm, he wanted my e-mail so he can send me a copy of the video."

"Tell me you didn't give it to him?" His voice is angrier now.

"Umm." I turn red and look down at the ground.

"You did?"

I nod.

"Fuck, Keera! Quit being so naïve. He only wants it so he can keep in touch with you. Tell me you didn't give him your phone number or address."

"No."

"You sure?"

"Yes, Bryce!" Now I'm mad. I start to walk away.

"Where are you going? We're still talking."

"I'm done talking! Anyway, you're not talking. You're yelling."

"I'm sorry," he says, lowering his voice a couple of decibels. "I didn't mean to yell. I lose my mind and get so worked up when he's around you." He hurries to get in front of me and holds my arms. "I said I'm sorry. Please, talk to me. I won't yell."

I stop moving and look at him through narrowed eyes. "Fine," I say, my jaw clenched. "What do you want to talk about? The weather?"

He tries to smooth things over by hugging me, but I stand with my arms at my side not hugging him back. When he pulls away he holds onto my shoulders, bends his knees, and looks deep in my eyes. "You said you were pissed when you woke up. Why?"

Now he's trying to get me to talk so he can fix this. I've got your number, buddy.

"I had a bad dream."

"What was it about?"

"You. And Fiona."

"Continue, please."

"I searched for you everywhere and when I finally found you coming out of the elevator with Fiona, you ignored me. And then you left me, for her. That's why I wanted to go jogging this morning."

"Were you mad at me?"

"I was, until I realized it was a bad dream."

He wraps his strong arms around me again and I feel myself melting. "Next time you have a bad dream, wake me up. I don't want you alone, especially with the shark around."

I look up at him. "The shark?"

"Colton."

"Ah. Got ya."

Bryce wraps his arm around my waist and smiles down at me

as we walk back along the beach. "You know I only want you. She does nothing for me. When she comes around, all I'm thinking about is where you are and that I need to find you."

I stop and hug him. "You always make me feel better. And don't worry, I only want you. I love you, Babe."

"I love you, Angel."

And just like that, our fight is over.

Bryce's hand slides across my lower back and into my hand, and we stroll along the beach, like an old married couple, until I dart away from him. "Catch me if you can!"

I run along the hard sand at full throttle, but when I look back he's almost caught up to me.

Damn, he runs fast!

As I start giggling, I feel an arm around my waist and the next thing I know, I'm tackled and we're sloshing around in the ocean.

Sliding under the water, I surface and flip my hair out of my face. Bryce tugs me close, caressing the back of my neck and bringing our foreheads together. "I'll always catch you. I love you so much."

"I love you, Babe."

"Oh, shit."

"What?"

"This is not a bikini you should swim in." Bryce's eyes are staring directly at my nipples.

"Why?"

"I can see everything when it's wet."

I look down. The bikini top is clinging to my skin and my nipples are standing erect from the water. "Oh yeah, I guess."

"If we see anyone when we walk back to the bungalow, I want you behind me."

"Oh, Babe, you're too cute. I thought you wanted me naked?"

"Only when we're alone."

As we walk up to the boardwalk, Bryce steps backwards, his eyes raking over my wet white bikini.

I glance toward one of the tiki huts and see Colton videotaping again. What the hell? Seriously! What's with this guy? I look up at Bryce, who's still staring at me. He doesn't see him.

"Race you back." I take off full tilt. Bryce's attention is on me. He doesn't notice Colton.

When he catches me again, he scoops me up into his arms and holds me tight. "You're always running away from me."

"Yeah, but you always catch me and it makes me hot and horny."

"Good. Let's go do something about that."

We've almost reached the door of the bungalow when we notice Leena banging on it.

"Hi, Leena," Bryce says. "Something we can do for you?"

"Where the hell have you guys been?" she asks as she turns around. "I kept banging, thinking you were having a quickie."

"Well, we were going..."

"Oh, no!" Leena cuts me off. "No time for that. Get in the shower and meet us at our bungalow in one hour. We're going horseback riding."

Bryce rolls his eyes, as he usually does when Leena's being a pushy little broad, and I push him through the door. "Okay, one hour," I say, giggling.

As Leena leaves, we close the door behind us and Bryce peels my bikini off, tugging me toward the bathroom. The water is warm as we climb in and he strips off his shorts, tossing them on the counter with my bikini.

We start out washing quickly so we can meet Leena's deadline, but when Bryce washes my back and buns, he slows down, pulling me close.

Bryce reaches around and circles my nipple, caressing it, until it's sticking out three quarters of an inch. "Do you know how sexy it is seeing how big and hard these get under a wet bathing suit?"

I turn to look at him. "You like that don't you?"

"That's why I'm always hard."

I run my hands down his chest and tug his nipples as I head downward. "Babe, I love every inch of your body."

"You do, eh?"

"Oh, yeah." My hands skim across his washboard abs and down to the sexy V at his hips. When I take his cock in my hands, his head falls back slightly and he braces himself against the wall.

"Damn, woman, what you do to me." Bryce grabs my head with both hands, pulling my mouth toward his in a heated rush. When we separate, we're breathless. "Fuck Leena! I'm fucking you. She can wait!"

Bryce takes his cock and directs it to my opening.

Lifting my leg, I plant my foot on the side of the bath tub and Bryce pushes his cock in, inch by inch, until I'm full.

I hold onto his shoulders and he slams me against the tile wall, then he reaches down to sling my leg over his arm to open me wider.

Our movements are frantic, my dream about Fiona and his anger toward Colton lubricating our lovemaking.

Bryce sees the way Colton looks at me and it drives him insanely jealous-the same way I feel about Fiona. We have a desperate need to show our love to one another, especially after our fight, so the intensity of our love-making shoots up a few notches and it's the best make-up sex ever.

Bryce fucks me hard against the wall of the shower. I have no idea how much time passes. He's fucking me so hard he almost comes, but he's not ready yet, so he stops and kisses me, his tongue probing deep in my mouth. He holds my face in his large hands, our foreheads touching. "I don't ever want to lose you."

I think Bryce feels a little insecure and worried that I'll leave him for Colton because he's a rock god, but that would never happen.

"You won't. I love you too much. But what if you decide one

day that you want another woman, like my dream? I'd die if I lost you, Babe."

His hands roam down my body, skimming across my skin. My body tingles; every touch excites me. I do the same to him and can tell by the way he shivers a little that he feels the same way.

"Never. I'll always want you, Angel. I'm obsessed with you."

Bryce's hard cock twitches inside me. He pulls out slowly and then slams back into me. His fingers grasp my butt cheeks and dig into my flesh, holding me in place as he thrusts into me, over and over.

"Angel, I don't know how much longer I'm going to last." His breathing is harsh and laboured.

I know he's close so my fingers find their way between our slapping groins and I massage my clit. "I'm with you Babe" I say, staring into his eyes as he stares into mine.

His features strain as he struggles for control. "Now Angel!"

I clamp down on him and my head falls back. "Babe! That's it. Don't stop fucking me!"

He tries to hold out as long as he can. He slams into me a few more times, rearing up in the process, lifting me with his cock to my tip toes. I feel his cock twitch, releasing his warm cum inside me. He wraps me in his strong muscular arms, so I don't fall from my weak knees buckling, and he runs his tongue along my neck and bites gently.

"I love fucking you."

"Mmm, yes, neither one of us could do without this, I'll never get enough."

"I could eat you alive and fuck you to death." He bites me again and I giggle. "Come. We better get moving."

13

WE RUSH TO make Leena's deadline and we're only ten minutes late. Instead of us meeting them, they meet us at our bungalow.

Leena walks into the bathroom as I'm spraying my perfume on. "It's about time. Are you done yet?"

"Yup, done."

She watches Bryce leave, disappearing into the living room with Austin, then gently closes the door and whispers, "What the hell is going on with you and Bryce, and what's with Colton? Christ, the guy can't stop staring at you."

"Umm, Bryce is a little jealous of Colton, but we're fine. Everything's good."

"Come on, Keera, throw me a bone. I know something's going on. Spill it!"

"Well, I was also going to tell you, and this is hard to admit, but I'm jealous of Fiona. I don't know what it is about her, but the second she's around Bryce, the claws come out."

"Yeah, that bitch is getting on my nerves, too. Every time me and Austin separate for even a few seconds, she's right there flirting with him."

"She wants them bad."

Bryce sticks his head in the door. "We ready? Austin's chomping at the bit."

"We're ready," I say as I pass by Bryce and give him a wink and a gentle touch on his hip.

"Hey, guess what? We're riding in style today. My Dad said we can use his limo."

"Great."

We hear the band playing as we lock up and head to Leena and Austin's bungalow to grab the address she forgot for the horseback riding excursion.

I try not to look at the band too much as we wait on the front porch, but I do notice when the band takes a break that Fiona is flirting with Reese now. I guess she's moved on.

I glance over at Colton and his eyes are locked on us as we pass by. I gaze up at Bryce and he tightens his grip, pulling me closer.

We make our way through the gardens and into one hotel, then out to the front entrance.

The sleek black limo waits out front with the driver standing by the door.

Austin whistles. "We're riding in style today."

"Much nicer than the NASCAR bus," Leena replies.

"I liked the bus," I say, smiling. "We met all kinds of different characters. Remember the old guy and his monkey?"

"Grayson at your service." The driver opens the door and waits for us to climb in.

Bryce holds out his hand for me to go first.

"Thank you," I say as I climb in and scoot across the seat.

When we're all situated on the plush, L-shaped white leather seats, Leena hands Grayson the address. "Two hours and we should be done."

"Can I call you Leena?"

"Yes, please do."

"I'll fuel up while you're horseback riding, if that's okay with you, Leena."

"Great, thank you, Grayson."

Grayson shuts our door and climbs into the driver's seat.

Leena hits up the mini bar for us and distributes drinks all around.

I have a ridiculous smile plastered across my face. Before I tell Bryce this is my first limo ride, he knows. He gives me a squeeze and cuddles closer, smiling down at me.

When we pull up to the ranch, Grayson opens the door for us and I almost feel like a princess receiving the royal treatment. "Thank you," I say.

"You're most welcome," Grayson replies.

Sauntering over to the corral where the horses are, we take pictures of the magnificent creatures and wait patiently for our ride to begin.

We over-hear from a few people that we get to select the horses we want, so I wait for Bryce to choose. He picks the tall black male stallion and I decide on the white female Arabian that stays close to the stallion.

My adrenaline is pumping now that everyone's climbing on their horses.

Bryce helps me up. "I want you to wear a helmet, but that's probably going too far."

"Babe I'll be fine. I've ridden horses before."

"I want you safe."

I reach down and run my hand down his cheek. "Always watching out for me."

Our tender moment is interrupted by our tour guide, who wanders over to talk to Bryce after helping some people climb on their horses. He asks Bryce if he's ever ridden before, because the stallion that he picked can be ornery when he's not close to the white Arabian. Bryce tells him he's ridden before and it seems to pacify our guide.

The tour guide holds out his hand for Bryce to shake. "Max. And you are?"

"Bryce. And this is my girlfriend, Keera."

I lean down and shake his hand. "Pleased to meet you."

He nods his head and goes back to talking with Bryce. "If Goliath gives you any problems, we can bring him back and trade him in for a tamer one. He should be okay because he's beside Beauty." Max pats Goliath on the chest. "You be good for Bryce." Max walks over to someone else to talk to them, but his eyes stay glued to Bryce.

Bryce puts his foot in the stirrup and climbs onto the huge stallion with ease. Damn, the man is fine-so sexy. It doesn't matter what he's doing; it's the way he carries himself. Sex appeal oozes out of every pore he has. It's not only women who watch him intently; men too, study the way he moves. I observe how some men watch him and then instantly engage in conversation. I wonder whether they're admiring or if they're curious to find out if the gorgeous Greek god has a brain to match the body. They soon find out he's the perfect male specimen.

Bryce maneuvers Goliath beside Beauty and rubs my leg. "Yes, I am beside Beauty. My beauty."

"Babe, you're so sweet." I reach over and rub his thigh.

Austin brings his big burgundy, almost black horse close to us. "You two cut that shit out."

Leena pulls her tan horse beside Austin and touches the inside of his thigh. "Austin doesn't like to show too much public affection, but I think maybe I can change that."

Austin looks like he melting from her touch.

Our tour guide takes us through scenic areas with hills, trees, and cactus. When we reach an open area, he lets us run the horses. Bryce gets Goliath running at full speed and Beauty follows. I hold my hands straight out and squeeze my thighs tight to the saddle, giggling at the sensation-It feels like I'm flying. When we stop to regroup we're smiling and laughing.

Bryce's drop-dead gorgeous smile tells me he's enjoying himself.

We follow a trail to the beach and ride along the water line, taking pictures as we stroll at a leisurely pace on the long stretch of white sand. Then our guide surprises us by taking his horse further into the water. Our horses follow, running after him and cooling their body temperature.

When we make it back to the ranch, we follow each other into the corral where the horses canter over to the watering hole and drink. Our butts are sore when we get off, so Bryce wraps me in a hug and reaches down to rub my buns. I do the same to him.

"Christ, you guys are embarrassing," Austin complains.

Leena hugs Austin and reaches down to rub his cheeks. "Oh, come on, my buns are sore, too."

Austin rolls his eyes, but then gives in to her request, rubbing her butt.

Bryce moves us close enough to them so Austin can hear. "Just two words: pussy whipped."

"Screw you, asshole." Austin playfully punches Bryce in the arm and we all laugh.

I spot Max, our tour guide, staring at Bryce again and my gaydar goes off.

Forget it buddy-he's mine. Not only do I have to worry about women throwing themselves at him, I have to worry about men, too!

Max strolls over. He barely glances at the rest of us before turning one-hundred percent of his attention to Bryce. "So did everyone have a good time?"

We all answer at once. "Oh yeah, great time." "That was fun." "For sure, I'd do it again."

"I do a little survey with my customers. Where are you guys from?"

Since his question is directed at Bryce, he answers. "Canada."

"Long way from home."

"We're on vacation. Aruba is beautiful. We'll definitely be back."

"That's good to hear. What do you do for a living back home, Bryce?"

"Firefighter."

"Damn, that sounds exciting." Max switches his attention to Austin. "How about you, big guy?"

My eyes roam up and down his body, taking inventory. He's built-tall, muscular and good-looking. He has a masculine voice. Not effeminate in the least. Hmm, maybe I'm wrong.

"Ontario Provincial Police officer," Austin answers.

Max smiles. "A firefighter and a cop."

His wheels are turning. He licks his lips and then his eyes scan both Bryce and Austin's bodies.

Bryce must feel uncomfortable. He tugs me close and his voice deepens. "Nice meeting you. Had a great time."

"Nice to have some Canadians. I hope you'll come back."

We turn and head out to the parking lot. "That was strange," I say when we're out of ear-shot, hoping someone else will express their thoughts on the situation.

"Yup. He's gay," Austin says plainly.

"I got the same impression," Leena pipes up.

Austin teases Bryce. "He wants you bad."

"Fuck you, I saw him eyeing you up." Bryce playfully punches Austin in the arm.

We're all laughing as we come upon Grayson waiting for us at the door of the limo. "Looks like everyone had a good time," he says, smiling.

"Yes, that was fun," I say as I climb in.

He drives us back to the resort and Leena tells him we'll need his services again tonight to go clubbing. They discuss a time as we exit the limo and Bryce and Austin slip Grayson a generous tip. We thank him and make our way through the resort.

As we're walking back to our bungalows by the pool, we see Colton directing people around to get into position for the video, pointing, instructing his crew members about what he wants. He glances over and sees us, but doesn't skip a beat. He keeps talking as his eyes freeze, locked on us.

Bryce's hand slides possessively to the small of my back, sending delicious tingles down my spine as we walk through to our bungalow.

It's mid-day and hot. The wind has whipped up, so we decide to go play in the waves, but Bryce wants me to wear a bikini that has a little more material than my other bikinis. I lay them all out on the bed and he picks my black grommet suit, but once I try it on he still doesn't approve because the top shows cleavage and the boy shorts show exposed butt cheeks. He tries to tug up the top and pull down the fabric over my butt.

"Pretty soon my crotch is going to be showing," I say, holding in a laugh.

"Fucking thing." Bryce re-adjusts it, to the way I had it.

I keep remembering Bryce saying, "I want you naked," before we came to Aruba and it makes me chuckle how possessive and over protective he's being. He's done a complete flip, trying to cover up as much of my skin as possible. I have to hold back the smirk on my face.

In the water, the waves reach four feet high. When Leena and I are not ready for them, they re-adjust our bathing suit and knock us on our asses. A couple of times, Austin has to hurry to fix Leena's bikini top.

Bryce holds me in his arms as we observe. "No public affection, eh?" he teases Austin.

"I can't let my puppies hang out for the world to see."

We laugh and Leena and I get knocked on our butts again.

Exhausted, we stroll over to lay on the lounge chairs for a mid-afternoon siesta in the shade and it surprises me that I actually fall asleep for a bit.

Bryce doesn't say a word when I come out with my white, mini, spider-web, pearl-neckline dress on. His eyes widen and he grins, mouthing, "Wow." He stands in front of me, drinking me in, then runs his hands over my curves and hugs me. "I told myself that I need to zip my mouth and trust your judgement in clothing."

"What's wrong with the clothes I wear?"

"Nothing. That's what caught my eye the first time we met. But now that I have you, I want to keep you all to myself. I'm a selfish bastard, I know."

"No, you're not. I love you for it and I love your honesty. You'd tell me if I looked like crap, right?"

"Angel, you always look good. Good enough to eat." He playfully licks his lips and nuzzles in my neck, making me giggle.

I can't take my eyes off his lips and it stirs dirty thoughts of that sinful mouth on me. "Tease. You keep doing that and we'll never get out of here."

He chuckles and pulls me to the door. "Leena's going to be banging on the door any second. We'd better go."

We meet them half way and are standing in a circle talking by the pool. "Look at you, you sexy bitch." I say to Leena as I check out her black mesh cut out dress.

Leena's eyes scan up and down my dress. "I'm borrowing that someday. Damn girl, that's hot!"

"As long as I can borrow yours."

We're the same size, though Leena's a little taller, so we trade clothes all the time.

As we're talking by the pool about what's on the agenda for tonight, Reese slips in the middle of our circle, popping up into our conversation. "You guys are coming to the big video party tonight, right?" He looks around the circle at all of us, searching the expressions on our faces. "Tell me you're coming?" He gives us his pleading puppy dog eyes. "Please, you have to." I glance over and see that Colton's watching us.

"We're going clubbing right now, but we might see you later," Leena says, smiling.

"Okay, I'm going to hold you to that. See you guys later." Reese rushes over to tell Colton.

Leena continues talking, telling us that Pops wants us to join him for dinner before we go clubbing, so we head toward the entrance of the hotel.

I glance over as we walk by and see Reese relaying the message to Colton.

Colton's head and eyes follow us the whole time and I feel very uncomfortable from his scrutinizing stare.

Bryce tightens his grip on my waist.

I think Bryce would like Colton if he would stop staring at me. From what I've observed, Colton has a great personality and every person who comes in contact with him, loves and admires him. He's got a sexy cool, I'll stand-back and observe until the right moment, and then, take-charge kind of personality. The light bulb comes on as I realize he's exactly like Bryce.

Pops waits anxiously for us at the door and ushers us to his table. Can't keep the man waiting. We should know better, but I think Leena likes to push his buttons.

After dinner, Grayson holds the door to the limo for us and we file in to head to the first club. We sit and have our first drink, but no one's dancing, so we leave and Grayson recommends another club.

The dance floor is packed, so we ease our way through a sea of people to make our way to one of the many bars.

The club is very modern, with bird cage dance floors suspended high above us and sexy girls dancing around stripper poles in scanty outfits. The music is loud and the coloured neon lights give the club an electrifying vibe.

Bryce tightens his grip on my waist as we pass by a few guys, who hoot and holler, yelling out comments while eyeing Leena and me.

Bryce protectively pulls me in front of him and plasters my body against his as we inch closer to the bar.

The music is loud, so Bryce talks against my ear. "You've got boyfriends everywhere."

I turn in his arms to face him as I inch backwards. "I only have one boyfriend and he's oh-so-hot!" My eyes scan the length of his body and I give him my I-want-to-fuck-you-now smile.

"You keep looking at me like that and were going back to the bungalow. Like pronto!"

The atmosphere is hopping. It super charges me. I feel like the Energizer bunny. Bryce smiles down at me as I start to dance. He squeezes my hand, giving me the impression that he enjoys seeing me like this.

We finally make it to the bar and, after a short wait, the bartender distributes our drinks.

Leena's eyes scan the crowd and then she yells in my ear. "This place is rocking!"

I take a few sips so I don't spill my drink, nod my head, and keep dancing.

Leena tugs my arm and we head to the dance floor. By the time we make it, we're done our drinks and place the empties on a nearby table.

They play one good song after another and we work up a sweat, getting a great workout in the process. We keep dancing until Leena says she has to go to the ladies room.

Bryce shakes his head and twirls his finger at us. "We all go together."

Austin doesn't disagree. He follows holding Leena close.

The lineup for the women's washroom is long and we have to wait for a bit, but the guys slip right in.

"Now that I have you alone again, what the hell's up with Bryce, he's a little over-protective, don't you think?"

"No, he's making sure I'm safe."

"He's smothering you. I hardly get any alone time with you."

"I know. He'll probably relax in time. He's placing the blame on himself for not being there when I was abducted."

"I can see him doing that, but he has to share you."

"You've got to understand what he's been through."

Leena gives me that face. The angry, annoyed one. "I'll let it slide for now, but if he's still like this in six months, I'll be speaking my mind. That is if I can hold out that long."

Two stalls become available and while I'm doing my business I think about Bryce's over-protectiveness and Leena tugging me in the other direction, whining that she doesn't get any alone time with me. I can see Bryce and Leena butting heads in the near future and I'll have to be the referee in the middle.

While we wash our hands, a loud woman standing in line belts out, "Hey, who's the lucky bitch that gets to fuck the gorgeous twins outside."

Leena grabs a paper towel to wipe her hands and says, "They're not twins, and we're the lucky bitches."

"Well, you better hurry. Some bitches are flirting with them."

"Thanks," Leena says as we pass by to exit the washroom.

Bryce and Austin stand against the wall, leaning with their legs and arms crossed in a relaxed position waiting patiently for us. What a sight to behold-muscles flexing and the pronounced bulge between their thighs catch the appreciative eyes of every female who looks their way.

Closing the gap between me and Bryce, my hand automatically reaches down and I cup his balls. He doesn't flinch, he stays in the same position with a smile on his face.

I give him my most seductive smile. "Where'd your girlfriends go?"

He looks at me surprised. "The ones that were trying to pick us up?"

"Yeah. We heard from a loud woman in the washroom that some bitches were flirting with our gorgeous fuckable twin boyfriends."

Bryce chuckles. "Austin shut them down right away by saying we're taken."

I whisper in Bryce's ear, leaning my body against his and running my hand along his cock, which is growing with my touch. "I want this."

"You can have it as soon as we get back to the resort."

I look at Leena. "Do you want to stay here or do you want to go back to the resort?"

Leena looks at Austin and Bryce. "What do you guys think? Too crowded in here?"

They both agree and we head for the exit.

Back at the resort, Colton's attention slips away from Fiona and a few other women as we walk by the pool to our bungalows. He struts over to Reese and talks to him. Before we make it to the bungalows, Reese is standing before us. "You guys are coming for the barbeque and fireworks on the beach, right?" He tilts his head and twines his fingers together in a begging motion, looking to Austin and Bryce for conformation.

Who could resist that? He's so cute with those eyes.

Austin looks at Bryce and then at Reese. "Yeah, we'll be back. Have to get out of these clothes and into something a little more comfortable."

"Okay, I'm going to hold you to that. We want to party with the Canadians."

Austin playfully slaps Reese on the back and walks past him with Leena closely behind. We follow, with Bryce wrapping his arm around my waist and planting his hand on my hip, guiding me over to our bungalow.

He opens the door and we slip inside. "Do you want to go to the party or do you want to stay in tonight?"

"We did promise Reese. We could go for a bit and then sneak away."

His expression changes, like he's in deep thought. "Will you do something for me?"

"Sure," I say quickly, although I'm confused.

Bryce saunters into the bedroom and I follow, hoping he's not going to tell me what to wear.

He stands in front of his suit-case and rummages through it. In his one hand is a pink egg. "Can we have some fun with this?" In his other hand is the remote.

Right away my muscles clench and a tingle runs through me. I smile. "I'd love to."

"Good. Let me help you with this."

He unzips my dress and I shimmy out of it. He picks it up off the floor and stands back admiring me, his eyes scanning appreciatively. "Christ, I'm getting hard already."

He spins me quickly and bends me over the bed. "Hold tight. This is bigger than the balls, so if it hurts let me know." His finger slips inside me and I moan from the sensation. I push back onto his finger, wanting it deeper. I start to circle my hips.

He pulls his finger out quickly and smacks my ass. "Tease."

I look back at him from my bent-over position with only my high heels on. "Who's teasing who here?"

He slaps me on the ass again. "Eyes forward."

I smile and do as I'm told.

Bryce pushes the egg in and I feel it stretching my walls. The feeling is exquisite. He pushes it up further, inch by inch, and then it starts to vibrate.

I've felt this before.

This is what he used when I was in the swing with the blindfold and headphones on, when he played that amazing music that teleported me to a different world. That was fun. I think tonight will be just as exciting as that night.

I grip the comforter and circle my hips. My head rests on my arm and I moan. "Feels so good. Oh, oh, God, Babe."

"Aw, fuck, you're, killing me, Angel." He slaps me on the ass. "Get dressed."

Turning, I see his cock straining against the material of his pants. "Look what I've done." My fingers caress the length of his cock. "Here, let me help you with this." I undo the button and unzip his pants. When I pull his boxers and pants down to his ankles, his cock springs free, almost hitting me in the face from my crouched position. I look up, my eyes bulging. "Wow, look at that!" I take his cock in both my hands and caress it gently.

His eyes close and he moans. "See what you do to me?"

I take his cock deep in my mouth and look up to see his reaction.

"Fuck! That mouth of yours."

I suck his cock for a bit and then he snatches it away from me and pulls me up by my arms. "You keep doing that and we're not leaving." He says in his deep husky voice.

Wiping my mouth with the back of my hand, I quickly stand. "Okay, I'm getting dressed."

It is still fairly warm so Bryce wears only his jean shorts, which look absolutely amazing on him. I wear the slinky little sun dress that Bryce loves-the one with plenty of cleavage showing-and no thong for easy access later. We both go barefoot because we'll be in the sand all night.

On our way out of the bungalow, Bryce tests the remote to see how much distance he can get with the egg inside me. It has quite a few different vibrating modes, seven in all, and I love every one of them. A smile spreads across my face every time he starts it up because it surprises me. This is going to be fun.

We meet up with Leena and Austin along the pool and then make our way to the beach where all the festivities are taking place. Bryce activates the egg for a few seconds and then shuts it off. When I'm not paying attention, he surprises me by activating it again.

Reese is at the bar with Fiona and Colton when we squeeze through to get a drink. "See, I told you they'd come." Reese playfully slaps Austin on the back. "Shaun take care of my Canadian friends right away." Shaun, takes our drink order and while we're standing there waiting, out the corner of my eye, I see Colton move away from Fiona to stand right next to me.

His arm rubs against mine. I try to ignore his touch by not skipping a beat with my conversation to Leena, Austin, and Bryce.

I reach for my drink and my arm leaves Colton's.

Now I feel his butt and back pressing against me.

I move slightly and he moves with me.

Okay that didn't work.

Bryce's ring tone wails with the sound of sirens. He quickly takes his phone off his hip to see who is calling and then hands me his beer. "I'll be right back. This could be important." He makes his way through the crowd to find a quieter spot so he can hear the conversation over the loud music and I watch him go.

Colton, standing in front of me now, takes both drinks out of my hand and places them on the bar next to Shaun. "Watch these for me, buddy."

Colton turns. "Dance with me. Please." He hesitates for a second, and before I can confirm or deny, he takes my hand and pulls me to the dance floor.

14

COLTON WRAPS ME in a tight embrace and whispers in my ear, "I'm going to remember how you feel against my body for the rest of my life." He runs his nose along my neck. "And the sweet smell of your skin." He inhales and runs his lips along my jaw line.

I stiffen and pull back, but he holds me steady at the waist.

Colton notices my reluctance. "I'm sorry I can't help myself, I've been thinking of you constantly from the first time I met you."

"I don't think Bryce would appreciate it."

"I can tell. He won't let you out of his sight. Can't blame him, though. If you were mine, I'd never let you out of my sight either."

I don't know what to say so I try to change the subject. "You dance really well."

"Thank you. So do you. I've been watching every move you make and I've got to tell you, I can't get enough."

He pulls me closer and I feel how hard his cock is.

Oh no!

He grins down at me with his gorgeous dimple.

He knows I feel it.

Shit! Bryce, where are you? Save me.

Colton's hand slips down to the small of my back and then down further to just above my butt cheeks.

Aw, crap! He's searching for panties. He knows I'm not wearing any.

He holds me close and we dance for a bit until he breaks the silence. "You are beautiful! And those lips-I want to kiss them."

"Not a good idea. Bryce will be back any moment."

His eyes lower to my cleavage and then back up to mine. "I've never felt someone feel so good in my arms."

What do I say to that? "You don't have a girlfriend?"

"Not yet. But so you know, I'm a very stubborn and patient man. When I want something this bad, I'll wait. And I always get what I want." Colton slowly drawls the last part of his sentence. He knows how to get a woman's attention.

The determined look in his eyes makes me shiver because he's clearly dead serious.

Looking away, I see Bryce over by Leena and Austin. From his creased forehead and thin lips, I'd say he's seething with anger. He glares at Colton, but Colton doesn't notice.

The song ends and I see Bryce maneuvering through the crowd of people in our direction.

Colton reluctantly eases away, but not completely, he still holds my arms. "Thanks for the dance, beautiful."

"You're welcome."

"Maybe later we can dance again."

Bryce rests his hand on my lower back. "May I have this dance, Angel?"

"Sure." I smile and Colton moves away.

Bryce holds me tight and whispers in my ear, "He's really getting on my fucking nerves."

"I'm sorry he asked me to dance."

"You could've said no."

"I didn't get the chance to answer him. He pulled me to the dance floor." I try a diversion to get his mind off of Colton. "Who called you?"

"Grant." His voice is clipped and angry as he gives me a one word answer.

"What did he say?"

Bryce hesitates. "Do you really want to know?"

"Yes, I want to know. I need to know."

Bryce makes eye contact with me and I can see he's still angry. But then his face softens and he holds me tight again. "Shit, I'm sorry Angel." He hesitates. He doesn't want to tell me. But eventually he does. "They got him."

"My stalker? Where'd they find him?"

"Sorry, Angel." Bryce is searching my eyes again. "They found him in your bed."

"What? In my house?"

"Yes."

"How? The security system failed?"

"No, it worked. He broke a window to get in. The security company alerted the police, and they just happened to be in the vicinity when the call came in."

"Jesus! Do I have to install metal bars on my windows?"

I hesitate and take a deep breath. "So is he going to stay in jail this time?"

"He's in jail as we speak."

"Good. Ma's okay?"

"Yes, she's fine. She went to your house and cleaned up the glass. She called to have the window replaced the moment Grant told her about it."

I take another deep breath. "Great. So let's forget about this and move on."

Bryce looks deep in my eyes. "You're amazing. Do you know that?"

He kisses me slowly and I savour the taste of him.

When we pull apart, he looks over my shoulder. "You're right! Let's get back to me seducing you." He hits the remote in his pocket and flips through all the different vibrating modes.

Bryce looks down at me and grins.

When he spins me around, I see that he's been looking over my shoulder at Colton, who's sitting on a concrete wall, watching us.

Bryce grinds against me. "You like?"

"Yes, I love. I love you."

"When you smile, you light up the dance floor," he says, and I smile even more. "I love you, Angel. Too much."

Leena and Austin join us on the dance floor for a few songs and we have a great time, joking and laughing. Then later, Reese dances his way between all of us and makes us laugh by the way he's dancing. His playful personality is infectious.

Colton appears shortly after and gently touches my back where Bryce is not. "The food is ready, if anyone would like some?"

I turn to look at him. "Thank you," I say, because I know Bryce won't say it.

Colton's eyes rake over me hungrily. "You're welcome," his voice is a deep baritone sound.

"Oh yeah, I'm starving." Austin pulls Leena over to where the barbeque and tables are set up, full of food, and Bryce and I follow.

Two lines form on each side of the tables and we wait our turn with everyone else.

Bryce must be bored because he hits the remote every once in a while to see my reaction.

The line moves steadily and when Bryce is preoccupied, dishing the food onto his plate, someone slips in behind me, touching my lower back. He leans against me and whispers in my ear, "I need to touch you, to be close to you."

I turn and look up to see Colton's smouldering eyes staring back at me.

Oh no! I've seen that look before.

Colton disappears before Bryce sees him and I'm relieved that he's gone.

We take our plates over to the concrete wall and settle down on it to eat. I look down to my right. Colton, Reese, and the rest of the band are sitting and eating with us. They tease each other and I laugh to myself at the irresistibly cute relationship among all the band members. They get along great.

The ribs and chicken are mouth-watering. Austin devours his plateful and goes back for seconds. He's an eating machine.

After our late night barbeque, we grab another drink and saunter over to the large bonfire to dance.

Later, the band brings out fifty sky lanterns that they want to fly off at the same time for the video. They distribute lanterns and lighters to the fifty people on the beach and Colton yells out instructions about how to light them. The final instruction is, "Let them fly!"

Bryce takes his phone off his hip. He takes me in his arms and we watch in awe as he uses his phone to video all fifty white lanterns lighting up the sky and floating away. What a beautiful sight. He flips his camera around and takes a picture of himself holding me with the lanterns in the background.

The band members and crew set up the fireworks in the sand, while we watch from a distance on the concrete wall. My eyes wander over to Colton when he's in a bent-over position. He playfully nudges Drake, one of the guys in the band, and Drake falls over.

Bryce notices my gaze and hits the button on the remote. I turn, smiling, and my attention is diverted back to Bryce.

I pull him down so I can whisper in his ear. "That feels so good."

"You're so cute. Every time I turn it on, you jump and then you give me that adorable smile."

"That's because it surprises me."

He shuts it off and jumps off the wall, taking my hand in his. "Come with me. Let's get another drink."

"Are you trying to get me drunk?"

"Maybe."

Maybe his plan is to take me away from watching the hot guys setting up fireworks. Leena was enjoying herself, too. Damn it.

This is my fourth drink and I'm really feeling the effects. Bryce holds me steady as we walk back to the concrete wall from the bar. "I think you need to sit."

"I think so, too."

Bryce lifts me and gently places me down on the wall. I giggle. "Look at that. We didn't spill a drop." I place my drink beside me.

He stands between my legs with his back facing me and I wrap my arms around his chest and squeeze his meaty pecs.

I giggle again. "I love these."

"Look, she's got a glow on," Leena says. "She's shit-faced already."

"No, I'm not. But I'm getting there."

The long-awaited first firework lights up the sky and its reflection lights up the water, making a spectacular display. The band members eventually set them off faster and in unison. The show lasts for about fifteen minutes. During that time, Bryce hits the remote a few times and it makes me giggle. He spins to face me and then kisses me until we're hot and breathless-or until Austin makes some remark like, "Will you two watch the damn fireworks and cut that shit out?"

Afterwards, we help clean up the beach. I hold the bag, so as not to bend over with my short dress on, while I push the sand around with my foot to find any casings left behind. Bryce picks them up and throws them into the bag. Then we say our goodnights, thanking the band for the entertainment. "You're not leaving yet!" Colton and Reese say simultaneously.

Before Austin can answer for us, like he usually does, Bryce says, "It's been a long day."

Reese pipes up. "Oh, come on guys, the night is still young."

Who is he kidding? It has to be at least one or two in the morning.

"One more drink." Reese pulls Bryce by the arm toward the bar and we all follow. "Shaun, set me up with ten China Whites."

Shaun, the bartender, starts to pour different concoctions into the shot glasses and we marvel at his speed and efficiency.

"Everyone gather round. We're doing a shot," Reese insists.

I've already had too much to drink, but Reese distributes a shot glass into our hands. "To good times."

"To good times," we all repeat and drink up.

"That's good," I say, surprised that it doesn't taste terrible.

"Shaun, one more round," Reese says, plopping his shot glass down on the bar.

"Oh, no! I'm done," I say quickly.

"But you said it was good. Just one more. We can't celebrate without you." Reese's convincing voice is so smooth.

"Fine, but that's it," I insist.

Reese distributes the shot glasses again. "To good friends."

"To good friends." We all suck it back and place the shot glasses back on the bar.

"Crap, I feel that already."

"Then let's go dance it off," Bryce says as he ushers me to the dance floor.

It's a slow song, so Bryce wraps himself around me and holds on tight. We sway to the rhythm and savour the feeling in blissful silence. When the song ends, Colton appears out of nowhere beside us. "Bryce, can I have this dance with Keera?"

Oh crap!

Bryce hesitates. There is no emotion on his face.

How awkward is this?

Bryce finally nods at Colton and reluctantly backs away, then he stands next to the bar, watching.

Colton holds me at arm's length with his hand on my hip. "So, are you enjoying yourself tonight?"

"This is amazing. I'm having a great time. Thank you."

Colton looks over my shoulder. "You're welcome."

We dance for a couple of minutes in silence as he stares in my eyes.

I turn away.

All of a sudden, he wraps me in his arms and holds me like Bryce was. *Oh, no! Bryce is going to lose it.*

I search for Bryce and see that he's dancing with Fiona, but he's holding her stiffly at arm's length and watching us.

That bitch! As soon as I'm preoccupied, she moves in.

Fiona tries to talk to Bryce. He answers quickly and then looks back at us.

Colton steals my attention away from them. "Did you hear me earlier when I whispered that I need to touch you and be close to you?"

"Yes."

"I can't think straight. You're all I think about right now. And I keep trying to figure out a way to get you alone, without Bryce."

"We came to Aruba to get our minds off of something that happened back home that we're still dealing with. So that would be why Bryce is a little over-protective with me."

"Oh, I'm sorry to hear that. Did someone die?"

"No, no one died. I don't like to talk about it. I want to forget and move on."

"Okay. But you know you can tell me anything, right? I want to know you better."

"Colton…" How do I break this to him gently? "We'll probably never see each other again."

He pulls away to look in my eyes, but tightens his grip. "Not if I can help it!" He frowns and his eyes are intense, staring into mine. "What we experienced…"

The song ends and Bryce is standing right beside us waiting for Colton to release me.

"May I have this dance, Angel?" Bryce holds out his hand and I take it.

It's bloody amazing how Bryce keeps his cool around Colton when inside, he's probably fuming. He must be using everything in his power to hold back from losing it.

Colton backs away and heads to the bar.

Bryce holds me even tighter now. *Jeez, you're going to suffocate me!*

I idly wonder when the shit storm will hit and Bryce will accuse me of having too much fun in Colton's arms. But then it occurs to me that Bryce is no better at saying no to Colton than I am. After all, he's the one that said Colton could dance with me and then backed away. *So don't even think of blaming me, because I'll give it right back!*

Bryce releases me a bit, reaching in his pocket to hit the button on the remote. When he sees my smile, he relaxes and hugs me again. "I love you so much."

"I love you, Babe."

I frown slightly, knowing he can't see the expression on my face as I try to figure him out. *Okay, this is weird-Bryce is in a good mood.*

He stares off to our right every once in a while, so my line of sight follows his.

I get it now. Bryce is putting on a show for Colton. He doesn't want Colton to see how angry he really is.

He places both hands on each side of my face and kisses me with all he has.

What a kiss! I'm breathless and needy now and he knows it because he's searching my eyes.

He hesitates for a few seconds before saying, "Come!" He takes my hand and we walk off the dance floor.

As we pass by Leena and Austin, Bryce says, "Were calling it a night!" and keeps walking with me in tow.

"We'll see you tomorrow," I blurt out as I follow him.

We walk from the beach to the wooden pathway and through the gardens. Somehow I've caught up to Bryce and pass him, and I'm now in front, deliberately stopping, bending to fix my toe ring, which has swivelled upside down.

"Christ, help me," I hear from behind.

In my bent-over position, I can feel the cool breeze on my exposed skin. I turn to see Bryce standing back and admiring the view. I almost topple over, but Bryce catches me.

"Easy, now." His one hand grips my hip and the other rubs the globes of my ass. "You don't know how bad I want you. Right here, right now!"

I straighten, holding him in my arms, pulling him down so I can whisper against his ear, "So take me."

"Fuck!" slips from his lips as he lifts me in his arms and carries me to the bungalow.

As soon as he puts me down and closes the door, he pulls my dress up and off. I'm blown away by how fast he is. He picks me up in his arms again and walks through the living room to the bedroom, where he throws me down on the bed. I giggle in delight.

I pull the comforter and sheet down to the end of the bed and as I'm settling into a comfortable position, Bryce hovers over me, gloriously naked and holding a rope.

Damn, that was fast! When did he get undressed?

In a flash, I'm lassoed like a calf at a rodeo and it takes me by surprise. What the... ? I giggle.

Both my wrists are tied together and somehow my ankles are tied to my hands. My knees are against my chest with my feet up in the air and my butt is exposed.

Damn, this is hot! And erotic. And oh shit, that look? Holy moly!

His intense eyes pierce right through me. *There he is. My dominant lover.*

"Do you want him?" he says angrily, his tone accusing.

Oh, shit! Here we go.

"No! I only want you. I love you, Babe. Probably too much. So much it hurts. Can't you see what you do to me?"

"Well, obviously he does it for you too."

"No, he doesn't. Only you can get me this turned on. Christ you've been teasing the hell out of me all night. Vibrating me."

"Good answer," Bryce says sarcastically as he pulls the egg out of my body. He replaces it with his hard-as-steel cock, thrusting deep inside me, making me cry out in ecstasy.

"Oh, God, Babe, that's what I want. It's so hard."

"That's what you do to me." His shaking hands are the telltale sign of his desperate need for me. "Fuck, Angel, you make me crazy. I can't handle this. You're fucking with my head. So now, I take what I want!"

"I'm sorry, I don't mean to."

"And what I want, is you! You're mine! Every inch of you. Mine to do whatever I please."

He slams into me repeatedly, and then hesitates. "Do you want his cock inside you?"

"No."

"Do you want him to fuck you?" He slams relentlessly into me, again and again. "Fuck you, like this?"

"No."

"Do you want him to blow his load inside you?"

"No!" His tone has become vicious and nasty so I try to push him away, but I can only move a fraction. A tear slips down my cheek and then another. "Stop!" I spit out.

Bryce notices and stops abruptly. "Aw, Christ, I'm sorry, Angel." He quickly unties me, pulls me onto his lap, and rocks me back and forth.

"Please forgive me. I didn't mean to hurt you." He kisses the tears off my face. "I'm sorry, Angel." He hugs me and we stay like that in silence, listening to each other's hearts beating, lost in our intimate moment for a couple of minutes.

I know exactly how he feels-how the mental images can form in the brain and get blown out of proportion, clawing and ripping out your heart until you're in a jealous rage.

I try to stop crying.

"I'm okay," I say, wiping away my tears. "But I want you to quit blaming me. I never asked to dance with him. He asked you. And you let him. I was quite happy and content in your arms."

"Yeah, but the way you were smiling and the way he was holding you. I'll never get that out of my head."

"I can't be rude to him. I find it impossible. And obviously, neither can you. You didn't tell him no."

"I'm trying to have patience with the guy, but he's overstepping his boundaries."

"Can we forget about Colton and get back to this." My lips cover his and I kiss him slowly and sensually.

Bryce moans in my mouth and lowers me to the mattress with our mouths still fused together.

I'm feeling the effects of those two shots now and I get a little aggressive. I grab a handful of his hair and pull him back so I can look in his eyes. "I like the way you tied me up there. Babe, that was so hot!"

He hesitates for a second, searching my eyes, and then moves quickly, but deliberately. His whole demeanor changes before my eyes as he becomes the dominant sex god again and I am lassoed like a calf at the rodeo once more. I giggle.

"You like this, eh?"

"This is hot! And so are you." My eyes scan the length of his body.

"You want this?" He kneels, thrusting his hips forward, grasping his hard cock in his hand and stroking the length of it. I watch as it grows thicker and harder.

"Yes, please." Before I can say anything else, he tunnels into me, one delicious inch at a time. "You feel so good." The connection is surprisingly intense as he sinks balls deep into me.

I gasp, taking it all.

His desperate need to have me shows in his shaking hands and impatience. He gives it to me hard, pounding relentlessly for quite a while.

When he wants to change positions, he pulls out and unties me, throwing the ropes on the floor.

Bryce falls down on me. "Christ, Angel. I lose my mind over you." He buries his face in my neck and kisses me, running his tongue along every sensitive nerve there.

"Don't. I'm right here with you. Always."

He kisses and licks his way down to my breasts, capturing my nipple between his teeth. "I want to eat you alive."

Whenever there's an obstacle in the way of our relationship, Bryce has a desperate need to show me how much he loves me. Hard, explosive, mind-numbing sex is one of the ways he drives his point home.

My orgasm builds like a storm. A fast-moving storm. I focus on him and his hard cock scraping my sensitive tissues inside.

His lips surround my nipple and he flicks it wildly with his tongue. The sensation arrows directly down to my pussy. I clamp my muscles down on him and relish the feeling. I try to hold out.

Bryce is soaked with sweat and breathing hard. I know he's close. "Angel, give it to me."

I can't hold out any longer. My legs start to shake and my back arches. I scream out. "I'm coming, Babe!"

Bryce rears up and grunts something I can't quite make out. He closes his eyes and opens them again, slamming into me a couple more times as he spurts long and hard into me. When he's done, he slips out and pulls me back onto his lap holding me in his big, strong arms. "I love you so much it hurts, you know that?"

"I know. I know exactly how you feel." I think about Fiona swooping in on him as soon as I was preoccupied with Colton.

Damn vulture.

"Did you ask Fiona to dance?"

Bryce frowns and presses his lips together, giving me his irritated look. "No. She asked me and then pulled me onto the dance floor."

"That's what I thought."

Bryce shimmies me off his lap and gets out of bed with his hand extended to me. "Come with me."

I take his hand and follow him out the French doors to the hot tub. I sink into it.

Bryce turns on the music, starts the jets, and then lowers into the water. Slowly.

I scoot beside him so I can feel his body next to mine.

We lean our heads back and relax every muscle for a few minutes and then my hand works its way between his thighs and I run my finger up his balls to wake him. He's a little too relaxed. His head flies back up and he smirks at me. "You ready for round two?" he asks.

You are not going to sleep yet.

I stand in front of him pouring the water over my breasts. I circle my hips and run my hands down my belly.

"So sexy when you dance for me." He slides his hands behind his head in that sexy pose that drives me wild, and watches me intently with his half smile that I love.

I've got his undivided attention now.

I spin and shake my ass provocatively at him, then lift both arms in the air. I turn just a fraction, curving my body and peeking through my bent arm at him with my mischievous smile.

"Christ, that's sexy."

All of a sudden we hear a loud noise on the other side of the privacy fence and we both look that way. "What was that?" Bryce asks, sitting up.

15

"I DON'T KNOW." I quickly cover my breasts and lower into the water, listening for any sound of movement beyond the fence for a minute. Bryce and I exchange concerned looks. When I'm satisfied that no one is intruding on our special moment, I rise and start to move like I was before we were interrupted. "I don't hear anything now."

My hands go back to sensually caressing my hips, my belly, the curves of my butt, and when they reach my breasts, I squeeze them together and pinch my nipples.

Bryce relaxes again, sinking in the water with his fingers locked behind his head. His eyes narrow.

"Come here." He crooks his finger at me.

I turn to face him and straddle his leg, rubbing on him.

Bryce watches me for a bit, struggling. "That's it! Side of the tub."

He stands, gesturing for me to sit. "Place that sexy little ass right here."

I sit on the edge of the stamped concrete with my feet in the hot tub and lean back on my hands.

Bryce lifts one foot on the ledge and then the other, so I'm spread wide open. He stands back admiring, shaking his head. He smirks at me. "Such a tease. You know what happens to little teases?"

"No. what? I get what I want?" I smile, cocking my head slightly, trying for a mischievous look.

"What am I going to do with you? You're irresistible."

"Good. I'm glad you like."

"Not just like." He sinks back down in the water and settles between my thighs. He opens my juicy folds and looks on in amazement. His gaze comes back to mine. "I love. I love everything about you. Even when you make me crazy with jealousy." His attention goes back to my pussy as he intimately inspects it.

I find myself straining toward his finger because the gentleness of his touch is too much to bear. I crave more.

He smirks at me.

I'm soaked with his semen, but he doesn't seem to care. His mouth seals warmly over my sensitive tissues and his tongue flicks and sucks furiously on my clit. His finger slides in and out of me, driving me closer and closer to orgasm. My head falls back and my legs start to shake uncontrollably. I hold his head steady while I rub out one of the fastest and strongest climaxes of my life-must have been from the way he was teasing me all night with the vibrating egg. But then my mind flashes back to how the night unfolded with Colton telling me how he thinks about me constantly, the way he was holding me and how he'd remember it for the rest of his life.

Why is he saying that to me? Stop thinking about him Keera. Enough!

The timer for the jets on the hot tub expires and it is now quiet except for the music Bryce turned on earlier.

He stands in front of me, looking down. "What are you thinking about, Angel?"

I quickly stand. "This." I take his cock in both hands and run them down the length of it. "I want this." I stare deep in his eyes and reach down, cupping his balls in my hand. My finger slides on his soft skin and his balls tighten immediately.

His body jerks from my touch. "You can have it, anytime, anywhere. You've got me in the palm of your hand. Literally."

I drop to my knees in the water and look up. "Good." I peer at him with one eyebrow raised, giving him my devilish look. Then I lick my lips and drive his cock deep in my mouth.

Bryce groans. "Your mouth is amazing, Angel."

I pull his cock out and lick all the way around it, getting it wet with my saliva. I take him to the back of my throat, in and out, while I stroke the shaft, giving him a good work over.

His fingers weave through the hair at the back of my head with exactly the right amount of pressure from his large hands. We move together in unison. I feel his grip tighten as he lifts and lowers my mouth onto his cock. His thighs tense, and when I grasp his balls, they draw up firmly, puckering on command.

"Angel?" He releases an almost silent cry to let me know he's ready to come and if I don't want it, I'd better stop now.

I don't stop. I milk him until his warm cum shoots to the back of my throat. I swallow quickly and take more.

I watch every expression on his beautiful face and how every muscle in his body tightens and bulges, how he gasps for air and the sounds he makes.

I'm ready for round three.

Watching him come is such a turn-on for me. I can't get enough. I always want more.

He pulls me up from my crouched position and holds me in his big, strong arms.

I wipe my mouth quickly.

He stares deep in my eyes with adoration. "You are so good at that. You amaze me every time." His lips seal over mine and we kiss slowly.

He takes my hand and helps me up from the hot tub. "Let's

go to bed. It's late." We walk back into the bungalow to the bedroom and he flops down on the bed. "I'm tired."

"Sleep then. I'm going to wash my face. I'll be with you in a second."

When I turn the water off after cleaning up, I hear Bryce breathing deeply from the bedroom. *Jeez, that didn't take long.* I shut off the bathroom light and search for the bed in the darkness, stubbing my toe, trying to contain my outburst before snuggling in next to his naked body.

He wakes slightly and wraps me up in his arm and leg. "I love you."

"I love you, Babe."

We fall asleep like that.

I wake to a light shining in my face and open my eyes to see Colton standing over me. I close my eyes, rubbing them with my fingers. When I open them again and focus on the room, Colton is gone. What the frick?

Jesus, tell me I'm not dreaming of him! I close my eyes and start drifting back to sleep, but I can't take the bathroom light glaring in my face.

Throwing back the sheets in a huff, I stumble out of bed, over to the bathroom to shut off the light.

I know I turned that light off. Maybe Bryce got up and forgot to turn it off. I climb back in bed and fall asleep.

In the morning, the sun shines through the blinds, waking me. I turn to see Bryce sound asleep. Not wanting to wake him up, I lie motionless, thinking about last night, and every aspect of our lovemaking-how aggressive he was from his jealous rage and then the regret he showed after making me cry. I can see how he struggles with his feelings, how it consumes him and he can't think of anything else but me. He truly loves me.

My mind wanders to Colton and the things he said. And now that the fog is lifting from my night of drinking, it hits me like a ton of bricks. Did I dream that Colton was here or was he really standing over me? I try to clear the fog further. I remember shutting off the light before I climbed in bed because I stubbed my toe in the dark.

Bryce rolls over and blinks at me. "Good morning, Angel. Sleep well?"

"I woke up once. How about you? Did you sleep good?"

"Passed out and never woke up until now."

"Oh, that's good." Okay, that answers my question-it wasn't Bryce that left the bathroom light on. *Was Colton really here, standing over me?*

"Must have been all that booze we had last night. And the great sex. Made me sleep like a baby."

"I'm feeling it this morning, but that was fun. I had a good time. Did you?"

"I always have a good time with you. As long as I'm with you, Angel. I'm happy."

"So am I."

The day starts with Leena banging on the door, wanting to go for breakfast.

As we enter the buffet, I notice the band and crew members at a large table in the far corner. Bryce steers me to a table on the other side of this massive room, and we settle in there, waiting for our waiter to bring us tea and coffee. After taking a few sips, Bryce and I go our separate ways, collecting our food at different stations. Later, as I'm reaching under the glass canopy to scoop some scrambled eggs, I feel Bryce's hand on my hip and I run my hand over his.

I turn to see his reaction.

I'm shocked to see Colton smiling. "Good morning, beautiful."

I quickly move my hand away. "Good morning. I thought you were Bryce."

"How'd you sleep?"

I frown. *Why is he asking me this?* "Good. And you?"

"Not sleeping much." His eyes float up and down my body. "I've got someone on my mind."

"Oh." I turn and continue loading my plate, not knowing what to say.

His hand moves to my hip and he leans his body against mine, talking next to my ear. "Tell me you're coming to the final video shoot today and the after-party?"

I turn back and see Colton grinning at me. "The way you dance. I could watch you forever. I also want another dance."

"I don't know what's on the agenda for today. Leena usually takes care of that."

"All right, then. I'll talk to her. I'm not taking no for an answer. You have to be there. I had a good time last night. I want more."

I move out of the way to reach for some bacon and his hand drops off my hip.

His hard body leans into mine once again, and he whispers in my ear, "I can't stop thinking about you."

I turn and he's got that look in his eyes. The look that says he has it bad.

I feel Bryce approach before he touches my lower back. "I got you some toast." Bryce nods and stares icily, throwing darts with his eyes, but Colton doesn't seem to notice. "Colton." Bryce says in his deep, irritated voice, which is almost a growl.

"Thanks, Babe," I say, taking the toast from Bryce's plate.

Colton backs up. "How are doing this morning, Bryce?"

Bryce doesn't answer.

"I'm sorry," I say as we move out of the way of the scrambled eggs so an older gentleman can load his plate.

"See you later, Colton," I say, not wanting to be rude as I turn and we head back toward our table.

"No, you won't," Bryce mumbles.

Back at our table, Bryce and I settle in again and then Leena and Austin join us.

"Reese asked me and Austin if we're going to the final video shoot today."

"Steak barbeque and seafood feast tonight," Austin says, rubbing his hands together.

"I told him we wouldn't miss it. It'll be a repeat of last night. I had a great time."

"Don't you want to do something else?" Bryce grumbles.

"Oh, come on, Bryce. Don't tell me you didn't have a good time."

"It was fun, but I think we should do something else. I'd like to jet ski before we have to leave."

"I'll reserve those as soon as we leave here," Austin says.

"I'd like to go jogging on the beach this morning," I say.

"We can do that." Bryce wraps his arm around my shoulder and kisses my hair.

"Okay, so we'll do what we want to do this morning and then we'll go hang with the band later this afternoon and tonight," Leena concludes.

Bryce groans in disapproval, but no one else pays attention.

The waves crashing in along the beach and the seagulls squawking in the distance is a sound that is soothing and will be fixed in my mind, remembering this trip as a special time in my life. It is hot already and it's only mid-morning. We work up a sweat jogging along the beach, but every once in a while we feel an exhilarating breeze. This time we go farther than what we have before, and when we jog back, Leena and Austin are waiting for us, talking with Colton.

Jeez, he's everywhere.

Bryce grumbles. "Fuck's sake."

Colton's scrutinizing eyes float up and down my bikini-clad body, making me feel self-conscious, so I look to make sure nothing's popping out.

"I thought you'd never get back. Where'd you go?"

"Past six hotels this time," I say breathlessly.

"Come on, we've got the jet skis for one hour." Leena pulls me down the beach and Colton follows.

Bryce seems to enjoy strapping me into my life vest as Colton looks on. When Bryce guides the strap between my legs, he makes sure he feathers my pussy lips. I look up to see him smiling mischievously at me.

Climbing aboard, Bryce hoists me up out of the water. I sit behind him wrapping my arms around his hard body. "Hold on tight, Angel. This is going to be a wild ride."

My heart's racing and adrenaline courses through my veins as we fly over the crashing waves.

Austin attempts a couple of tricks, swinging the ass end of the jet ski around, while Leena holds on for dear life. Bryce observes, but he's holding back for some strange reason. He takes it easy, circling around Austin and Leena's jet ski.

I tap Bryce on the thigh. "Why are you driving slowly?"

"I don't want you hurt."

"Babe, I'll be fine. I'll hold on tight. They look like they're having a lot of fun."

"All right. Hold on!"

Bryce attempts a couple of quick maneuvers and when he sees I'm still hanging on, he attempts more.

Fifteen minutes later, we float over to Austin and Leena who are shutting their engine down.

"Had enough?" Leena asks me.

"Yeah. We'll let you guys take them out, and we'll watch."

"I want you to come to the boutique with me and tell me what you think of the dress I want to buy."

"Okay. So I guess were going to the boutique," I say, grasping Bryce tighter from behind, giving him a hug.

When the guys drop us off at the beach, Bryce noticeably relaxes as he sees Colton has disappeared.

Leena and I watch the guys do tricks, jumping the waves two feet in the air, playfully splashing one another.

I shake my head in disgust. "Oh sure, look at him now. But would he try that with me on the back?"

"You should know what Bryce is like by now."

"Yeah, I know. Safety first."

In the boutique, Leena pulls me over to a rack where she's hidden the dress she saw earlier. "This is it!" she says excitedly, holding the dress up against her body. "Isn't it beautiful?"

"Nice! You should try it on."

She's gone in an instant to the dressing room and I roam around the boutique, looking at all the fabulous dresses. I hold a few dresses up to myself, looking at my reflection in the mirror, deciding which one I should try on. I come back repeatedly to the same short, off-the-shoulder, peach-chiffon creation with fabric gathering across the breasts, giving it a ruffled look.

Something in the mirror catches my eye. It's Colton hiding behind a tall rack of clothes. I know it's him from the tribal tattoo on his arm. I ignore him and try the dress on.

When I come out, he's disappeared and Leena is twirling around, checking out the dress she has on in the mirror.

"Wow Leena, you have to buy it. Looks great!"

"How'd you do?" the sales woman behind the counter asks.

"Good. I like the way it fits, but I'm going to think about it for a while." I do the same as Leena, hiding my dress on the rack so no one finds it. My mother always told me, leave the store and if you can't stop thinking about it, go back and buy it.

Leena pays for her dress and then we head back through the botanical gardens to the beach to find the guys.

When we have them in our sight, they're playfully slapping each other on the back, laughing, as they hand the keys to the attendant.

"Looks like you guys had a good time."

Bryce chuckles. "Yeah, that was fun." He wraps me in a hug and kisses me.

"Kicked his ass," Austin says laughing.

"Now what do you want to do?" Leena asks.

"I'll reserve the sail/surf boards for us," Bryce says quickly. "They look like they're a good work-out."

I'm sensing Bryce wants to keep us busy so we won't make it to the video shoot with the band.

"While you guys do that, me and Keera will drop off my new dress at the bungalow." Leena grabs my hand and tugs me toward the boardwalk.

"Be back in a flash," I call out to the guys.

As we're walking up the front deck of our bungalows, I notice a box wrapped in colourful paper with a bow, leaning against our front door. "What's this?" I pick it up and look at Leena, confused.

"Is there a card?"

I flip it all around, searching for one. "No."

"Open it."

"Here." I hand it to Leena. "You do it. What if someone left it at the wrong bungalow?"

"That's their problem. It's ours now."

I chuckle as Leena rips through the paper and box.

Leena holds up the same peach dress I hid on the rack. "Isn't this the dress you tried on?"

"Yes, same one."

She examines it and when she sees the look on my face, she freezes. "What's that look for?"

I take it from her. "Colton!"

"What about Colton?"

"I think he was in the boutique when I went to try it on."

"Colton bought you this?" Leena asks.

"How else would it get here?"

"Tell me you're going to keep it!"

"No. I'm taking it back right now." I turn and head toward the boutique. "Meet you back here." I yell back to Leena.

Bryce kept us busy as long as he could with morning and afternoon activities, but he had to give in to Leena's request to go hang with the band after she complained enough.

On our way to the other end of the pool, the camera man walks backwards, trying to get a shot of us. When he stumbles over a chair, we chuckle, reaching quickly to hold his camera while he recovers. He follows behind us as we make our way to the stage, still video-taping us. It's strange that he's spending so much time with us when he usually spreads himself out, capturing everyone. *I wonder if Colton told him to do that.*

The band is singing and the crowd of people is growing, due to Colton's sexy baritone voice. When Colton's eyes lock on mine, he smiles down at me and continues singing.

Bryce notices and guides me to the bar. "We stay together."

"Okay," I say, knowing how much it irritates Bryce when Colton looks at me that way.

After waiting at the bar for five minutes in the sweltering sun, it's time to take shelter, so Bryce guides us over to an empty spot under a colourful sunshade and we watch the band from a distance.

Later on, the band takes a break, exiting the stage one by one and make their way to the bar. Then each one sits around our table, hanging out with the Canadians, and shading themselves from the sun.

Reese and Drake keep us entertained as they recapture some of the hilarious events that happened during their tour. When I hear Bryce chuckling, I glance over and notice he's having a good time with them.

My mind wanders to the anonymous person who bought me that beautiful peach dress.

When I went to return it, the sales lady said she'd just started her shift and had no idea who bought it for me. It was paid by cash so there was no paper trail showing who purchased it. I stood there holding it, wondering what I should do. Then I carried it back to the bungalow, where I hung it up in the closet.

Looking up, I see Colton staring at me again.

Did he buy me the dress?

I look away and listen to the conversation that's unfolding.

The guys in the band are trying to convince Bryce and Austin to come back up front so they can get their final shots of the video. Now that we have significant cloud cover, they agree. We all head to the bar first to get a drink, and then Reese makes sure he physically places each one of us up front when they continue playing their number one hit.

We dance and raise our drinks high in the air, enjoying the music and the day. When they get their final video shots, the director yells out, "That's a wrap," and we all cheer, clapping our hands.

The guys in the band exit the stage and come over, thanking everyone who participated in the video.

A playful shoving match ensues and Reese and Drake tackle one another, falling into the pool.

The temperature is hot-feeling well over ninety-five degrees and there is no breeze to cool us. One by one, we dive into the pool and swim up to the bar for a drink.

After three, Reese organizes a water volleyball game and we can't help but laugh when the band members pretend to drown each other. They switch the teams up several times and Leena and I get to play on the same team twice. At dusk, just before the sun slips behind the trees in the tropical forest, they switch the teams again and Colton occupies the space next to me at the net.

Bryce is on the other side now with Leena and Austin. As the game progresses, I find Colton inching closer to me. When the ball comes my way and I'm just about to spike it over the net, Colton reaches for it at the same time and we collide. I'm dragged under the water, where he kisses me. When I surface, I convey my displeasure by scowling at him. *What is he thinking?*

Shaking it off, I resume the game. I glance at Bryce who seems preoccupied. He didn't see the kiss or the look on my face.

Reese has been throwing playful insults in Bryce's direction the whole game, deliberately antagonizing him, and when Bryce has had enough he wraps Reese in a head lock like he does with his friend Dante. While Bryce's back is turned, Colton wraps his arm around my waist and pulls me into him, staring at my lips. "Those are kissable lips. I want more."

The moment Bryce turns toward us, Colton moves back to his original spot, looking sideways at me, smirking with a sneaky mischievous smile on his face.

What is he up to?

Bryce lets Reese go and we continue the game until it's too dark to play anymore.

We agree to head back to the bungalows for a quick shower before meeting the band back at the pool for the barbeque.

Bryce stays right beside me all night, not giving Colton an opportunity to get close. By midnight, we are exhausted, so we say goodnight to everyone and head to our bungalow.

In the morning, I'm full of life again. Bryce watches me from the bed as I search for my bikini bottoms.

"What do you say we go shopping in town today? I heard the flea market sells t-shirts, dresses, and jewellery. I want to buy you something."

"Sure, but do you want to go for a jog first?"

"I don't know, Angel. My head is still in a fog. How about we go for breakfast and then take a shower and head to town. We can see if Leena and Austin want to come with us."

"Okay." I give up looking for my bikini bottoms and slip a sun dress on after my shower.

Bryce leads me through the flea market, from one vender to another, with that simple touch at the small of my back. Then we head to a plaza nearby and somehow end up standing outside a jewellery store, looking in both directions. "Where did Austin and Leena go?" Bryce asks.

"They were following us. They must have slipped into one of the stores."

"Come with me." Bryce tugs me inside and veers to the left. We stare into the glass case, admiring the wedding rings. I glance up at him, smiling.

"What?" Bryce says, his dimple showing as he smiles back.

"Nothing. You're just adorable, that's all." I glance back down in the case. "Oh, this one's nice... and this one."

"Angel, they're too small. You deserve a huge diamond engagement ring with gemstones all the way around the wedding band."

"Babe, all I need is something small. Look how tiny my fingers are. A big one just wouldn't look right."

"So you like something like this one or this one?"

"Still too big. Oh, wow, this one is beautiful."

"Would you like to try it on?" the sales woman asks.

"Oh, no. We're just looking."

"Try it on, Angel. You'll never know until you try it."

Before I can confirm or deny, the sales woman has it out of the glass case and is holding it for me to take.

"Oh, okay, thank you," I say.

Bryce takes it from me and slips it on my finger. "To have and to hold from this day forward."

I glance up at him, his eyes glimmer and shine. He smiles, deepening that sexy dimple, and what a smile it is. He takes my breath away.

I stare lovingly into his eyes, smiling so much my cheeks hurt. I reluctantly turn away to look at the ring on my finger. "Wow, that's nice. Not too big, not too small. It's perfect."

"Like you." He holds me from behind and kisses my hair.

Oh, my, this is turning him on. I feel his hard cock rub against my butt.

I turn to glance at him again, and he hugs me harder.

Bryce takes a picture of the rings on my finger. "For future reference."

"And what kind of a ring would you like, Babe?"

"Just a plain wedding band. Maybe something like this." He points to a simple band with cut gold that would look simply gorgeous on his large, strong hand.

We head out the door to the street to find Leena and Austin. After about fifteen minutes, we catch up with them. Leena shows me her purchases and I show her mine. We find an outdoor café and have a tropical drink they are famous for and we share a nacho supreme that could feed an army.

Bryce suggests we keep shopping and I look at him, wondering why. He's not the shopping type and neither am I, but I don't say anything, just follow his lead.

Leena calls Grayson to pick us up at the café and drop us off at the mall. We walk from store to store, not really buying anything, yet Bryce seems to be content. Odd.

When we walk into Swarovski, Leena and I look in the glass cases at the magnificent figurines. I tear my eyes away for a second to see Bryce and Austin roaming over to the other side of the store.

When I look back, a huge, colourful peacock catches my eye. "Leena look at this one." I point.

"Look at the price tag."

"Eleven-hundred dollars? Oh, but it is beautiful."

We're both mesmerized as we make our way around the store, pointing at everything, until we meet up with Bryce and Austin.

Leena sees a Swarovski bag in each of their hands. "What'd ya buy?"

Austin holds the bag behind his back. "Nothing you need to know about."

She tries to grab for it, but Austin twists so she can't reach.

Bryce smirks down at me and when I realize that he's bought something for me, I reach for the back of his neck and pull him down. Our foreheads meet. "I like surprises."

"You're going to like this one."

I give him a sensual kiss. When we separate, Leena is still reaching for the bag behind Austin's back and he's dodging her.

Austin wraps one arm around and tugs her tight to his body, restraining her. He whispers in her ear and she seems to melt in his arms.

I guess he is taming her. *I wonder what he said to calm her down.*

She turns to kiss him and then pulls him out of the store. We follow them, our hands entwined.

When we get back into the limo, Grayson asks, "Where to?"

Bryce suggests we drive around to see the sights and if anything catches our eye, we'll pull over.

Everyone agrees.

While we're driving and our minds are on the beautiful sights we're seeing, Bryce suddenly swivels in his seat.

His eagle eyes have caught a glance of something else, and he abruptly hits the button and tells Grayson, "Pull over," then he quickly opens the door and darts out.

The three of us exchange surprised looks and Austin blurts out, "What the hell is he up to now?"

16

WE ALL FOLLOW Bryce out the limo door and see what's caught his eye.

On the side of the road, a mom is cradling her daughter trying to console her after what looks like a scooter accident.

Bryce bends down to talk to the mom. "We were driving by and saw that you may need some help."

The mom glances up. "Thank you, but I think..." She stops speaking mid-sentence and then continues. "Oh, my! I... I think she'll be fine."

We all stand behind Bryce, including Grayson. "I'm a firefighter back in Canada. I might be able to patch her up," Bryce says.

"I have a first aid kit in the limo," Grayson offers.

The mom appears to relax as Bryce speaks to the crying little girl, who looks about four years old. "Hey, sweetie, can I look at your arm? I might be able to make it feel better."

She tries to stop crying. "You can fix my bow-bow?"

"I'm sure going to try. What's your name, sweetie?"

"Alyssa." She sniffles.

"Alyssa, sweetie, let me take a look."

She holds her arm out to Bryce and winces in pain.

Bryce glances sideways at me with a worried look.

I kneel beside him and rub his back, assuming that look means that her arm may be broken.

"First aid kit," Grayson says as he hands it to me.

I open it to find some antiseptic ointment, Q-tips, bandages, gauze, scissors, and a tensor bandage. I try to clean up the blood as best as I can and then Bryce places the bandages over top and secures them. "How's that feel, Alyssa?"

"Better, but I still have a bow-bow on my arm."

"You know what we're going to do? We're going to make you a sling for that arm."

I wrap the tensor bandage around her arm gently, while Bryce pulls his t-shirt over his head and takes the scissors to it. He then gently wraps it around her arm, tightening the make-shift straps he's cut and secures the sling around her neck.

I look at the mom and she periodically glances at Bryce's washboard abs.

I smile up at Leena and she smiles down at me.

"How's that feel, Alyssa?" Bryce asks.

"It feels better."

"Good. How would you like to go for a ride in that big car with us and we'll get you checked out by a doctor."

"What are we going to do with the scooter? I can't leave it here." Alyssa's mom sounds anxious.

"My brother Austin will drive it behind us to your house and from there we'll go to the hospital to get Alyssa some X-rays."

Austin does a double take at Bryce with the funniest look on his face. His neck extends and he twists his head sideways, frowning, but he doesn't say a word. He grumbles and goes to pick the scooter up from its side.

"Alyssa, honey, is it okay if I pick you up so your mom can get up?"

"O-kay." Alyssa hesitates, but then climbs into Bryce's arms.

Leena and I hold out our hands to Alyssa's mom and help her up.

Watching Bryce carry Alyssa to the limo and thinking about the care and compassion in his voice when he talks to her makes my heart swell. I never thought I could love him more, but somehow I'm falling for him, deeper than before.

Alyssa stays on Bryce's lap in the limo. I sit beside Bryce, and Leena sits beside me with mom across from us.

I glance across and see blood dripping. "Bryce, Alyssa's mom is bleeding."

"Alyssa, honey, I'm going to put you on Keera's lap while I fix your mom's knee."

"Okay," Alyssa says softly.

"Please, call me Jenny."

Alyssa scrambles onto my lap while Bryce goes to work wiping the blood off of Jenny's knee. "I'm going to try not to hurt you, but I've got to pick the stones out and then I'll be able to clean it up properly."

After Bryce is finished wrapping Jenny's knee, he settles back on the seat next to me and Alyssa climbs back onto his lap and hugs him.

Bryce gives her his mega-watt smile and hugs her back, then turns to me and shows off his sexy dimple.

Seeing this side to Bryce makes my eyes water. Can he be more admirable than he is right now?

I can't stop smiling at him.

"What?" Bryce asks.

I whisper in his ear. "You're irresistible! Do you know that?"

He smiles and then directs the attention away from himself. "Look at Austin. He looked tougher on the Harley."

We all look out the back window at Austin trying to keep up to the limo as he maneuvers through traffic. It's comical and we can't help but laugh.

After we drop the scooter off at Jenny and Alyssa's house, Austin climbs back in the limo and we take Alyssa to the hospital.

We all go in to make sure she'll be fine, but also because Alyssa is holding on tightly to Bryce's neck. She doesn't want to let him go.

Bryce receives a lot of strange looks from people because he's bare from the waist up, but he doesn't seem to care or pay attention.

When the X-ray technician says she needs the little girl on the table, Alyssa tightens her grip around Bryce's neck.

"I've never seen her like this. Usually men frighten her. This is very odd." Jenny pries Alyssa's fingers from Bryce's neck. "Alyssa, Bryce has to go. This nice lady is going to take care of you now."

"But, Mommy, I don't want Bryce to leave."

"Yes, I know. Bryce is nice and he's been very helpful."

"He's pretty, too. Don't you think he's pretty Mommy?"

Jenny's cheeks turn red. "Yes, sweetie, he's pretty."

"Maybe he could be my daddy!"

Jenny becomes flustered and her cheeks turn to a beet red. "No, sweetie he can't be your daddy." Turning away, I hear her say quietly, "Unfortunately."

Leena and I look at each other grinning.

As Jenny turns back to Bryce, she says nervously, "I'm so sorry."

"No problem," Bryce says as if he hasn't heard a thing. "Always happy to help." Turning to Alyssa, he says, "You get better soon, and be a good girl for your Mommy."

"Okay, Bryce," she says in her adorable little voice.

We all wave to Alyssa. "Bye, Alyssa," We say in unison, but Alyssa is only interested in one of us.

"Bye, Bryce," she squeaks.

As we walk through the emergency room toward the exit, the nurses' reaction to Bryce makes us laugh. One of them stops dead in the doorway, looking him up and down, "Oh dear! My, my, my!"

"I bet you've made her day a happy one," I say, turning back to see if her eyes are still glued to Bryce.

"Oh, you're funny." Bryce tucks me into his side and squeezes me.

Back in the limo, Bryce pulls me close. "Alyssa is a smaller version of you, with that long blonde hair. She's so cute."

"Yeah, she's a cutie. She loved you, but who doesn't?" I gaze lovingly into his eyes, admiring everything about this man.

"She didn't want to let me go."

"Just like every other woman who comes into contact with you."

Bryce looks at me with an expression that suggests he's about to roll his eyes, but he stops himself. "I hope our kids are that cute."

Leena pipes up. "Oh, they will be-maybe cuter."

Back at the resort, Austin and Bryce give Grayson a large tip and thank him for all his help.

"Thank you for making my day exciting," he says tipping his hat.

As we walk by the pool to our bungalow, I note that it's deserted. The stage, the backdrops, and the equipment are no longer around the pool. The band finished the video last night, but I hope they haven't left the resort to go back on tour. We didn't get to say goodbye. We were becoming really good friends after spending three days together partying.

Bryce notices too, but he doesn't say a word.

Okay, now I've figured you out. You kept me occupied in town, away from the resort, so I wouldn't be able to say goodbye to the band, especially to Colton.

Once inside the bungalow, as we're putting away our purchases, Bryce pulls me into his arms. "This was a good day."

"Yes, a very good day."

"Did you feel how hard I was when we were looking at rings?"

"Yes, did that turn you on?"

"Yes. I can't wait to make you mine."

"I am yours."

"I mean officially. I don't want to pressure you, I just want you to get used to the idea."

"I'm getting there."

There's a knock at the door and Bryce and I go to see who it is.

Leena stands in the doorway. "Before you guys get busy, I thought I'd come to tell you my dad wants us to join him for dinner in half an hour, so get dressed and I'll be back in twenty-five minutes."

Bryce gives a low grumble.

Leena notices and backpedals. "My dad's bumming that we've only got tonight and tomorrow morning with him and then we're leaving. He wants to spend as much time as he can with us." Leena looks at us with those puppy-dog eyes, almost begging.

"Okay," Bryce agrees. "We'll take a quick shower and get ready."

I rub his back, knowing he wanted to spend the night alone with me, but he gave in to Leena to make her happy.

After we've showered and dressed, Bryce takes out the box from Swarovski. As he opens it, my eyes widen and my mouth drops open. I look up to see his eyes glimmering. "Do you like it?"

"I love it. Babe, it's beautiful."

"Here, let me take this off," he says, reaching behind to unclasp my necklace. "I want you to wear this one tonight."

"Okay." I hold the box and Bryce takes off the two-heart necklace that he bought me, skimming his fingers gently across my skin as he fastens the new one. The tear-drop crystal earrings match the necklace, and the light bouncing off of them is mesmerising. We stand back from the mirror, admiring them together.

"You've got great taste. Thank you." I give him a hug and a kiss.

"You're welcome." He takes my hand and runs his finger over my left ring finger. "You're missing something. But we'll fix that soon enough."

I glance up into his eyes, which are sparkling as much as my new jewellery.

I'm finding that Bryce is mentioning marriage more often since my stalker abducted me. That incident not only marked me, it scarred him too because he wasn't there to protect me.

He takes my hand. "Come, we'd better go. We're late, as usual."

Pops is at the door, ushering us in for dinner at his table. He's not mad that we're a bit late, but glowing and happy. He holds Leena's hand and rubs it with his thumb.

When we ask where Brooke is, Pops waves his hand and says, "She's a little under the weather, so I told her to stay in and relax."

The conversation flows easily throughout dinner, and then after dessert we take our drinks and follow Pops beyond the two large double doors outside.

The dance floor is dotted with tables around the outer edge and dimly lit with strings of white lights, setting the atmosphere to intimate. It is crowded, but Bryce and I find a spot and dance there.

Pops can't hide the smile on his face as he holds Leena on the dance floor.

My mind floats off, thinking about how heart-wrenching it must have been for Pops to leave the only woman he's ever loved and his only child to follow a dream. I wonder how many other people have done that in life, and whether they regret it.

"Earth to Keera."

"Sorry. I was lost in thought."

"What were you thinking about?"

"I was thinking how difficult it must have been for Pops to leave Ma and Leena when she was only six."

Bryce whispers back. "A little selfish, in my eyes." He shrugs his shoulders. "Just saying."

"I wonder if he regrets it. I mean, look at him. He doesn't want to let her go. You can see the love in his eyes."

"I'd put money on it. He regrets it." Bryce holds me tight. "I could never do that. I'd never be able to live without you."

My eyes start to water from his heart-felt declaration. "I love you, Babe. And I want to tell you how grateful I am for taking the time off of work to be with me and for this unbelievable vacation. I'll never forget it."

"You're welcome. I love you, Angel." He holds me close as we dance, and I melt into his embrace, relishing our intimate moment.

Pops and Austin take turns dancing with Leena, and Bryce and I stay out on the dance floor for most of the night, enjoying each other's touch and improving our dance skills. We thank Pops for a wonderful evening and he tells us to meet him in the paradise lounge for a late-lunch before we leave.

We all agree and make our way back to the bungalow.

Once inside, Bryce steps closer to me. He runs his finger along the material that's gathered across my breasts. "This sexy little dress has been driving me-and every other guy on the dance floor-nuts all night."

Oh, sure. You notice when men stare at me, but you don't notice when women look at you. I think he does. He just doesn't let on he knows. Not a conceited bone in his body. I love that about him.

"So you like my dress?"

"I love it, but you already knew that by the way my hand was travelling up your leg." His hands slip underneath and he runs them over the globes of my ass. His finger slips inside me while his palm massages my clit. His mouth takes mine and I moan from the intense feeling of him pushing his tongue and finger deeper and deeper. "Damn woman, the sounds you make. I love them all."

To my surprise, he steps back, but then he pulls me into the bedroom. His hands go to work stripping my dress off of me. It falls to the floor in a puddle of fabric. He holds my hand and I step out as gracefully as I can.

Before he can protest, I grab the hem of his shirt. "Let me undress you."

He holds up his hands surrendering. "I'm all yours. Go to it."

I pull his shirt up and over his head and toss it on the chair. My hands skim down his chest, feeling every ripple and well-defined muscle. "All of it?" I kiss one meaty pec muscle, gently running my lips to the other.

"Every inch, Angel. My body is all yours."

My sight lands on the smattering of hair on his well-defined chest and I kiss gently.

I bet those nurses would love to be doing this right now. But I keep that to myself.

"Babe, I love your body," I glance up into his eyes, which are staring intently back at me. My gaze travels down his body taking in the sight of his eight-pack abs, my hands caressing gently. When I reach the button on his pants, I undo it and unzip him. I pull them down with his boxers and he steps out of them, kicking them away.

"Back to where I was." My fingers slide along the indent of his sexy V. The muscled indent that cries out to be touched. His cock is so hard, it stands at attention stiffly. I desperately want to take it in my mouth, but I want to seduce him, like he does to me, so I run my finger across his belly button and down my happy trail. My hands fan out at his groin and caress downward, making sure I miss his vital organ.

"Enough! You're driving me mad."

I sigh. "But I'm having so much fun."

"My turn." His gaze becoming more intense.

My belly flutters with anticipation as Bryce lowers his luscious lips to mine and we kiss slowly, sensually, tongues dancing, exploring.

His lips continue kissing the corner of my mouth, then following a line to that soft spot behind my ear. He runs his tongue down my neck and surprises me by quickly spinning me around. He's behind me now, pressing his hard cock against my butt. He pulls my hair back and runs his tongue along my neck, sending shivers down my spine.

I move only to tilt my head giving him maximum exposure to my neck and the sensitive spots. I'm frozen, totally Immobile, hypnotized by his touch.

His cock rubs deliciously against my lower back and butt. "You love this."

"Mmm."

He continues for a bit and then switches to the other side. His arm snakes across my belly, up to my breast. His large hand cups it, feeling the weight. He tugs my nipple between his two fingers, sending a hot line to my groin.

I lie in bed listening to Bryce breathing deeply, my mind wandering to the way he made love to me-how gentle he was while taking the time to drive me into a wild frenzy until I was almost shaking with need, how aggressive he got when he was close, and the expressions on his face when he let go, but only after making sure he'd satisfied me first. And the affection he showed afterwards. It all makes me smile.

The bathroom light is still on, so I rise out of bed, careful not to disturb Bryce, and tip toe over to the vanity. I wash up, brush my teeth, and run a brush through my hair. Turning off the light, I make my way through the dark back to the bed, making sure I don't stub my toe this time, and gently lower myself into bed. Bryce doesn't stir.

It feels like I've only been sleeping for a couple hours when I'm awakened by the bathroom light shining in my face. Colton is standing over me, shaking me awake. As the grogginess fades, I see him holding one finger over his lips.

Panic stricken, I turn to see Bryce still in a dead sleep.

What the heck! I thought they left to go back on tour? Am I dreaming again or is he really here, standing over me?

I turn back and he's crooking his finger at me to follow him.
No. I'm not dreaming.
I go to get up and remember I'm naked.
He smiles, his drop-dead gorgeous smile.
I try to shoo him away, but he doesn't move. His smile changes to a mischievous grin. His head tilts, his eyebrow lifts and he smirks at me. Almost like he's daring me to get up.
I deliberately widen my eyes and tilt my head toward the door, motioning for him to get out.
He rolls his eyes at me, and walks into the next room.
I shake my head.
Once I see Colton's disappeared behind the wall, I gently rise out of bed and grab the closest thing to me, which is the sexy little dress Bryce bought me. I step inside, sliding it up my body adjusting it so it covers my breasts. I slip into the bathroom and swirl some mouthwash around so I don't knock Colton over with bad breath.
I look in the mirror. *I knew he was here the other night. I wasn't dreaming.* I spit out the mouthwash and turn off the bathroom light before going to find Colton.
He stands at the front door with it cracked open so we can see in the darkness. When I pass by him, he places his hand on my lower back, like Bryce does, and steers me out onto the front deck.
"I'm sorry for waking you, but I had to see you one last time."
"I thought you left to go back on tour."
"No. I wouldn't leave without saying what I need to say to you." He steps toward me. "The guys conjured up a plan to get me away from you. They said I'm not thinking straight. They tried to hook me up with Fiona and every other woman at the club, but they finally gave up when I told them I only see you. You're the one I want."
He steps closer and holds my hips.
"Colton-"

"Wait! Before you say anything, hear me out. Give me one night. One night with me and I could change your mind. I could make you happy. I'd give up this crazy life for you. I've made enough money that I could retire right now if I want to. We could build a luxurious home where ever you want, have maybe five kids, travel, see the world. I want you to see what I've seen. We could be so happy. You do want kids, right?"

I hesitate as he waits for my answer. "Someday I'd like to have kids, but Colton-"

He holds his finger over my lips. "I knew it. You've got that motherly vibe to you." He moves closer and lifts my chin so I'll look up at him. He gazes down in my eyes and holds me tight against his growing erection.

"Damn, the things I could do to you. I've imagined them in my head from the first day I met you."

I lean back, but he holds me steady.

He runs his hand down my cheek and neck. "I know our relationship won't happen right away, but when you and Bryce break up, give me a chance. Let me be the one." He searches my eyes. "Just think about it. And think about this." He holds the back of my head and dips me backwards, holding me in a helpless position. His tongue slides in my mouth, expertly dancing around my tongue.

I quickly pull away.

He reluctantly pulls me back up so I'm standing.

"Colton!" I say, scolding him.

What a kiss. I'm stunned. Frozen in place.

He kisses me again, taking me by surprise. Then he steps back and begins to back away. "Think about that kiss, and my lips and tongue all over you, and how good I could make you feel. Until I see you again. And I will, see you again."

"Bye, Colton." It's the only thing I can say because I'm in shock.

"Uh-uh." He shakes his head. "It's never goodbye. I'll be seeing you. Soon."

He flashes that gorgeous smile again and turns. I can see by the way he's strutting back to his bungalow that he's quite proud of himself.

What just happened here? I tried not to kiss him, but I was helpless, bent backwards and couldn't defend myself.

The taste of his kiss remains on my lips. I touch them. "Thank God I used mouthwash." I shake my head and tip-toe back into the bedroom. I'm relieved to see Bryce is still asleep.

I slip my dress off, lower my body back down onto the mattress, and cover myself with the sheet. Letting out a sigh, I lie there asking myself how I could have prevented what just happened.

Couldn't be done.

Bryce would have woken up if I hadn't gotten Colton out of here.

I lick my lips and I can still taste his kiss. It tastes of cinnamon.

Was that pre-meditated? Did he come here knowing he was going to kiss me?

I think about the kiss from beginning to end. How soft his lips were, how deftly his tongue moved, how he held me so I couldn't resist him. And then his last quick-but-powerful kiss.

He knew exactly what he was going to do before he came here.

My thoughts roam to everything he said to me. How he imagined doing all sorts of things to me from the first day he met me. How he'd give up touring for me, build a house wherever I want.

Five kids! Is he for real? He doesn't even know me. He can't possibly mean all that. Can he?

Shake your head Keera. He'll forget all about you once he goes back on tour and meets other women. Sleep. Get to sleep.

I turn to look at Bryce's perfect features in silhouette against the light of the alarm clock. His profile is amazingly beautiful: his strong jawline, long black lashes, perfect nose, and luscious lips. How I'd love to kiss him right now to let him know Colton's kiss didn't mean a damn thing, that only his kiss means the world to me.

17

SUDDENLY, I'M GUILT stricken.
What if he finds out?
He won't. Not if you don't tell him.

My mind's a scrambled mess and it takes me half an hour to fall asleep.

I wake a short while later, my chest heaving for my next breath. My eyes dart around the room frantically. Sweat forms at my temples. I'm physically shaking.

When I see Bryce lying next to me in a dead sleep, I realize I've had a bad dream-a nightmare.

I take a deep breath, gather my thoughts, and try to relax. I'm reliving those terrifying hours held in captivity by my stalker all over again.

My nightmares of Jake almost raping have grown less frequent lately, but my most recent ordeal has obviously affected me. I've been in denial, thinking it was no big deal now that I'm safe. I was wrong.

Just then, Bryce rolls over and wraps his arm and leg over me. I glance sideways to see if he's awake, but he's not.

I sigh contently. I'm safe in his arms. Right where I want to be.

I can't tell Bryce about my nightmare. He'll want to send me to a shrink and I don't want to go.

The rest of the night I was unable to fall into a deep sleep, due to Colton showing up in our bungalow and then the horrifying nightmare. By the time we sit down for our late-lunch with Pops, I'm yawning.

Pops' mood is mostly upbeat, though it sways a few times when a couple of his employees interrupt him with Leena. But I can see him struggling, trying hard not to be sad because Leena is leaving to go back home. He doesn't fool me.

Pops shakes Bryce and Austin's hand firmly and tells Austin to take care of his baby, then he turns to hug me.

His voice falters when he holds Leena's face in his hands and a tear slides down my face.

Bryce rubs my back and I wipe away the tear.

Saying goodbye is harder than I thought it would be, but we thank Pops for a great vacation and the use of the limo. He asks us to come back as soon as we can and to bring Leena's mom.

I haven't seen Brooke. I wonder if they broke up?

We check to make sure we haven't forgot anything in the bungalow, grab our luggage and then lock up. Standing on the front deck, I get a flashback of that kiss with Colton, and I'm guilt stricken again. I shake my head to get the thought out and roll our luggage to the main hotel.

Bryce and Austin stand to the right of the concierge desk talking, while Leena and I stand in line gabbing, waiting to hand in our key cards.

The room's noise level rises a couple notches, so I glance over to see what the commotion is. The band is shaking hands with Bryce and Austin.

My elbow nudges Leena's side to get her attention.

"Check out Bryce," Leena says. "His whole demeanour

changes when Colton comes around, but you can tell he's trying to play nice even though Colton wants to steal his ball."

"Ball? Meaning me?"

"Oh, yeah, any idiot can see that. And you will be telling me everything that went on here. When the boys go back to work, we're having a girl's day, just you and me, and you're spilling it-all of it! And you better not leave anything out. I won't tell Austin. This is between you and me. Promise."

Shit!

We hand in our keys and tell the concierge that everything was perfect, then walk over to Bryce, Austin, and the guys in the band.

"There you are, the beautiful Canadian girls." Colton hugs both of us. His hug lasts longer than it should and then he nuzzles his nose-against my neck, breathing in deeply.

I hope Bryce didn't see that.

"We had a good time partying with you guys. If we come back to Canada, we'll have to look you up." Reese gives us a hug and slaps Austin and Bryce on the back.

"You should," Austin says. "So where's the tour taking you now?"

I glance over at Colton. His intense inspection makes me feel self-conscious about what I'm wearing.

Bryce quickly tucks me into his side, wrapping his arm around my waist.

"Detroit, Ohio, Indiana, Illinois, and then we get another week off." Reese smiles.

"Damn, you'll be close to us. Only five hours away," Austin says.

Bryce is gathering up our luggage and Austin knows that's his cue.

They seem to know each other's moods without speaking. "You guys have a safe trip!"

"You too," Reese says.

I gather my luggage and turn to wave goodbye.

Colton lunges toward me and runs his hand down my arm to my elbow. He mouths, "I'll be seeing you."

Bryce, furious now, can't get me to the limo fast enough.

Grayson places our luggage in the trunk and even though Bryce is pissed off, he shakes Grayson's hand and asks him how he is. Bryce is always respectful.

Bryce doesn't say much most of the way to the airport; he just holds me close. Leena and Austin are busy talking, so I quietly ask Bryce if he's mad at me.

"No, I could never be mad at you." Bryce kisses the top of my head.

Once we get to the airport, Bryce seems to snap out of his bad mood.

We make our way through inspection and then Bryce steers us to a restaurant that serves alcohol. He must have noticed I'm a little anxious.

We talk and have a few drinks while we wait for our dinner, trying to kill time until our plane arrives.

As we walk through the terminal toward our gate, we see a crowd of people and in the middle is Von Jobin signing autographs. My eyes meet Colton's and he freezes as he watches us walk past. Some of his fans turn to see what has his attention and their eyes follow us too.

Our gate is approximately seven down from where we last saw Von Jobin signing autographs. We find a seat and wait. Bryce and Austin check their e-mails now that we have Wi-fi and exchange what's been going on at the cop shop and fire department.

After a long flight followed by the drive from Pearson Airport to Barrie, we leave our luggage in the foyer of Bryce's house, climb into bed, and fall asleep instantly.

I wake to the gentle touch of Bryce's cock against the crack of my butt, and his arm strung over me, holding my breast.

The sound of his breathing makes me think he's asleep, so I

don't move except for the slight push back so I can feel his cock firmly against me.

I lie there, relishing the feeling of it and of his hand cupping my breast. I think about our trip and how hard he got when we were looking at wedding rings. It makes me smile. He wants to get married. To me. And soon too.

His cock grinds hard against my butt and he pinches my nipples between two fingers. "Good morning, Beautiful."

I turn my head to look at him. "Good morning to you, Mr. Tall, Dark, and Gorgeous."

He rolls me over and climbs on top, surprising me with how quick he is. He takes his cock in his hand, pokes my pussy with it, and we're off to the races. It's a beautiful morning delight that lasts almost two hours.

When we sit at the breakfast bar, I can feel the after affects. I'm deliciously sore, but have no complaints.

I call Gramps to let him know our trip went well and to tell him I'll be coming to visit in a couple weeks.

Bryce overhears and surprises me by saying, "I'll come with you."

"Okay. Gramps would love to meet you."

"You think he'll let us sleep together? He might be old-fashioned."

"I've never brought anyone to meet him, so I guess we'll find out. He should be okay with it, though."

"So I'll be your first?"

"You're my first for a lot of things."

"Good!" Bryce says, content with my answer.

After our shower we head to the grocery store to stock up on a few things and later we go see Bryce's family.

"There they are." Deana walks from the kitchen to the living room archway. "Look at the tans on you two!"

"Hi, Ma." Bryce hugs and kisses his mom.

"Hi, Mrs. Hamilton."

"Deana." She corrects and gives me a hug. "It's so good to see you." She rubs my arms up and down. "I'm so sorry I couldn't make it to the hospital. I wanted to see you, but they wouldn't give me the time off work."

"Oh, it's okay. I was only there one day and I didn't want to stay that long."

"I'm so happy you're okay."

"Oh, yeah, I'm fine."

Deana hugs me again and I can feel all of the emotions she had felt for me during that ordeal, without words.

She leads us into the kitchen. "Austin and Leena are here already."

Bryce's dad and Ciara get up from the table and come over to hug me. Ciara gives Bryce a disgusted look and mumbles, but then she smiles and punches him in the arm.

Garrett pats Bryce on the back. "Good to see you two."

Austin nods. "It's about time you got here."

"We brought gifts." I hand them each a bag.

"You didn't have to," Deana says, surprised.

Garrett pulls out the tissue paper, unwrapping a t-shirt and a firefighter cup. Deana and Ciara, each unwrap a t-shirt, necklace, and earrings.

"Thank you," Deana says.

"I love it." Ciara runs her fingers over the crystal bling on the Aruba t-shirt. "Thank you."

"You didn't have to, but thank you. This is my new favourite cup," Garrett says, holding it high in the air.

"That's Keera. She loves buying gifts for everyone." Bryce wraps his arm around me and drags my chair closer.

I run my hand up his thigh underneath the table cloth.

"Keera, these are beautiful," Deana says, admiring the earrings. "Look at the detail."

"They caught my eye. I had to get them for us."

"You're staying for dinner, right?" Deana asks, as she tucks her gifts back in the bag.

"Only if you have enough," Bryce says as he goes to the fridge to get drinks for everyone.

"Of course. I was hoping you'd be coming over today."

As we start to tell them about our trip, Leena pulls out a stack of pictures and hands them around.

"This is our Harley excursion. Doesn't Austin look hot on a Harley?"

"Maybe I'll get one, since you like it so much." Austin wraps his arm around Leena's waist and pulls her close.

"Over my dead body!" Deana says loudly. "You know I don't like them. Too many people die. You of all people should know that."

Austin takes Deana's hand in his. "I was kidding, Ma. Calm down! I know you don't like them." He pats her hand reassuringly.

Deana relaxes. "Well, at least you were wearing helmets."

"You went horseback riding?" Ciara looks through a few more and when she sees the band she goes nuts. She stands with the picture in her hand, shaking it. "You did not meet Von Jobin!"

"Oh, yeah," Leena says. "And we're supposed to be in their new video."

"Get the hell out of here!" Ciara grabs the pictures away from Bryce. "Let me see those. Oh my God! Colton, Reese, Gavin, Drake, and Ryker."

"You know who they are?" I ask.

"And you guys didn't have a clue, right?" Ciara shakes her head in disgust.

"No, we didn't."

"Unbelievable! And you didn't get me an autograph?"

"Sorry, we didn't think." I shrug my shoulders.

"This picture's mine." Ciara holds it to her heart and then looks at it again, pointing at each one. "Look-every one of them is hot! So gorgeous." She glares at me and Leena. "You lucky little bitches."

"Ciara!" Both Deana and Garrett raise their voices at her.

Leena rubs it in more. "We got to spend three days with them. This is at the beach when we set off fifty sky lanterns for the video." She flips to another picture. "And the fireworks and the food."

"You took a picture of the food?" I ask.

"Hell, yeah! That was a nice spread." Austin says.

I smile. "Austin and his food."

"Keera got to dance with Colton?" Ciara asks loudly.

I cringe. Holy crap! Leena took a picture of that?

"I bet you didn't like that too much, eh Bryce?" Ciara looks at the picture and then at Bryce, waiting for an answer.

She always has to irritate him, at least once every visit.

Bryce slides his chair out and goes to the fridge. "Anyone want another?"

"Yeah, I'll take one. And get Leena a wine cooler." Austin says in that deep voice of his, leaning back on his chair as he looks over at Bryce digging in the fridge.

Bryce ignores Ciara's comment.

Ciara whispers in my ear. "Lucky little bitch."

I glance over at Bryce rummaging in the fridge and then give Ciara a half smile.

"And this is my dad's resort."

"Leena, this is beautiful." Ciara flips through the pictures. "Who's the little girl?"

"That's Alyssa. Bryce patched her up when she and her mom were in a scooter accident."

"Oh, Bryce, that was so nice of you." Deana walks over to rub Bryce's back.

"Wow, she really took a liking to you," Ciara states.

"She was cute," Bryce says.

"She didn't want to let Bryce go when we took her to the hospital." Leena adds.

"Her mom said she's usually afraid of men, but she loved Bryce." I pat Bryce on the inside of the thigh now that he's come back to sit beside me.

"And this is Austin driving the scooter back to Alyssa's house."

"What a geek," Ciara says, getting her dig in.

"And here's us on the Harleys again. He doesn't look like a geek here. He's hot!" Leena says.

"Thanks, Hun, for sticking up for me." Austin rubs Leena's shoulders.

I'm surprised how at ease Leena is, considering this is her second time meeting Austin's family. That's her personality, whereas I'm shy and it's harder for me to be at ease. But I'm getting there.

Garrett finally speaks. "Well, it looks like you had fun."

"Yes, very nice pictures," Deana says as she walks around the kitchen island. "It all looks so beautiful."

As we help Deana with dinner, I go to the fridge to get some cheese out and Leena comes to whisper in my ear. "I'm coming over tomorrow for our girls' day and you're spilling it-every last detail."

I glance sideways at her. "All right."

When I close the door and place the cheese on the counter, I glance over at Bryce and see the curious expression on his face.

Our night goes well. Dinner is delicious and laughter fills the room.

Ciara gets her digs in with Austin and Bryce and then they tag team her, throwing insults back and forth, and we stick up for her.

Ciara's smiles when we support her.

We thank Deana and Garrett for everything, give hugs and kisses as we say our goodbyes, and then walk down the driveway, gabbing with Leena and Austin. When we look back, Garrett is holding Deana, and Ciara is standing a few feet away on the front porch, waving.

As we're backing out of the driveway, Bryce's attention seems to be elsewhere, like in the rear view mirror. He waits for Austin to pull out in front of him.

"I had a good time, I love your family."

"They love you. And, yeah, we always have a good time." Bryce glances continuously in the rear view mirror.

"That was nice that your mom wanted to come see me in the hospital."

"She was pissed when they wouldn't give her the time off."

He keeps glancing, obviously preoccupied as we drive a few streets over.

Bryce opens the garage door and backs in. "Damn it!"

"What?"

"Lindsay's here. Stay right there."

Lindsay pulls her car in the driveway right in front of Bryce's truck. Bryce gets out and walks over to her door and talks to her through the rolled-down window.

I watch his every move, paying attention to his body language, looking for any signs that he still loves her. This is our first encounter with Lindsay since our huge fight where we almost broke up. I promised myself at the time that if I saw any signs, I'd call it quits, but now that we've been through so much together, how could I?

Bryce shows no emotion through most of the conversation and it surprises me that Lindsay is not throwing a fit. She's calm.

This is really strange.

I have a sudden urge to get out of the truck. *Should I? Or should I stay? If I get out it won't be a good situation for Bryce because he'll have to referee a cat fight. I better stay here.*

Lindsay looks straight ahead at me and then Bryce turns to look at me. Then they continue their conversation.

They're obviously talking about me. I wish I could hear what they're saying.

It looks like their conversation is over. Bryce backs away and Lindsay rolls up her window. She looks straight at me again with an intense look of hatred and then backs out of the driveway.

I get out of the truck and walk to Bryce. "That went well. What'd she say?"

"She said she won't be bothering us anymore. She says she has a new boyfriend."

"Oh? And do you believe her?"

"I hope she does. Then maybe she'll leave us alone."

"What else did she say?"

"That she's sorry for all the drama."

"Oh." I don't ask anything else. If he wants to tell me, he will.

We walk into the house with Bryce guiding me with that simple touch.

Once were in bed, we spoon and cuddle, but Bryce quickly falls asleep and I lie there wondering why he didn't want to have sex. Is it because he has to wake up early to go to work? Or was he thinking about Lindsay and her new boyfriend. I quickly dismiss thoughts about Lindsay.

Bryce has just left for work when Leena comes knocking at the door.

"Damn, you're up early," I say, opening it wide.

"Yup, couldn't wait to get here." Leena slams the door and pulls me upstairs to the kitchen. "Spill it!"

"Would you like a tea or a coffee?"

"You're stalling. Keera, I promise I won't say a word to Austin or Bryce. This is between you and me. No one else."

"Fine." I pause collecting my thoughts. "Remember when we were in Colton's arms taking that picture and his hand was on my hip rubbing it?"

"He was rubbing your hip? He wasn't rubbing mine."

"Colton had his finger behind my bikini bottoms rubbing me and Bryce saw him."

"Shit, eh?"

"Bryce was pissed. He dragged me into the trees and asked me if I wanted him." I hand her a tea and take a sip of mine. "We argued for a bit and then he said I know what we need. He pulled me further into the trees and fucked me against a huge boulder."

"Nice."

"But someone snuck up on us and was hiding behind a tree."

"Really? Who?"

"Colton."

"Get out!"

"I couldn't say anything because Bryce would have beaten him to a pulp."

"So what did you do?"

"Nothing. We had mind-blowing sex with Colton watching, and when I looked over he came out from behind the tree with his shorts dropped to the ground and he was stroking his cock."

"Holy fuck! What a turn on. How frickin' hot was that?"

"Mind-blowing, like I said. He shot up in the air so high. I swear the man hasn't had sex in a year."

Leena shivers. "Holy crap I'm having a visual right now." She opens her eyes. "You are one of the luckiest women I know."

"He wasn't done yet. When we switched positions, I looked behind and he was going at it again."

"Damn, I wish I could have been there. That man is so hot!"

"I know. That's what probably pisses Bryce off the most, and I know how he feels. Every time Fiona came around him, I wanted to kill her."

"Yeah, me too. That bitch was just too perfect."

"I know. I had a bad dream about Fiona and Bryce."

"You did?"

"In my dream they were coming out of the elevator hand in

hand. I called out his name. He stopped and looked at me, but that bitch pulled him away. He left me for her, so I had an awful urge to go jogging to look better than her. So as I'm jogging back down the beach I see someone sitting on a lounge chair. I was thinking it was Bryce because I left him a note to join me when he woke up, but it was Colton. He was videotaping me as I was jogging in my white bikini."

"No!"

"Yes. And then he got close to me. I told him he might want to back away because I was all sweaty, but he said 'Do you think sweat bothers me? The closer I get to you, the happier I am.'"

Leena's eyes widen.

"He held me close and looked in my eyes and said we shared something beautiful together and he wants more."

"Oh, no!"

"Thank God Bryce came jogging up and saved me."

"Bet it didn't go over well with him that you were alone with Colton, the rock god."

"No. It didn't. Bryce was pissed that I hadn't woken him up and Colton was the last person he wanted to see me with. Oh, and also he couldn't believe how naïve I was for giving Colton my e-mail address."

"You gave him your e-mail address?"

"I did. But only because he said he'd send a copy of the video to me. Maybe I am naïve, but he was so smooth about it. You would have given it to him too."

"Probably. I would've given him anything. The man is hot!"

I chuckle. "So after our fight, when we calmed down and were back to normal, I took off running down the beach and told Bryce to catch me. He tackled me in the ocean. When I came out of the water with my wet white bikini, Colton was hiding behind a tiki hut, videotaping me again."

"Bet he got a good shot there. Did Bryce see him?"

"Bryce was too busy checking out how my bathing suit was clinging to me."

"Hit that button for the kettle. I think I want another tea."

"So remember when Bryce took the call from Grant and Colton asked me to dance?"

"Yeah."

"Colton held me close and said he'd remember how I feel against his body for the rest of his life. Then he ran his nose along my neck, inhaling, and when I stiffened, he said, 'I'm sorry, I can't help myself. I've been thinking of you constantly from the first time I met you.'"

"Get out! What'd you say?"

"I said, 'I don't think Bryce would appreciate it.'"

I hand Leena her tea.

"Thanks."

"So then he pulled me close and was feeling my butt and when he felt I had no panties on he grinned down at me with that irresistible dimple of his. The bugger knew I could feel how hard he was getting."

"Damn, girl, this is getting juicy."

"So during that conversation, he'd said he's never felt someone feel so good in his arms. I didn't know what to say so I asked, 'Don't you have a girlfriend?'"

"What'd he say to that?"

"'Not yet, but just so you know I'm a very patient and stubborn man and when I want something this bad, I wait. And I always get what I want.' Leena, the intensity in his eyes made me shiver. He seemed like he was dead serious."

"Really?"

"That's when Bryce saved me again. Later, when we lined up for the barbeque and Bryce was occupied with his food, Colton slipped behind me, holding my lower back, and said 'I just need to touch you, to be close to you.' Leena, you should've seen the look in his eyes."

"He always looks at you like that."

"Yeah, so anyway, later on that night, when Bryce and I were dancing, Colton cut right in and asked Bryce if he could dance with me."

"I bet that was awkward."

"Real awkward, especially when Bryce hesitated for a bit. I thought there might be a fight. Only because the last time after Colton was done dancing with me Bryce whispered, 'That fucker's really getting on my nerves.' But Bryce held it together and backed away, giving Colton permission to dance with me."

"Shit, Keera, I had no idea what you were going through. I mean I saw a few things, but for most of it, I was in my own little world with Austin."

"So Colton held me at arm's length for a bit and then, all of a sudden, he tightened his hold on me. I'd turned to see what Bryce's reaction was and Fiona was dancing with him. I bet Colton sent her over to keep Bryce busy."

"I saw that. She came over with that flirty expression on her face and pulled Bryce onto the dance floor, but she probably regretted it because he was so stiff and she could only get one-word answers out of him. Austin was laughing his ass off. He kept saying 'Look at him, look at him.' Bryce's attention was one-hundred percent on you and Colton."

"Anyway, while we were dancing, Colton said I was all he could think about right now and he was trying to figure out how he could get me alone, without Bryce. So then I told him Bryce was a little over-protective because of the ordeal we had gone through before going to Aruba. Well then, of course, he was digging, but I didn't tell him anything."

"Oh, shit."

"What?"

"Colton asked us later on that night when you and Bryce left and we, uh, kind of told him."

"Great."

"Sorry." Leena shrugs her shoulders. "It's not like you'll ever see him again."

"True. So that night I woke to the bathroom light shining in my face and Colton was standing over me."

Leena's eyes widen, but she waits for me to continue.

"But when I focused again he was gone, so I thought maybe I dreamt it, but I didn't because he came back the last night we were there and was shaking me awake, motioning for me to come with him."

"What? Did Bryce see him?"

"No. He was sleeping."

"How'd he get in?"

"I don't know. Maybe he hopped the fence and came through the door where the hot tub was. We might have forgotten to lock it."

"Got lots of use out of that hot tub, too, eh?"

"Yeah." My mind wanders back for a few seconds. The loud noise we heard behind the fence when I was giving Bryce a personal dance-was that Colton?

18

DID COLTON SEE me naked? Was he looking over the fence hoping to see me and Bryce have sex again?

"So what'd you do?" Leena brings me back from my wayward thoughts.

"I panicked and turned to see if Bryce was awake. Thank God he was sleeping. So then I went to get up, forgetting I was naked and you should have seen Colton smile."

"Oh yeah, I bet."

"He finally left and I got dressed, then I went to find him. He was waiting for me at the front door. We went outside to talk. He said, 'Sorry for waking you, but I had to see you one last time.' I said, 'I thought you left to go back on tour.' He said, 'No, I wouldn't leave without saying what I need to say.' He said his band took him to the club to get him away from me. They tried to hook him up with Fiona and every other woman at the club. They finally gave up when Colton told them that he only sees me, that I'm the one he wants."

"Keera, he wants you bad. What'd you say?"

"I didn't know what to say except-'Colton!' But he quickly

shut me up with, 'Please just hear me out. One night. Just give me one night and I could change your mind. I know I could make you happy. I'd give up this crazy life for you.' He said he's made enough money to retire right now if he wanted to. He said we could build a luxurious home wherever I want."

"He said that?"

"I'm not done yet. He wants five kids, and to travel and see the world. He wants me to see what he's seen."

"He's really thought this through, hasn't he?"

"Apparently he doesn't sleep well, so he's got a lot of time to think."

"He thinks of you while he jacks off."

"Leena, that's what I love about you. You have no filter. Whatever comes to your head, you say."

"What? I'm serious. He probably replays you getting fucked in the jungle in his head over and over again, while he's jacking off. That's definitely in his spank bank and it's never leaving."

"You crack me up."

"You love me."

"I know I do. So then, he got even closer and pulled me against his hard on. He said, 'I've imagined all the things I can do to you in my head.'"

"See, I told you. Spank bank." Leena gets off the bar stool and tugs me to the couch. "My ass is getting sore, but seriously, think about what it would be like to fuck his brains out. I'm getting wet just thinking about it." She squirms on the couch and clenches her thighs.

"Leena, you're one of a kind."

"You can't tell me you haven't thought about it. I'll call you a liar right to your face." She glares at me with those eyes. "Well... I'm waiting."

I hesitate. "Okay, so I've thought about it."

"Ha! I knew it. And?"

"And he's hot. And I know he'd be great in bed by the way he is. He's got that sexy cool personality like Bryce and Austin have."

"They definitely have it."

"So anyway, he ran his hand down my cheek and neck."

"Ooh. Intimate."

"He said, 'I know our relationship won't happen right away, but when you and Bryce break up, give me a chance. Let me be the one.' He said, 'just think about it and think about this.' And then he dipped me backwards and kissed me."

"Holy shit! He slipped you the tongue?"

"Yes! And then another quick kiss, and he told me to think about his lips and tongue all over me and how good he could make me feel."

"So how was it?"

"I try not to think about it."

"Yeah, right! Did you kiss him back?"

"The man can kiss."

"But did you kiss him back?" Leena repeats.

"I tried not to. I was in a helpless position, bent backwards."

"Bullshit! You did."

"It all happened so quickly."

"Good answer. So what'd you do then?"

"I said, 'Goodbye, Colton,' because he was backing away from me with that devilish smile on his face."

"Oh, that tease!"

"He said, 'Uh-uh. It's never goodbye. I will see you again.'"

"Keera, you've got to tell me if he contacts you. I mean right away."

"You know, after he spilled his heart out to me I thought, he doesn't even know me. How could he possibly mean all that?"

"Keera, haven't you ever heard of love at first sight?"

"Yes, I've heard of it. Bryce said he had it with me, and technically I guess I had it with him too. I mean, I thought he was gorgeous from first sight, but love… you need to know the person first."

"It sure as hell sounds like he meant every bit of it."

"He'll forget about me when he goes back on tour with all those women."

"Maybe."

"You have to promise me you won't tell Bryce or Austin. Not one thing I've told you."

"Did I tell them where you were when you had your meltdown over Lindsay?"

"It wasn't a meltdown. And you would've flipped out if Austin looked at Sydney with love in his eyes as he was bringing her back home after her meltdown and then left you behind with his family and didn't say a damn word."

"Okay, it wasn't a meltdown." She rolls her eyes like she's not convinced. "I promise, I won't tell a soul. So that's it? You didn't forget anything?"

"No, that's pretty much how it happened. Anything happen to you on our trip?"

"Reese would rub up against me a few times when Austin wasn't looking and then he'd grin at me. The horn dog. That's another one that's irresistible. Bet he'd be fun."

"Like Ciara said, every one of them is hot."

"So what's for breakfast?"

"I could make bacon and eggs, or we can go out. I need to buy some new bedding. The first thing I'm doing when I get home is burning the stuff I have now."

"Think he jacked off in your bed?"

I shake my head. "Leena, you are something else."

"Don't tell me you haven't thought about it? I'm just saying it out loud."

"I try not to think about it."

"They most likely took your bedding for evidence. You know that, eh?"

"Maybe."

Monday with Leena is a fantastic day filled with shopping and laughter. Tuesday, she drives home to Huntsville because she has to get back to work. Wednesday, the guys have their hockey game and I sit with the Hamilton's. Bryce's team ends up winning that one too, but not by much-the final score is Firefighters 1, Cops 0. Dante and Jax tease Bryce, saying he's lost his touch from too much vacationing, and Bryce retaliates by holding them in a head lock and banging their heads together. Their playfulness makes me smile. They've definitely missed him.

Wednesday, after the game Bryce gets to come home with me and sleep. The rest of the week he has to sleep at the station again, working around the clock.

The week goes by quickly, and then Bryce has a couple days off again so we travel to my house in Huntsville.

Bryce watches me intently as we enter my house, probably to see if I'm freaked out about my stalker being found in my bed. Last night, I woke up in a panic, sweating, from another nightmare of my stalker hovering over me again. Bryce wasn't home to feel my reaction to it, which I'm thankful for. I'm hoping these nightmares will pass and I won't have to tell Bryce how this has affected me.

I observe everything that's out of place as I inch my way to the bedroom, peering in.

Leena is right; the cops have stripped the bed for evidence. With Bryce's help, I make the bed with my new sheets and comforter. I inspect the new window and then notice a few things out of place, which I quickly restore to their rightful places.

I feel Bryce watching me cautiously.

"You keep looking at me."

"We can go to the cabin if you want to."

"If we do that, the bastard wins. No. I will not let him hold me hostage, unable to live in my own house. I need to feel comfortable." I step toward him and lift his shirt a fraction to play with the hair below his belly button. "Can you help me forget by making love to me in my bed?"

"Angel." He holds me close. "You're the strongest woman I know."

"That's because I have you."

"Anything you could ever want, I will give you. Let's start here."

His hands slip under my shirt and rub my back while he lowers his lips to mine and kisses me softly, knowing exactly what I need.

His gentle hands and the tenderness of his kiss make my heart quiver and melt.

We spend two days tangled in each other's arms.

With every passing moment, I feel more at ease in my home. Bryce doesn't want our days of bliss to end, so he convinces me to go back with him to Barrie, though it doesn't take a lot of convincing. I love spending time with him.

During the week, when I go grocery shopping, I find myself a little paranoid, thinking I see Lindsay's car in Bryce's rear-view mirror. But then as I walk around the store, I realize I'm not being paranoid. She's here. She's watching me from a distance. When I catch her, she quickly turns away. What is she up to?

When I get back to Bryce's, I text Leena to ask her opinion. She tells me she's on her way to visit Austin and she'll see me tonight at the hockey game.

Leena and I sit with the Hamilton family and I'm stuck between Leena and Sydney who are throwing darts at each other. Leena still wants to straighten her out. To let Sydney know not to waist her time thinking about Austin. He's taken.

Bryce's team wins again: Firefighters 2, Cops 1.

We gather in the lobby, when the game is finished, unthawing from the cold arena. Leena misses her opportunity. Sydney slips out the side door before Leena has a chance to talk to her.

The next morning, Leena bursts through Bryce's door without knocking and comes upstairs, where I'm preparing tonight's dinner. "Hey, girlfriend?"

"What the hell! You don't even knock anymore? What if me and Bryce were having a quickie on the stairs?"

"Listen to you. Have you ever done that?"

"It starts out there, but they're a little uncomfortable so we move to other rooms."

"No cushion on those stairs. What are you making?"

"Thought I'd try to make Deana's famous Au Gratin potatoes."

"Yum. You're getting comfortable with them."

"Yeah. Do you want a tea?"

"Sure. So about Lindsay since I didn't get to talk to you about it last night. I think she's bullshitting. She doesn't have a boyfriend. If she did, she wouldn't be following you around."

"That's what I thought."

"Did you tell Bryce?"

"No, I haven't. Only if she gets weird again."

Leena sits on the stool at the breakfast bar behind my lap top and fires it up. "So what's on the agenda today?"

"Well, I was supposed to go hand out resumes, but things have changed. Do you want to go jogging? I need a workout." I hand Leena her tea."

"Thanks. Resumes? Why?" Leena takes a sip.

"I've been thinking while I'm here in Barrie, I could work while Bryce is working."

"What the hell for? You don't need the money."

"To keep busy. I clean the house, exercise, make dinner, but it gets a little lonely when Bryce has to work around the clock. It feels like I should do something with my life."

"I don't think Bryce is going to like that. He likes having you home when he gets time off. He doesn't have to work around anyone's schedule except his own. And he likes you waiting on him."

"I told him my idea and he held me and said, 'I like having you here with me.'"

"Smart man. He didn't slam your idea. He's hoping you'll forget all about it and it'll pass."

"Yeah, well, maybe tomorrow I'll go hand them out."

Leena focuses on the laptop screen and says, "Hey, I heard this song on the way over."

"Oh, yeah? Who is it by?"

"The pretty reckless. Remember *The Grinch Who Stole Christmas?*"

"Yeah."

"This is little Cindy Lou Who." Leena turns the lap-top so I can see.

"Get out! She grew up." I come around the breakfast bar to watch the video. "That's it, you go girl. Show what your mama gave you. Dang, that's a skimpy outfit."

"Ya think? It's a couple pieces of tape across her tits and crotch. What's this?" Leena clicks on something else and we both watch the video playing.

"Is this Von Jobin?" As I'm asking, I realize it is.

"That's it? Only a thirty-second preview?" Leena says, clicking away at my keyboard.

"Play it again."

"Okay." We're glued to the lap-top screen. "Oh crap, that's us. I didn't realize it the first time." Leena adjusts the screen to maximize. "That's better, let's play this from the beginning again. This is us walking along the pool." She points to the screen. "Check out the sexy butts on those two. Christ, where the hell was that camera man. Lying on the ground?" Leena slows down the video.

"Damn, that's a good shot he got from underneath." I turn my head sideways as I focus in on our butts.

"Yeah, I'd say so."

"Look. That's when Bryce got pissed off that Colton was rubbing my hip." I point to the screen.

"Look how the camera man zooms into that. Jesus, Keera, look at the way Colton's looking at you."

"Bryce is not going to like this video."

"We all knew that. Hey, look, there we are again. That was when we laid out in the sun that day, when the guys left us to get a drink, and before Colton and Reese came over to ask us to be in the video."

"That's when I undid my top."

"You knew they'd show that. Male photographers."

"Where the hell was the camera man? I didn't even see him."

"He was close," Leena points out. "He got a shot of Reese sitting on your chair… us diving in the pool… us coming out of the pool."

"Oh, shit. Remind me not to where my pink bikini in the water."

"You can't see that much… I guess." Leena bites her bottom lip and her eyes widen. "Okay. Yeah. I'll remind you next time."

"That's it? It's done?"

"It's a preview to see if the fans like the song and the video. Keera, look at the comments."

"Love it. Want more." "Amazing song." "Can't get enough of it."

"Damn, Keera. They've got a million hits and it's only been out two days."

"I wonder if Colton sent me a complete version of it." I reach for my purse on the counter, pull out my phone and search through my e-mails. "Nope. Nothing."

"Maybe they haven't finished it yet?"

"Yeah, maybe."

"Let's play this one more time and listen to the words."

I knew the day I met you,
I'd never be the same.
From that first touch,
Knew I'd never want,
Anything so much.
I watch the video I made of you every day,
And my heart breaks.
Give me a chance,
Whatever it takes.
Let me be the one to kiss you,
Let me be the one to touch you.
These other women, I see none.
You're the one I want,
The one I need,
Someone real in my life.
Let me be the one to hold you,
Let me be the one to make you smile.

"Grab me a pen and paper," Leena says. "I'm writing this down."

"It is a good song." I hand Leena the pen and paper and go back to finishing my potatoes.

She goes through the video several times until she gets it all down on paper. "Keera, have you been listening? This is about you. He wrote this song for you. He's spilling his heart so you'll listen to him."

I read what she has written and it hits me, but in my mind I'm denying it. "Maybe it's for someone else."

"Keera." She shakes her head with a disgusted look on her face.

"What? He could have found someone else. Or maybe he had someone else in mind when he wrote this."

"You don't actually believe yourself, do you?"

"If he wrote this for me, Bryce is going to snap. Tell me you won't bring this to Austin or Bryce's attention."

"Not if you don't want me to."

"Thanks." I place the lid on the crock pot and turn it on low. "Okay, let's go jogging."

Leena claps her hands together, looking excited. "I can't wait to hear the rest of the song. This is getting interesting."

"You're enjoying this, aren't you?"

"Hell, yeah." Leena closes the lap-top. "We'd better dress warmly. It's cold out there."

As we're jogging down the sidewalk on Bryce's street, I spot a blue car trailing behind us.

"When we cross onto the other side, check out the blue car that's hanging back a little."

"All right. Who is it?" Leena asks.

"Lindsay."

"Maybe she's planning on running us over." Leena chuckles.

"Never thought of that."

We run through the side streets until we get to a bike trail and stay on that for a couple miles, losing Lindsay, but when we head back and come off the trail, Lindsay's waiting for us. "There she is. You have to give her points for being so patient," Leena says.

"We'd better keep an eye on her so we can jump out of the way," I say, looking in her direction.

"Can you picture the headline? 'Joggers have near miss as car plows through them. Driver says gas petal got stuck.'"

"What imaginations we have." I giggle.

"I'm telling you, don't put anything past her. She's following you for a reason."

"Yeah, I've seen her in full-crazy-mode. But she's supposedly on her meds."

Lindsay hangs back and watches us with no incident, so I don't see a reason to bring the situation to Bryce's attention.

Dinner at the Hamilton's is great and before we know it Bryce has a couple of days off again.

The temperature drops considerably during the night and we awake to a significant amount of snow on the ground. I call Gramps to let him know we're on our way to North Bay, and he tells me to be careful because they already have close to a foot of snow and more is on the way. He asks me if I want to postpone the trip for another time, but Bryce says we'll be fine. He has four wheel drive and they'll be out with the snow plows already.

I've already packed our bags and left them in the foyer, so we can grab them and go. The traffic moves slowly as we drive through Barrie, but we pick up speed once we get to Highway 11. One lane is clear and the other is snow covered. Bryce passes the slower cars and then gets back in to the clear lane. He doesn't seem to be nervous driving in this bad weather. I know I'd be white-knuckled and tense the whole way, but I still would have driven. Bad weather makes me nervous, but it doesn't stop me.

Once we get to Gravenhurst, the snowflakes are huge-the size of a golf ball and it's a total white-out. We can only see about ten feet in front of us.

Bryce slows down and pulls over. When I look to my right, I can vaguely see an accident has just occurred. "Angel, call 911 and tell them there's an accident with a car and a transport truck. Tell them to send fire and ambulance. Highway 11 at the Gravenhurst exit." Bryce springs into action, grabbing his coat and gloves and heading over to a badly damaged car, trudging through the deep snow. He disappears into the storm and I can no longer see him.

I call while I bundle up and grab a blanket from our luggage in the back seat. The 911 operator tells me they've received a couple of calls and fire and ambulance have been dispatched and are on their way.

The snow is deep, so I head in the direction Bryce went, following his footsteps, running and jumping to get to him. The truck driver is out of the cab and helping Bryce pry apart the metal roof, which has partially collapsed on top of its occupants. When I look through the broken passenger window, I see a woman with blood on her face and hands, and she's asking for her husband, Ken. With further inspection, I see Ken pinned and the metal wrapped around him. He's bleeding heavily and not responding to his wife's questions.

I wrap her in the blanket and try to console her by telling her my name and Bryce's. She tells me her name is Susan and I tell her Bryce is a firefighter in Barrie to reassure her that he is capable of getting her out.

Bryce stands on the hood of the car yanking some metal up and out of the way with the metal bar the truck driver handed him. "Angel, cover her face. Some glass might fly."

I do as I'm told and then look away.

After Bryce gets the metal free, he jumps down off the hood and comes to the passenger door. I move out of the way so he can get some leverage as he tries to pry open the door. The muscles in his neck strain as he pulls, but it still won't budge. He shoves the pry bar between the frame and the top of the door and reefs on it, pulling it down with all his weight. It loosens a bit, so he repositions the pry bar and pulls on it again. It finally opens.

I'm so proud of him that tears start to form in the corner of my eyes.

We quickly attend to Susan, making sure she is okay and checking to see if she's pinned elsewhere.

The sound of sirens wailing in the distance is welcome to my ears and relief washes over me when fire and ambulance arrive at the scene. I tell Susan it won't be long and they'll have her in the warm ambulance. I give her good arm a gentle squeeze. Bryce and I move out of the way and the firefighters go to work extricating her from the vehicle.

Now that the adrenaline rush is over, I'm freezing and start to shiver. Bryce wraps me in a hug to warm me up as he tells police that the accident had already occurred when we came upon it.

A few firefighters greet Bryce and shake his hand as they walk past us.

Bryce sees the confused look on my face, and he answers my silent question. "Gravenhurst fire college. It's just around the corner. I've done quite a few courses here and got to know a few guys."

"Oh."

I watch as the firefighters set up the Jaws of Life and they work diligently to extricate Ken from the car.

"Angel, go hop in the truck. You're freezing. I'll be there in a couple of minutes."

"Okay." As soon as I get in the truck, I start the engine and crank up the heat. The ambulance attendants load Susan onto the gurney and then into the ambulance. I watch Bryce as he talks to the fire chief for a few minutes. The chief shakes Bryce's hand and then Bryce makes his way back to the truck. Once he climbs in, he grasps my knee and gently squeezes. "Thanks for your help, Angel."

"No problem. Is Susan's husband going to be okay?"

Bryce shakes his head.

"He died?"

19

"YES. HER HUSBAND died."

"Oh, my God!"

Bryce pulls me close. "Is this the first death you've encountered besides your parents?"

"And Gram. Yes."

"I'm sorry you had to see that."

"You see this all the time?"

"It was tough at first, but it gets easier. You sure you're okay?"

"I'm fine."

Bryce gets back on the highway. The snow has slowed down a bit, so he drives faster.

My thoughts are scattered. "My parents went through that. I hope they didn't suffer."

"Hopefully they went together, fast."

"Yeah." I sit in silence, thinking about my mom and dad and our life together instead of the accident. I can't change anything, so why torture myself?

After a couple minutes of Bryce glancing at me with a concerned look, I finally snap out of it. "You were amazing back there. You saved her life."

"I hope she'll be okay."

"I hope so too. Her whole life has been changed in a split second, not to mention the lives of her children and grandchildren, if they have any."

"We see how accidents change people's lives forever." Bryce squeezes my knee.

We drive in and out of white-outs, and just as were passing Burk's Falls, we see another car that's slid off the road. Bryce pulls over, jumps out, and checks on the occupants. When he climbs back in the truck, his hair and eye lashes are covered in snowflakes. "No one inside. They must have gotten a ride."

"Nice eyelashes."

"You think it's funny, eh?"

"Babe, you're the Guardian Angel of the Highway. The White, Guardian Angel." I chuckle

"Aren't you cute?" He tugs me close and holds my knee.

"This is a little crazy out here. Maybe we should've postponed," I say, a little worried.

"We'll be okay. Another forty-five minutes and we'll be there."

Gramps is standing at the front door when we pull in the driveway. We grab our luggage and head inside.

"Give your Gramps a kiss. I was worried about you."

"Hi, Gramps. This is Bryce." I give Gramps a kiss. "We're fine." I move out of the entrance and more into the living room, so Bryce and Gramps can shake hands.

"Good to meet you, sir. Keera's told me so much about you."

"Good to meet you, Bryce. Call me James. Come in, come in."

The kitchen is at the back of Gramps house and down the

hall to the right is Gramps bedroom, laundry room and his wood shop. To the left of the house is my room, and the large bathroom.

"It's bad out there. We saw an accident-a car and a transport truck. Bryce pried open the passenger door, where Susan was pinned and Ken, her husband, died."

"Come in the kitchen so we can talk about this."

We tell Gramps everything that happened at the accident as we eat soup and sandwiches. I watch as Bryce transforms, shedding his nervousness to feeling very comfortable around Gramps. Then we show him the pictures of our trip, minus any shots of Von Jobin. Leena gave those to Ciara.

Gramps comments on the beauty of the island and that it looks like we had a good time.

Later we bundle up and go back outside to push snow with Gramps snow blower. I take the shovel and push the snow off the sidewalk leading to the house while Bryce clears Gramps driveway, and his two neighbours.

Gramps thanks Bryce as we sit by the fire warming up, watching a movie, and sipping hot chocolate. Then Gramps goes back into his wood shop to work for a couple more hours.

When it's time for bed, I motion for Bryce to come with me to my room, but he shakes his head. "I don't think that's a good idea. I'll sleep on the couch."

"Babe, he'll be fine with it."

"Tonight I'll sleep on the couch and if he says we can sleep together tomorrow night, then great. I don't want to over step the boundaries."

"The perfect gentleman. Your mama taught you right." I lift his t-shirt and run my hand backwards down his washboard abs, grinning at him. "But I'm going to miss you."

He stops my hand abruptly. "Oh no, you don't. I know what you're up to. Not here in your grandfather's house."

"You're no fun. You said anytime, anywhere. Remember?"

"Okay, one exception to the rule. Not at your grandfather's house. Anywhere else."

I sigh. "Fine." I go to get Bryce a blanket and pillow and when I come back, I give him my sad eyes and pout.

"Come here." He takes the blanket and pillow from me and throws them on the couch. He wraps me in a hug. "We'll see each other in the morning. I love you."

"I love you." I kiss him and head for my room.

I toss and turn thinking about Bryce on the couch wondering if he's comfortable. After about half an hour of thinking, I finally get up and shimmy in next to him on the couch. He's asleep, but he instinctively wraps his arm around me, holding me close. I fall asleep right away.

In the morning, the sun shines brightly through the living room window, waking me.

I glance up at Bryce to see him looking down at me with a smirk on his face. "What?" I say softly.

"Couldn't sleep without me?"

"No. I tossed and turned for half an hour, but as soon as I came in here I fell asleep right away."

Gramps clears his throat. "Well, good morning. You two ready for breakfast?"

"Good morning," Bryce says as he starts moving to get up.

That's my cue. He doesn't want Gramps to see us lying together, so I quickly get to my feet and go into the kitchen.

"Gramps, I could have made breakfast."

"Tomorrow you can. You looked too cozy to wake you. But you'd probably be more comfortable in your own bed. It's a little bit bigger than that couch for the two of you."

I saunter over to where Bryce is standing at the archway between the living room and kitchen and nudge him. I mouth, "See, I told you." Then I take his arm and pull him into the kitchen. "Sit. Let's eat and then we'll go push some more snow. Looks like we got another four inches."

"I think we got more than that. Looks to me like at least six inches." I place a plate in front of Bryce. "Thanks, Angel."

"Angel?" Gramps asks.

"Yes, that's one of my many nicknames. Giggles, Angel, and Bryce's brother Austin calls me Blondie."

"Well, eat up."

"How's Mary, Gramps?"

"She's doing good. That was her soup we had last night. She made it for us before she went to the hospital. They were short-staffed because of the storm, but I got her there and home with my four-wheel drive."

"That's a nice truck you have. I was thinking maybe I'd trade mine in for a new one."

Gramps hands Bryce the key fob. "Take her for a spin. She's great in the snow."

"Okay, maybe we'll do that."

Gramps finishes his breakfast. "I'll be in the wood shop."

"We'll get the driveway done," I say as he rounds the wall to go down the hall.

"Thank you," He hollers back.

I sit on Bryce's lap and wrap my arms around his neck. "See, I told you he'd have no problem with us sleeping together."

"You had no clue how he'd react."

"You're right. I didn't."

While I'm shoveling the heavy thick snow off the sidewalk, Bryce disappears. A few moments later, from the corner of my eye, I see snow falling from the roof. I look up to see Bryce straddling the peak, shoveling almost a foot-and-a-half of snow off the edge. "Be careful up there."

"Angel, back up. I don't want you getting hurt."

"Always looking out for my safety, but never your own!"

I do as I'm told and start from the road, keeping a watchful eye on Bryce. When he finishes and comes down, I relax.

He moves his truck onto the road and then honks Gramps's horn, stealing my attention away from shoveling. I get in the truck so we can take a spin around the block. Bryce is like a kid in a candy store, playing with all the features his truck doesn't have. "Nice truck," He says as we pull up behind his.

"Yeah, he really likes it."

As we're storing the snow blower in the garage, Bryce checks out Gramps's old truck. "Nice." Bryce opens the doors to see if there is any rust. "He's kept her in good shape."

"That's his baby. There are a lot of memories with that old truck."

Bryce then looks out the back window and sees a huge wood pile that needs to be split and stacked. "You think your Gramps would mind if we split his wood for him?"

"I could ask him."

Back in the house, we grab a beer and then go see what Gramps is working on in the wood shop.

Bryce hands Gramps his beer. "Nice truck you have there."

"Did you take her for a ride?"

"Yes. It has a lot of features that my truck doesn't have. She's a beauty."

"What's that you're working on Gramps?"

"A kitchen table for Mary."

"She's going to love it. Keera talks about hers all the time- what good quality it is." Bryce smiles at me.

My mind wanders to us making love on my sturdy kitchen table. "Yes, I wanted to thank you again for my kitchen table. I love it."

Bryce searches around, looking at different things. "Very good quality." He glances sideways at me, smirking.

"Hey, Gramps, we saw your wood pile out there. Or I should

say your snow pile. Would you mind if me and Bryce split and pile your wood?"

"No, I wouldn't mind at all. I've been too busy to get back to that."

"Hey, are we going to see Mary at Tim Horton's tonight?"

"Indeed, we are. She wants me to pick her up."

"Great. We'll let you get back to your work."

Bryce and I exit the wood shop and go back into the living room.

As I'm handing Bryce wood to place in the wood stove, I say, "So do you think my Gramps and Denis Leary look a lot alike?"

"Oh, yeah. Even their personalities are almost the same."

When Bryce stands, I close the gap between us, lifting his shirt to run my finger down his happy trail. "Since Gramps is busy, maybe we could…"

Bryce chuckles. "You've got a one-track mind, Angel. We could go split some wood?"

Shut down instantly!

"Fine." I don't press the issue.

We get three-quarters of the way through the wood pile and then go into the house to get warmed up and make dinner-moose burgers and poutine. After dinner, I take a quick shower and get ready for our nightly outing to Timmy's. I had offered for Bryce to join me in the shower, but he shut me down again and took one after me. I have no idea why he's so uptight.

Mary's waiting at her front door when we pull into her driveway.

Gramps gets out of the truck to get her and Bryce climbs in the back seat with me.

I run my hand up his leg until I get to the bulge in his jeans and then I grab a handful, grinning mischievously. I raise my one eyebrow and show him my dimple.

"Well, hello there, dear." Mary climbs into the passenger seat and twists to look at us.

I move my hand quickly to Bryce's thigh. "Hi, Mary. How are you?"

"I'm good. And you must be Bryce."

"Nice to finally meet you Mary." Bryce shakes her hand.

On the way over to Timmy's, Gramps tells Mary how good our moose burgers were. "Melt in your mouth. So tasty."

"Mary, he ate two. And they were big."

"I guess you liked them if you ate two." Mary looks lovingly into Gramps's eyes as he turns sideways to look at her.

Mary and I talk away while waiting for Bryce and Gramps to come back with our coffee and cappuccino.

"Your children will be gorgeous." Mary stares off at Bryce and Gramps talking at the counter.

"Thank you, Mary."

"He will love you forever. I can see the love he has for you in his eyes."

"Yeah, we love each other."

"How are you and Gramps doing?"

"We're doing great."

"That's good to hear."

Our night at Timmy's goes well. We show Mary the pictures of our trip and all four of us laugh and have a good time. It's nice.

When we get home from Timmy's, Gramps goes back into the wood shop for a bit and Bryce and I cuddle on the couch watching a movie.

When the movie ends, Bryce and I say goodnight to Gramps and head to my bedroom. While I strip naked, my phone alerts me of an e-mail, and I read it. Bryce sees the expression on my face and asks, "What is it?"

"I don't know if this is bullshit or not."

"Let me see."

I hand the phone to Bryce and notice he's still wearing his boxers. "What are you doing? You never wear anything to bed."

"We're in your grandfather's house."

"Babe, he's not going to come in here."

Bryce reads the e-mail and frowns.

The e-mail is from Chaz Vanderbilt, the president of Alaina modelling agency. He says he saw a Von Jobin video and hunted me down. He'd love the opportunity to work with me at his studio, modelling some designer clothing. It will be a long day of ten hours, but the end result for me will be a portfolio of beautiful pictures and three-thousand dollars for a day's work. The modelling agency will make copies of the pictures and I'll have to sign a contract giving them the rights to distribute the photographs. They have studios in Paris, London, Los Angeles, New York, Montreal, and Toronto.

He wants me to e-mail him back to let him know if I'm interested in his offer and whether I have any questions. He says this is a great opportunity and almost every new model that he hand picks moves on to bigger and better opportunities.

I wait for Bryce to finish reading. "You think it's a scam?"

Bryce's expression tells me he doesn't like it. "Might be." Bryce hands back my phone.

I place it on the night stand and climb into bed next to him, cuddling into his side and laying my head on his chest. My hand travels to the waistband of his boxers and my finger slides just inside across his lower belly. "You sure you don't want to take these off?"

He grins down at me when I turn my head up to look at him, but he's silent, just grinning at me.

What are you thinking?

I try a different tactic, running my hand up his washboard abs and feeling every ripple until I get to his muscular pecs. I cup each one, testing the feel of them in my palm. I look down to see his growing erection and my muscles clench instinctively.

"We're supposed to sleep. This is your grandfather's house."

He hardly gets the words out before I take him by surprise by climbing on top of him.

I grind suggestively on his cock and dangle my hair across his chest to the side, blanketing both our faces. Our eyes meet and I smile down at him. "He won't hear us. I promise. I'll be quiet."

Bryce starts to say something and I shut him up with a sensual kiss. I don't stop. I pin his arms and go wild on top of him, keeping my lips fused to his. When I see his defensive wall come crumbling down, I pull away. "You don't want me?" I ask.

His mouth opens again and I shut him up for a second time with an aggressive but effective kiss. When we pull apart, he's breathless like me.

He tackles me down onto the bed and climbs on top, pinning my hands at the side of my head.

"Damn! You've got ninja skills."

He whispers in my ear. "You won't give me a chance. Yes, I want you. I always want you." He kisses my neck and then runs his tongue along it. "But we'll have to be quiet. No sudden movements." He lifts up and off me, balancing with his strong arms and toes as I slide his boxers down and I use my feet to kick them off.

"That's better. I can feel you, feel your beautiful cock against me."

"Christ, Angel, see what you do to me? I could never deny you." Bryce's movements are slow and unhurried, tender and sensual.

My legs open wider to accommodate him as he slips deep inside me.

I try to be quiet, but the feeling of his big cock stretching my walls emits a satisfied sigh. My nails scrape lightly down his back, and then I follow down the curve of his perfect, tight ass. When I grasp his butt cheeks and pull him deeper into me, he lets out a low moan.

We find the perfect slow rhythm which jumpstarts the incredible sensations into overdrive, but then the bed creaks. I giggle slightly and Bryce shuts me up with a scorching hot, tongue-on-tongue kiss.

When he pulls away, he places one finger over my lips. "Shhh."

He continues rocking his hips expertly, then switches it up by pulling out to the tip and easing gently back in. He's torturing me. He withdraws, then inserts. With an expert roll of his hips, I'm all sensation.

Damn, the man can fuck.

His lips lower to one nipple and he sucks gently, switching to give the other the same amount of attention. He bites on my nipple, making it grow to twice the size. The sensation is like a hot line to my groin, electrifying me-in a good way. As he lifts, my hands splay across his chest, caressing every well-defined muscle. I pinch his nipple between my finger and thumb and my mouth latches onto his other nipple.

His satisfied groan tells me he likes it, so I continue nipping and sucking while he expertly rolls his hips. He tilts me a fraction so he hits that perfect spot inside me.

My back arches, letting him know I'm ready without words.

He takes my hand, places it where we're connected, and whispers in my ear, "Play with yourself. I want you to come."

The single bed creaks every once in a while because it's not used to having the combined weight of both Bryce and I, but Bryce instantly adjusts to keep it quiet.

He's misted with sweat and his breathing has changed to a deep pant. I know he's struggling for control, so I quickly vibrate my clit with my finger. I don't know if it's because were being naughty in my grandfather's house or if the slow, sensual movements are turning me on, sending me over the edge instantly.

"Babe?"

"I'm with you, Angel."

I lift and angle my pelvis so he'll go deeper and at my silent request he shoves his cock in farther, as far as it will go. I gasp.

My hands grip the sheets, my toes curl, my back arches, my head tosses and turns, and all the while my body convulses with such a strong orgasm that I'm breathless when I finally come down.

When I open my eyes, Bryce is gasping for air. Every muscle in his body tenses. He closes his eyes and opens them again as his cock jerks, filling me with his warm cum. When he finishes and falls down on me, I run my hands down his back and whisper in his ear, "Babe, you're amazing."

He lifts up to look at me. "Yes, that was amazing, but that wasn't supposed to happen." He reaches for the Kleenex box on the nightstand, pulling out a few placing them between my legs when he withdraws. He lies back down gently so the bed won't creak.

Jeez, why is he acting so strange?

He tucks me into his side and I rest my head on his chest again. He kisses my forehead. "So you're good now?"

"Yeah." That's it? That's all?

"So we can sleep now?"

"Yeah." I sigh.

"What? What's wrong?"

"I don't understand why you're acting so strange."

Bryce lets out a huff of air. "I don't want your grandfather thinking that something's going on in here. I need to give him the best first impression imaginable. I want him to like me."

"He does. Can't you tell?"

"Let's just say I'm still trying to read him. He's a tough old bugger."

"Yeah, that's the way my Gramps is, but you know what? If he didn't like you, there's no way he would have offered to let you take his truck for a spin."

"I'll take your word for it."

"And I'll cut you some slack-this time."

Bryce gives me a throaty low chuckle. "That's very generous of you."

"Thought you'd like that."

"Angel? What am I going to do with you? You're too irresistible."

"Love me."

"I do. Sometimes it feels like my chest might explode."

"Here, let me rub it." I rub across his chest and look to see his reaction while I lick and bite my bottom lip. That always gets him.

"You know where that's going to go, don't you?"

"I don't mind."

"Sleep. Close those pretty little eyes of yours and sleep." Bryce reaches over to close my eye lids.

Shot down again. "Fine." I lie awake, thinking about the e-mail wondering if it's legit. If it is, I could make a little money modelling some clothes, while Bryce is working. This could be the job I've been looking for.

When I wake, I find that I'm lying in the same position that I fell asleep in. My head rests on Bryce's shoulder and the thought of his arm asleep has me shifting to my side to give him some relief. He moves with me, wrapping his arm over me. His heavy breathing tells me he's still asleep. I don't want to wake him so I lie there thinking.

After what seems like ten minutes, I reach toward the night-stand for my phone and send Leena the e-mail to see what she thinks.

Leena texts me:

If you don't call, I will! This could be the job you're looking for. And when you get your foot in the door, tell them you have a beautiful friend who would love to model.

I text back:

Yes, you are beautiful and not conceited at all. Okay, I'll send him an e-mail first to see if it's legit. I'll see if he'll send me a phone number to call.

Let me know what you find out.

Will do. TTYL BEAUTIFUL!!!

I place my phone back on the nightstand and Bryce stirs. His large hand reaches to grab a handful of my breast and I feel his morning erection rubbing deliciously on my butt.

"Well. Good morning, big boy."

He snuggles into my neck. "I love waking up like this."

"Mmm, me too." I reach behind and run my fingers over the length of his shaft.

Bryce groans against my ear. "If we were home, you'd be mine, but right now I have to pee." He climbs over me and out of bed and searches for his clothes.

I lie there watching the glorious show of muscles contracting as he hurries to get dressed. "You kill me, Babe."

"What?"

"How anal you are about having sex in my grandfather's house."

"Shhh," Bryce warns me. "Seriously, I need to go."

"Okay. I'll make breakfast." I climb out of bed and Bryce's eyes scan my body from top to bottom. I move around the room, pretending I'm looking for something.

Bryce shakes his head. "Christ, Angel, you're not making this easy for me."

Mission accomplished. I smile.

"Tease!" He slaps my butt hard enough to force me forward and I jump.

When Bryce comes into the kitchen after showering, the smell of his cologne and body wash manipulate my senses. I can't resist. I step toward him, admiring how good he looks, holding his butt cheeks in his snug-fitting jeans, tugging him into me. "Mmm, you smell delicious. I'd rather eat you than breakfast."

"You've got to quit doing that. I've already taken one cold shower."

Gramps clears his throat as he enters the doorway to the kitchen and Bryce and I quickly separate. He's caught us a couple times in an intimate moment so now he signals when he's coming into a room.

"Good morning! Everyone sleep well?"

"Yes." Bryce sits at the table.

"Slept good, Gramps." I stand in front of the stove, holding the flipper in my hand. "Breakfast will be ready in two minutes."

Gramps sits and I pour them coffee and a glass of orange juice and then add the finishing touches to breakfast while they talk about specifications on a new truck for Bryce.

After breakfast, Gramps goes back to the wood shop, Bryce heads outside to finish splitting the wood pile, and I take a shower.

Just as I'm about to hop in, I get an e-mail back from Chaz, giving me his phone number. When we talk on the phone, I ask enough questions to realize this job is a dream come true. I had asked him how he found out about me and he said his employees hunted me down and got my e-mail from Mike, Von Jobin's manager.

At the end of our conversation, Chaz tells me he's in New York at the moment, but Tuesday morning he'll be in his Toronto studio and we can do the photo shoot at eight-thirty a.m.

I hang up content and happy.

On the phone, I didn't want to sound too excited, even though I probably couldn't hide it.

I call Leena right away, and she's excited enough for the both of us. She asks me how I'm going to break the news to Bryce. "You know he's going to freak out."

I have to admit, that kept running through my mind while I took my shower.

How do I break it to him?

As I'm about to enter the wood shop, I hear Bryce telling Gramps it was love at first sight and he's never felt this way about anyone.

I halt and hold my position as I eaves-drop.

"She's the one I want to spend the rest of my life with."

20

TEARS THREATEN THE corner of my eyes as I try to keep it together when it finally registers why Bryce has been acting so strange.

"I want Keera to be my wife. I love her and I'd really like your blessing."

Gramps clears his throat again. He's deliberately hesitating, torturing Bryce with his silence. After what seems like an eternity, but is only ten-long-seconds, he finally speaks, "You haven't known each other very long."

"I know, but when you find the one you want to spend the rest of your life with, you don't want to waste any time. I'm twenty-seven and I want to start a family in a couple of years. Or when Keera's ready."

Silence fills the room again until Gramps speaks. "Sounds like you've thought this through."

"Definitely. She's all I think about."

"I can see you love her." Gramps pauses, the way he does when he's gathering his thoughts. "She's all I have. Her heart better not be broken."

"Never. That's a promise. I'll make sure she's happy for the rest of her life."

"Have you asked her yet?"

"Unofficially, yes. She told me we have to get to know each other better."

"That sounds like my Giggles. She's just like my Lily. Independent-takes her time with big decisions. If you ever need any advice, I might be able to help."

"Thank you."

"You have my blessing as long as she still comes to visit me after you're married."

"Thank you. That won't change. She loves to visit you. I've had a good time too. Thank you for having us."

"Anytime you want to come back. I love having the company."

I hurry back to the bathroom and look in the mirror, fixing my make-up. "That's why you were so nervous. Oh, Bryce…"

My mascara has run a bit from crying, so I quickly fix it before making my way down the hall to the wood shop.

"How'd you make out with that wood pile?" I ask Bryce, trying to disguise my voice so it doesn't sound like I've recently been choked up, crying.

"All done and piled against the fence."

"Thank you for shoveling off the roof too," Gramps says.

"If you ever get that much snow again, just call Keera. We'll come up and I'll shovel it off for you. You shouldn't be up on that roof, whereas I'm used to it."

"Can you do me a favour before you pack up and go?"

"Anything. What do you need?"

"I cleaned Mary's driveway twice, but I think it needs one more pass."

"Consider it done. Keera and I will shoot over there right now."

"Giggles, you've got a good man here."

"He's a keeper."

On the way home to Barrie, my mind wanders back to how Gramps never said a word about his and Bryce's conversation. He had plenty of opportunity when we were alone, but he kept silent. Bryce hasn't said anything, either, even when I brought up how Gramps told me he liked having him at his place. They sure can keep a secret when they want to.

I've been trying to figure out how to tell Bryce about my new job and the only thing I can come up with is to blurt it out. "I sent Chaz an e-mail to see if he'd send me his phone number so I could ask some questions and see if it's legit. He sent me back his phone number, and I called."

Bryce turns to look at me. "Oh yeah… and?" He sounds annoyed.

"He said he's in New York at the moment, but he'll be in Toronto on Tuesday at eight-thirty a.m. for the photo shoot."

"Oh, no! You're not going!"

"What?" I can feel the blood rising in my face.

Bryce backpedals. "Settle down. I mean, you're not going alone. I'm sorry, but this could be a set-up to get a young, beautiful girl alone."

When I realize he's only looking out for my safety, I calm down. "Fine, I'll see if Leena can come with me."

"I'd go with you, but it's short notice and I can't take more time off."

"No problem."

"What else did he say?"

"He told me not to bother with hair and make-up. They'll do that in the studio."

"And… what else?" His voice is sounding angrier by the moment as a low growl escapes.

"He went through what I'll be doing and then he gave me the address of the studio."

"I don't like it."

"Why?" I can feel the heat rise in my face. A clear sign it's turning red.

"If you and Leena get there and something doesn't feel right, just leave and call me right away."

"I think you're worrying too much. This sounds like a great opportunity. If you would have talked to him, you'd be more relaxed. Everything's going to be fine."

"Are we forgetting that less than two weeks ago you were kidnapped by a stalker?"

"He's in jail. I'll be fine."

"I don't have a good feeling about this."

"I've wanted a job for a while now and this is the perfect opportunity. I'm pretty excited about this, so don't burst my bubble." I'm feeling increasingly impatient.

"Remember what happened the last time I had a bad feeling?"

Yes, I was being stubborn then, too, but I didn't see that until I was kidnapped. Point taken. "Yes. I'll be cautious okay? If something doesn't feel right, we'll leave right away and call you."

Bryce is silent as we drive.

"Babe, would you feel better if you talked to Chaz yourself?"

"No, I don't need to talk to him."

I move back to my side of the truck and stare out the window. After about five minutes, I look over at him again. "Um, I'm going to need my Journey. Can we stop at my house?"

He hesitates before answering. "Fine," He grumbles.

We drive in silence for the fifteen remaining minutes to Huntsville, with Bryce lost in his thoughts and me in mine.

Before I get out of Bryce's truck, he grabs my knee and looks in my eyes. "Wait! Angel. You've got to understand that I'm worried about you."

The look of concern in Bryce's eyes has me physically relaxing. I run my hand over his cheek. "Babe, don't worry. I'll be okay. I'll keep you updated. Everything's going to be fine."

Tuesday morning, I punch the address for Alaina modelling agency into my navigation system and it tells me the trip will take approximately one hour and ten minutes. I've got a little over an hour-and-a-half to get there, so whenever I can speed a little, I do.

As I drive, I think about how Bryce reacted when I told him Leena had to work and I'd be going by myself.

He's had quite a few mood swings since then. His reluctance to let me go this morning showed through with every kiss and every touch. Before he left for work he held me in the driveway for a long time, and kept reminding me to call and let him know I'm safe as soon as I arrive.

Traffic is slow in spots, but I make it there with six minutes to spare. When I pull up to the tall, blue, mirrored-glass building, there's a valet to greet me and take my car. The doorman, in a sharp suit with a top hat, escorts me inside to a large marble desk. I'm surprised the receptionist knows my name too. She says Chaz is waiting for me on the twenty-first floor and points to where the elevators are.

When the elevator doors close, I fish out my phone and text Bryce:

Made it here safe. Valet, doorman-in-top-hat, and receptionist all knew me by name. On my way up to the twenty-first floor. Everything seems fine. I'm so excited. I love you! I'll text again when I get a chance.

Bryce texts back before the elevator makes it more than a few floors:

Good. I'm relieved and I love you.

Short and sweet. That means he's still mad.

People enter and exit the elevator all the way up and I glance at my phone and grimace.

I've got two minutes. Come on people! I don't want to be late.

The elevator pings at the twenty-first floor with one minute to spare. I exit and go to the large marble desk.

My eyes are drawn to the magnificent blue lights shining through a large, etched-glass sign for Alaina modelling agency on the wall. When I tear my eyes away, I see a beautiful receptionist sitting attentively behind her computer screen.

"Good morning, Keera. Chaz is waiting for you in his office. This way, please."

"Oh, okay thank you."

As we walk down the hall, I notice how modern the offices are. The large, life-size pictures on the walls show beautiful models in different poses. I watch how people stand at their desks in their glass offices to watch us walk by. Some wave and I wave back. Others just watch.

Jeez, I'm glad I got up early to get ready for this.

Chaz's glass doors are huge-ten feet tall with beautiful etchings so those outside can't see in. They open automatically. I look at the receptionist, strangely.

"They open and close on a sensor." She smiles at me.

"Oh. I was wondering."

Chaz is looking out the window when we enter his large modern office. He slowly turns and nods to his receptionist. He's tall and lean with muscle. Very good looking, as if he started as a model himself. His blonde tipped, short and spiky hair looks really good on him. His black dress pants and a white dress shirt show a nice body underneath. He looks like he works out, though maybe not as much as he'd like. Just an observation.

Chaz comes around his desk as I walk toward him, holding his hand out for me to shake. "So glad to meet you, Keera."

"Nice to meet you, Chaz."

He motions for me to sit in the large executive chair and the receptionist disappears.

I glance out the massive windows and notice his view of the city is amazing, and with the light snowfall makes it very picturesque.

"We just have to sign these release forms. This gives Alaina the rights to touch up, alter, and distribute the photos as we see fit. You'll get to see the finished copies before you leave and we'll send you a portfolio of your own." Right down to business. Okay, he might be a little pissed that I was almost late.

"Sounds great."

He hands me the legal documents. "Take your time reading them. Would you like some orange juice?"

"Yes, please." That'll keep him busy.

While I'm reading both sides, I glance up as he walks over to his bar which is lit up with the same mesmerizing blue lights as on the Alaina sign.

"The last page is for contact information, including name, address, and phone number."

"I guess you'd need all that."

Chaz comes back and places the glass of orange juice in front of me. "Here you go."

"Thank you."

"Take your time. I have to make a couple of phone calls, so just ignore me."

"Okay." I keep reading.

Chaz dials his phone. "Hey, it's Chaz. Good, and you? Yeah, as we speak. Gold mine."

I look up at Chaz, who's staring back at me. Grinning. *Okay, this is weird.*

I go back to reading, but I can't concentrate. I'm side tracked by Chaz's conversation.

"Oh yeah, definitely. Yeah, alone. No, no one else. Your pictures are ready. You're in the air right now? All right, I'll see you later. Bye."

I take a sip of the orange juice and go back to my reading.

Once I've finished reading and see everything looks fine, I pick up the pen and sign. I fill out the last page and then shuffle it across his desk and finish my orange juice while he speaks with someone else.

When he hangs up, he looks over the documents. "Okay, let's get you over to the salon. Not that you need it. You're beautiful just the way you are."

"Thank you."

"And polite, too. Not very punctual, but polite." He grins at me.

"What?" I shrug my shoulders. "I made it right on time. I tried to get here earlier, but traffic."

"I'm kidding." Chaz taps his hand on my shoulder and keeps smiling at me. "He said you were irresistible."

"Who?"

"Colt, um, I mean, Mike."

"Mike who?"

"Von Jobin's manager."

"Oh."

He guides me to the door and then we head down the hall.

The salon is huge and when everyone notices Chaz, they all turn.

A beautiful woman with big, auburn hair comes toward us. "Keera, nice to meet you."

"This is Josie. Josie, not too much. I like the natural look." Chaz takes his hand off my lower back.

"Hi, Josie. Nice to meet you." We shake and she motions me over to a chair.

Chaz comes walking over. "After makeup and wardrobe, Josie will take you to the studio. I'll look in on you every once in a while."

"Thanks, Chaz."

"It's good having you here."

"Thanks. It's good to be here."

Chaz disappears and Josie takes over, telling me how beautiful I am with hardly any makeup and how she loves my eyes and my lips, all the while working her magic.

I pay attention to how she applies everything and what products she uses and when I'm done, I'm stunned. Not too much. And I look good. Not like some of the models in expensive magazines with their freaky, over-emphasized make-up. This is perfect.

"We'll keep your beautiful, long, blond hair straight for now and later we'll bring you back in here to curl it."

"Oh, okay."

"Come with me, beautiful." Josie holds out her hand and helps me out of the seat.

We walk over to a rack of clothes and she runs her hands through it, showing them to me. "I picked these out for you with a little help from Colt… um, from the picture Chaz gave me of you." She turns red and seems a little flustered. Odd. "And Chaz approves. Let's try this one on first." She hands me a pant suit and leads me to the dressing room.

"That was very strange," I whisper to myself while I'm changing.

When I come out, Josie adjusts my collar, then she searches for shoes and accessories to complete the outfit.

"Perfect, let's go." I'm whisked away to the studio next door, where a few people are scurrying around doing last-minute preparations.

"This is Brent. He's one of the easiest photographers to work with."

"Hi, Brent. Nice to meet you."

"Nice to meet you, Keera." Brent shakes my hand. "I don't mean to be rude, but we're a little behind schedule, so if you could come over here."

I follow him and do exactly what he wants me to do. We go through all the poses, left, right, give me a smile or a laugh, look away from the camera, and he praises me when I do it perfectly.

"Okay, back to wardrobe." Brent orders.

After the fourth wardrobe change, Chaz comes to check on me. "How's she doing?"

"Great. Easy to work with. We're moving right along," Brent says as he adjusts his camera.

"That's good to hear." Chaz looks over some of the pictures already taken. "Very nice."

"We're just going to get this shot with the kitten and then we'll break for lunch."

"All right, see you in there." Chaz leaves in a hurry.

"Busy man," I say softly to Josie, who's fiddling with my hair.

"You have no idea."

Brent's assistant places a fluffy, white, Persian kitten on my lap. As I start petting it, it quickly falls asleep.

When we're done with the kitten shots, I follow Josie into a large meeting room.

In the middle of the room is a massive, round, smoked glass table with comfortable-looking, leather, executive chairs around the outer edge. There's a buffet set up on black granite counter tops against the full length of the wall. There is fruit, sandwiches, bagels, cereal, bacon and eggs, waffles, and yogurt.

I line up with everyone else and take a little fruit and yogurt, feeling like everyone's watchful eyes are on my plate. All eyes turn as Chaz comes through the door and he walks toward me. "How's everything going?"

"Good," I say, feeling a little shy.

Brent slides in to the conversation, saving me. "We're getting some great shots."

"Good." Chaz lines up to get some food.

After lunch, they send me back to get my makeup touched up and my hair curled. As I'm sitting in the chair, I notice the snow outside the window falling more heavily. In the background, the oldies and country music that's been piped in throughout the day has now changed to mellow rock. At the moment a love ballad is playing.

I listen to it for a minute and then it hits me. I feel my face turn red and my body stiffens. *Oh, God!*

Josie notices. "Are you okay?"

"Yeah."

"Nice song, eh?"

"Yeah."

"They've been playing it a couple times a day now and we love it. Von Jobin is one of our clients."

"Oh, yeah. Nice." I don't want to give anything away so I stay quiet and listen to the rest of the song.

Josie returns to curling my hair, while humming along to the music.

It's the full version of the song, which Leena thinks Colton wrote about me, so I listen intently to the words.

Holy fuck! Colton mentions the kiss. Please tell me this song isn't about me.

If it is about me and Bryce hears this, it will break his heart. What am I going to do?

Deal with that crap later. Right now you have a job to do.

When Josie finishes, she hands me a beautiful red dress, but when I change into it, I struggle to get it on. I yell out to Josie, "I think this is one size too small."

"Keep trying. It's supposed to be snug."

I wiggle into it, grunting and groaning, trying to suck in everything as quickly as possible because I know Brent is waiting for us. "K." I finally get it over my breasts. I adjust, but they're still gushing out the top. Now I know why there are no straps. My boobs hold it up. It just covers the nipples.

When I emerge from the dressing room, Josie gasps, holding her hand over her open mouth. "Oh, my! Look at you. You're stunning!"

"Thank you." I look in the mirror. The material gathers across each breast, opening up between them, showing the top of my stomach and maximum cleavage. It flows to the floor with the red fabric gathering at my right hip. Red jewels are strategically placed across the breasts and down the right side, and they sparkle and shine in the mirror almost blinding me. I've never seen such a beautiful dress. "Wow, this is beautiful. Shows some major cleavage, eh?"

"Yes, but look at you. You're gorgeous. Chaz will love it. He told you that you get to keep all of the clothes?"

"What? No! I couldn't." I twirl, looking at it in the mirror. "This dress would be in the thousand-dollar range."

"I little bit more than that, sweetie. And yes, all of our models keep the clothes. They're made exclusively for their perfect measurements by the best designers."

"I get to keep this dress?" I run my hands down it. Bryce is going to love this.

"No, I can't keep this. It's not right." A thought breaks through my mind. "Unless I pay for it. Could you find out how much I owe for all these clothes and I'll pay Chaz?"

"Oh, Keera, you're adorable. Come with me. We've got to get a move on."

When we enter the studio, mouths drop and I hear a lot of good comments.

Brent stands before me. "Magnificent! Stunningly beautiful!" He moves to his camera. "Okay, people, let's get some shots of that long, gorgeous hair and then we'll send you back to the salon to get an up-do."

I get into position and as I'm turning this way and that way, posing perfectly, my attention shifts to the commotion unfolding just outside the glass wall, with a crowd of people gathering to look into the studio.

I get a split-second glimpse of Chaz speaking with someone who looks a lot like… Colton?

"Keera, just ignore them," Brent says. "Attention over here, sweet-heart. I want you to face the backdrop, turn forty-five degrees, and look over your shoulder at me."

Crap, busted! I do as I'm told.

"Turn just a bit more. Great shot. It shows the back of the dress and your beautiful hair. Back to the salon for the up-do."

When I get a chance to look again, they're gone.

Damn it. You're seeing things, Keera.

Back in the chair, I sit with the red dress still on as Josie pins my hair up.

Anna, Josie's assistant, comes rushing in with a worried look on her face. "Have you seen how much snow is out there?"

"No," Josie replies.

"Everyone's talking about how bad the roads are. First they said eight to ten inches, now they're saying twelve to fifteen. The storm was supposed to skirt us, but it turned and stalled, and now we're getting the brunt of it."

I have to drive home in this shit.

"We might get to go home early," Anna says hopefully.

"Okay, help me pin a few more curls and we'll bring her back in." Josie hands Anna some pins.

From that moment on, everyone is rushing to finish the photo shoot, including Brent.

Brent loves the up-do with the dress and directs Josie to make some of the curls fall loosely. He sends me back to wardrobe with instructions to wear the elegant one-piece bathing suit with high heels, and then back to the salon to take a bit of my hair down, followed by two more bikini changes.

Another crowd of people gathers outside the glass wall, staring in as we do the final shoot. I'm feeling a little uncomfortable because of the lack of clothing I'm wearing, but I convince myself it's because they're all anxious to go home early as they wait on us.

I get a glimpse of Chaz and that man as they walk up, but the crowd instantly turns to look at them, covering my view. Dang it! I wanted to see who's with Chaz.

"Over here, Keera. We're almost done."

Crap, busted again! Pay attention, Keera.

Brent instructs me to hold a volley-ball in the air, as if I'm playing on the beach. They have real sand and the back drop is a turquoise and navy-blue ocean with a volley ball net and palm trees off to the side.

"Great shot, Keera." Brent takes a couple more pictures and then yells out, "That's it. We're all done. Great job, people. Great job, Keera. I'd work with you any day."

"Thank you."

We finish the photo shoot in seven hours instead of the ten Chaz expected.

Everyone is hugging and thanking each other. When Chaz enters the room, Josie whispers "Chaz" in my ear and unwraps me from a tight hug.

"Great job, Keera." Chaz touches my elbow to get my attention.

I turn to look at him. "Thank you."

I'm shocked to see the man standing beside him.

21

"COLTON? WHAT ARE you doing here?"

"I'll take one of those hugs." He wraps me in a tight embrace, lifting me off the floor and twirling me in a circle. Josie and Anna can't contain their smiles-and neither can anyone else. All eyes are on me and Colton.

When he puts me down, I stare up at him, waiting for an answer, but he's just smiling down at me.

"How have you been, beautiful?"

"Good, and you?"

"I'm good now." He stares deep in my eyes.

"What are you doing here?" I ask again.

"I heard you were here, so I thought I'd pick the pictures up from the band's photo shoot, personally."

"Oh," is the only word I can think of because my brain is going a hundred miles a minute.

Chaz, told Colton I was here? Yes, when he was talking on the phone this morning, when he was smiling at me.

And then it hits me. *Was this photo shoot a set-up so Colton could see me?*

Colton eyes me up and down hungrily, like he did in Aruba, bringing me back to the present. "You look beautiful."

"Thank you."

"God, Keera." He picks me up and hugs me again, swinging me around once more. "I missed you." He holds me, looking deep in my eyes.

Please don't kiss me, not in front of all these people.

I look around the room and everyone's frozen, staring at us. *This is awkward!* I can feel my face turning red from embarrassment. "How's the video coming along?" I say, trying desperately to distract him-and everyone else. *I wish everyone would go about their business and ignore us. And I wish he'd put me down!*

"How I've missed you and your beautiful smile." Colton finally sets me down. "You didn't get a copy? I told Matt, my computer geek to send it to your e-mail."

"No. Nothing."

I'm grateful when the other people in the room begin to direct their attention elsewhere.

"Okay, people, great job, the pictures look great. One last thing. Group photo."

They must do this all the time, because all the people in the room quickly gather at the backdrop.

"Keera, come stand right here," Josie says, signalling for me to stand beside her. Colton keeps his hand on my hip as he follows me.

Brent sets up the camera and hurries to get into position, next to Chaz. "Smile everyone."

After the flash goes off, Chaz moves to the table and inspects the pictures from the shoot. Then he turns to make an announcement. "Be careful going home, everyone. There's a lot of snow out there. Have a good evening."

Brent, Josie, and Anna hug me again and tell me they loved working with me. Then, the people in this crowded room disperse, leaving Chaz, me, and Colton. I go over to the table and look at the pictures with Chaz. Colton follows, placing his hand gently on the bare skin on my lower back. I feel his thumb moving back and forth.

"These turned out great," Chaz says, praising the pictures before him. "All of these, but this one is amazing."

I try to move so Colton's hand drops off, but it stays secure, draping my hip. "Yeah, that's a beautiful red dress," I say, distracted by Colton's thumb caressing my skin. "I enjoyed wearing it."

"I'll have my receptionist send the portfolio of pictures, your cheque, and the clothes to the address you gave me."

"Chaz, let me pay for the clothes."

"Keera, you're adorable. Designers donate the clothes to the models so their creations will be seen in magazines. None of my models pay for the clothes."

"Oh, okay. I'm going to get changed. Thank you so much, Chaz."

Chaz hugs me. "No. Thank you. These are going to make a lot of money."

As soon as I get into the dressing room, I text Bryce, but I get no response. He's not even reading the text, which leads me to believe he doesn't have his phone with him or it's turned off.

I text Leena:

The photo shoot went well, but a major snow storm. I can't get a hold of Bryce. Can you let him know I'm leaving now?

Leena responds quickly:

No! You can't! Bryce didn't want to interrupt your photo shoot. He told me to tell you he's busy because of all the accidents. He says to get a room for tonight and then drive back when the roads are clear. He said **do not drive in this!**

I reply:

Okay, I'll get a room and stay put for tonight.

I decide to see how bad the roads are for myself.

When I emerge from the dressing room, Colton is staring

at his phone, leaning against the wall in a bulge defining pose, which is an obvious tactic to get my attention. Unfortunately, it's succeeding-I'm distracted. He looks up at me through the long hair dangling across one eye. Would you look at that? He's wearing perfect designer jeans and a white dress shirt that clearly shows off his muscles. *Crap! I'm screwed!*

"All done?"

"Yeah." I grab my purse and head for the door.

He slides in beside me, holding my lower back. "You took your hair down."

"All those pins hurt my head."

"You look beautiful with it up or down."

"Thank you." I keep walking down the hall toward the elevator, trying to show him I'm intent on leaving. "We'd better get going. You probably have a long drive too."

"How far do you have to drive?" Colton asks.

"Back to Bryce's house. It's about an hour away."

"You can't drive that far. They've shut down the major highways."

"What?" I stop walking. "How am I going to get home?" My stomach grumbles from hardly eating all day.

"How about you come with me to dinner? You're obviously hungry, and then we'll figure out how to get you home."

I place my hand on my stomach, embarrassed that he heard it. "I didn't eat that much because everyone was staring at my plate."

"What have you had today?"

"A glass of orange juice, a yogurt, and some fruit."

"Oh, Keera." Colton shakes his head, unimpressed by my lack of food. "Come with me. Let me feed you. I'm taking you to my favourite restaurant."

I hesitate. *What should I do?* "Colton? I can't. Bryce wouldn't like it and I don't want to lead you on. I love Bryce."

"I know. This is just dinner. Me and you eating in a good restaurant."

I hesitate again, thinking for a bit. "I don't think this is a good idea."

"Why? You need to eat. You're hungry." He puts his hands together in a begging motion, like Reese does. "Please?"

It is just dinner. Then after dinner I'll grab a room in the nearest hotel and make my way home tomorrow.

"Okay," I say hesitantly.

"Yeah?" His face lights up and he shows me that gorgeous dimple.

The elevator doors open and Colton guides me in, holding me close with his hand on my hip. He calls his driver to pick us up at the door and when he hangs up he stands in front of me staring down. "You don't know how happy you've made me."

He picks me up and holds me against his body.

Yes I do. I feel how happy you are.

His lips come close to mine, but I turn and give him my cheek.

"Oh, no!" I wave my finger at him, but I can't help the slight smirk on my face. "No kissing me."

His smile suggests he's up to something.

The elevator pings and he puts me back down and takes my hand, leading me out the doors and through the massive lobby. Snow covers the large windows, so we put our coats on and bundle up. I place my hood over my curls to save them, and then Colton takes my hand.

As we step outside, the door-man tells us to take care. The wind whips up the snow, making it very hard to see.

Colton's driver stands patiently at the door of the hummer limo and I slip inside.

I watch as Colton climbs in after me and the snowflakes engulf the doorway falling onto the carpet and seat. The driver has to use force to shut the door behind us. "Wow! It's bad out there," I say.

"I can't believe that. I've never seen so much snow."

"I guess you wouldn't, living in Las Vegas." I take off my hood and get comfortable on the seat.

"You normally get snow like this?"

"Oh yeah, a few times a year, especially where I live."

"And where do you live?"

"Huntsville. It's further north. A lot more snow."

His driver climbs back in and starts to drive.

"Jeez, you could have a party in here." I say smiling.

Colton, looking amused by my comment, moves to the mini bar to get us a drink.

He hands me a Bud Light Lime and I look at him, surprised that he knows what I drink. In Aruba, it was mixed drinks or Corona beer. Not much variety.

He answers my silent question. "Leena told me when we were in Aruba."

"Oh." I take a sip and then I'm distracted by what's going on outside the limo. "Colton, look outside. There are cars everywhere."

Colton looks outside and then he hits the button on the console to talk to his driver. "Jim, how are the roads?"

"Not good. There's only one lane open and there are cars stuck in snow drifts, obstructing my way through," Jim says with a heavy Scottish accent.

"Okay, let's see if we can make it to the hangar."

"What if we get stuck?" I ask.

Colton squeezes over right beside me and places his arm around my shoulder, pulling me into his side. "Don't worry, I'll keep you warm."

"I know you will."

"This thing is a tank. It should make it through anything."

"I hope so." I take a few sips of my beer.

I think about Bryce and what he's doing. He's probably on top of a car ripping it open like a can opener to get the occupants out safely, not even worrying about his own safety. He's probably cold and hungry-I hope he's okay. Meanwhile, I'm riding around in a limo with an arm around my neck, and I'm toasty warm.

Guilt overwhelms me.

Now that it's almost too warm inside the limo, I move to take my coat off, using the opportunity to put a little space between Colton and me. His arm reluctantly drops off my shoulder. "Everyone at Alaina is so nice, I say. "I hope they all make it home okay." I shake the snowflakes, which are turning into raindrops, off my coat and move a bit farther away.

"Yeah, I hope so too."

The hummer stops and our attention turns to what's going on outside. Colton hits the button again. "How are you making out there, buddy?"

"There's a huge drift covering the road and cars are stuck all along the side. I might be able to make it between two cars if I get a running start, but I'm worried about the two of you."

"Go for it. Just plow through it." Colton turns to me. "Here, let me hold you to brace for impact." He scoops me up so I'm sitting like a baby in his arms.

Well this isn't working out.

The hummer backs up as Colton stares down at me. "I love holding you."

I don't know what to say, so I stay quiet.

The hummer guns it. When we hit the snow drift, it bogs down slightly, pushing us forward in the seat, but Colton holds me tight and the hummer keeps going, pushing through the drifts as if it's a snow plow. Colton hits the button again. "Way to go Jim, you made it!"

I raise my arm in the air and yell excitedly, "Woo-hoo Jim. You're awesome."

"Thank you, Miss Johnson. Everyone okay back there?"

"Oh yeah, we're fine." Colton says pressing the console button. "Better than fine." He says next to my ear.

I move slightly and he holds me tighter, his eyes smoldering with the look of love.

Shit! He's not going to let me go.

"Keera, when we left Aruba, I tried to keep my head in the game, but all I could think about was you. I couldn't eat, I couldn't sleep-not that that's anything new, but it was worse. I went through the motions of trying to live. The guys are a little worried about me. They kept calling me on my cell when you were getting dressed, until I shut it off. They haven't got a clue where I disappeared to."

"Colton, you should let them know you're fine."

"Yeah, maybe later."

The hummer slows and then stops. I look out the window and we're in what looks like a huge garage with a very high roof.

"We're here. You should put your coat on."

"Oh, okay." I pull my coat on and take Colton's hand as he helps me out.

He smiles as he guides me to a helicopter.

"We're going in that?" I ask, hesitating mid-stride.

"You don't like helicopters?"

"I've never been in one."

"Really?"

"I don't get out much. That was the second limo I've ever been in. The first was in Aruba and I was like a kid in a candy store."

"Keera, I think I love you. You're adorable."

"Thanks." *Okay, we'll let that I–love-you part slide. What have I gotten myself into now?* "Where are we going?" I ask, hesitating again as I climb up the steps.

"You'll see." He guides me up onto the seat and climbs in beside me as the pilot starts the rotors, making it impossible to hear or say anything. He pulls the three-point harness over my head and motions for me to open my legs so he can slide in the clip. He grins down at me. "Spread 'em." He says, next to my ear.

I can't help but smile at how cute and playful he's being.

Suddenly, he turns and reaches to hold my face while talking above the sound of the helicopter. "Don't worry. Everything's going to be fine. How do you think I got here so quick." He places head phones over my ears and kisses me quickly on the lips. Then he adjusts the microphone so it's in front of my mouth.

I wait patiently for him to get his headphones on and microphone positioned. He grins down at me, taking his time. *The brat.*

The helicopter lifts off the ground and flies away from the hangar into the snowstorm before gaining altitude. "Oh, my, God! This is so cool." I giggle and when I look down, I see that my hand is clenched on Colton's thigh, so tightly my knuckles are white. I ease up and try to take my hand away, but he holds it there.

He smiles down at me.

"What did I tell you? No more kisses. Can you hear me?" I bang my finger over his left headphone.

He lifts his hand to his headphone and shakes his head mouthing, "I can't hear you." Then he smiles again.

"You can hear me. I mean it. No more kisses!"

"You're so beautiful when you're angry." His voice comes in loud and clear through my headphones.

"Don't pull that shit with me. Where are we going?"

"To my favourite restaurant."

"This thing is okay to fly in this crap?"

"Oh yeah, my pilot's flown many hours in the snow. He's good. No worries."

"I don't know."

"Is it the helicopter ride or me you're unsure of?" He turns slightly in his seat to look deep in my eyes as he runs his hand down my thigh to my knee. "Leena and Austin told me what you've been through. I'm sorry. I wish I could change what happened. Trust me, I'd never do anything to hurt you. But let me tell you one thing: If that jackass ever gets out of jail, he's dead!" By the expression on Colton's face, I can see he means it.

"Can I tell you the truth?"

"Always. Wouldn't want it any other way."

"Umm, I guess it's a little of both. We are in a snow storm and I know you wouldn't hurt me." I try to collect my thoughts. "It's just that I'm trying to be a little more cautious in life. So that..." The unwelcome thought of my stalker, naked, and hovering over me, floods my mind and I hurry to shake the thought. "So that it never happens to me again."

Colton takes my hand in his. "I just want to spend time with you."

"Okay," I say softly.

I look out the window, but all I see is snow, so I glance back at Colton and his smile lights up the cabin of the helicopter.

"So how do you like your first helicopter ride?"

"I'll let you know when we land."

"You really are nervous."

"When we went to Aruba that was the first time I was on a plane and I was scared shitless until we landed."

"You're so cute. Jesus, Keera..." Colton shakes his head slightly and grins from the side of his mouth. "You make me so happy."

"Well, I'm glad my discomfort makes you happy."

Colton places his hand over mine and stares lovingly at me, boring right through me.

If I didn't love Bryce, I'd really enjoy the way he's looking at me, but this is too much for me to handle. I have to turn away. When I do, I see the snowfall is slowing down enough that I can vaguely see what's below. I see lights, tall buildings, and a bridge. The helicopter turns and when I look farther, I can see different coloured lights shining on a huge waterfall.

And then, it hits me.

"Is that Niagara Falls?" I turn to look at him.

He grins.

"Your favourite restaurant is in Niagara Falls? You brought me to Niagara Falls?" My voice is high pitched and angry.

22

"CALM. RELAX. BREATHE. I'll take you back to your car after dinner."

I stare out the window again at the beautiful sight below us and try to calm down.

How am I going to explain this to Bryce? You don't. Colton said he'd take me back to my car and then I'll get a room and drive to Bryce's when the roads are clear. Good plan.

"Are you mad at me?"

I turn back to Colton. "No. Just a little irritated."

"Good. I don't ever want you mad at me."

Not even five minutes later, the pilot lands at a nearby airport and I notice how smoothly he sets us down.

"See, I told you he was good."

I loosen my grip on Colton's thigh.

He unclips his three-point harness and pulls it up and over his head. "I get to do you now," He says in that sexy tone. He reaches between my legs and I instinctively open wider. He takes his time as I sit with my legs spread, with him pretending to have a hard time with the clip.

"Need some help?" I ask.

He chuckles. "You wouldn't believe the things going through my head right now."

"Oh, I can imagine."

He unclips me, pulls the harness over my head, and slips in another quick kiss.

I hold up my finger, scolding him again. "What did I tell you? No kisses."

He puts my finger in his mouth and gently bites. "But you're so beautiful, I can't resist."

I shake my head and try not to smile at how cute he is.

"You can't resist me either. Can you?"

My smile breaks through, betraying me. I shake my head. "Colton-"

"I know. Bryce."

"Are we going for dinner?"

"How I'd love to know what's going on in that pretty little head of yours."

"Dinner. Starving."

"Come with me, beautiful." He helps me out of the helicopter.

The pilot comes around and Colton moves them both away to the front of the helicopter, out of ear shot, so I can't hear, I presume. I see him pull out a credit card and hand it to the pilot. He says a few more things, then slaps him on the back. Colton turns and comes back to me. "Ready?"

"Yup."

He guides me by my lower back to the limo. "Third limo," he says with a smile.

"Yes. You're spoiling me."

"I could spoil you for the rest of your life, if you'd let me."

We climb into the limo, and settle in on the luxurious white leather seat, and Colton reaches for the mini-bar.

"Would you like a drink?" He asks, holding a Bud Light Lime in his hand.

Now what are the odds of both limos having Bud Light Lime stocked in the fridge?

"Are you trying to get me drunk?" I ask as I hesitantly take it from his hand.

"You're more at ease and you talk more when you've got a few drinks in you. I noticed that when we were in Aruba. I noticed a lot of things about you in Aruba."

I ignore the last part of his sentence. "Yeah, I had a glow on a few times."

"Did you enjoy yourself?"

"That was my first trip. I'll remember it for the rest of my life. The island is beautiful, Leena's dad's resort is amazing, and we all had such a good time. Did you have a good time in Aruba?"

"Definitely. I met you."

As I look up at him, I feel my face blushing. "You're sweet."

"And you're so beautiful when you blush." Colton looks outside, now that the limo has stopped. "We're here. Drink up."

I guzzle my beer, plop down the empty in the cup holder, and take Colton's hand as he helps me out of the limo.

We walk through the massive, beautiful lobby of what looks like the Hilton Hotel and we head straight for the elevators.

Once inside, Colton hits the button for the thirty-fourth floor and then stands close to me. As the other occupants leave on the nineteenth floor, Colton quickly turns and presses me against the wall, holding me close to his body. "Have you ever done it in an elevator?" His voice drips sensuality and he gazes at me with dark, mysterious eyes, waiting for an answer.

"No. Have you?"

"I'd like to." His eyes glimmer and shine.

We're stuck in an awkward moment again, but the ping of the elevator saves me and it has Colton releasing his dark stare as he quickly stands beside me, smirking. We walk into a beautiful foyer entrance to the restaurant. Colton guides me, his hand wrapped around my waist, holding my hip.

"Good evening, sir."

"Reservations for Johnson."

I glance up at him with a silent question, but don't say a word. We follow the maîtres d' to our table and Colton pulls out my chair, surprising me at how considerate he is. The crisp white linen table cloths, the navy candle burning, and the navy blue napkins in the shape of a fan at each table, catch my eye.

"Your waiter shall be with you in one moment." The maîtres d' disappears.

We sit and stare out the window at the spectacular view of the different coloured lights illuminating the falls.

I turn back to look at Colton. "This is amazing. You can see everything from here."

"Everything I want to see is right in front of me."

I let that comment slide. "So you like this restaurant for the view and not the food?"

"The food's very good too."

"So why did you make the reservation for Johnson and not Von Jobin?"

"No one needs to know where I am and no one needs to be bothering me right now."

"Oh." That reminds me to text Leena. I quickly look over the menu. "Can you order the Veal Parmesan for me? I need to hit the ladies room."

"Yes, I can. Washroom is in the far right corner." He grabs my hand when I stand. "You're not going to take off on me are you?"

"Colton, I wouldn't do that." I pat his hand, reassuring him.

As soon as I get into a stall, I text Leena:

My phone's about to die. I'm safe. Have a room. Will head home in the morning as soon as roads are clear. Tell Bryce I love him.

I hit send and hope it goes through. Fortunately, my phone shows it's delivered, so I start to text something else, but the battery runs out. "Crap!"

Oh, shoot, I hope no one heard that.

I do my business and the normal ritual of washing my hands, fix my makeup and hair, apply more lipstick, and a squirt of perfume, and then stroll back to our table.

Colton stands and pulls out my chair. "Thank you."

"You're welcome." He nuzzles his nose against my neck and kisses it. "You smell delicious."

I hope no one saw that.

The waiter places our beers on the table and says, "I'll be right back with our warm bread and dipping sauce."

My mouth waters at the mention of food and my stomach growls loudly enough that I think Colton hears it. Embarrassed, I try to talk over the noise. "Thank you, that sounds great."

The waiter disappears and I hurry to take a drink to defuse the grumbling.

"I guess you're hungry."

"You heard that?"

"I think everyone in the restaurant heard it." He says smirking.

I nudge his leg under the table.

"Oww."

I smile at him. "That didn't hurt and you know it."

"That's okay. You can beat on me any time you'd like. I'm here to take any abuse you want to inflict on me."

His eyes move down to my cleavage, where I obviously have too many buttons undone, and then back to my eyes.

I can just imagine what's going on in his head.

I have to look away, so I look outside at the changing colours of the waterfall.

"Would you like to go for a walk after dinner to see the falls?" Colton asks.

"We came all this way, so we have to see the falls. I'd love to."

"Look at you. You're so beautiful."

"Thank you. I think I was five or six when I came here with my parents, so I don't remember too much."

He takes my hand in his and rubs the inside of my palm. "I'm sorry about your parents."

"How'd you find out about that?"

"Leena told me. When she's drunk, she can talk. I learned so much about you."

"Should've known."

The waiter brings the warm bread and disappears again.

My eyes devour it, but I hesitate.

"Dig in," Colton says, "You're starving."

I grab a piece of warm bread, dip it in the sauce and take a bite. "Umm." I moan and chew for a bit and then swallow. "Colton, you've got to try this. It's delicious."

"I can see that. I thought you were having an orgasm right here at the table."

I nudge his leg again.

"Oww."

"That didn't hurt."

"No, it didn't. But I do love it when you touch me. Even if you are beating on me."

"Aren't you funny."

"And charming."

I chuckle. "Yes, and charming."

He dips a piece of bread in and takes a bite. "That's good. Almost orgasmic."

"Are you teasing me?"

"No, I wouldn't do that," he says sarcastically.

I smile at him and take another bite.

He stares at my lips when I chew, making me feel self-conscious.

"What?" I ask.

"Nothing."

"All right." Another awkward moment, so I look at the falls again.

From the corner of my eye, I see and feel him staring at me.

After what seems like an eternity, but is really only about ten seconds, I turn to look at him. "You keep staring at me. Don't you think the falls are beautiful?"

"Not when I have such a beautiful sight before me. I only see you. I want your face and body imprinted on my brain. I want to remember everything about you." As he takes my hand in his, our waiter brings our dinner. Colton lets out a regretful groan and lets go.

My meal looks and tastes delicious. "This is amazing," I say between bites. When I glance at Colton, I see he hasn't even touched his food. He's watching me. "Are you going to eat?"

"I'm enjoying watching you."

I put down my fork and knife. "I'm not eating until you do."

"Okay, will this make you happy?" Colton picks up his fork and starts to eat.

"Yes." I continue to devour my Veal Parmesan.

When Colton finishes, he takes my hand again. His eyes, fixed on mine. "I have to go to the washroom, but I'm afraid you'll leave me."

"Colton, go to the washroom. I'll be right here when you get back."

"Promise me."

"I promise."

He squeezes my hand and heads for the washroom.

Throughout dinner, I've been noticing a woman at the next table with her friends has been staring, and now she stands before me and touches my arm. "Sorry to interrupt your dinner, but I had to come and tell you what a beautiful couple you two make. The love in his eyes for you is something that comes along once in a life-time. Some people have never experienced that. Treasure it. My girlfriends and I were also commenting on how beautiful your children will be."

She's telling me this because they see the love in his eyes, not mine. *Do I tell her were not a couple? Nope. Don't get into it.* "Thank you."

Colton comes back and stands next to the woman. She gets flustered and touches my arm again. "I just had to come and tell you that. Sorry for bothering you."

"No problem."

As she returns to her seat, Colton sits down with a questioning look on his face. All four of the women wave at us. We wave back and then Colton turns to look at me. "What was that all about?"

"They said we make a beautiful couple and they were discussing how beautiful our children will be."

"Oh yeah, what'd you say?"

"I didn't want to get into it with a complete stranger so I said thank you."

He smiles at me.

When the waiter brings our receipt, Colton fishes three one-hundred-dollar bills from his pocket and places them on the table. I've also noticed him giving the limo drivers hefty tips. *Does he always tip like this?*

By the time I gather my purse and turn to get up, Colton is already standing and holding his hand out for me to take.

"Thank you," I say, surprised at how courteous he is.

He smiles down at me and tucks me into his side. He spins me around so we are facing the women.

"Ladies." He bows his head. "Thank you very much. We do make a beautiful couple. And our children are going to be gorgeous. Don't you think?"

That's what he's up to, Mr. Smooth has a hidden agenda. My face turns red from his comment.

All four of the women make their own comments as they smile up at Colton, clearly impressed at how good looking and charming he is.

"Ladies, nice meeting you. Have a good evening." He guides me through the restaurant with his hand on the curve of my back.

I glance up at him. "They loved you."

He reacts with a dimpled smile.

The elevator doors open and we slip inside to the back corner. Colton holds me close and I can feel the anxiety dripping off of him. I think he wants to get me alone again, but he misses his opportunity, due to the number of people coming and going in the elevator. I'm relieved when we make it down to the lobby. He takes my hand and leads me out of the elevator, then pulls me to his side again. He glances down at me. "You ready to see the falls?"

"Crap, my phone died. I can't take any pictures."

"No worries. I'll take care of that." We pass a store in the hotel lobby and he guides me to the counter, where he buys me a disposable camera.

"Thank you." I glance up at him as he places the camera in my hand. "Colton, you're so sweet. You know that?"

"Anything for you, darlin'," he says with an exaggerated southern drawl.

The limo driver waits patiently at the door of the limo just outside the overhang of the hotel, greeting us with, "Good evening, where to?"

"To the falls." We hop in and Colton goes for the bar right away. "Drink?"

Since he already has the cap off of the beer and I don't want to be ungrateful, I take it. "Thank you."

I drink quickly because I know the falls are close and I don't have much time to finish it.

The driver moves the limo into traffic and Colton slides in beside me. "I'll have our driver wait for us down the street while we walk along the falls."

I guzzle my beer because the driver has pulled over and is waiting by the door to let us out.

It's now nine-thirty and the snow is still falling, although much more lightly. With the lights shining on the falls, it's mesmerizing. The ice buildup on the rocks from the mist is something to see. When I stop to take a few pictures, I feel Colton stand close behind me. For some reason, he always has to be touching me. As we get closer to the falls, I feel the mist hitting my face. With the temperature just below freezing, I start to shiver. Colton notices and wraps me in a hug. "Let me keep you warm."

I look up at him. "I'm okay."

He picks me up anyway and holds me tight to his body. "Well then, let's keep each other warm." His lips move toward mine and I quickly turn so he'll hit my cheek.

I give him my shaking finger again. "What did I tell you? No kisses." This time he takes my finger in his mouth and sucks on it. I retrieve it. "Especially in public."

"So when were behind closed doors, I can kiss you?"

I shake my head. "No. You can't."

"You're irresistible, and beautiful, even when you're trying to be pissed off at me." He kisses my lips.

"Colton, you've got to quit doing that."

"What? Making you fall in love with me. This is the place for lovers, you know?"

23

"OH, COLTON." I shake my head. "Put me down."

"But I like holding you."

"Can we walk?"

"Whatever you want." He puts me down.

I turn away, pretending to look at the falls so he can't see my face, and mouth, "Holy fuck." *This is awkward.*

I take a few more pictures and before I know it, Colton is leaning against my back and holding me around my stomach.

He whispers in my ear. "I just need to touch you."

I let him hold me for a few seconds and then wiggle away. That hold is too intimate. "Come with me. Let's get a better look at the falls." I take his hand and tug him down further, trying to distract him.

"Look at you. You're really enjoying this, aren't you?"

"It brings me back to my childhood with my parents. I remembered bits and pieces before, but seeing the falls brings it back clearly. I remember standing right here." I climb onto the wall, lean against the railing, and hold my arms straight out like I'm flying as I stare at the falls. "And my mom had a fit, telling me to get down. She grabbed my arm and pulled me down. She looked scared, I think that's the only time she ever got that bent out of shape."

"I can see why! How about you come down? You're scaring the hell out of me, too."

I jump down. "Aren't you going to look at the falls? They're breathtaking."

"I've seen them before. But watching you, how happy you are, I can't take my eyes off of you. You're breathtaking."

I change the subject. "Who'd you come here with, a girlfriend?"

"No. The guys. We had a gig in Toronto and then we played here in Niagara Falls. I always said I'd come back."

I shiver again.

"Hey, what do you say we get out of here and go somewhere warm, so I can show you something else?"

"Okay, sounds good."

Colton turns on his phone, which alerts him of probably twenty e-mails and texts. He ignores them and calls the driver. "Hey Tom, we're ready."

I look at him not saying a word, but thinking, *Shouldn't you be answering your texts and e-mails?*

"He's on his way."

The limo pulls up to the curb and the driver rushes to open the door. I slide in to the warm, luxurious interior, waiting for Colton to climb in after me.

Colton whispers something into the driver's ear before sliding in.

When we exit the limo, Colton pulls more cash out of his pocket and slips the driver a tip. That's when I see we're back at the Hilton Hotel. We make our way through the massive lobby, then take the elevator to the top floor.

As we walk down the hall, Colton wraps his arm around my waist and leads me to one of the three double doors on this floor.

I tense. "Colton, I don't think this is a good idea. Is this your room?"

"Yes, this is my room."

Clearly you haven't been planning to take me back to my car tonight.

But you are going to take me back or I'll find my own way to Toronto.

He rubs my back. "I just want to show you the video. My camera crew did a fantastic job. Got some great angles."

I pull away from him, hesitating-thinking.

He steps close and holds my hips again. He leans down and tilts his head. "I won't try anything."

I search his eyes to see if he's telling the truth. "That's it. Right? Just the video?"

"I promise."

I hesitate for a few more moments.

Colton tries harder to convince me. "We worked day and night perfecting that video and the results are a masterpiece. You've got to see it."

"Fine."

When he opens the door, I step into the foyer of the huge presidential suite.

He tugs me in farther. "Come and check it out."

I glance around the room noticing it's been newly remodeled. The kitchen and bathroom are to the left and the bedroom must be behind the door to the right. I roam through the living room, checking out the décor and then go to stand in front of the massive windows, which overlook the falls. The view is better than the restaurant.

He comes to stand beside me, holding a Bud Light Lime. "It'll help you relax."

I don't really want it, because I've already had too much, but I take it anyway and stare out at the falls.

He takes a swig of his beer, goes over to his laptop, and fires it up.

I walk over to stand behind his chair. "Thank you for taking me to the falls."

He pulls me from behind his chair and wraps his arm around my waist, pulling me up against him. "You're welcome. I had a good time watching you."

Colton clicks on YouTube and then pulls a chair over. He pats the seat. "Come, sit. You'll be more comfortable."

"Okay." I sit and look at the computer screen.

His hand slides down my thigh and he rests it on my knee. He clicks on a few things and then the video starts playing.

I pay attention to every detail of the video because I know he'll probably only play it once-not like Leena, playing it over and over again. I really pay attention to the words in the second half of the song.

What we've shared
Is something I'll never forget.
Can't get you out of my head.
That touch,
That kiss,
Let me be the one,
Let me be the one, to make love to you.
He can't love you like I do.
I'll steal your heart from him
And drive you wild.
You'll never need another.
Let me be the one,
Let me be the one to love you.
Holding on to the thought
I might see my angel eyes again.
Let me be the one,

Let me be the one.
Your touch,
Your kiss.
If I had you, I'd give up this crazy life.
Until then, I'm a broken man,
Holding on for my angel eyes.
Let me be the one,
Let me be the one... To love you.

Oh God! He mentions what we've shared together.

Is he talking about watching me and Bryce have sex in the tropical forest?

He also mentions the kiss and how he'd give up this crazy life if he had... me?

I glance up at him and his stare holds me there. He's waiting for a comment.

"Nice song, it's very good. Nice shot of me coming out of the water and how you zoomed in to my wet bikini top, by the way."

"You like it?"

He's talking about the song, ignoring my comment about zooming in.

"Yes, it's a nice song."

"I wrote it for you." He hesitates and I wait for him to finish. "So every time you hear it, you'll think of the words and how much you mean to me."

Aw shit. What do I say? "Colton, it's the nicest thing anyone could ever do for me. It's a great song, I love it and I love the video." A few embarrassing moments, but I'll get over it. I hesitate, collecting my thoughts, but he cuts me off.

"Look at how many hits we've had," Colton says excitedly. "And the comments people are writing about it." Colton clicks on them and I read:

"Great song and video."

"My favourite new song."

"Can't get enough of it."

"Play it over and over again."

"Who's the blonde bitch, Colton?"

"Love the shot of the blonde in the white wet bikini, and the ass shots of the babes walking along the pool."

"We play your song in the office at least four times a day and everyone loves it."

"Colton, you're mine, stay away from the dumb blonde."

"Okay, don't read those comments. But most are good." Colton clicks a few more things that catch his attention.

At the top of the page in large bold letters it says, **Colton Von Jobin Missing. Band Members Worried.** Posted eight hours ago.

"See," I point to the screen. "You should call them. Let them know you're fine."

He clicks on the next one. **Have You Seen This Man?** There's a picture of Colton. **Lead Singer for Von Jobin Missing. Band and Family Members Fear for His Safety.** Posted six hours ago.

"For fuck's sake! They're blowing this way out of proportion."

He clicks on the next one. **Colton Von Jobin Sighted at Canadian Modelling Agency.** Posted five hours ago.

He keeps clicking. **Colton Von Jobin Disappears in Toronto Blizzard.** Posted four hours ago.

The next one says, **Colton Von Jobin Sighted in Niagara Falls, Safe in Arms of Blonde Model from Singers New Video.** Posted forty-five minutes ago.

Colton scrolls down to look at the pictures.

"Colton! Someone was taking pictures of us as we were walking along the falls. And at the restaurant. How did they get those?"

"You'd be surprised how they get pictures. Been caught skinny dipping a few times. One photographer got a pic of me taking a shower in my own house. Still don't have a clue how he got that one, two stories up."

His attention returns to the computer screen. "I like this picture. Might have to get this one blown up." He points to the one where he's holding me and I'm smiling down at him.

"And this one." He's holding my hand in the restaurant, looking like he's in love.

"Oh, I like this one, too. Kind of erotic, don't you think?" It's of him holding me in his arms and sucking on my finger at the falls.

I stand quickly. "Colton, I'm in deep shit! Do you not understand?"

He looks at me, concerned. "Bryce?"

"Yes." I start pacing back and forth. "Oh my God, he's going to lose it."

He stands in front of me holding my arms. "I'll protect you."

I glare at him, stunned by his comment. "He'd never hurt me. He might yell a bit, though."

"I don't know. I've seen his temper."

I stare at him again, wondering what he's insinuating.

"You can call me anytime, anywhere and I'll hop on the next plane to get to you."

I shake my head. "This was supposed to be just dinner. Now look at the mess I'm in! I knew this wasn't a good idea."

He holds my shoulders, keeping me in place. "This was a great idea. I got to spend time with my Angel Eyes."

I spin out of his hold and start pacing again. "Don't you see how serious this is?"

He tries to stop me from pacing by putting his arms around me. "If you want, I'll talk to Bryce."

I cut him off and push him back. "Oh hell, no! That would make it ten times worse."

"He's got to understand that you were in a blizzard and couldn't get home and all you did was go to dinner with a friend."

"Yeah, a friend who the paparazzi follow around taking pictures. And the said friend, can't stop touching me."

"Just tell him the truth. I'm in love with you and I can't keep my hands off of you."

"You're not helping." I drop down onto the couch and let out a huge sigh.

"Well, just think. If he breaks up with you, we can be together."

I look up at him, stunned again. Did he plan this? Is he trying to break me and Bryce up? No, he wouldn't do that. Would he? He wants me that badly? I place my hands over my face and rub my forehead in circles.

"Do you have a headache?"

"No. I'm trying to think."

"Don't worry. It'll all work out. Maybe he won't see the pictures."

I glance up at him with my, you've got to be shitting me look. I lower my head back down and rub my forehead again.

He comes to sit beside me and rubs my knee. "I hate seeing you like this."

I stand up and grab my coat and purse off the chair. "I've got to go."

"Go where?" He catches up and steps in front of me before I make it to the door. "The storm is just ending. The roads are still pretty bad. The only way to get you back is by helicopter and my pilot might be asleep now."

"Where is your pilot?"

"Next door."

"Can you see if he'll fly me back?"

"You don't want to stay here with me? I promise I'll sleep on the couch, you can sleep in the bed. I just need you near me. Please? Stay?" His voice is so convincing.

"Colton, I can't."

"I understand." He hesitates a moment, probably waiting for me to change my mind, but I glare at him. "I'll go see if he's awake."

Colton steps out the door and I go to the bathroom.

When I come out, He's standing at the window, looking out

at the falls. I come up beside him. "Um, he uh, has someone with him."

"Okay, so maybe when he's done."

"I could check in a couple of hours."

I turn away from Colton, sighing. "What now?" I mouth silently as I walk into the living room. *Fuck!*

I flop down on the couch, grab the remote, and turn on the TV.

Colton sits beside me and pats my knee. "You don't like my company?"

"Yes, I like your company. But It's late. I should be getting back now. I got up early and I'm tired."

He puts a pillow on his lap and pats it. "Put that pretty little head of yours right here and take a quick nap."

"I'm okay." I start flipping through the channels and see a picture of Colton's face plastered across the TV screen.

The news announcer says, "Colton Von Jobin, lead singer for the rock band Von Jobin went missing for eight hours today. Band members, family, and friends have not heard from him, but there have been reports of him visiting this Toronto modeling agency." They show the tall, blue, mirrored-glass Alaina building. "He then disappeared in the Toronto blizzard to show up in Niagara Falls with this beautiful model, who appears in his newly released music video." They show a couple shots from the video of me in the water flipping my hair back and running on the beach in my white bikini. Then a shot of Colton picking me up by the falls and sucking on my finger.

I can't believe this!

"All of us at the station are relieved to know you're safe, Colton. Moving on to more entertainment news…"

I lower my face into my hands and shake my head. "I can't fucking believe this."

Colton pulls my hands away from my face. "I can't hear you when you mumble like that."

I look at him and say, "I said, I can't believe this! I hope they don't play that news cast in Barrie."

"Usually it's just the local area."

"I hope so. Colton you've got to call Reese and let him know you're okay."

He lets out a deep sigh. "Fine."

"I'm sorry, I don't mean to bitch at you, but put yourself in his position. If he went missing, you'd be losing your mind."

"You're right." He turns his phone on and checks his texts and e-mails. After a few minutes, he comments, "Yeah, they were freaking out. Thought I lost my shit and off-ed myself."

"Why would they think that?"

"Because I've been a little depressed the last couple of weeks, but I'm good now." He tugs me into his side.

I look up at him, and cock my head to one side raising my eyebrows.

"What?" he asks, as if he doesn't know what I'm getting at.

"Reese?"

He's stalling, but I don't say another word.

"Right. Call Reese." He hits a number on his phone. "Hey it's me. I'm fine." He puts the phone next to my ear and leans close to me.

I hear Reese shouting. "Everyone shut the fuck up. It's Colton! Where the hell have you been? You asshole! You scared the shit out of everyone. From what we've seen on the news, it looks like you're getting cozy with Keera."

So much for the theory that the news stays local.

"Yeah, I'm fine now that I'm with Keera. She can hear you, by the way."

"Hi, Keera."

"Hi, Reese."

"You taking care of my big bro?"

"He seems to be fine."

"That's good news. Colt, when you coming back?"

"I'll be in Detroit for tomorrow night's concert."

"You'd better be."

"I will. Promise."

"Okay. Have fun! Bye, Keera."

"Bye, Reese."

"Bye, Jackass." Colton gets his dig in.

"Bye, Asshole." Reese insults Colton and they hang up.

I hold my hand over my mouth and yawn. "Excuse me. Brotherly love. You guys are too cute together. Very comical."

"Yeah, but sometimes you just need a break."

"I know, I'm that way with Leena." I yawn again.

"You're tired. Just put your head down right here." Colton pats the pillow on his lap.

"I probably won't fall asleep." I lie my head down on the pillow and watch as he flips through the channels.

When I wake up, I rub my eyes until I can see clearly. I'm lying in a bed. I look around and see I'm in a hotel room, and there's an arm wrapped around me. I turn slightly and see the arm belongs to Colton. I stiffen. Holy fuck! His hand is pressed to my stomach. His left leg is slung over both of mine. I'm stuck. I can't move without waking him.

He's sleeping? What time is it? I search for the alarm clock, but can't see it. I lie still, listening to his breathing, thinking as I glance over the room. My gaze stops abruptly when I see my pants and blouse draped over a chair on the other side of the room.

Panic stricken, I lift the covers and see that I have my bra on, but can't feel whether I still have my thong on.

Oh no, we did not! I don't remember anything after lying my head on the pillow. *Relax, Keera. You'd remember if anything happened. Especially with Colton. Right?*

Oh, God, I don't know. Wake him up and ask him. But he's sleeping so soundly. He probably just crawled into bed beside me and went to sleep. *What the hell did he take my clothes off for then? Why didn't he wake me when the pilot was ready?*

Because he had plans for you, that's why. Ah Jesus, why does this shit always happen to me? Okay, enough torturing yourself, Keera. Time for him to get up.

I lift and turn my head so I can look over Colton and see the clock. It says eight-thirty. I try to roll over and he lifts his leg and arm without waking up. Once I'm settled in facing him, he places them back down over top of me.

I stare at his beautiful features. He seems to be sleeping still. His dark brown silky hair flops across his forehead. He has long dark eyelashes and a sculpted face with a perfect nose, full lips, and a slight indent in his chin.

He looks a lot like Kurt Russell.

What woman wouldn't want him? He's gorgeous. Am I the only idiot? He would be the perfect boyfriend, husband, and father.

If Colton had come along before Bryce, would I be in love with Colton?

Colton stirs and then opens his eyes. He kisses me before I have time to react. "Good morning, beautiful."

"Good morning? Is that all you have to say? What did I tell you about kissing me?" I cover my lips with my finger.

"I thought it would be okay after last night."

"What? What do you mean?" Panic stricken, I feel my eyes widen. "What happened?" My heart is pounding. Fast.

"You don't remember?"

"Colton, quit fucking around. What happened?" I'm horrified.

"Relax. I only wish there had been some fucking around, going on. You fell asleep and I carried you in here."

"Why'd you take my clothes off?"

"So you'd be comfortable."

"How'd you get my clothes off without waking me up?"

"That wasn't easy." He chuckles. "Every time you moved to

wake up, I'd stop and wait for you to fall into a deep sleep again. It took me a while to get those clothes off."

"Why didn't you wake me when the pilot was done with his sexcapade?"

"Because he's probably still going at it. When I called him, he said 'She's a wild one, she could suck the chrome off a trailer hitch,' so I figured I wouldn't bother him anymore."

"So when you took my clothes off, what did you do?"

"What do you think I did? I stood there and stared at you. Fuck Keera, I've never been so turned on, except of course when I watched you and Bryce fucking in Aruba. Damn woman, you stir up all kinds of dirty shit in the back of my head. I had to go take care of myself in the bathroom after that."

I try not to smile, but fail miserably. "Then what'd you do?"

"Then I came back and stared at you again. You're so beautiful. I tried to leave the room to go sleep on the couch, but I thought, hell no, I'm not missing the opportunity to hold you all night, so I climbed in bed with you. And obviously fell asleep. Of all the fucking nights to fall asleep. I fell asleep with you in my arms. I can't believe this!" He shakes his head in disgust. "But I did get eight hours of sound sleep for the first time in-well, actually, I don't know how long it's been since I slept eight hours."

I smile at his honesty.

"Promise me you'll never tell anyone we slept in the same bed."

"Trust me I won't, because then I'd have to explain why I didn't get any and had to go jack off."

I laugh and start to get up.

"Wait." He holds me tight in his arms. "Can I just hold you for a bit?"

I relax in his arms and he kisses my forehead.

"Keera?"

I look up at him. "Yeah?"

"If you and Bryce ever break up. Will you call me?"

"In a heartbeat. You'd be the perfect boyfriend. You sure do know how to treat a girl right. Thank you for everything. I had a great time."

"You're welcome. I have to say this has been the best two days I've had since we came back from Aruba."

Some of the things he says, breaks my heart. "Colton, you're so sweet." I take his face in my hands and kiss his cheek. "Thank you for not taking advantage of me."

"If you only knew the things that were going on in my head last night, you wouldn't be thanking me right now."

"Oh, Colton. I love your honesty."

He holds my face in his hands and looks deep in my eyes. "I love you."

"Oh, no you don't!" I wiggle out of his embrace and get out of bed. "Colton, you will find the right girl and she will love you forever, but I'm not that girl!"

His eyes rake up and down my body hungrily.

He throws the covers back and gets out of bed.

"Jesus, Colton, you're naked!" I cover my eyes, but look through my fingers.

24

COLTON CHUCKLES. "YOU'RE not covering your eyes very well."

I turn and face the wall. "You were lying next to me naked all night?"

"Well, yeah. That's why I'm surprised I fell asleep." He pauses. "Lord have mercy! That is the perfect ass, by the way."

His voice, deep and sexy, grabs my attention and I look over my shoulder at him. He's leaning against the door jamb in a pose that screams dominant sex god. He's totally naked, and staring at my ass. "Colton, put some damn clothes on!"

I rush over to the chair, holding my hand up like a blinder so I won't be tempted to look at him, and slide my pants on. I pull my blouse on quickly. As I'm fumbling with the buttons, I feel the heat from his body behind me.

How'd he move that fast from across the room, and without a sound?

"What are you getting flustered for?" he asks in a husky tone, right next to my ear.

Because you're too close with that body. That gorgeous naked body. "I'm not," I say, trying to disguise my wayward thoughts.

"Yes, you are."

I keep trying to do up my buttons, but my fingers are useless.

He leans his body against mine and hovers over my shoulder, looking down my top. "Fingers not working?"

I turn to get a better look and see he's grinning at me.

He wraps his arm around my waist and tugs me hard into his steely erection. *Oh, my!* Then he whispers in a voice that makes my knees go weak, "I like it when you have fewer clothes on. That body of yours and that bra and thong?" He shakes his head and his long hair tickles my sensitive skin. "Mmm, so sexy."

"Colton. I gotta go." I twirl out of his arms. "I've got to get out of this bedroom."

"Wait!"

When I get to the door, I look back and see he's not covering up at all.

Why is it, men always feel the need to get naked in front of me? I cover my eyes again. "What?"

"Don't leave. I'm sorry. Wait for me in the living room, I'll get dressed."

I pull my hands away and look him straight in the eye. "Good." As I'm about to turn, I do a once over, checking out his body from head to toe.

I shake my head, smiling and walk out. "Fucking tease."

That body of his. Holy mother of god!

Shake it off Keera. Get that vision out of your head. But I don't want to. Pay attention. It's time to go home now. Right! I can't even think straight.

Crap. I have to go pee. While I'm in the bathroom, I do the normal ritual to freshen up and swirl some mouthwash around.

As I leave, Colton is coming out of the bedroom fully dressed and our eyes meet.

Good. This is much easier when he has clothes on.

"Ready to go?" I ask, grabbing my coat, eager to get out of here.

"I have to see if my pilot's ready."

"I'm coming with you."

"Don't trust me?" Colton says, winking.

"Let's just say… you're stalling."

He chuckles. "You're getting to know me well."

He holds my lower back and guides me to the pilot's door.

He knocks and a short, bubbly, half-naked blonde answers the door. "Two more?" she asks, looking surprised. "You ready to join us now, Colton?"

"Where's Craig?" Colton steps inside, tugging me into the foyer, which looks the same as his room except for all the naked bodies lying on the floor in the living room.

I look at Colton. "Yeah, Craig's into some freaky shit. But just so you know, I'm a one-woman man, into just one woman—and that's you."

"Come on." The bubbly blonde leads Colton and me to the bedroom. "I'll show you where Craig is."

The pilot is passed out across the bed, naked.

"Oh, that's just fucking great!" I can't contain my outburst.

Colton tugs me over to the bed with him and slaps the pilot across the face. "Wake up, it's time to fly. I don't give a shit that you've only had a couple hours sleep. Get your fucking ass up or you're fired!" Colton slaps him in the face again.

"Okay, I'm up." Craig falls back to sleep.

Colton lets go of me, picks Craig up, and throws him over his shoulder. He carries Craig into the bathroom and, when I hear what sounds like a little girl screaming, I assume he's put him in the shower and turned the cold water on. "Fucker!" Craig yells. "Turn it off! Turn it off!"

"I'm telling you, if you're not at the chopper in half an hour, you're fired and you won't ever work again. Got that?" Colton's voice is loud and angry.

"Okay, okay."

The bubbly blonde looks me up and down. "So your Colton's girlfriend?" Her voice is spitefully unpleasant.

I'm just as snotty back. "What's it to you?"

"Because, I just fucked Craig all night so I could get close to Colton."

"Well, that was your first mistake! He won't even look at you now. He likes good girls. The ones who are a challenge."

Colton overhears our conversation, I think, because he gives me a reassuring squeeze. "Let's go for breakfast."

"Sure, let's go."

Colton takes my hand and leads the way as he storms out of the penthouse and heads for the elevators.

I've never seen him this angry, so I stay quiet, waiting for him to calm down.

He hits the button for the elevator and then hugs me. "I'm sorry you had to see that."

"I'm okay," I say, but my mind is replaying the picture of all those naked bodies scattered across the living room. *Yup, that was a little freaky. And yet... arousing. Am I weird to think that?*

Colton releases my hand, pulling me from my strange thoughts as the elevator arrives.

The ride down is a bit awkward as Colton tries to regain his composer and return to his normal personality.

As we wait to be seated at the restaurant near the main lobby entrance, Colton expresses his thoughts. "That fucker's been getting on my nerves for a while now. He thinks that just because I'm a rock star, I'm into that shit. But he's wrong. He's got another thing coming when he gets us back. His ass is fired! I'll get a new pilot!"

Holy! Don't piss Colton off, he's all business. I see that now.

Curiosity is killing me. "I don't know how to ask this, so I'm just going to say it. Did he want you to join them?"

"Yeah, he pulls this shit all the time. You'd think he'd get the hint when I turn him down every time."

"Sounds to me like maybe he's gay and he wants you."

"Craig doesn't care where he gets it."

"Oh."

During breakfast, I get Colton talking about his parents and I can see him physically thawing after his disagreement with Craig. I learn that he has a younger sister who plays the violin very well. I ask if she's ever played on stage with them at a concert and he says, "Maybe someday." We talk about Reese and then we talk about the instruments Colton plays. As well as singing, he plays guitar, drums, and piano. He also organizes and mixes all their recordings, and writes most of their songs. The man is very talented.

He then turns the tables and asks me how long Bryce and I have been going out for. After I tell him, I can see the wheels turning in his head. He asks me about my life. I say there's not much to tell, but I tell him how my parents died and how hard it was. He asks me if I have any brothers and sisters and I tell him I'm an only child and Gramps is the only family I have left. He asks where I live again and I keep it short, only telling him Huntsville again. Do I like living there, he wants to know. It's the only life I know, I respond.

During breakfast, Colton maintains steady contact with his leg against mine. I experiment by moving my leg occasionally, but he always finds his way back to touching me. In the limo he did the same, touching me constantly, and I felt sorry for him that I couldn't return the gesture.

When we get to the airport, Craig is just finishing up fueling the chopper. Colton's whole demeanour toward Craig has changed from yesterday, almost like he has no use for him. I think Craig notices, because he's awfully quiet.

On the ride back to Toronto, Colton is all business again, staying quiet even though we have headsets and microphones. I stay quiet too. His leg leans against mine and he holds my hand. I let him, knowing he just needs to. He looks down at me and smiles every once in a while and I look up and smile back. He points down to certain things he wants me to see and I nod, letting him know I've seen them.

When we arrive at the airport in Toronto, Colton calls for another limo and tells Craig to wait with the chopper because he'll be back in one hour. There's no mistaking the harsh tone in Colton's voice, so I hope Craig listens for his own sake.

On the limo ride over to the Alaina building, where my car is parked, Colton takes my hand in his and kisses my palm. "Do you know how bad it's killing me to let you go again? To let you go back into Bryce's arms?"

"Colton." I hesitate for a second, not wanting to hurt his feelings, but he starts to speak again.

"I know I don't have the right to claim you as mine. Yet. But I will."

I turn away slightly and open my eyes wide. *Jesus, he just doesn't give up.*

"Keera?"

"Yes?" I look at him.

"I don't have much time to tell you everything that's been on my mind. So will you do me a favour?"

"Sure," I say, before I have a chance to think about it.

"Will you listen to Von Jobin's music? I mean really listen to the words, because everything that's in my heart I put down on paper and then I create a song. And don't think it's about someone else, because I know what you're like. You keep denying my love for you. There's only you. You're the one I want. I will only write about how I feel for you."

Jeez, if that isn't clear, I don't know what is. "Yes. I'll listen to the words."

"Really listen?"

"Yes."

"Thank you."

I have to lighten the mood, so I try the southern drawl he used on me. "Anything for you darlin'. How's my southern drawl?"

"Needs some work."

I tickle his side. "What do you mean? I thought I did pretty good."

"But you weren't sincere, like I was."

"Colton, I try to please people. I like to make people happy. I'm sorry I can't give you what you want. I wish I could be more sincere. But-"

He cuts me off. "I know. Bryce."

"Yes."

The limo slows and then stops. "Come with me, beautiful." I take Colton's hand and slide out of the limo. He fishes out another hefty tip for the limo driver.

I search for the tag in my purse and hand it to the valet to retrieve my car.

Since it's cold outside, Colton and I slip inside the double glass doors of the Alaina building and wait for the valet to bring my car around.

He invades my space, making me back up against the glass wall, unable go any further. His left hand rests on my hip, while his right hand gently holds my neck as he strokes his thumb back and forth along my jawline.

"Keera, I'll be back in three weeks, unless you need me before then. Say if Bryce pisses you off. He'd better not touch you over this. I'd have to kill him. I'll drop everything to see you. Just call me. Here's my number." Colton hands me a piece of paper with a number on it and I slip it in my coat pocket.

He's coming back in three weeks. How do I explain this to Bryce?

"I know calling is out of the question, but can I e-mail you?"

"Umm."

"Just hide it from Bryce. What he doesn't know won't hurt him. I'll e-mail. I need to stay in contact with you."

The valet saves me by pulling up in my Journey. I look over Colton's shoulder so he sees they've brought it. He takes my hand and leads me to my car.

A lone paparazzi surprises us when we step outside. He moves in quickly, getting closer, clicking away to get as many pictures as he can.

Colton quickens his pace. "Keera, get in and drive." He moves fast, hopping in the passenger side as I jump in the driver's seat. He hands me a tip for the valet and I roll down my window and give it to him. "Drive, baby! Drive!"

I pull out of the parking structure, sliding sideways because the roads are still slick, but I quickly recover it. When I look in my rear view mirror, the paparazzi is taking pictures of us driving away.

"Nice driving!" Colton shouts. "Were you a NASCAR driver in a previous life?" I chuckle.

As I drive us back to the airport, Colton runs his hand over my knuckles. "See? Something else I know about you now. This is a Dodge, right?" His other hand rubs the dash.

"Yes."

"If you were mine, I'd buy you whatever car or SUV you want. A Benz or an Audi? What about a Ferrari? I could see you in a red Ferrari."

"Colton, I'm a simple kind of girl. I don't need much. That's why I think you'd be better off with someone more compatible with your lifestyle. I can see you with a Victoria's Secret mod-"

"Nope." Colton talks over me. "That's what I love about you. I know you wouldn't take me for a ride. You're not a gold digger. Like I told you before, there's only one woman for me and that's you."

This is getting me nowhere.

"Thank you for the ride back," he says.

"Colton, you spent way too much money on me. All the limos, a chopper, the restaurant, and taking me to see the falls, thank you for everything. Do you spend money like this all the time?"

"Not usually, but this was a special occasion. I've learned a lot about you on this trip. There will be more to come. I'm not giving up, Keera. We'll get to know each other, real well. And if you and Bryce break up, I'm coming for you!" His eyes bore into mine, intensely. "You will be mine!"

Oh, crap!

Colton hugs me. "God I'm going to miss you."

"Thank you for everything, Colton."

He kisses my cheek. "You're welcome. Be careful going home."

"You too."

He hugs me again. "I don't want to let you go. I'm worried about you! If Bryce loses it, if he touches you, call me right away and leave him."

"He'll be fine. He'll be mad and yell, but he should be-"

Before I finish my sentence he kisses my lips and gives me a little tongue. "Gotcha! Be safe. I love you, Keera."

He hops out of my Journey and I watch him strut happily to the chopper.

I smile. "Bugger! He got me again."

Just as Colton's about to get in the chopper, he hesitates on the first step. Looking back at me, he salutes with two fingers to his temple.

I smile and wave.

He ducks his head and climbs in. The rotor blades start turning.

"Lord, help me. He is too sexy."

The helicopter takes off and I start to drive away, shaking my head. "Why does he think he loves me? He hardly knows me."

Once I'm out of traffic and on Highway 400, I think about Bryce and how he's going to react to this. *What if he breaks up with me? I'm overreacting. Maybe he hasn't seen the pictures. Yeah, right!*

I have to prepare myself for the worst. *Shit, what do I say? I just need to tell him the truth from beginning to end.*

How nothing happened. How I told Colton not to kiss me.

How I tried to keep my distance. Colton's just a touchy-feely kind of guy. *Nope, don't tell him that.*

By the time I make it back to Barrie, my nerves are shot from worrying about Bryce's reaction.

I had a spark of hope that he might be here because the driveway is cleared of snow, but once I open the garage door, I see his truck is not here. My hope fades. *Damn! I want to get this over with.*

When I punch in the code and the door opens, I'm surprised he hasn't changed it.

First thing I do when I get upstairs to the kitchen is plug in my phone and then call Leena on Bryce's home phone.

"It's about time you called me." Leena's voice sounds a little angry. "Bryce was texting me, asking where you were and if you got a room."

"And you told him I was safe and had a room and I love him, right?"

"Yes. I also told him your phone died and that's why you weren't texting after the photo shoot was done."

"Good."

"So tell me about it. How was the photo shoot?"

"Good. Very impressive. Everyone knew me by name, including the valet. Chaz is very nice. Good looking, like maybe he was a model himself."

"Oh, yeah?"

"After signing the paperwork, he sent me to Josie in the hair salon and we got to work right away. Brent, the photographer, was easy to work with, but he had me change I don't know how many times. Josie and Anna curled my hair and then did an up-do for the red dress, which was amazing. Then they had me in a few bathing suits and when I finished with the last bikini change, guess who showed up?"

"Who?"

"Colton."

"What?"

"I know. I couldn't believe it. I thought I saw him a couple of times during the day, but I wasn't sure. I thought maybe it was just someone who looked like Colton. I was shocked. I asked him why he was there."

"What'd he say?"

"He said he heard I was there at Alaina, so he thought he'd come pick up the pictures of the band, personally."

"And do you believe him?"

"No. Colton and Chaz were talking on the phone earlier when I was filling out the paperwork, or at least I think he was because of the way Chaz was talking and smiling at me."

"You think Colton set up the photo shoot to see you again?"

"Yeah. That's what it looks like."

"Holy shit, this is getting interesting. What happened then?"

"Everyone in the office disappeared and went home because of the snow storm and left Chaz, me, and Colton. I got changed because it was a little cold wearing that bikini, and when I came out of the dressing room, Colton was waiting for me. I was booking it to the elevator so I could see how bad the roads were for myself, and he told me the major highways were shut down. So then I thought, okay, well, I guess I have to get a room now."

"Tell me you didn't drive in that shit? Stubborn!"

"No. My stomach was growling so loud from lack of food all day-"

Leena cuts me off. "They didn't feed you?"

"They had a huge buffet set out for everyone, but they were all staring at my plate so I only took fruit and a yogurt."

"Oh, Keera. You have to quit worrying about what people think of you. I would have dug in and chowed down until I was full."

"I wish I could be more like you."

"Yeah, fuck 'em. If they don't like it, don't look. Right? Then what happened?"

"After Colton heard my stomach growling, he asked me what I'd eaten all day. When I told him, he shook his head like he was unhappy with me, so then he said, 'You're obviously hungry. Let me take you to my favourite restaurant.' I was pretty hungry. And he was very convincing. So I thought I'll go for dinner and then find a room right after and drive home in the morning."

"Oh yeah?"

"Why are you saying it like that?"

"No reason. Continue."

"The hummer limo was having a hard time making it through the snow with all the cars stranded, so Colton thought of different transportation. A helicopter."

"What? Get the hell out of here."

"I was surprised too, and scared shitless. I couldn't see anything out the windows until the snow storm mellowed out, and at that point we were over a huge waterfall with different colored lights."

"No frickin' way. He took you to Niagara Falls?"

"Yeah. I lost it. I said, 'Your favourite restaurant is in Niagara Falls?' I was thinking, 'How am I going to explain this one to Bryce?' But he told me he'd take me back to Toronto to get my Journey, so I calmed down."

"What was his favourite restaurant?"

"The Hilton Hotel. He had reservations overlooking the falls. I think he was trying to impress me."

"And were you?"

"Yeah, it was very nice."

"He took you to Niagara Falls in a helicopter for dinner? Sounds to me like the perfect boyfriend. Just saying."

"Yeah, yeah, whatever. So dinner went well, the Veal Parmesan was excellent, except he was staring at me the whole time and not looking at the falls. He asked me if I wanted to take a walk along the falls later. I said, 'We came all this way so we have to see the falls. I'd love to.' I remember being there with mom and dad when I was five or six, but I couldn't remember much of it. Once I saw the falls, it all came back to me. It was nice except there was a paparazzi taking pictures of us, which I found out later when Colton showed me the completed version of his video back in his room."

"What! Whoa! Hold up here! Let me get this straight. You're at dinner overlooking the falls in some ritzy restaurant, he takes you to the falls, and somebody's taking pictures of you and Colton together, and you only find this out because you go up to his room and he's showing you his new video on the computer and you see it then?"

"Yes, that's when we saw all the pictures."

"One second. I'm getting my computer so I can see this. How the hell did he convince you to go up to his room?"

"I was cold at the falls so he offered to show me something else where it's warm and I had no clue until we were standing at his hotel room door. He told me to relax, he just wanted to show me the video."

"I know what he wanted to show you. And you believed him?"

"You know what Colton is like. He's smooth, very convincing, like Reese."

"Yeah, Reese, I'm telling you, if Austin hadn't been there in Aruba with me, Reese would have convinced me to drop my panties in a second."

"Ho!"

"Oh, yes, I am. Keera, what the hell is this? Colton Von Jobin missing?"

"That's another thing that was going on. He told me that after we got back from Aruba, all he thought about was me and he got a little depressed. While I was in the dressing room, everyone in the band was wondering where he disappeared to and was calling, worried about him, so he shut his phone off. I told him he should let Reese know he's okay, but he said, yeah, maybe later. He said he didn't want anyone bothering him right now."

"Well, yeah, he had you all to himself and Bryce was nowhere in sight."

"Yeah." I let out a huff. "Then the story escalated to Colton missing in the blizzard and Colton found in Niagara Falls in the arms of the model from his new video."

"I can see that. Holy crap! Keera, there are pictures of you two at the restaurant with Colton kissing your neck, and you guys walking along the falls. Oh crap! Wait until Bryce sees this one."

"What one?"

"The one where he's picking you up in his arms. And… is he sucking on your finger?"

"I was pointing and told him not to kiss me, because every once in a while when I wasn't paying attention, he'd slip one in."

"This is getting really interesting."

25

"I'M SCREWED, LEENA, don't you see that? Bryce is probably going to break up with me."

"You haven't talked to him yet?"

"No. I'm waiting for him to get home from work."

"Umm… I hate to make this worse, but did you see the video?"

"Von Jobin's video?"

"No, the video of you and Colton."

"What video?"

"It shows you and Colton in an intimate moment inside two glass doors."

"That's the Alaina building where he handed me his phone number and said he'd be back in three weeks. Then he proceeded to say, unless I need him before then, say if Bryce pisses me off. He said he better not touch you over this and that he'd have to kill Bryce. He said he's worried about Bryce's temper and if he loses it, to leave him. He also said it was killing him to send me back into Bryce's arms. At that point it crossed my mind a few times that maybe he was trying to break me and Bryce up."

"Don't you remember when Colton said that when he wants something, he'll wait? And he always gets what he wants?"

"He looked serious." My mind wanders back to when he said that. "But I fluffed it off."

"You need to quit being so naïve. The man means business. Obviously. He hatched this whole plan to see you again."

"I think he did."

"Here's another video of you and Colton getting into your Journey in a hell of a hurry."

"That's because Colton told me to get in and drive. The paparazzi was right there when we came out of the building."

"I see that. There's a good shot of you handing the valet a tip and you can hear Colton say, 'Drive, baby, drive!'"

"That's when I took him back to the chopper at the airport."

"Keera, you have got to check out these pictures."

"I've already seen them. Saw the news cast."

"It was on the news?"

"Yes. Reese saw it all the way in Detroit, so I'll put money on it that Bryce has seen it. How do I get myself into situations like this?"

"You're too fucking nice, Keera. You've got to start saying no and quit being so goddamn naïve."

"Thanks." I say sarcastically. "You're really making me feel better."

"If Bryce loves you, he'll believe you."

"If Colton wasn't famous and he was just another guy, no one would be taking pictures and no one would have a clue that I went out for dinner. That's all it was supposed to be. God, I've got shitty luck."

"Just a couple pictures show him kissing you and then you can show Bryce the one where you're giving him shit for it."

"That doesn't help because I'm smiling when I'm giving him shit."

"See, you're too nice. Well, you know, if Bryce breaks up with you, you could always go out with Colt-"

I cut Leena off. "Don't even say it."

"What? Look at these pictures. You're obviously having a good time with him."

"See, if you think that, what is Bryce going to think? I should never have gone with him."

"Pictures can be deceiving."

"I'm royally screwed!"

"It might not be that bad. After that picture, he took you back to Toronto, right?"

"Umm, not exactly."

"What happened?"

"Well, after the news cast, and after I made him call Reese, that's when we saw the pictures and the headlines about Colton missing. I had a fit and told him I had to go back right away. He said he'd see if his pilot was awake. I asked him where his pilot was and he said in the penthouse next door. When he came back he said the pilot had someone with him and he'd check back with him in a couple hours. I was tired, so he convinced me to take a nap."

"Oh, no!"

"Oh, yeah. Promise you won't tell anyone what I'm about to tell you."

"What happened?"

"Promise me or my lips are sealed forever."

"Okay, okay, I promise. I won't say a word. This is between you and me."

"No Austin, no Bryce, no Ciara, and no one else, for that matter."

"I promise. Spill it."

"I fell asleep on the couch with my head on a pillow in his lap. And when I woke up, I was in bed, with Colton wrapped around me, asleep."

"Oh, fuck."

"And then I looked over and saw my clothes on the chair."

"What?"

"So I looked under the sheets and found out I had my bra on, but I couldn't feel if my thong was still on. I didn't want to wake him because he was finally sleeping. So then I was losing my mind, thinking I fucked him. But I'd remember fucking Colton. Right?"

"Oh, hell yeah, I hope so. Honey, he could eat crackers in my bed any day of the week. Or anything else he wanted to eat in my bed. He's one of those guys you know can fuck real good."

"I know, eh? Someday I'll kick myself in the ass for this. So when he woke, he kissed me before I had time to react. I said 'What did I tell you about kissing me?' He said, 'I thought it would be okay after last night.' I panicked. I was like, 'What do you mean, what happened?' You should have seen the devilish smile on his face when he said, 'You don't remember?' The expression on my face must have been pure horror. I told him to quit fucking around and asked again, 'What happened?' He told me to relax, he only wished there was some fucking around going on. He said I fell asleep on the couch and he carried me to the bed. I asked him why he took my clothes off. His answer was so I'd be comfortable."

"Yeah, right. How'd he get your clothes off without you waking up?"

"He said every time I started to wake up he'd stop and wait for me to fall into a deep sleep. He laughed and said it took a while. I think it was because of all the Bud Light Limes he was feeding me in the limos. Oh, thanks for telling him everything about me by the way."

"Who would have thought you'd ever see the guy again. I mean really, he's Colton Von Jobin, the rock god."

"Yeah, so then I asked him what he did when he took my clothes off. He said, 'Fuck, Keera! I've never been so turned on in my life, except of course when you and Bryce were fucking in Aruba.' He said, 'Damn, woman, you stir up all kinds of dirty shit in the back of my mind.'"

"Oh, I bet."

"He told me he went to the washroom to take care of himself and when he came back he stared again."

Leena talks over me. "And jacked off, all over again."

I chuckle and then continue. "He said he tried to leave the room to go sleep on the couch, but he wasn't missing the opportunity to hold me all night."

"I bet he tried real hard. Colton had a plan and he succeeded."

"I don't know, he was pretty bummed that he fell asleep. He said, 'Of all fucking nights to fall asleep, with you in my arms.' Then I thanked him for not taking advantage of me and he said, 'If you only knew what was going through my head, you wouldn't be thanking me right now.' I told him I love his honesty and then he held my face and said, 'I love you.'"

"What?"

"I know. It freaked me out. He said it before, but indirectly, so I fluffed it off. But this time, Leena, I think he meant it. I jumped out of bed and said, 'Oh no, you don't. You'll find the right girl and she'll love you forever. I'm not that girl.' He threw the covers back and I got a big surprise. I said, 'Jesus, Colton, you're naked!'"

"Get out? He was naked?"

"I covered my face and looked through my fingers. Leena, oh my lord! What a body!"

"I thought you said you saw it before in Aruba?"

"I did, but he was thirty feet away. This time he was only ten feet away. So anyway, he said, 'You're not covering your eyes very well.'"

"Busted!"

"Yeah. So then I turned to look at the wall. I said, 'You were lying next to me naked all night?' He said, 'That's why I'm surprised I fell asleep.' Then I heard that voice of his."

"I know that voice-the one that fries your brain and has you clenching your thighs together, thinking of wild, extraordinary sex with the god himself."

"That's a good description of what I felt like at that moment."

"Yeah, you were! You were probably dripping."

I chuckle. "Anyway, in that voice he said, 'Lord have mercy, that is the perfect ass." His voice made me curious so I turned around and he was leaning against the door jamb in the sexiest pose. I yelled at him to put some damn clothes on! Holy fuck, Leena, it was too much to handle, so I rushed over to get my clothes on and as I was buttoning my blouse, I could feel the heat from his body leaning against me. He said, 'Why are you getting flustered?' I said I wasn't. 'Yes, you are.' he said. I couldn't get my fingers to work, so he leaned over my shoulder and looked down my top, smirking at me. He said, 'Fingers not working?' Using that sexy-as-hell voice again. Then he pulled me against his hard cock and whispered, 'I like it when you have fewer clothes on. That body of yours and that bra and thong… so sexy.' Leena, I think my thong disintegrated at that moment. I couldn't take anymore. I twirled out of his arms and ran to the door. I said, 'I gotta go.' He yelled, 'Wait!' I turned to look him straight in the eye and said, 'What?' He said, 'I'm sorry don't leave, I'll get dressed.' But before he did, I had to run my eyes over his body, from head to toe, once more."

"I don't know how you did it? There's no way in hell I would have had enough will power to ever resist that."

"He's such a tease, I couldn't even think straight when I left the room. I still have that vision in my head."

"I just shivered. I think I had a mini-orgasm thinking about him."

"Leena, you crack me up. Anyway, when he came out of the bedroom, he was fully dressed. Much easier to resist him. He said, 'I'll go see if the pilot's ready.' I said, 'I'll go with you.' He said, 'You don't trust me?' I said, 'Let's just say you're stalling.' Then when we got to the pilot's door, a bubbly, half-naked, little blonde greeted us and said, 'Two more? You ready to join us now, Colton?'"

"What does that mean?"

"I guess the pilot has these parties all the time and invites Colton to join him, but Colton says he's not into that freaky shit. He says he's into one woman and that's me."

"Well, he liked it when he saw you and Bryce fucking."

"Yeah, he did. He's mentioned it a few times. So anyway, Blondie brings us through a sea of naked bodies sleeping in the living room to see Craig in the bedroom."

"What? You mean there was a fucking orgy going on? Keera, you lucky little bitch. I knew I should have called in sick. I could have gone with you. I fucking missed all the action."

I giggle. "So Craig is passed out on the bed naked. Colton smacks him across the face and tells him to get the fuck up or he's fired. He falls back asleep. Colton lets go of my hand, picks him up, and throws him in a cold shower. So then Blondie looks me up and down and says in a snotty voice, 'So your Colton's girlfriend?' I said, 'What's it to you?' Just as snotty."

"I'm so proud of you. It's about time you stopped taking people's shit."

"So then Blondie says, 'Because, I just fucked Craig all night to get close to Colton.' I said, 'That was your first mistake. He won't even look at you now. He likes good girls. The ones who are a challenge.'"

"Well, way to go, Keera! My shy little friend isn't so shy anymore. I'm so proud of you."

"Thank you. So when we got to the elevator, Colton pulled me into his arms and said, 'I'm sorry you had to see that.' So then, of course, I reviewed it in my mind and, you know what? I got a little aroused. Is that weird?"

"No, not at all."

"Says the one who likes orgies."

"Hey, I never said I wanted to participate, but don't you think two guys doing you all night long would be the ultimate? Both working you into a frenzy. Oh fuck, I think I just had another mini-orgasm."

"I think you need to go see Austin."

"Yeah, I need it. Bad!"

"So, anyway, we went for breakfast and I got him calmed down by talking about his family, the instruments he plays, and other things. He kept touching me. It was constant from the time I first saw him at Alaina, until he got out of my Journey."

"How many times did he kiss you?"

"I don't know. Six or seven times. I lost track. He'd slip them in when I wasn't paying attention."

"How many times did he slip you the tongue?"

"Once. And he was quite happy with himself. That was just before he got out of my Journey to go to the chopper."

"Anything else interesting happen?"

"Colton asked me to listen to Von Jobin's music. He wants me to pay attention to the words. He said he wrote that song for me."

"I told you! I fucking told you!"

"Yeah, yeah."

"Did you have fun?"

"Yes. He spoiled me. He spent way too much money on me. Five limos, a chopper, dinner. He bought me a camera, he gave huge tips to the limo drivers and in the restaurant. He was the perfect date, a gentleman. He was funny, charming, and considerate. He pulled my chair out for me every time, helped me in and out of the limos, strapped me into the chopper harness, which I think he enjoyed way too much. Leena, if I didn't love Bryce, he'd be the perfect boyfriend, husband, and father."

"Well, ya know…"

"Don't even say it. I love Bryce. I couldn't live like Colton does-on the road all the time, in the public eye, paparazzi taking pictures right in your face. It's a hard life, and you know what I'm like. I'm that shy little girl from the small town of Huntsville. I told Colton I could see him with a Victoria's Secret model. They're used to that kind of lifestyle."

"And, of course, he wasn't listening."

"No, I don't think so."

"Anything else you forgot to tell me?"

"I think that's pretty much it. Now I have to prepare myself for the worst."

"I'm here for you if you need me."

"Thanks."

"Okay, call me after you talk to Bryce."

"Will do."

Once my phone charges a bit, I text Bryce. I get no response at all, so I convince myself that he's busy still from the snow storm.

To keep myself occupied until Bryce gets home from work, I prepare dinner, work out, take a shower, and clean up. When five o'clock nears and Bryce still isn't home, I text him again and wait for a response, pacing the floor anxiously. After ten minutes, I call his cell and get no answer, so I get dressed, trying to look my best.

I fix my hair differently by pulling just a section up into a pony tail and leaving the rest long, the way Bryce likes it. I place a Swarovski crystal at the base of the pony tail. I wear my black bustier, with the silk ribbon running through, which shows major cleavage, and slip on the jeans that always makes Bryce say he can't keep his hands off me. Then I throw on my short black leather jacket and little high heel boots. I take one last look in the mirror, satisfied with my appearance, and head out the door.

When I pull up to the fence at the fire station, Dante and Jax are just getting in their trucks. I note that Bryce's truck is in between, but I don't see him.

As soon as I get out of the driver's seat, Dante is over to me in a second. Jax slowly makes his way toward me as Dante wraps his arm around my shoulder. "Wow! Look at you, Keera. You look hot!"

"Thanks, Dante. Is Bryce still here?"

Jax makes it to my side and runs his hand down my back. "Hey, Keera."

"Hi, Jax."

"He's inside. We'll take you to him."

Jax walks behind while Dante slides his arm around my waist and guides me to the door.

Once inside the door, they bring me in between two fire trucks.

And there he is.

Bryce.

26

BRYCE CLOSES THE door of the fire truck, which was obstructing my view, our eyes meet. We hold our stare on one another and I drink him in. Damn, he's sexy with his uniform on-black hair shining in the light, gorgeous hazel eyes, face sculpted and shaved. My eyes inspect those luscious full lips that have been on mine-and elsewhere-sending me to some hot, erotic, memories of our beautiful lovemaking. That tingle I always feel when he's near slides deliciously through my body, making my nipples peak and harden. My eyes wander to his huge hands which set me to reminiscing about how they've touched me and how magical they are. I check out the whole package. His sleeves are rolled up and I see his muscles and the thick veins bulging in his forearms. His large thighs tighten in his uniform and my eyes focus on the bulge in his pants, my happy place. I can see the outline of his beautiful cock where his pants strain in that area, probably because he's a little bit larger than your average male.

Dante and Jax look good in their uniforms too, but not like Bryce. He fills it out to perfection.

That spark is still there, running rampantly through my veins.

It's like an electrical charge pulling us toward each other. My eyes devour the length of his body again.

His eyes do the same to me.

But then, he looks away.

When he looks back at me, the look in his eyes has changed to one of pure hatred.

Oh, God! I've seen that look before. But it's always been directed at my stalker, Jake, or Colton. Never at me.

I wait for him to speak. But with the look on his face, I need to say something quick. "Babe, nothing happened. I had no idea he was going to be-"

"Keera, just quit!" he says, cutting me off and talking over me. "I don't want to hear it. The pictures say it all. But there is one thing I want to know. Did you arrange this rendezvous with him when you were in Aruba?"

"No. I had no idea he was going to be there."

"Stop talking!" His voice is loud and angry. "Leave! Get out of here! I can't even look at you!"

If he'd slapped me in the face, it might have been better, because right now I'm numb and I can't breathe. Tears threaten in the corners of my eyes, so I turn quickly and head for the door.

Make it to the door, Keera. Don't cry.

In my blurred vision, I see Jax and Dante scrambling to do something, pretending like they haven't been listening. I truck right past them. *You're almost there. Don't cry.* I burst through the door and the flood gates open. Tears fall, wetting my shirt, almost turning to ice pellets from the cold, but I keep going through my unfocused vision to find my Journey for a quick escape.

"Keera, wait!"

I don't stop. I keep booking it for my Journey.

Dante runs up from behind and slips in front of me, holding my arms. "Keera, I'm so sorry. I was the one who showed him the pictures, but only because they were all over the internet and TV. He would have seen them, there was no hiding it."

I turn away so he doesn't see me crying.

"Damn it. You're crying. Jesus, I'm so sorry." He hugs me.

I feel Jax rubbing my back to console me, but he doesn't say anything.

"Nothing happened. Colton showed up at the end of the photo shoot and wanted me to go for dinner because I was starving from hardly eating all day." I reach into my pocket, pull out some Kleenex, and wipe my tears before continuing. "It was just supposed to be dinner and then I was going to get a room, wait out the snow storm, and drive home in the morning. But the snow was too deep for the limo. I had no idea his favourite restaurant was in Niagara Falls. Listen to me. I'm rambling. Can you tell Bryce I think Colton is trying to break us up?"

"Hey, jackass, Cap wants you." We all turn to see Bryce hanging out the door.

Jax and Dante both point at each other. "Who? Him?"

"Both of you." Bryce disappears back inside the fire station.

"Shit! We better go."

"Sorry again, Keera."

"It's okay, Dante. He would have seen them eventually. Tell him I'm going back home and I love him."

"Will do." Dante hugs me and then wipes a tear off my cheek.

Jax shoves Dante. "My turn, dickhead."

Dante moves out of the way and Jax gives me a hug. "Don't worry. He'll snap out of it and come to his senses. And he better do it fast or someone else will be standing in line. Like us."

All I can muster is a small smile. "Thanks, Jax."

"Now!" We all turn in the direction of the yelling. Bryce is hanging out the door again, directing them inside. He sounds furious.

"Shit, better go. Bye, Keera."

"Bye, Dante."

Jax rubs both my arms. "It'll work out."

"Thanks, Jax."

They both hurry back into the fire station. I get in my Journey and drive back to Bryce's.

When I get inside, I shut the crockpot off and put Bryce's dinner in the fridge. I collect my things and sit down at the breakfast bar with a paper and pen to write down what happened from beginning to end. I leave out the part about Colton sleeping with me. It would break his heart. At the end, I tell him I think Colton set up the modeling shoot so he could see me and I'm not sure, but I think he's trying to break us up. "So please, don't do this," I write. "We have to have trust in this relationship." These are the exact words Bryce used when we started this. Hopefully he remembers.

I also write in the note that I won't bother him or cause a scene. "If you don't want me, I will move on with my life." By the time I tell him I love him and love can conquer anything, my tears are saturating the page. At the very end, I write "P.S. I would never cheat on you. I gave you a second chance. Give me one please. Babe, I love you! I always will!"

Just before I leave with my bags in hand, I take an eight-by-ten picture off the wall. Deana took the picture a couple years ago of Bryce at a firefighting competition and had it framed. The picture shows him bare chested with only his bunker pants on, opening a fire hydrant. It's her favourite and mine. I hold it to my heart. "You're coming with me."

I leave the note on the breakfast bar for Bryce to see and leave his house, making sure I lock up.

On the way back to Huntsville, every time a song mentioning a relationship in any way, shape, or form, comes on the radio, I have to switch stations, so I can drive without losing my vision from tearing up.

As I'm driving, I play back in my mind when Bryce first looked at me, and the spark I felt. And then how his look changed before my eyes today, from one of love to one of pure hatred, how he yelled at me to stop talking, how he couldn't even look at me.

When I remember how he raised his voice telling me to leave, I start to cry all over again. The tears welling up in my eyes make it near impossible to see the road. I wipe them away quickly and breathe deeply. I think about Bryce's reaction to seeing the pictures for the first time with Dante and Jax over his shoulder and anyone else who was in the room at the time. He must have been so embarrassed. I hate myself for putting him through this.

Leena calls me on the way home and I tell her I'll call her back in fifteen minutes when I arrive home.

By the time I get home, I've beaten myself up pretty good.

When I pull into my driveway, Leena is sitting in her car waiting for me. When I get out of my car in the garage she's standing by my door waiting to give me a hug. "You're always here for me."

"So what did he say?"

"Well, our eyes met. We were frozen, staring, trying to figure out what was going through each other's minds. My eyes travelled his body. His did the same to me. I saw it. We had that spark like we usually do, that electrical charge between us. I know I saw and felt it, but then he looked away and when he looked back at me, there was pure hatred in his eyes. You know that look he has for my stalker, Jake, and Colton? It was directed at me this time. Leena, I can't get it out of my head."

"Then what happened?"

"I had to explain fast. I told him nothing happened and I had no idea Colton was going to be there. He cut me off. He said, 'Keera, quit talking. I don't want to hear it. The pictures say it all, but there is one thing I want to know. Did you arrange this rendezvous with Colton when you were in Aruba?' I said, 'No. I didn't know he was going to be there.' He didn't let me finish. He yelled at me to stop talking and said, 'leave! I can't look at you.'"

Leena hugs me again and the flood gates open wide. My chest heaves for my next breath. I try to calm down and she waits patiently for me, rubbing my back.

"I had to get out of there before I cried, but of course Jax and Dante caught me before I made it to my Journey."

"What did they say?"

"Dante apologized for telling Bryce. But he said Bryce would have seen the pictures anyway, because they were all over the internet."

"Well, that was nice of him," Leena says sarcastically.

"I can't blame Dante. He's only looking out for his best friend. And he is right. It was only a matter of time before Bryce saw them."

"So do you think Bryce broke it off?"

"I don't know. He can't stand to look at me. He hates me. So, yeah. I think we're done."

"You can't be! You've been through so much together. If your love can survive a crazy ex-girlfriend and a stalker kidnapping you, then it can survive Bryce thinking you've cheated on him. You'll have to tell him that nothing happened until he listens."

"I did. I wrote him a two-page note telling him everything that happened from beginning to end. That is one issue Bryce has always expressed that he would not tolerate. And right now, he believes I cheated on him. Leena, I can't get it out of my head. The look on his face was pure hatred." Tears slide down my cheeks once again and the lump that's formed in my throat chokes me, stopping me from speaking.

"He hates me," I whisper.

COMING SOON!

Look for book 3 of the Unforgivable series.

Unforgivable Lust & Release.

If you like the Unforgivable series, help spread the word. Authors need reviews, so please, take the time to write a review on, Goodread's, Amazon, Indigo/Chapter's, Kobo, Google, iBooks, and Barnes and Noble.

Thank you for buying the Unforgivable series.
I appreciate it more than words can say.
I would love to hear if you like it. Please find me on
Facebook, Twitter, and Instagram or
check out my website @ www.shayleesoleil.com
for more information and upcoming news.
Lots of love from Shay Lee Soleil

CPSIA information can be obtained
at www.ICGtesting.com
Printed in the USA
LVOW03s1517250418
574834LV00001B/168/P